TOO GREAT A SKY

TOO GREAT A SKY

a novel

LILIANA COROBCA

Translated by
MONICA CURE

Seven Stories Press
New York • Oakland

Seven Stories Press
140 Watts Street
New York, NY 10013
www.sevenstories.com

Library of Congress Cataloging-in-Publication Data

Names: Corobca, Liliana, author. | Cure, Monica, translator.
Title: Too great a sky : a novel / Liliana Corobca ; translated by Monica
  Cure.
Other titles: Capătul drumului. English
Description: New York : Seven Stories Press, 2024.
Identifiers: LCCN 2024029421 | ISBN 9781644214176 (trade paperback) | ISBN
  9781644214183 (ebook)
Subjects: LCSH: World War, 1939-1945--Deportations from Romania--Fiction. |
  LCGFT: Historical fiction. | Novels.
Classification: LCC PC840.413.O763 C3713 2024 | DDC
  859/.335--dc23/eng/20240627
LC record available at https://lccn.loc.gov/2024029421

College professors and high school and middle school teachers may order free examination copies of Seven Stories Press titles. Visit https://www.sevenstories.com/pg/resources-academics or email academic@sevenstories.com.

Printed in the United States of America

9 8 7 6 5 4 3 2 1

TRANSLATOR'S NOTE

Translating *Too Great a Sky*, the third novel by Liliana Corobca that I've translated, was especially challenging. If while working on *The Censor's Notebook* I was exceedingly aware of the possibility that a translator could also be a censor, while translating *Too Great a Sky* I felt the additional burden of accuracy in bearing witness, especially given the ongoing war in Ukraine. Though it is a fictional story, many of the events and details closely follow the facts of the Soviet deportation of Romanians from what was then part of Romanian Bucovina, now Ukrainian Bukovyna, during World War II. In her academic work, with Dumitru Covalciuc, Corobca edited a volume of over eighty oral histories of survivors entitled *The Romanian Golgotha: Testimonies of Bucovinians Deported to Siberia* (*Golgota românească. Mărturiile bucovinenilor deportați în Siberia*, Vestala, 2015). These oral histories and others inform many of the incidents narrated by Ana Blajinschi in the novel.

Bearing witness is difficult and often complicated, a reality that is heightened in this novel. At first, I had no intention of getting overly involved in the "facts" of the story. My engagement started simply enough—I wanted to render the Romanian spellings of foreign words into their most common spellings in English. Almost all place names in the novel are real. I felt that leaving the

Russian and Kazakh ones in the Romanian spelling would seem inconsistent with the character Ana having learned Russian and Kazakh as she does in the novel. Finding the Russian and Kazakh names is easy enough for rivers such as the Irtysh and Ob. But then I couldn't find which steppe the "Anarhai" steppe could be. Liliana sent me the spelling in Cyrillic and luckily a blog post on the writing of Kyrgyz author Chingiz Aitmatov came up allowing me to match it to the Anarkhay steppe, which would have been obvious had I been more familiar with that part of the world. Then came Central Asian foods and customs. Without having intended to, I found myself looking up every unfamiliar word, place, and name. In the process of doing so, I noticed several discrepancies that I wouldn't have otherwise. Fortunately, Liliana and I have a collaborative working relationship as well as a friendship. We cross-checked Central Asian details with information that could be found online. We found the names of dishes that more closely resembled their descriptions in the novel. We changed the name of the Kyrgyz teacher, again thanks to Chingiz Aitmatov. We made it clearer that people from that part of the steppe happened not to have a ready supply of apples rather than never having heard of them, a detail that had come from the testimony of a deportee to Siberia rather than Kazakhstan.

I could have chalked up any errors to Ana Blajinschi not understanding certain words at the time of her deportation when she was eleven, or to her forgetting or confusing things in her old age while explaining them to her great-granddaughter in the novel's present tense. But I realized I wanted Ana's account to be as accurate as possible so long as Liliana felt the same way that I did and agreed with the changes. Ana as a character is somewhat otherworldly at the same time as she is very human—I wanted errors to be anyone's but hers, even as I recognized no memory or testimony is perfect.

I also knew that Ana's story, while based on real events, is fiction and that this is a source of power in the book. The emotions come from the way the story is told, how it draws the reader close. Though I was tempted to consult a Kazakh language specialist, I limited myself to imposing only once on the writer Maria Rybakova, who was living in Kazakhstan at the time, to help me find an appropriate word in Kazakh that could sound like an insult in English, since the word had to be changed from the Romanian version regardless. I'm grateful for her assistance in polling thirty people for options. Moreover, though I researched every unfamiliar word, I thought including notes would detract from the story (a decision supported by the editors at Seven Stories). Often, I added a couple words of description to Romanian words I left untranslated, such as *cojoc* and *sarmale*, to help readers without distracting them from the story. These changes were easier to make because Ana often explains things to her great-granddaughter rather than simply narrating them.

The songs included in the novel were based on songs actually composed by deportees and sung by survivors. Corobca found them in the journal *The Land of the Beeches* (*Țara Fagilor*) dedicated to the history and culture of Romanians in that area. She altered them slightly when writing them into the narrative and I was somewhat more liberal in my translation. For most of the songs I prioritized a folksy tone and rhyme, or at least half-rhymes. The only song fragments for which I adamantly created a regular meter were the songs the deportees danced to when they got off the train.

Liliana also read a range of religious books in preparation for writing the novel since several of the main characters, especially Ana Blajinschi, are marked by their Christian faith. In some ways this aspect was less of a challenge for me since my grandfather had been a Romanian Baptist pastor who had been imprisoned for his faith in the early years of the communist regime and so the language of Christian faith was already very familiar to me. In several of the prayers I preserved what may seem to be awkward syntax since it accurately depicts the rhythm of extemporaneous spoken prayer, with the common interjection of the word "Lord." Specifically Orthodox aspects, which show up in the novel in layered ways, were less familiar to me. A *troiță* is a large wooden or stone cross set up at crossroads or to mark an event, but Troiță de Sus is also the (fictional) name of the village in Moldova where Ana settles, and *de sus* can be translated either simply as "upper" in geographic usage or as "from above" in a metaphorical sense. Part Three was entitled "Troiță de Sus" in Romanian and we decided that the most important meaning to keep was "roadside crosses," especially since Ana had just shared the memory of the invisible crosses she saw along the train tracks.

Throughout the novel, Orthodox and folk practices and beliefs are often intertwined, as they continue to be in reality, especially in rural areas. Liliana collected many of the folk beliefs present in the novel during fieldwork in her own village in Moldova, especially those mentioned in the book during the burial ritual performed with words on the train. Ana's last names also hold both religious and spiritual connotations. Her maiden name is Zeiță, which means "goddess," while her married name, Blajinschi, and its affectionate diminutives (Blajinica, Blajina, and Blajâna), has at its root the word *blajin*. The word means a combination of gentle, peaceful, kind, and forgiving, which calls to mind Christian virtues. The gentle mother in the train and Anton, Ana's husband, are described using this word as well. But *blajin* can also refer to fairy-like creatures from Romanian folklore, also called Rohmani, as Ana notes. The syncretism of Orthodox and pre-Christian beliefs is especially present in the day in which the dead are honored, which I translate here as the

"Feast of the Peaceful," but a literal alternate translation could be the "Easter of the Blajins."

Too Great a Sky is comprised of countless liminal spaces: between heaven and earth, both literally and metaphorically; different peoples; different languages, including words in Russian, Kazakh, Kyrgyz, Uyghur, Polish, and Karakalpak; and different eras. Passages about various sewing machines and fabrics, and the process of manually preparing hemp, make sense in the context of Ana's desire to bridge the gap between past and present. In telling her story to her great-granddaughter, Ana is both witness and translator. The further apart the spaces are, the more challenging the translation is, but also the more rewarding.

—MONICA CURE
Bucharest, April 2024

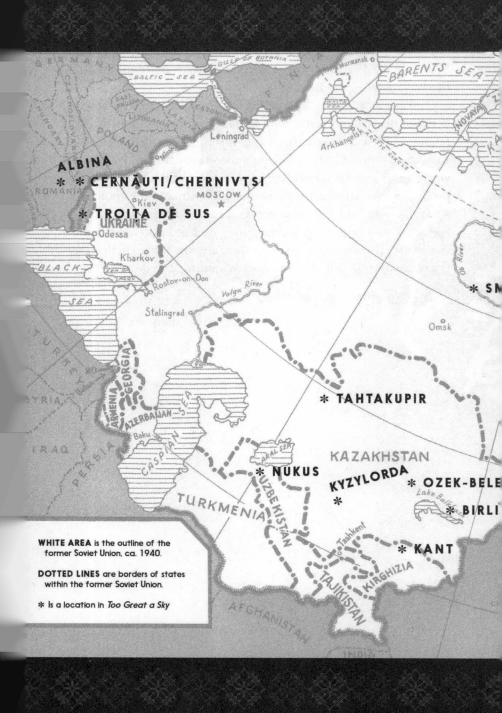

ALBINA

* * CERNĂUȚI/CHERNIVTSI

* TROITA DE SUS

* TAHTAKUPIR

* SM

* NUKUS

KYZYLORDA

* OZEK-BELE

*

BIRLI

* KANT

KAZAKHSTAN

WHITE AREA is the outline of the
former Soviet Union, ca. 1940.

DOTTED LINES are borders of states
within the former Soviet Union.

* Is a location in *Too Great a Sky*

- PART ONE -

THE TRAIN

At the end of the road are the heavens. Above, below, to the left, the right, and in every direction, sky, nothing but sky! The train was slowly departing, it was melting into the horizon, going back where it came from. Beyond this point there were no train tracks, they ended here. And us, after the long journey in that hellish, godforsaken train, they abandoned, cast us off, threw us straight into the heavenly skies. As if God had heard our repeated prayers and, after a month of torment, led us here, to this heaven of limitless sky. The sky began right above the blades of grass, which were short, feeble, and sparse, there was nothing else around as far as the eye could see! God, we've reached the end of the road which is right in the middle of Your kingdom! So much air for our shriveled lungs and so much beauty for our grief-stricken eyes after the crowding and darkness of the train car! Air, air, air! We breathed, yelled, jumped up and down, those of us who were younger; the others could hardly move, shaking from weakness and all the emotion. We thanked God that we had arrived here.

You sorely tested us and long was the test, but that was Your will, God! We thank and praise You, God, for helping us survive and for not losing our faith. We looked all around, enchanted, so much overskyness it was almost scary! That's not how we had imagined the end of our journey. Not this beautiful. A high heaven spilled over our heads, and around us spread a giant expanse of land, rounder than we had ever seen. All the royal azure had gathered above us and was waiting for us here at the end of our suffering . . .

The best possible place to die, we thought as we saw the train slowly depart, then disappear, as if it had never existed. We had come here to die as well, those of us left alive, because many had died on the way. No need to wait for our souls to ascend. Our bodies, so slight and thin, almost transparent, like this grass, had been brought straight into heaven. Maybe we've already died and, behold, this is our well-deserved place in heaven! We shouldn't have arrived in such pure, azure spotlessness so lice-ridden and unkempt, though. We felt a kind of shame, as when you step on a brand new carpet with shoes tracking dirt or mud. It's too much for us, God, Your gift is too great for us, the unworthy and a month unwashed! We breathed slowly, so as not to choke on air so abundant and clean. You don't load up the plate of a starving person after a long period of hunger, because it could kill him. That's how it was with us, we breathed little by little, so we wouldn't die from so much air, fearfully, in disbelief, exhausted by our many and difficult trials. Here we were, we'd been abandoned under these foreign skies. But we never lost hope, we knew that You were somewhere nearby, never far. That there where no one was waiting to receive us, You, God, were waiting for us! Do not forsake us, merciful God, for You are holy, and we lift up praise to You, to the Father, and to the Holy Spirit—now and forever and ever. Amen.

⚬

When word spread in our village that the Russians had crossed the Nistru, advancing toward the capital of Bucovina, we didn't become too alarmed, knowing that only two counties, Cernăuți and Storojineț, would be occupied, and that the villages in Rădăuți County would continue to remain under Romanian administration. In that June of 1940, along with the Romanian troops that were retreating, the civilian population was leaving as well. When the soldiers passed through villages, the people would yell: "Brothers, don't leave us! Don't abandon us in our time of need! Help us!" The most terrified actually seemed to be the Ukrainians who had come to Bucovina from the so-called communist paradise and knew better than we did what was in store for us. Landowners kissed their doors and gates, they left their houses with doors thrown every which way, the yards remained desolate, on the road you saw animals freed from mangers, abandoned to their fates. With loaded up carts or with only the slightest fraction of their wealth in satchels, people followed after the soldiers. Many headed then toward Romania, after they heard that the Russians were approaching our ancestral land.

> *The Prut is wide, the Nistru tight, oh,*
> *And Romania has lost the fight. Oh, oh!*
> *The Nistru's tight, the Prut is wide,*
> *Romania surrendered us to the other side*
> *But we mustn't lose heart,*
> *They gave up only a part,*
> *May God make the flood rise higher*
> *May the Bolsheviks burn in a fire*
> *Romania, Romania*
> *Don't give us over to foreigners!*
> *Oh, oh!*

But the Soviets, greedy for foreign land, also invaded the villages in Dorohoi and Rădăuți counties. So the setting of the border between the Soviet Union and Romania caught many of our fellow villagers on the other side: at schools in Siret, Rădăuți, and Suceava, at the mobilization of reserves that had just been announced, at relatives' houses, entire families finding themselves dismembered overnight, the majority of them remaining that way forever.

Many, like us, had children and relatives all over Romania, not because they had any hostile intentions toward anyone or because they didn't like the new regime, but because we had been one country until 1940 and everyone had gone wherever they wished. My older sister, Domnica, had studied in Cernăuți, that's where she met her intended, and after their wedding, the young couple decided to build their little nest near Rădăuți, where her husband was from. Nestor, our brother, was studying in Iași, we were all proud of his academic accomplishments, and he was happy to be a university student. Our other brother, Teodor, was studying at a high school in Cernăuți, but that summer he was helping build Domnica's house, then he never returned. Father had bought wood for our sister's house, for the doors and windows, he had found workers. He had made many trips throughout our region and, when he saw that it was better to get out of the antichrist's path, he loaded up the wagons with everything and drove to Domnica's house, with the idea that we'd move to her place until the situation became clear. First, he took our grandparents, one had died in the war, the other was still in good health, so two grandmothers and a grandfather. He set them in wagons and they were taken safely to Rădăuți. It was the summer of 1940, when you could still leave. He was supposed to come back to take us as well. Not only our father and grandparents left then, but other families from our villages too.

My father's parents were from Horecea, near Cernăuți. I hadn't known my grandfather on my father's side because he had died in the war, along with his two brothers. My father, Andron Bojescu, also had a sister who had gotten married and settled in Zastavna. My grandparents on my mother's side had been the richest couple in our village and were very respected. My grandfather, Constantin Zeiţă, had also been the mayor; he possessed countless sheep and cows, even horses of the splendid kind, and he had a great deal of land. They brought four children into the world, he and my grandmother, two boys and two girls. My mother was their first child and they gave her in marriage to the school principal who had just moved to our village. "Aspazia Zeiţă will you accept Andron Bojescu?" her parents asked her. She did. They built a large house in our village and they lived together in peace and harmony. The boys, my mother's brothers, were sent by my grand-father to study, one became an important gentleman in Bucharest itself, the other was a doctor in Cernăuţi. I visited him in Cernăuţi twice. The youngest daughter, Sancira, also remained near her parents, marrying a respectable rich landowner from the village, Haralambie Isopescu. Our grandparents helped them build a large, bright house, too, next to ours. And Domnica, my older sister, was the first granddaughter at whose wedding my grand-parents danced, and they went to help build her a house as well. That's how it was back then, all the relatives would gather together and help the young couple however they could. They built a beau-tiful house, fit for a noble family, right next to Rădăuţi where the groom was from. Domnica's husband was a good doctor who was in high demand, from what my mother said, because I can't remember him. But I was the flower girl at their wedding, that I do remember. When the times became troubled, Father told them all to stay there, not to come back to our village. They had just finished that mansion.

We gathered our things, got ourselves ready, and waited for Father and the other men to return. We waited nervously, especially

Mother, but he never made it back home. A man from their group had left late but had made it to the village before them. According to him, Father and our grandparents had arrived safely at their destination in Romania and that they had settled on a meeting point for the return trip. But the man who hadn't reached the spot in time didn't know where they might be now. Out of the group of four men who were supposed to return, only that man reached the village. If someone from the new government were to catch them, they could arrest them for carrying weapons or just because, for no specific reason. When they had left, it had been easy to cross to the other side. But on the return trip, for anyone setting off, no one knew what could happen, because the Russians had already taken over. Suddenly, our Bucovina, which was so small, became two different territories that belonged to two countries. People from the same village were separated by the new border and were no longer allowed to pass from one side to the other. By the time my mother finally agreed to leave, as the women in the village kept urging her to do, it was no longer possible. She had continued to wait for Father, how could he return and find our little house deserted? Mother expected him home at any moment. Three children and her elderly parents were in Romania, but we didn't know anything about Father. The first arrests were made a few months after the Russians arrived and you were found guilty if you had relatives in the neighboring country. In our village, there was not one person without relatives in Romania. It must have been difficult for my siblings, alone over there, without their parents, with no news of us, the oldest had been on the front lines, he returned and then left with the youngest brother to cross the border. And my sister was deported to the plains in southeastern Romania, so she wasn't able to enjoy the house built by our parents for very long. Once taken away from Rădăuți, she kept moving until she settled in Iaşi, the most beautiful city in Romania, as my brother who studied there would say proudly.

While Mother waited for Father, she took care of my grandparents' farm as well. The neighbors stole, they had no shame once everything was abandoned. Mother was afraid to let me go see what was happening. She was scared someone might bash in my head because I caught them stealing. We brought over Grandmother's two fluffy cats, a neighbor had taken the dog. They'd also rip out the fences, the windows, and it wasn't foreigners who did that, but the stribocs from our village, the new activists who had gotten in good with the new rulers, you couldn't be around these people anymore, you couldn't reason with them . . . A woman all alone, with a small child to boot, Mother could barely get by. She asked some people from the village to take care of the house and the animals, she found some neighbors with a bit of humanity. Luckily, the most valuable things had already been sent to Romania in the wagons, because people would steal even the tiles off roofs.

At first, no one knew for sure where the border was, those of us from Albina, for example, were certain that we were still in Romania, it was rumored that the Russians had stopped two villages away and were staying there. Then they'd reconsider and advance, they'd stop, and then advance again. The new border was marked in the beginning by some long sticks stuck in the ground, with a bunch of hay or some rags tied to the tip, straw dummies they'd call them. When it was just straw dummies, which looked more like scarecrows than something you'd use to scare people, you could still cross to the other side, but when soldiers with guns appeared, with dogs, that was it, forget about leaving. The Soviets set themselves up on two hills not far from us, one was Berlinţu Mic, and the other, Arşiţa, and for three days straight they shot at each other thinking the other was the enemy. You couldn't leave the house. Then things calmed down.

On an ugly overcast evening, it was a Friday, a man from the
other end of the village came to tell us that they were forcing his
family out of their homes and taking them to the train station,
that everyone on that road would be rounded up, meaning all the
families with bigger and better-looking houses from that neighborhood. It had become terribly dark, a strong wind was blowing,
and then it started raining. It stopped raining around midnight
and a great rumbling of carts crisscrossing the village started up.
The hunt for everyone began that hour. You could hear yelling and
the voices of women and children quickly stifled, gunshots, and
dogs barking. From another part of the village came the sound
of wailing, and from time to time a horrified scream cut short.
The communists had surrounded the village so they could catch
everyone on the list for deportation to Siberia.

The people's voices were silenced, but the animals revolted
and kept screaming in all kinds of ways. They had shut up the
villagers, they were threatened, forced not to scream, so others
wouldn't find out, but how could you tell an animal to shut
up? The animals made a huge racket, though they didn't want
anything to be heard or seen. They silenced the children, they
covered the wives' faces with rugs. The men were struck so they
wouldn't resist. Everyone was asking themselves who would be
next.

They started by taking people from the outskirts, so it wouldn't
be too obvious, then they reached the center of the village. When
someone from the center yells, the entire village hears, but it was
already too late, whoever was supposed to be taken had already
been taken, they had rounded up everyone. They took my aunt
Sancira toward morning, around four something. Even though
they had covered her mouth afterward, the entire village had still

heard her screams. At one of her shrieks, as if they had stabbed her, the chickens squawked too, all the cows bellowed, and all the dogs started howling as well, like an echo, you couldn't even tell anymore if it was her screaming or all of Bucovina, every person and animal, grief-stricken and terrified by our cruel fate, sensing what would be theirs, that of abandoned animals who would lose their kind owners. When she started screaming for help, a soldier stuffed the edge of a pillow in her mouth to shut her up. We were close by, one house over, I was watching from the window with Mother, but how could we help her? We understood roughly what was about to happen, Sancira grabbed a rug, a pillow, a small sack of corn flour, some food, and put it all out on the porch. Then the children were also told to come outside in the yard. The house was surrounded by soldiers, as if they had come to a house of robbers, not to a single mother with three small children, one of them not even weaned. I remember her screams, the screams of her children, my cousins, who I had been running around with everywhere until just the other day. I can almost see it now, how she, wearing a heavy sheepskin cojoc, went to the backyard and freed the geese, mournfully saying to them: "Go on now and fly away to warmer countries!" Sancira's geese flapped their wings and kept honking sorrowfully behind the cart, like people who didn't want to say goodbye to their loved ones. Even when a soldier shot one, the others didn't turn back but kept following their owner. Maybe they wailed after her all the way to the train station, I didn't see until where. Mother was able to keep from groaning, so she wouldn't scare us, but she couldn't stop her tears, and they rolled down from her chin onto her skirt, where they became two stains. If they had reached the ground, they would've turned into two small puddles. Sancira was my mother's youngest sister, and my mother was the oldest of the four children of my grandparents in the village. Mother's children were big, but Sancira's were small, little Profira was about two months old then, just a baby.

From that moment on, we were expecting them to take us too. On the 13th, it rained, the sky was dark, all of nature was crying, even the sky was spilling tears, from seeing such heartbreak and misery. And Sancira's cow was bellowing at our gate as well, she wanted to be milked and hoped we would help her. We would help her, but for how long? The next day, Mother rushed to bake bread which she then dried. First she sliced it, then she laid the slices out in the sun so they'd dry out faster, and in the evening, she put them into sacks. Why save up anything anymore, if you'll be taken somewhere from where you'll never return? Many were taken, but as for returning, no one ever came back. She was getting ready because she felt our turn was coming too, but she sent me and a neighbor's child to the train station, loaded with bread. I found Sancira and gave her one of the small sacks. Then I gave another one to a man who begged me to give him one as well, I didn't know who he was but he seemed distraught and hungry.

Such a ruckus at the train station, the entire village had gathered there! Yelling, crying! Some whimpered, some wailed, some were silent. Children stayed close to their parents, as if they were sheep scared by a wolf. In the blink of an eye, our most important land-owners, the ones most respected by the villagers, had become pitiful and the object of scorn, hunted down by Stalin's dogs. They had done nothing against the new rulers, who had it in for us because of their mission of uprooting Romanian landowners in Bucovina.

I remember the men's faces. At the train station, I saw how families were separated, women and children went into one railcar, able-bodied men and teenage boys, in another. Children were taken from their father's arms and the little ones screamed, the fathers were barely able to hold back their tears. Only a few, a small number, bowed their heads and allowed tears to stream down their cheeks. The men didn't take any provisions, they left everything to their wives and children. Some men were made to take off their cojocs and thick clothing, I saw piles of winter clothes in the train station. But why? They were sending them to the taiga! Here it was summer, it was hot, but where they were going, without thick clothes, death awaited them. I was afraid to see my father among them, I was afraid, but I kept looking for him. I didn't see him. I gave the rest of the bread to those men. I couldn't reach them, but I handed it to those who were near me and they passed it down toward the railcars. People were crying and I burst into tears as well, I came home crying. "Let's gather up our courage, let's prepare ourselves," Mother said, "with hope in the power of holy prayers. Let us pray earnestly with a broken heart, and weeping hot tears! Lord Jesus Christ, our God, You who give invincible strength to those who believe in You, forgive us and strengthen us, rid us of our despair and unworthiness, so that we may praise Your Glory. Help us, Lord, in our time of trouble!"

The next day, I didn't go back to the train station, and then on the third day we were there unwillingly. They took us on the morning of the 15th, Sunday, when we should have been at church, worshipping and praying, but they came at three in the morning, and at nine, the train started for Adâncata. It didn't rain on Sunday, it was a clear day, only on Friday had it poured.

Here begins my tune, toward the fifteenth of June, oh,
At night, at half past three, soldiers armed to the teeth,
Burst into our house and at my mother shouted:
—Move your things and get out!
Cursed at and seized, as if we'd been thieves,
Taken from our village home, on a harsh road to roam.
Oh, Oh!

"We have to bear the burden for our family," Mother said. "Look, all the family members are being taken, even grandparents who can barely walk, even babies who were just born. But I'm hopeful that our family is living peacefully, all together, and that they won't have to experience this brutality. We're going through what we're going through, but the oldest is married and is carrying a new soul in her belly, the other two are at good schools, they have a roof over their heads, they're healthy, they'll get by. Maybe even your father, my husband, is alive! I have only you left," Mother stroked my head, "but people are going with five, with ten, I'll be able to manage with a single child. We'll get through it all, God willing. I'll keep my brave little girl safe." And Mother did keep me safe! What choice provisions she put into that trunk which seemed small but which two soldiers were barely able to lift into the cart, that's how heavy it was! The foreigners who had knocked on our window had told Mother to take lots of food, because the road would be long. Mother was afraid to bring out the food and clothes she had prepared, but one of the soldiers, to encourage her, set his weapon on the porch, with its barrel leaning against the wall, and helped her carry out the things that we might need. They also helped us when we had to get on the train, because Mother had been nice to them, she didn't yell, she didn't insult them. She served them pastries, since the pastries were there steaming on the table anyway. But not for a second did we think that they wouldn't take us as well.

Mother had baked pastries that evening, they were warm when we got the knock on our door. The soldiers pretended to search for weapons, they rummaged through everything, but there was nothing for them to find. The whipping around of their cloaks caused the lamp to go out and then, in the darkness, we were scared they'd kill us. We relit the lamp. I don't know what Mother had been thinking about in that moment, but when we had loaded everything, she swooped down like an eagle and grabbed me by the hand, pulled me after her into the house, and lifting her eyes to the icon of St. George, she prayed earnestly, holding me by the shoulders, then she pushed me outside, picked up something else, and hid it under her cojoc. The Bible? The children's book by Coşbuc that happened to be there, which I later found in my pouch, because I don't remember taking it.

"Wait for me to free the dog."

She freed the dog which almost tore those long, black cloaks. We thought they'd shoot him, but they just kicked him and he whimpered and continued barking, then he followed us for a bit, but Mother told him to leave: "We're being taken away by troppos," meaning we're being taken away by force.

"Austrian gendarmes were called troppos," Mother explained to me on the way to the train station.

"What, these soldiers are troppos, Mother?"

"A kind of troppos."

I didn't live during those times, but I know that the troppos would take one person, fine, two, from a village, but these ones were sending the entire village to that Siberia of theirs. Who was left?

"They loaded up people randomly, but at the train station there were still lots of empty railcars, and I'm sure they aren't there for nothing," I said to Mother. They would've loaded even the roofs from off houses into their railcars, if the war hadn't started, when they had to take off themselves, along with railcars of cattle. Mother had brought with her colored thread for embroidering, a needle and scissors, but she didn't embroider on the way.

When I saw the train was coming, the fear was numbing, oh,
When I saw the railcars, I knew the people would be taken.
They took hundreds, thousands, to Siberia the forsaken;
They took thousands, millions, to die without provisions.

The honest landowner who had worked all day,
Set the table straight away, with his family ate the spread,
Then, exhausted, went to bed.
He couldn't have imagined what an hour later happened.
We had all just gone to sleep when the hooligans came to do a sweep,
They had come for us, for our little ones, with weapons, with guns.
They burst in the house and wouldn't let up, shouting:
—Mister, right now, get up!
Come on, mister, wake up and pack up the lot,
We're arresting you, those are the orders we got.
Now, pack—you, your wife, and kids are never coming back!
To the train station they took us all, like sheep to the shearing stall;
They pushed in every son and daughter, like cattle to the slaughter,
Without bread to help us bear. Without clothes to wear.
And what was left behind?
You could cry yourself blind. Every street lined
With houses whose windows are now all boarded,
Stables and barns deserted, and all the cattle hoarded
By the thugs who learned the trick of serving the Bolsheviks.
Ah Stalin, you murderer, may your tears be just as bitter,
Ah Stalin, Ah Stalin, may the earth split open and you fall in,
You brought us misery, but not one good thing, not any.
You deported so many.
Oh, Oh!

Mom, Dad left and now it's just me and Cuța. Dad fixed the fence, got a lock for the basement because there hadn't been one, and put in a new bolt on our door. Cuța complimented him, she said: "My dear grandson is so handy, he knows how to do everything!" He even hooked us up to the internet, with some boys from here in the village. Skype works fine. But he didn't say one word about the nursing home, he left all the hard stuff to me. I'm waiting for the right moment. Let me know when you want to talk.

Mom, at first I thought that our little great-grandmother had no idea what was going on, sometimes she thought she was in a cattle car, sometimes in the steppe, sometimes she'd yell: "I got off and I saw heaven." Sometimes she thought she was in a boat on the water . . . at first I couldn't understand a thing, she talked nonstop, she mumbled nonsense, she repeated words: *train, Kot, Jenica, the wheels turn, bread, cigarette page, grain, wolves* . . . I thought she was delirious. Poor thing, I told myself, she must be really sick if she doesn't even know what she's talking about! But she does know where she is, she knows and she's telling her story, because she can now, she doesn't have to hide it anymore and she believes she'll die in her own house, *at my hearth*, is what she keeps repeating. She had gotten so wrapped up in her story, in all that had happened, it was as if she were seeing it all again, as if she were back there, and on my first day here I thought she had gone crazy.

Mom, why didn't you tell me that our Blajinica had been deported to Siberia? I thought that she was asleep and talking in her sleep, except that she'd start talking whenever I'd come in the room and stop when I'd leave. She'd watch out of the corner of her eye if I was coming or going. After a few times of coming in and out, she said to me:

"My little dear, has Cuţa been talking too much? Forgive me if I'm bothering you. I've never talked about this before, I didn't tell anyone, at first because it wasn't allowed, then when it was, I didn't have anyone to tell it to, because all my children and grandchildren had scattered to their own nests. It has been a long time since a grandchild or great-grandchild has stepped foot in my home. And now that you're here . . . Stories come over me day and night, they won't let me live my old age in peace. Maybe if

I say them out loud, they'll stop flashing before my eyes. As if I were living them over. But if you don't want me to, if they tire you out, Cuţa won't tell you any more stories. So many stories, so many moments from my life that I thought had been forgotten, resurface in my mind, untold to anyone until now! It's as if God has sent you to be my witness of those long-ago days."

Mom, Cuţa tells such interesting stories. Do you want me to go on Skype so you can listen in? Just don't say a word!

❦

It was 1941, in the distance boomed the cannon:
Cruel was the harsh decree, ordered then by Stalin,
The accursed villain who emptied out our village. Oh, oh!
In the middle of the night, deep, the people were dead asleep,
But they woke up terrified, with soldiers on every side,
Loaded into carts and taken away, taken to the railway.
Sent off without warning, the village for us was mourning.
In tears, both men and women, in tears, the little children,
In the sky cried a lark, my house stood in loneliness stark.
When at the train station we arrived, my parents almost died.
What worse fate than ours, getting shoved in cattle cars . . .
Rosemary battered by the rain—come down, God, on earth again,
Come down gently, God, and stop their train!
Oh, oh!

In our railcar there were also landowning families from Putila, Sinăuţi, Dihteniţ, Plaiu, Huţa Veche, Tereblecea, and other Romanian villages in Bucovina. Many old people, many children. Young wives separated from their husbands, and only one family, with five girls, with their father and mother, the Gherman family, who I later ended up with in the same aul. They all told of how they had been arrested in those dark days and terrible hours for the pick of the bunch of Bucovina. They rounded up people from all our villages into carts or cars specially brought over and they took them to the closest train station. In our railcar there were many who were seized only at the end, on June 15, more to fill up the railcars and complete the number of people on the lists than anything else. Here were grannies left all alone, girls who themselves had written up the lists of deportees, single mothers whose children had run away to Romania. There were also families who weren't at all rich, who weren't involved in politics either, who hadn't taken in farmhands, who didn't have relatives abroad, such as the Ghermans with their five children. Then we figured it out, the Ghermans had a large house in the center of the village and the stribocs were looking for a place for "the village committee." Some had managed to escape, they disappeared from the village, others had been warned and hid, and in their places whoever they happened upon were deported. In Cernăuți, they even picked up passersby from off the street near the train station and loaded them straight onto the railcar. It was terrible luck for those people who were passing by right there then.

In Rădăuți, my county, which had two cities, Siret and Rădăuți, both of which remained in Romania, of its two cities and eighty-six villages, eighteen townships, comprising thirty-four villages, were ceded. Among them Bahrinești, Fântâna Albă, Gura-Putilei, Plaiu, Oprișeni, Șipotele Sucevei, Tereblecea, Prisaca, Sinăuții de Sus and Sinăuții de Jos, Seletin, Câmpulung-pe-Ceremuș . . . They took us to the train station in the neighboring village, Tereblecea. Landowners from nearby villages were also brought there. The train waited there until it was full, then started in the direction of Adâncata.

In Dorohoi County, the new powers occupied the city of Herța, along with the townships and villages of Buda Mare and Buda Mică, Pasat, Godinești, Slobozia, Horbova, Cotu-Boian, Bănceni,

Hreaţca, Lunca, Molniţa, Proboteşti, Târnauca, and others, a total of twenty-six villages. The people from Dorohoi were also brought to the train station in our Tereblecea.

In Storojineţ County, there were three cities, Storojineţ, Văşcăuţi pe Ceremuş and Vijniţa, and fifty-two rural townships, made up of sixty-seven villages. Beautiful, large villages: Berhomet-pe-Siret, Carapciu-pe-Ceremuş, Crăişoara Veche, Drăcineşti, Ispas, Jadova, Iordăneşti, Prisăcăreni, Răstoace, Şipotele Sucevei, Zamostea, Mesteceni—all of them invaded and occupied. In this county, trains were formed in Pătrăuţi, Adâncata, and Storojineţ. At the train station in Pătrăuţi (Pătrăuţii-de-Sus pe Siret), people were rounded up from the villages of the Siret Valley, Broscăuţii Noi şi Vechi, Cupca, Cerepcăuţi, Crasna Ischi. Also, forty-two families from Suceveni were brought here in trucks, strong-armed and thrown into the vehicles to be crammed into railcars along with hundreds of other families. On the evening of June 13, 1941, the locomotive pulled the railcars from off the sidetrack. They kept the people at the train station until an hour after midnight, when they thought everyone was sleeping. Then, in that total silence, the locomotive started up. But as if anyone could sleep? When they heard the chug of the locomotive, everyone who had been moaning behind locked doors became agitated. The voices of thousands of women and children cried and screamed.

And in Adâncata as well, waiting on the sidetrack were dozens of railcars, brought over from Russia for deportations. When it became lighter outside, the train filled with people from Vadul-Siret arrived. That's where people from the townships of Vadul-Siret, Volcineţi, Bahrineşti, Fântâna Albă, and Petriceni had been loaded up. These railcars then were coupled to the ones from Pătrăuţi. Each railcar had an assigned guard. In the evening, the train from Ciudei and our train from Tereblecea were added, and these railcars were coupled to the other ones. Each train also had two or three railcars made up of only men who had been separated from their families when they had been boarded. After that, the train from Storojineț arrived, which they say was the longest one, made up of sixty-five railcars, of which five were of men isolated from their families. These railcars were linked up and they headed toward the train station in Cernăuți. In Cernăuți, the railcars with men were switched to a different line and together they formed a special train, of only men, which took off in a different direction, somewhere in Ukraine, with most of the Bucovinian men ending up in the Republic of Komi or in the depths of Siberia. The poor people were crying that they'd never see their blessed land or their parents' graves again. In the morning, we arrived in the Cernăuți train station, and here, like in Adâncata, there were many empty railcars, which I think they hadn't managed to fill anymore because the war broke out.

At the Cernăuți branch train station, the train in which a huge number of people from the Romanian villages in Cernăuți County and the Herței region had been loaded was waiting for us. Cernăuți County was made up of three cities, Cernăuți, Cosmeni, and Sadagura; a suburban township, Horecea; and sixty-one rural townships, composed of ninety-three villages, all of them ceded, back in 1940. Some of the Bucovinians from this county had been loaded into railcars in Sadagura. All of the families taken from Cotul Ostriței had been put into carts and driven to the municipal building on the outskirts. Then, loaded into trucks, they were transported to Sadagura, where the men were separated from their families. After they rounded up scores upon scores of people from all of Bucovina, a line of railcars so long you couldn't see the end of it was formed at Cernăuți.

On June 15, we were at the train station and they still hadn't given us water. Some had been in the train for two days. The littlest ones were crying and asking for either food or water. Those at the bars of the railcars were all children, who would continually ask for water whenever they'd see an officer. Then some soldiers came and unlocked the railcars, allowing one person from each car to bring back water in a bucket. We stayed a while longer at the Cernăuți branch train station, then our train took off, headed east. The people there looked at us sorrowfully and waved at us in a friendly way. As we were leaving Cernăuți, the train stopped because the track was being repaired and it had to go very slowly. Then, I saw a group of women who were crying and motioning to us, and saying: "May God help you!" They were the ones who told me that another train had left from Cernăuți and that people had been picked up off the street and taken by truck to the train station to be deported . . .

My my, we who were rich, who had lived a life of plenty, we had lived in large, beautiful houses, our children had been rosy and joyful, and now we are wanderers, we have no one, hungry and dirty in this cruel, dark train! Lord, do not abandon us in this time of need, for our trials are greater than Job's! Because he, though he had lost his wealth, sat in his own dirt, while we are taken to foreign lands and we don't know where we will lay our heads and rest our bodies. He had friends who spoke the same language as him, who cared for him, encouraged him, while our children and parents die of hunger in cattle cars, and soldiers wave their weapons at us and speak to us in a foreign language, we can't understand a thing. Job, though sick and full of sores, received comfort from his beloved wife, while our husbands, O Lord, were parted from their wives and children, loaded into separate railcars and locked up far from us, without a word from them, without even knowing whether they're still alive or not, they were torn from the bosom of their families. And so, companionless and alone, we are carried away by this train on an endless journey, as reeds blown by the wind we are shaken by the storm of misfortunes and tomorrow's uncertainties . . .

The railcars had a single tiny window, but even that was grated. We were lucky to have gotten in last and so stayed near the door. As for sleeping, we slept on the floor, because it was the height of summer and we could barely stand the stifling heat, we each had a rug or a small carpet. We were given food about once every two or three days, a small piece of gummy bread as black as dirt, and we'd sometimes receive a salted fish or kasha, which is a cereal porridge. When we children first tasted that food, we all wrinkled our noses, accustomed to our sweet, fluffy bread. The second time, three days later, we ate it, though we didn't like it. And the third time it tasted good to us. But until we were able to eat our bread from Bucovina again, as the song says, long was the road, and down the Irtysh, Ob, Lena, and Volga much water flowed: "I begin my song just like the wheatear, perhaps we'll live another year, and when back home we'll go, mother will give us milk as white as snow. Her bread will be golden brown, not like this one you can hardly keep down." When our provisions were almost finished, the bread we received seemed a real treat, and we forgot the taste of our Bucovinian bread.

In our railcar, there weren't any very small children who were nursing, praise God! What suffering for the terrified, thirsty, hungry, dirty child, who was destined to die because of the conditions on the train, but also for those beside him, who were powerless to help him. What suffering to be next to a mother whose child is dying and who can't do a thing. After all the humiliations the poor people went through, they also had to witness the suffering of others. To watch how those around them, who were weaker, wasted away. When the train would park on the sidetrack and everything was quiet, when they'd leave us out in fields, far from human dwellings, we'd hear the crying of the children from the neighboring railcars. That crying tortured and horrified us, those of us nearby, and I don't even want to imagine how it must have been to be in there, in the same car. Then the crying got softer, and softer, until we didn't hear it at all.

On the train, I happened to end up next to a girl about my age with her grandmother. The two of us, and the two of them—Jenea and her grandmother Anghelina, me and my mother Aspazia— though we were from two different villages and we hadn't met before, became friends on the train and as close as sisters. Dear Jeni was the oldest in her family, while I was the youngest. Her mother had been taken earlier, along with all her younger siblings and her father. She had been at her grandmother's then, who she visited from time to time, to help her out on the farm, and sometimes bring her food. Jenea was sad and very serious, it wasn't hard to guess what she was thinking about, and I liked cheering her up. She didn't tell me at first how she had escaped from the initial invasion of the antichrists, how she had seen her entire family loaded into a cart, how she had followed her family all the way to the train station, while she escaped because her mother had made sarmale and sent her to take the warm cabbage rolls to her grandmother, and her youngest brother hadn't yet been registered at the village office, that's how little he was. The soldiers had counted: mother, father, three children, that's what was on their list, so they had gotten them all, they had rounded them up in one fell swoop and they didn't search for the oldest child. She, officially, didn't even exist. And the one who was only a few weeks old was probably among the first to die in the train, because those who were very young didn't make it. Her presence there wouldn't have saved the nursing baby, but I think she would've wanted to be with her parents and siblings. She missed them. With dear Jeni I shared all the joys and all the torments of that journey and only to her did I whisper my great secret about the treasure hidden away in the well.

Our chest on two wheels, how lucky we were to have it, it could've been used as a hope chest, maybe that actually had been its purpose, especially since my older sister had gotten married and had left it for me. I could've fit inside it, after we started emptying it of the provisions Mother had brought for the journey. It had a lid with a lock. It was a real lifesaver for us! That's where we kept the cat too. He didn't really eat much but he definitely kept growing, and he no longer fit inside the shoebox we had received him in. I was really afraid someone in the railcar might steal him.

The soldier who had pushed us into the railcar had whispered to me: "Don't move from next to the door and stay as close as you can to the wall of the railcar, under the window." Lord, what wise, life-saving advice! I had air! In a packed railcar, to be able to press your nose against the cool and less-stinky wall! We had a kind of window with so many bars that the light of day couldn't even get through. It was also too high up, so we couldn't look through it, we, children, couldn't reach it, only the grown-ups, who were taller, stood near that window. We carved out a little hole with a knife, we wore away at the space between two slats, no more than that, so it wouldn't look too obvious, then we tied a piece of metal to it with some wire, a kind of cover for the window, which would protect us from rain and soldiers.

A sunbeam! Our sunbeam made us happy, the way a gift makes you happy. The sun at the window, we'd crowd around it and line up to see it, smiling at each other. As if God Himself were revealing His presence to us, coming and greeting us. He is with us, we mustn't forget. We'd play by putting our finger on the sunbeam, catching something of its warmth and gentleness. We'd wait with our eyes fixed on our little hole, awaiting the miracle. Sometimes the light was stingy and it wasn't in a hurry to lift our moods. Arise and be done, oh brother sun, not over herds of sheep, nor over cattle sweep, but over our train black as coal, who us from our houses stole! Whoever sees it first, yells out: "My sunbeam! My sunburst! I saw it first!" It was our collective joy. Then we would sunbathe. Our eyes, lips, hands. Another time: our eyes, cheeks, noses. We'd tan ourselves in that sunbeam, we'd laugh, tell jokes. It was the most beautiful moment of the day and the one which passed by the most quickly. Great is your power, Lord!

The hole is also how we were able to stick a saucer outside when it rained, and after it filled with water, we'd pour it out for thirsty people into glasses and cups, then into a small jug to have some saved up for times of great thirst. But we'd a long time to wait until the first rain. In our railcar there was only one woman who didn't have any food left at all and she depended on our mercy and on that of the soldiers who would bring us something from time to time. We, the others, still had enough to eat, but they didn't bring us water and our thirst tortured us more and more. Mother couldn't help me when we didn't have any water left at all and I was dying of thirst so she'd start telling me stories; all of us kids would gather around her and listen with our mouths agape, forgetting about our thirst for a while. When mother didn't know any more new stories but the hardest part was just beginning, a long road awaited us, we were told stories by teacher Miss Eufrosina Procopovici who later also taught us words in Russian. The lady was the daughter of a learned man, and her father, an important professor, had gone to Transylvania. How it was that he left his daughter in the cruel clutches of the enemy, we didn't know. Maybe she had had a husband here, maybe a job. She was a young thing, pretty and gentle. We children were always by her side.

She would teach us after we had been fed and given water, but when we were thirsty and hungry she'd tell us stories. So that us little ones would forget our troubles and worries, but the grown-ups would listen as well, the entire railcar listened. When anyone made noise, the others would poke him: "Be quiet, keep it down, we can't hear!" Thanks to Eufrosina, we knew what places we were passing through and about where we were headed. She would read to us what she saw through the slits in the wall whenever we'd stop at a train station. When the soldiers would yell something at us, we couldn't understand them because they were Russian, but she'd translate for us. We really lucked out with her. Miss Procopovici was also the one who let us know that the war had started, she had heard people talking outside when we had stopped in a town. At first we were happy, we hoped that now they would take us back, that they'd free us. But that's not what happened and the train kept moving on. Then they bombed the railway, we heard the whizzing of planes, gunfire, as if our train were smack dab in the middle of the war, maybe some of our families had been wounded, maybe some railcars had been hit by bombs—how could we know?

<hr />

Mom! Hurry up and come get me! Cuța Ana is a witch! She walks through the forest and then disappears, with her cat and all. Her cat Sofron follows her everywhere, like a trusty dog, it wouldn't surprise me if he started barking at strangers one day!

I started shaking when I saw her do it. I'm afraid! I told myself at first that I'm imagining things, that maybe I'm hallucinating. She has me buy matches for her, 'cause I'm spry and quicker on my toes. I kept hauling back matchboxes, until the whole village was surprised. I, too, wondered what Cuţa could want with so many matches. I put them on a shelf, then she waited until I was rummaging for who knows what in the attic, and she stuffed the matches in a pouch and hurried out of the yard. I heard the gate and tiptoed out quietly after her. I saw her going into the forest, I saw the cat too, then it was as if she had become see-through, invisible, she went right down into the ground, I couldn't see her anywhere. I ran home to write you! I'm afraid! Come get me! I'm sure she's a witch!

Yes, Mom, you were right. I asked her about the firing lines, she said she wasn't from this village, that she came here when she was twenty years old, but she knows about the huts built by the partisans and all the trenches dug by them in the forest. We went there together and climbed down into a dark, deep one, she said she'd show me more, but that I shouldn't go alone, 'cause I might get lost. Do you know about them too? Did Dad show you? In some places, the ground could collapse and bury you alive. She said she's keeping a little place there for hard times. Mom, I think that hiding place is where she takes the matches. But why? Anyway, everything is fine now, Cuţa is telling me more stories about the deportation.

—Mom, Cuţa keeps a fast on Mondays, Wednesdays, and Fridays!

—You should too.

—But I'm dying of hunger! And we can't so much as sit down at the table without praying to God. God this, God that! I haven't heard His name so much even in church. On Sundays we go to church.

—Cuṭa's a believer, you should learn from her. You're a Christian, not a heathen.

—But we don't pray before meals at home. And aren't we believers?

—We are, but do as she does and don't upset her. Speak nicely to her, listen to her. You wouldn't have been born if it hadn't been for our Cuṭa's God. Cuṭa survived by having Him in her heart and mind, she made it through all the hardships and then took care of us too. Be respectful. And don't offend her.

After about a couple days, some furniture showed up in our railcar too, meaning some big straw bales, like a bunch of giant bricks, straight not round, which we stacked one on top of the other to the ceiling. The train had stopped in a field full of straw and we were told to gather it. We thought it was for us, but after about a week, the soldiers took all the straw and sold it to some local people. In our railcar, since we had a man, we also had more straw, because Mr. Gherman had gathered up more. There wasn't much space and we had to squeeze together. We'd sprinkle some on the floor too and, when the train would stop, we'd throw out the dirty straw and lay down others that smelled clean and fresh. Among the straw, we'd sometimes find an ear of wheat with a grain in it, which we'd keep in our mouth until it softened. The straw was our favorite pastime, for us children. Besides me and Jeni, there were also children who were bigger than us, and others who were smaller, not very many though, so we had someone to play with. I didn't count the child in the traitor's belly, because we couldn't play with him and, in any case, he was born dead, when the heat was at its most sweltering, and he quickly began to stink. We took the straw by storm, we made holes in it, a bale was set up to be a table, the older ones would lean against it, the younger ones slept in the holes we made, it was better than on the ground. For the older ones it was dangerous, if the train lurched more suddenly, we could topple onto the others or the pile of straw could collapse and it would bury all of us. Our parents would try to scare us, telling us to behave ourselves, or Tartaco with the beard down to his elbow would come and get us, stuff us in his red sack, and throw us to the rooster! But we weren't scared. Let's just see the terrible Tartaco get inside the railcar! Obviously Tartaco is afraid of the train and the soldiers.

On June 20, I celebrated my birthday, I turned eleven years old. Many days before that, mother and I, and then also Jeni, who I told the secret to and she joined us, saved up and set aside the bits of bread that we had received as food. We wrapped them in a towel so they wouldn't dry up, then we put them on a big plate and mother put a cherry on each of them from a small jar of jam we had brought from home which we had kept especially for my birthday. We hadn't yet lost track of the days and sometimes the soldier would also tell us what day it was. Meanwhile, Jeni had found herself something amazing to keep her busy, which I happily helped with. All the children helped, in fact, I mean all the girls. She started to braid a kind of mat out of straw. I'd never seen such skill before! I tried it too, but my straws would come loose, while hers seemed to obey and stick however she wanted them to. The girls would search for straws that were as long and thin as possible, then we'd hold on to the edges, as she instructed us. She made the first mat for her grandmother, Anghelina Țară, then one for my mother, then, in turn, she made them for others until no long, thin straws were left. When I told her I was saving bread for my birthday, she said she didn't need our help anymore for the mats and she hid in the bales and braided alone. On my birthday, I prepared the bread with cherries and gave a piece to each of the children which I had numbered beforehand with mother, I offered one to the child inside of the belly of the pregnant woman because I was sure he, too, must be craving goodies. When the door opened and they brought in the bucket of water, I gave some to everyone and then I said they should first eat and then drink some water, because jam makes you thirsty. How happy the children were! Mother said a prayer of thanksgiving to God as the other mothers tried to hide their tears. How happy they were to see us alive, eating bread and jam! And then, after I had passed it out and we had eaten it, it had melted quickly in our mouths, Jeni and all the children looked at me secretively and said: "The birthday girl will now receive a present." And they handed me a wonderful doll, it was big, made of straw, with a skirt from a piece of someone's headscarf, with hands, feet, and little boots made from twisted ribbons, with two blonde plaits done in French braids, it definitely wasn't Jeni who braided them, but Aglaie Gherman, who French braided her younger sister's hair, and in its hand was a flower, made of straw as well. It also had a face, with eyes, with a nose that was a bit big, and a mouth that grinned from ear to ear. So this was the mat Jeni was secretly braiding when I told her about my birthday! I had barely managed to admire my doll when everyone wanted to see it, touch it, admire and praise it, it passed from hand to hand and I could hardly wait for it to get back to me. I was afraid that someone might ruin it, or steal its flower or skirt. You never know. Jeni went to go look for it and she returned with my gift. Then she made smaller dolls for the other girls, without a flower or a headscarf skirt. I put my doll in a special place and I looked at it every day. It was the loveliest day of the entire journey! After she had made about five dolls for other girls, Jeni also made a boy doll, with a hat, also made of straw, and pants and a shirt, not made from a headscarf, but from straw as well. It was big and matched my doll. She also made a flower for it, but on its hat.

One day, I caught Jeni playing with our dolls, hers and mine, which she was pressing together, saying: "Ana and Jeni, eternal love!" At first, I didn't understand what she was doing and saying, then I started laughing, and Jeni got upset. I think that everyone in the railcar knew that Jeni was a boy, except for me. Only after she told me she was a boy did it start to make sense, the grown-ups probably knew, but we, the younger ones, had other things to worry about. Jeni also gave me his straw boy, who was in love with my straw girl. They were my old toys during my exile and I kept them for many years until they came apart and turned into a little pile of straw and dust. Jeni's hands were golden, he could make a miracle out of anything. He told us that in his village they would say about people who were rather simpleminded that they don't know how to tie two straws together. Then the soldiers took the straw from the railcars. But the mats and the dolls stayed . . .

A woman had managed to take a pot full of pork cracklings in lard with her. How our mouths would water whenever she'd eat some of them! She sat on that pot all day, as if it were a chair, maybe it was comfortable that way, maybe she was scared that someone would steal her cracklings. Mother saw that I was craving some and she gave me a small onion to take to her so she'd give me a crackling in exchange. I took it to her but received nothing back. Then, on my birthday, when I had passed out bread with cherries to everyone, she gave me a slice of bread with pork scraps in lard—a gift. The lard smelled rancid, but the meat was good. I didn't eat it all, I shared with those around me. A few children tasted it and there was still some left over for me. Then, after the end of the war, when we got back on our feet a bit, we, too, had a pig and Mother made cracklings in lard. Cracklings and lard on bread was then my favorite food. It seemed that nothing could be better. Though I remember that when I had worked on the farm, I thought milk was the best thing in the world.

When the doors would open and we'd receive either a piece of bread or a bucket of kasha, we'd all eat while looking at each other and at the portion each received. But, usually, we'd eat without looking into each other's eyes. When a mother would take out something good from what she had left for her child, the others would pull back their children, they'd turn them around so they wouldn't see and crave it. Some of the smaller ones would stare anyway and cry that they wanted some too. I didn't crave what others had, only once during the entire journey did I want cracklings and lard on bread. That woman's pot was huge, as big as a bucket, and I thought I'd like to taste some too. It was already rancid by the time she gave me some!

When we received kasha and had some greens on hand (we had gathered some when they had let us out of the railcars one day), we children and the girls who were a little bit older, started making little rolls with the leaves, pretending they were sarmale. Preparing the meal this way took a very long time and all the women in the railcar perked up. That was the only time I was able to pick greens, Eugen's grandmother said that it was coltsfoot and advised us to gather as much as we could. I put the leaves in a headscarf, our soldier let us. They were all amazed then, even Mother, at how I started making the sarmale. I could picture myself at home, in our sweet Albina in Bucovina, when the housewives would gather before a wedding or a funeral or another joyous or sad occasion and begin rolling the little sarmale. The smaller they were, the more skillful the cook. I rolled the leaf, folded the ends, even I felt as if I were making special sarmale, one end rounder and the other pointier, and small, as small as possible, the size of a finger.

Then I walked in front of the other children who were also busy shaping their sarmale and pretended to be the head chef, to the general amusement of all:

"More fat—sarmale without enough fat have no taste to them. What did you put in there? How come it tastes a bit sour?" I frowned at some little girl, imitating who knows which house-wife. "Ahhh, you boiled them in tomato juice, yes, they turn out really good that way . . . The fanciest sarmale are those that are as small as your finger. Look," I said and lifted up the miniscule sarmale of a girl. "Behold the ideal sarmale! Does anyone have a smaller one? No? Bravo, you're the best cook!"

"But you," I said to Eugen, who wasn't really able to make small sarmale, "made one in the Ukrainian style, as big as a fist. You eat two of those and you're full."

"What's this," I asked another child, "Lenten sarmale? Did you make it for a saint's day, or a memorial service?"

I moved on and pretended to taste one:

"What kind of meat did you use? Pork, beef, chicken? I can't tell." The girl, playing along, shyly said, "A little bit of rabbit meat."

I looked questioningly at Mother. "I've never heard of sarmale made with rabbit meat." Mother nodded. "People make them, but not that often."

"A white bunny, with red eyes," the girl added.

"Why were its eyes red? Did it cry because it didn't want to go into the sarmale? Poor little floppy ears . . ."

I moved on.

"Salt, girls, more salt . . ."

"What a cook! What a worthy housewife," the mothers praised me and whispered among themselves.

I saw Mother, proud, struggling to hold back her tears. After we finished with the kasha and filled a large pot with our sarmale, we stopped to catch our breath. "Let's go serve the guests." The mothers each delicately lifted, using two fingers, one of the so-called sarmale, they put it in their mouth, waited a moment, then slowly chewed it, closing their eyes in bliss, and they all said, one after another: "It melts in your mouth!" They said it with such conviction, that we believed them. What if, through some miracle, that tasteless kasha had transformed into rice and carrots with lots of meat? Then they invited us to taste the delicacies. I put a small roll in my mouth and its taste made me want to throw up, but so I wouldn't ruin the enchanting atmosphere, I closed my eyes and forced myself to eat it all, that's what the other children did too, we all struggled to swallow our marvelous sarmale.

—You tell such interesting stories, Cuţa! It was cheerful there in the train . . . Mom asked me to be careful not to laugh when you talk about the deportation. She said: "Cuţa suffered, and you're laughing about it . . ."

—Well, there are also stories that would make you cry, but we were children and we quickly got tired of crying and moaning. After two weeks, we acted as if we had been born in the train, as if that were our home. We played, we were happy, as skinny, hungry, and lice-ridden as we were, with the sunbeam, with the cat. We started learning Russian right from the start and it came in very handy. Then we'd repeat the words we knew from the previous lesson, that we had learned the day before. It didn't take much to make us happy. A person doesn't need a lot, a person who has God in their heart. It's a grave sin to allow sorrow and hopelessness to overwhelm you. Yes, people died of hunger, of thirst, but first of all because they had forgotten God or had cursed him, angry that they were badly off and He wasn't helping them. Only those who kept God in their hearts survived, the younger ones came back, they started families, they had children, they carried on the family line. We were children and we wanted to forget about all the sadness and hardships, we wanted to be happy, and now, in my old age, I still want to be happy and I don't remember every last thing we suffered. It's sinful to give in to sorrow. Cheerfulness dispels tiredness, and tiredness is what leads to hopelessness, and from it, all the other sins. Cheerfulness is not a sin. Lamenting your fate, cursing, rage, turmoil, immoral thoughts, all of them are born from a spirit of apathy. Troubles test us—they, too, come from God.

The railcar was alive, like a big animal, like a many-headed dragon that cries with all of its mouths, it sighed, it swayed. The howling of pain. You learn to ignore it. I filled my time with catching the sunbeam, counting what provisions we still had left and for how many days. I couldn't reach the bottom of the chest and I couldn't take everything out in the open, where others could see and crave what we had, but I would number the walnuts without taking them out, I'd number them a few times a day, but I wouldn't eat a single one. I'd mess up and start over again. Then, when the cat came into my life, he took up all my time. I'd take care of him, talk to him, explain what was right and wrong. I'd also play with Jeni and the other children, especially after they'd bring us something to eat and our bellies were somewhat fuller. I'd even laugh, through my tears, sometimes. With Jeni I'd play face's body— here's the cheek's cheekbone—here's the cheek's apple—here's the eyes' bags, the nose's nipple, the nose's bridge . . . I'd caress him, kiss him, thinking he was a girl, and he'd blush. We'd feel, pinch, tickle each other, we'd roughhouse. "Settle down, little foals," Grannie Anghelina chided us. Mother didn't say anything.

What we wished for most of all was that we'd lose our sense of smell, but it became more acute with each passing day. Each day, it stunk more terribly in the railcar. We were peasant children and had been raised in the fresh air, with fields, forests, flowers, trees in bloom in the month of May, the scent of acacia and cherry trees. Keeping us locked inside a stuffy railcar was the worst form of torture for us and more than we could bear. It was the same with the water. After about a week of being on the road, we were so thirsty that we were grateful even for the bucket of warm, murky water that tasted of swamp, especially grateful after having salted fish . . . Who could still remember the taste of cold and clear spring water?

The train sometimes slowed down and barely, barely kept going, like a cart being pulled by tired nags, and sometimes sped up, quickly, quickly, and flew like a rocket. Dazed by the perpetual movement of the wheels that continually rattled us, we were surprised that we didn't become completely tongue-tied. When the train would stop close to human dwellings, the people would come out, they'd cross themselves at the sight of us and they'd bring us something out of the little they had. Usually they'd bring us water, well water, not river water. When we stopped next to a pond, we rushed out toward it, though we weren't steady on our feet. We stuck our heads in the water, guzzled it, as if we were cattle. We couldn't get enough, we splashed ourselves, washed ourselves, and cooled off, because who knew when we'd have water again and how much longer it would be until the end of the road.

How terrible it was during the bombings . . . I hated stops when we were parked for a long time, on sidetracks, in empty fields, for entire days, forgotten by everyone. We'd yell, we'd beg for at least a little water, so we could moisten our lips, but no one would hear us. We'd ask for help, but not a soul was around, we didn't see the soldiers anymore either, was someone still guarding us, or had they left us there? We ended up being glad when the train started moving again.

"Water! Water!" the children first yelled in their different voices, high and low. When the train would stop for a bit, we'd all yell in unison, uniting all the voices in the railcar. Then we turned this word into a whole song: "Wa-ter, wa-ter, wa-ter! At least a little drop!" Our marching song, our hymn, our hope. At first, only the children, then everyone, from the oldest to the youngest. Others heard as well, the entire train sang this song of the thirsty deportees. Maybe the soldiers thought it was a rebellion? The train would stop, but the door wouldn't open. Especially in the cities. Water! Water! Then our song faded, we no longer had the strength we had in our first days. We employed our hands and feet when our voices weakened. Wa—*bang-bang*—ter—*bang-bang*, with our fists on the walls. Then with our feet as well: Wa—*stamp-stamp*—ter—*stamp stamp*, water, *stamp-stamp-stamp*! We thought it was the most beautiful song and when, finally, we received that holy water, we were sure that the good Lord Himself had heard our hymn.

In the railcar, it was dark more than it was light. We stood all day, by turns, with our faces up against our small window, for a breath of clean air, to see a ray of light. Many went blind when, after weeks of travel, they let us out. Their eyes couldn't take in so much light anymore. We were all unsteady from weakness, our legs were shaking, but those who were far from the light and any kind of window couldn't even see where they were going, someone had to take them by the hand. Some of them had been in our railcar as well, people who were in the middle of the car and didn't catch even a sliver of light. But slowly, slowly their sight came back . . .

———❧———

At first, Mother prayed for health, for a quick arrival at a destination, then I heard her pray: "Keep me, Lord, from holding my child in my arms as she dies. Give her life, Lord, take it from mine and give it to her. Lord, do not be angry with us, because we know the bitterness of life, but lead us on Your path with Your love, extinguish the flame of our grief, and with the hope of Your sweet goodness from heaven, cast out our bitterness! Keep us, Lord, from being overwhelmed by pain and hopelessness in this train and remember us, who with fervent tears pray to You! Strengthen, Lord, our brothers and sisters. Guide us all with Your Grace, until the end of the road, because without You we can do nothing."

Mother instructed me how to overcome difficulties. "Prayer," she said, "strengthens the soul and helps the body. Just as the body dies when it no longer has breath, the soul dies when it no longer prays. Prayer has to be awakened, it lies asleep in our souls, then when we light it, it's the fire that, once lit, must be watched over so that it doesn't go out. Cleanse us, Lord, from all bitterness, if our bodies are filthy and lice-ridden, may our souls be clean and directed toward You. Do not allow our fickle thoughts to race toward other things.

"When you start doing something, don't forget to begin with: 'Bless me, Lord!' and when you finish: 'Praise to You, O Lord!' Lord, have mercy on us sinners! Angel of the Lord, my holy guardian, watch over me and keep me! I feel an outpouring of warmth, mystery, and light when I pray, when the soul makes itself at home in the heavenly world. With prayer we can overcome all our enemies! With complete devotion I entrust myself into Your hands, our good and just Lord, our compassionate and merciful King. Come, Lord, with Your goodness, to warm my soul! May Your glory shine over all humanity and may we all know Your eternal love!

We fervently and earnestly pray that the gifts of words, love, prayer, and mercy not be taken from us, gifts which You, Lord, give. May Your Holy Spirit be our guide, Lord!"

In our railcar, no one had had lice, there were only respectable people, clean people. Even though we couldn't wash ourselves on the train, lice couldn't just appear from nowhere. Well, lice are lice . . . About halfway through the journey, after traveling for almost two weeks, our train, including our railcar, became a paradise for lice. All day, as long as we had a little light, we'd check each other for lice, we didn't even have time to play anymore. One day I found thirty, on Mother and Eugen, they had been in my area of delousing and the two of them were also checking me. Then I stopped, I said to myself that I'd leave some for tomorrow, because people had to keep themselves busy the livelong day. Even though we continually deloused ourselves, our chances of being rid of them were small, they came from all around, maybe they could fly, for years afterward I'd find lice in my hair, even in our Kazakh aul, even in Siberia, even at the vocational school for seamstresses, where they would check us once a month and take us to be treated. There was no shame in it, because they'd take all of us. Winters, when we'd stay at home, Mother would still sometimes find a random little louse who had gotten there who knows how, which I wouldn't even feel, after having experienced such a lousing on the train. At first, it made me queasy to crush them between my nails, I would only pick them off and give them to Mother. Then, I started enjoying killing them. Jeni would pop them so loudly it would echo throughout the whole railcar, I couldn't do it that loudly. In the end, I saw where we'd get re-infested with lice, where we'd be replenished with new species when we had thought we had killed all the ones on us: when they'd let us out of the train for water, we'd crowd together or we'd leave our clothes in a big pile if they let us splash around in some pond.

One day I caught the King of the lice, it was long and thick, the biggest louse in our railcar. It wasn't black or brownish like all the others but dark red, and it didn't run through Eugen's long hair, who at the time I thought of as my best friend Jenica, but stood there, planted right on the top of his head, as if waiting for me to find and admire it. All of us children gathered around and wondered what to do with it. Should we shut it up in a little box, kill it, let it go through the small window? In the end, after many proposals and much discussion, the fate of King Lice was decided and sealed. We would pass him on to Fedor, the soldier guarding us. He was fatter, jollier, and better dressed than us, our King would be well off. Mother let us whisper together, but we didn't tell her what we decided. We thought of a plan: as soon as Fedor would come inside our railcar, as soon as he bent down, someone would drop the dear louse selected for conservation right on his head. If any day now we were to kill all of licedom and the world would be left without lice, who and for what reason would anyone lovingly tousle a head, if lice didn't exist anymore? What tenderness when someone runs their hand through your hair in search of minuscule nits and insolent lice. What satisfaction when you crush them between your nails! Blessed lice!

Mom, Cuța gets so wrapped up in her story, it's as if she's seeing everything, as if she were there again. "Don't cry anymore, Cuța," I say to her when tears roll down her cheeks.

"The whole train is crying, not just me," she answers and continues with her story. "They threw the pick of the bunch of Bucovina to the dogs! They sent the old people to die far from home!"

Mom, I can't tell Cuța about your luxurious nursing home! She doesn't care about how much money you all are willing to spend there, or about how caring the nurses there are, or about its parks or how well the rooms are heated in the winter! She'll get upset if I talk to her about it.

Annie tried to reach you, she said she can never catch you on Skype. Apparently her boyfriend wants to show her around Bucovina, where he has relatives, then Annie wants to invite him here, to Moldova. Mom, Annie told me she loves him. He's that boy she met last year, they're classmates at the University of Iași. She said she'll bring me over to Romania too, to show me around the city. Instead of vacationing in Iași, I'm here with our Blajinica and fasting Mondays, Wednesdays, and Fridays!

When that woman went into labor in our railcar, we, children, were made to face the wall, the wall with the high window, we were to stay with our backs toward her and not turn around. A mother was watching us, "Don't look!" but they let us talk loudly, laugh, poke each other, we played belt snake, we were cheerful but maybe we were just trying to be cheerful and not hear what was happening there, in the middle of the railcar, that woman was screaming in pain, and her child was stillborn. We weren't to pay any mind. A child informed us that stillborn babies that are unbaptized and tossed out turn into "moroi," if you hear children crying at night you throw a handkerchief in that direction and say the Apostles' Creed, and that "strigoi" are old people who are unbaptized. Our old people are all baptized, so we don't have strigoi in our railcar, just one moroi.

That pregnant woman didn't want to give birth. We understood that and pitied her. She cried that how could she raise the child by herself, here in the train, she cried on account of many things which we, the cruelest among us, didn't really understand. We tried to work it out among ourselves: how could we find out if the pregnant woman would have a boy or a girl? If it's a girl, her face gets splotchy, her eyelashes and eyebrows fall out, her lower lip goes slack and she becomes uglier. If it's a boy, the woman is ruddy, beautiful, her face is smooth and spotless. Usually, a boy is carried on the right side, and a girl on the left. Our pregnant woman was splotchy and ugly, but we later found out it was a boy. So what the children said wasn't true. It's a sin not to let a pregnant woman taste the food she craves and we gave her some, because she was the only one in our railcar who hadn't brought anything to eat. If you nurse a baby from your left breast first, the baby will be a lefty. If in the first months a woman hides the fact that she's pregnant, the child will be born mute. If you wean the child and then breastfeed him again, he'll give people the evil eye all his life. If you let him nurse a dried-up breast to keep him quiet, he'll tell lies all his life. If the woman steals any object, a birthmark in the shape of it will appear on the body of the newborn. It's considered a sin to push ahead of a pregnant woman, because she has two souls, she's beyond a mere mortal. But ours was kind of mean, we didn't like her. Then she started looking for knives, she asked us for one, but we wouldn't give it to her. What did she want with it? She didn't by any chance . . . ? God forbid! Then Grannie Anghelina told her "The Story of God":

Out went a strong man, with a strong ax,
Into trees without number and chopped down hard lumber
And built a big monastery, with nine doors, altars just as many,
And nine holy tables in the sanctuary.
On the biggest altar was an icon of the Holy Virgin's death.
On the smallest altar was an icon of the Holy Virgin's birth.
Look in books, look in nooks, look in all the places,
He saw Saint John in the church.
Saint John sat, he read and prayers said.
The Mother of God came and asked him:
John, Holy John, have you seen my son, your godson?
I have not seen him, but I have heard him in the song of Jerusalem,
He was caught by pagan godforsaken dogs
On a cross crucified, nailed to each side,
A thorny crown put on his head.

When the Mother of God heard, her heart was scored,
And she almost fell to the ground.
She set off for the hill of Jerusalem,
In the dark valley of Gehinnom
And anon on the road she met with a toad:

What distresses you, Immaculate Mother?
I had twelve babies, each a darling button,
I took them out Saturday morning to get a little sun
And came a wheel pell-mell and all at once the twelve fell
And it did not distress me.
Go you to church Saturday morning

And come out on Sunday morning.
Over where your son will come to you
The fields will have dew, the trees leaves anew.
In haste your skies again will be blue!

And the Immaculate Mother came out of church on Sunday morning
And came the Lord Jesus Christ.
When the Immaculate Mother saw him, she ran and held him fast,
Kissed his face at last, and then finally asked:

Oh holy John, oh what he told me!
I knew you as worthy and mighty,
Why did you give yourself over to pagan godforsaken dogs?
But Jesus Christ answered:
Truly I did not give myself for me,
Truly not for thee.
For the law I gave myself truly.
Whoever died, no rites had,
Whoever was born, was not baptized,
Couples went without nuptials,
And mothers for their children didn't care.
But from now those who die will have rites,
Those who are born will be baptized,
Couples will have nuptials
And mothers for their children care.

Whoever knows this story and doesn't tell it
Each month, each week, each year, each half year,
God will take by the left hand
And on crooked paths steer,
To empty tables and unlit lamps!

Whoever knows this story and tells it
Each month, each week, each year, each half year,
God will take by the right hand
And on straight paths steer,
To laden tables, to shining lamps!

We learned this story as well and we kept saying it until that woman no longer wanted a knife and she went into labor.

—How can someone have a baby there, in the railcar?

—The way everyone does, except that it's on the train. A little water, a little brandy. Some rags, a woman who wasn't afraid to pull the baby out. We had a knife for cutting the newborn's cord. We even had a hoe and an ax that could be used in an emergency, if that would've ever made sense.

The first child to die in our railcar was Ştefănel, who had been hit by soldiers back then on the night of the 12th toward the morning of the 13th, he had also seen his parents being pummeled, yelling and crying. He had had such a fright that he never recovered. He wouldn't drink, he wouldn't eat, and Baba Tudoriţa's chants didn't help him. We'd hear her mumbling over him and we copied her, repeating:

Jiggery, pokery, what are you doing there?
I'm squashing the samca, the zaporniţa,
The great fright I'll beat
From Ştefănel's back, hands, and feet,
And throw from all his bones!
So Ştefănel will be left all clean,
Like water passed through a screen,
Like his mother who made him,
Like his godparents at his baptism,
Like God who gave him wisdom!

His mother would come up to us and stroke our heads, saying:

"Ştefănel dear, your little body was thrown out, but your soul is still here in the train, stuck to the children, I feel it when I touch their hair. Look, they even have cowlicks like you."

Ştefănel had been baptized, he didn't become a moroi.

It wasn't from hunger that people died in our railcar. The water we received was sometimes stagnant, fetid, we were allowed to drink from the ponds on the side of the road. Our stomachs would be churning afterward from water like that, we'd get sick, we'd need to use the toilet. We came from respectable families and it wasn't easy for us to relieve ourselves where the entire railcar could see and hear us. At least a hundred pairs of eyes and just as many ears tried not to see and hear what one of us was struggling to do inside a hole in one of the corners, with much embarrassment. We were even scared to eat knowing what was to follow. A mother hung a blanket to at least cover a little whoever needed to use our makeshift latrine. But there were older girls among us who were very shy. There were also a few old people, who back home had been respected fathers and the pride of their families. They used the latrine more often at night, bent over from shame, when they hoped that the others were sleeping. The children would cry that they wanted to go to the bathroom, but not here, their bathroom at home. How could they go here, while the train was racing, and in front of everyone? But when the train was still and it was quieter, it wasn't comfortable to go then either, because you were afraid you might let out some outlandish sound and others would laugh. Sometimes a child would break into muffled giggles. Then the shame among us would dissipate a bit but the stench in the train would thicken instead. When they weren't next to their mothers, the little children would lose their balance, they'd fall and get dirty. We didn't have water to drink, let alone for washing.

The ones who were a bit bigger would fall too, and the oldest among us. Whoever happened to be there would fall, when the train would jerk suddenly at some turn . . .

Meanwhile, our dragon raced on toward faraway places, and when it sometimes stopped in train stations, the soldiers would burst into the railcars and read off everyone's name from a long list, as if anyone could have escaped that death train. Each time the roll was called, those who were missing were children and old people who had died along the way, from thirst and lack of oxygen. In all that time, locals would come up to the railcars with bread, water, milk, and other good things. Whoever had money or a rug or headscarf to spare could receive something in exchange. Hunger made everything people had left cheaper. There seemed to be fewer and fewer soldiers guarding the train. Fedor was the only one guarding us. We once stopped at the edge of a small village, to get some water. Several people from that village came over to us, and we went to fill our buckets at a well. Those of us who wanted to sell or buy something got out too. Grandmother Anghelina and Nicanor Gherman were carrying water, and a girl my age came up to me. She handed me a box after she had looked inside it and firmly put the lid on, while saying: *Kot*. I can't remember if she said anything else, in any case I didn't know the language and "Kot" was the only word that stuck. I didn't know then that that's how you say cat in Russian.

I went back inside the railcar happily with my box and when I looked inside, I cried out and quickly put the lid back on! It never could have occurred to me that what was in the box wasn't the *hleb*, or bread, that we hungry deportees dreamed of, but an animal which no one in the girl's family wanted and she, afraid that someone might kill it or chase it away, decided to give it as a gift. Many came to the train with whatever they had, people would trade, she, too, brought what she had, but without wanting something in return, without getting anything in exchange, because I didn't have anything to give. The girl stayed there until she was convinced that I hadn't thrown the box under the train, something I had no intention of doing. I had gotten in quickly and the doors were firmly bolted, the train started off. Done, her Kot was safe, I thought that was the name of the scared kitty. That little girl had no idea what kind of train we were traveling in and where it was taking us. We quickly got used to the cat, and it got used to us. The children would come and pet it, play with it.

—I've forgotten the name of that woman, I'm forgetting things. My, how I'm forgetting, that's what old age is like. I can see her eyes, her face, I remember how her hands were always balled into fists, I thought she was hiding something valuable, I hear her voice, how she spoke, I can almost seem to remember even how her clothes rustled, but I can't remember the person's name. People from her village said she was related to someone named Şakaliuk. I think that's right, but what her name was . . .

—Why don't we give her a name?

—Alright.

—Maybe Maria was her name?

—No, it definitely couldn't have been Maria!

—Maybe Nicoleta?

—No, it couldn't have been Nicoleta either, names like that didn't exist in Bucovina back then.

—Cristina, Dana, Rodica, Dora, Viorica?

—Viorica suits. Or Dora . . .

That woman who had drawn up lists, only to find herself on one of them and put inside the same railcar with the women from her village who she hated, envied, and wanted as far away from her as possible. How hard must it have been for her to bear a burden like that! All of us prayed earnestly for her miserable soul. But she was also incredibly mean! We'd all be dying of thirst after that salted fishtail we'd received and the train wouldn't always stop to let us replenish our reservoirs, to fill up our dishes with water. Usually, when the train stopped a soldier would bring us a bucket and shut the door. Someone would use a cup to evenly distribute the water, so everyone would get some. If there was any left over, they'd continue to take the little that was left around to everyone again, or they'd leave the tiny bit in the bucket for emergency use. A bucket was, in any case, very little for an entire railcar full of people, especially since we didn't know when we'd get another. It could be even several days until the train stopped again and we received water.

One day, when the doors opened and we saw the long awaited bucket, Dora raced over from her corner, she elbowed everyone aside, and before we realized what she was doing, she stuck her entire head in the bucket, and then she did it again, hair and all, as if she didn't want just to quench her thirst but to drown herself in that bucket. She had completely lost her mind. "If you insist on drowning yourself, do it in your own water, not in our communal water." The women took her away from the bucket but strands of hair and snot remained in that murky water, contaminated by an unbeliever. Someone tried filtering the water as much as they could with a spoon, but we couldn't drink it, we were very thirsty but also nauseated, it was better to be thirsty. We poured the water into our cupped hands and wet our faces, and body parts that water hadn't touched in some time. It was such a pleasant feeling, Mother had wet a napkin and wiped me with it, that's what other mothers and other women did as well, so we forgot a bit about our thirst. Lucky for us, we soon had more water and we made sure some crazy person didn't contaminate it. When it rained, we stuck a small plate through our tiny window, one that wasn't very deep and could fit through the hole. After it was full, we stuck another one out, we did this by turns and then we poured out clean rainwater for everyone.

That was the only time we washed ourselves with water in the railcar, then they let us out near a pond, where the water was very cold and Mother said I shouldn't go in all the way, because I might catch a chill, that I shouldn't go in farther than my knees, because it's easier to die from a chill than from filth. Those who went in all the way later caught a fever and were thrown from the railcars in the hope that someone would bury them. Even though we were traveling during the summer, it was hot only in the first weeks, then it was warm only during the day and got cool at night. Our bodies, accustomed to the kind, gentle sun from back home, couldn't adjust to the freezing Russian summer. Ha, one month later, not even the freezing dead of winter could scare us, nothing could. People don't know how much someone can shoulder if they have a strong, faithful soul.

Dora seemed to have completely lost her mind after she lost the child. She would lean over the hole which we used as a toilet and stare into it, silently, as if waiting for a miracle. She didn't join in with the rest of the railcar, she didn't speak, didn't get upset or happy about anything, her gaze was absent, her entire being was absent, everyone avoided her, we, children, were kept away from her by our mothers. She was adrift, lost, with something cold and hardened in her expression. Then she stopped looking at the hole and instead laid down on the floor and acted as if she were dead, that's how it seemed to us, as if she were dead. Someone would dab her dry lips with water, she didn't ask for anything, she didn't cry, nothing.

I remember another incident with her, one I can't forget, how we prayed for her soul, all of us in the railcar, at first a few women who were next to her, then others joined in, then everyone prayed the same prayer. When we prayed, we'd touch each other's hands or bodies, we'd get close to each other, either we'd hold hands, or hold onto someone's shoulders, so that the prayer would be more powerful. The five Gherman girls stood next to her, it was hard for a bunch of children to be stuck there by her. Right then Aglaie, the eldest, holding her doll, happened to be next to Dora. We were praying and Aglaie must have thought, the way children do, that if we were all holding hands, maybe she would hold Dora's hand. Maybe the prayer would help her, if she touched her, squeezed her hand? The entire railcar seemed to understand what the girl was thinking and waited to see what Aglaie would decide. Would she be able to hold her hand or not? Silently, I, too, prayed that Aglaie would grab onto Dora's hand. *Come on, grab her hand.* But Dora might refuse it. Aglaie held out her straw doll to Dora while she prayed quietly, we couldn't hear her but we saw her lips moving, trembling. I don't know what Dora felt, but she took the doll and reached out for Aglaie's hand on her own, as if our thought had been transmitted directly to her hand, and held it. We, when we saw that, started to pray even more fervently, while tears sprang up in Aglaie's eyes, her hand hurt from being squeezed too tightly. I've heard that the grip of people on their deathbed is like a vice. And Dora began to cry quietly, gently, to our relief. She looked at Aglaie and I heard her say "forgive me" to her. And she also said: "Forgive me, Lord." Someone brought over a piece of a candle (we didn't have a whole one left, because there were many weakened and sick people and everyone kept a candle for those in their family, while Dora didn't belong to anyone). "Will you forgive me?" she asked Aglaie again. "Yes," Aglaie said. Our prayer turned into a barely whispered song. Dora let go of Aglaie's hand and she hugged the doll as if it were a child, maybe she actually thought she was holding her dead child to her chest, she rocked it in time to our song, she smiled, and died. "At least she died at peace," someone said. Death reconciles us all.

I wondered what would happen with the doll, Aglaie was looking at it as well, as if she were sorry to leave it with the dead woman. But when her mother asked her if she wanted us to take it from her arms, if she wanted it, Aglaie didn't, she didn't want to hold it anymore after Dora had held it to her chest as if it were her dead child. I wouldn't have wanted mine back either. Aglaie had dressed her doll in a piece of a cloth, pretending it was a dress, and she took back the dress, that's all. Then Dora was taken outside the railcar, because it was summer, the day was hot, and the body smelled, they set her down with the straw doll still in her arms. Something seemed off to the soldier and he wanted to take the doll from her arms and toss it, he tried to tear it away, but he couldn't. Dora was smiling and she no longer looked like a dead woman. Eugen didn't make Aglaie a new doll because we didn't have any straw left and we were already too exhausted, it was hard to do such painstaking work after being on the train for so long. After this incident, I kept my dolls carefully hidden, so there was no chance of anyone dying while clutching them to their chest.

Those first days, we didn't know that Dora was pregnant. The whole train found out about her when she lashed out at a wife with children, who was very gentle, from the same village as her. The young woman had been telling us how, in the hubbub, her husband had gotten lost, he had managed to hide and the soldiers left without him because they were hurrying to get them to the train station before the train left. Then Dora yelled hatefully:

"He ran after me. I'm bearing his child!" The middle daughter of the woman who was telling the story, a very beautiful little girl, started crying. We children didn't understand all of what Dora was saying, but the woman's children gathered around their mother, as if to protect her from the cruel and unjust words of the pregnant woman. She wasn't feeling well, none of us were feeling well, but that didn't mean we could attack our neighbor.

The night when Dora was in labor was torturous: she screamed, squealed, oh-godded, turned into her worst self, she ballooned, she curled up like a leech, snorted like a cow, but the baby still died. I don't even know if he was born alive, I never heard him cry and I don't think he could have anyway from the very first. And the formerly pregnant woman became just a shell. The face of a person abandoned by God changes, their empty eyes betray the existence of the inhabitants of hell, mirrored there as their light grows dim.

The train went on without stopping, no one opened the doors, no one came to take away the body. It stank and it reeked, the corpse started decomposing from the heat. We were suffocating from the lack of air and sultry temperatures, because the sky in June was still deciding whether or not to take off its sheepskin cojoc. Nights were cool, but days were very hot. Our pregnant woman's little baby was rotting. We hadn't seen how she had given birth, because we had been made to face the wall, so we wouldn't see anything, then we covered our ears as well, because of how loudly the woman was screaming, but what could we use to cover our noses? Where could we get more hands? That baby reeked so badly that I could see it turned even his mother's stomach. We went on like that for about two days, without a river or a deserted field along the way, without an open door to throw out the body. They once brought us a bucket of water, along with that salted fish, but they wouldn't allow us to take anything out of the railcar, they refused to let us throw out the body, because we were near a city. We kept our noses pinched, but didn't let out a single word. The hole we used as a toilet was always busy, so many times we vomited from the stench wherever we happened to be, the baby's mother couldn't stand it anymore and she let him slip into the latrine. I heard her sobbing as she let him go. Then she fainted, we thought she had died. We dabbed her lips and face with water and she came to.

The gentle mother kept crying and she'd give her tears to her baby to drink. I asked Mother to let me try one of her tears as well to see how they tasted. "But don't really cry, don't be sad, just let a couple tears fall and that's it." It wasn't hard to convince Mother and she let a few big tears roll down her cheeks. "You're a spring of crystal clear water," I said to Mother, licking her cheek. Mother, since I praised her, let flow another two tears, long as a couple of little streams, and she said, smiling, that she wasn't crying, that they were happy tears, she was happy she could ease my thirst. Then I thought that maybe she was thirsty too and I asked her: "Don't you also want to taste a couple happy tears?" She said: "*No*, I'm not thirsty." But her lips were dry, we hadn't received any water for about two days. We stayed next to and curled up against our tiny little window, but others, who were taller, stretched up to reach the barred window up top, where you could still get a whiff of air, you could still breathe a bit. But you can't stand all day in that uncomfortable position, and sometimes you had to let others have a turn. As soon as we moved away from the window, our stomachs twisted. But as soon as I saw that the small corpse had disappeared, the air in the railcar immediately seemed more breathable. And I don't think I was the only one who thought that. The dead really do stink!

It was peace and quiet for two days, then one night, before bed, the formerly pregnant woman leaned over our latrine, holding on with both hands to the very dirty and smelly edge of the hole, and stared into it. Then she started calling to her son, who she had thrown inside because she couldn't stand the stench anymore: "Dumitraş!" she yelled slowly and pitifully. "Mama's little Dumi-traş!" She called to him, asked him for forgiveness, waited for him to show up, she'd go over to his spot, see that it was empty, and take up her post at the toilet hole again. She screamed, wailed for him, she tore out her hair. The poor woman had lost her mind. No one could sleep that night. We didn't have medicine, we didn't even have water, what could we do? We were embarrassed to go relieve ourselves because we had the impression that she was watching what we were doing, that she was staring at us. She seemed to be guarding that spot. Then she got sick, she lay flat like a dead person, she no longer made any noise.

"If these I had, I'd break the spell, and from her illness make her well," we heard our dear Tudoriţa begin singing, "if I had three walnuts in their shell, willow from the river, meadowsweet for fever. The leaves or seeds at least of jewelweeds, arnica, horse-tail, valerian, yellow gentian, borage, lovage, sage, thorn of sloe, lady's mantle, mallow, burdock, and yarrow, some woodruff, wormwood's enough, viper's bugloss, bulrush, comfrey, dane-wort, smooth cicely . . . These in sweet Bucovina are found, in fields and gardens in the ground, plants that heal and take away the pain you feel . . . if I had at least one, her sickness could be undone . . . But in the train there's no chance . . . No sun for the plants, no water that's clean, prayers don't reach the Unseen . . ."

Train conductor, open the door or I'll die! oh, oh!
Train conductor, open up or I'll die of hunger!
The little children who died, through the hole they'd slide,
And the mothers would pray for someone to take them away
And put them in the ground so they wouldn't stay earthbound.
Hundreds, thousands died, only a few of us children left on this side

And we suffered there. Hunger, sickness, no clothes to wear,
But no one we told seemed to care.
For what fault of ours are you taking us from Bucovina in cattle cars,
Oppressed and distressed, and dispossessed? Oh, oh!

Make us, Lord, Your travelers on the paths of this life and bring us safely to the end of the road! Hold us tightly, Lord, in Your Holy Church, where we find all Your comfort! Guard us and protect us, Lord! After those difficult days, from lack of oxygen and food, maybe from the unsanitary water as well, two more old people died, they were unassuming and quiet, like two shadows, they were probably someone's parents or grandparents to some children. And once again it began to smell in our railcar. Starting about then, the stench of death accompanied us until the end of the road. It continued to follow us even when we lived in the barn, but at least there you could go outside for air whenever you wanted to and here you couldn't. When the door of the railcar would open, it was such a release, the air was like medicine, it healed you, we seemed to come back to life, we were happy. We, children, joyfully waited for the dead to be taken out of the railcar and we looked at the grownups with pleading eyes: all of you stop dying so much, hang on until the end! But they didn't listen to our silent appeal. Now I think about how wrong it is to be tossed out that way, what a sin for that to be your burial . . .

When the pregnant woman felt that she was about to die, she began talking. I don't know if she felt guilty, but she was trying to hold off death by telling her story. How the communist in her village, that striboc, promised to marry her, she slept with him, cooked for him. Her mother said it was a great sin, that they shouldn't be living together if they weren't married. If he's a decent, loving man, why doesn't he marry her? Her mother didn't like the communist at all. Who did? Then he made her write up the lists of "enemies," but he didn't tell her they would be deported, just to write those lists.

"He asked me: 'Who are the enemies of our regime?' 'There aren't any enemies in this village, only peaceful people,' I said to him. Then he asked, 'Who here doesn't love communists?' I couldn't well say to him the whole village. 'I don't know,' I answered. 'Who was a member of a party besides the communist party, who exploited the labor of others, and made farm hands work for them, who ran across the border, who are the most important landowners with the most land, who speaks badly of the communists and isn't happy enough about our new regime?' He said he needed a certain number of people and that's how many I should list.

"After I gave him the lists, telling him about everyone on them, because he was a newcomer to the village and didn't know people, my striboc started going around to people and you'd see him coming out with a horse, a carpet. When I told him I was pregnant, he didn't act as if he were happy. He told me to go to my mother's and give birth there, because I couldn't give birth in his house, which was actually the house of a rich landowner who had left everything and fled. That we'd see afterward what we'd do about it. He told me not to cry or yell so people wouldn't find out. I went back home and began waiting. My mother said to me: 'Your communist left you, you've barely walked out the door and he's already chasing skirts, but don't worry, we'll raise the child ourselves, we'll get by.' I didn't believe it, but I asked around, it's not hard to find things out in a village, people talk. He'd approach the rich and beautiful girls on my list and ask them directly or through their parents for their hand, saying if they refused . . . but the girls wouldn't hear of it, what kind of man is he, who lives with a woman and wants to marry a different one?

"I also ran into one of these girls and I told her not to marry him because he's a bad man, he promised to marry me and he's going after other women. I was really upset and I told her. As for your husband," she said to the sweet woman with the baby who she had yelled at in the beginning, "I really liked him. Every time I tried to put myself in his way, you'd give him another daughter! But he never answered my smiles, he had been my neighbor, we played together when we were children, together we'd steal the juicy white cherries from Baba Veturia, you know her too, he'd protect me from dogs . . . our mothers, both of them widows, got on well together, he was his mother's only child, I was mine, we were like siblings. But when you turned up, he confided in me: 'My dear sister, I'm in love and I'm going to get married!' What could I say? You also came from a wealthy respectable family. Who would look twice at me, a poor fatherless girl, a little sister?

"Then I fell under the sway of that communist who kept repeating that I should be proud of the fact that I'm poor and that I'm not exploiting anyone. And that the future belongs to us, the poor. Everything belongs to us. He used me like a doormat, with his lies about the future, after which, when it was no longer convenient for him, he punished me in ways you wouldn't punish even your cruelest enemy. And his eyes continued to be glued to his rich girls. He called me back, acted nice, he asked me what I had said to that girl. He wanted to know if I hadn't told her anything about the lists, because I would blow his cover, they would shoot him if his bosses found out. This is what he said: 'We're setting up our most important mission yet.' Two comrades, or whatever they were, had come with him then. They were thugs and bastards who gave me nasty, mean looks, and I didn't like them from the moment I set eyes on them. I told them that I hadn't breathed a word about the lists, I hadn't said a thing, I denied it all. I also told him that, even without knowing about the lists, the girl wasn't interested in him, because she wouldn't look at a good-for-nothing like him, a low-down liar. He hit me in front of his comrades, and told them that the village didn't know about the lists but that I couldn't be allowed to go, because I knew about them and might let something slip. He yelled that I would be the first name on the list, that he would write me down himself. The comrades didn't say anything. Then they took me into a dark cellar and they tortured and abused me, it made no difference to them that I said I was pregnant with the baby of their friend, the communist. I called out to him, I begged him, then they took me to jail.

"At the train station, I saw my mother. The village had gotten wind of what had happened and my mother suspected that the communist dog wanted to get rid of me and send me as far away as possible, so he could go after fresh young things. She had gone to the jail, and had also gone to the communist to convince him, to ask him to free me, she assured him that he didn't have to marry me, that we could raise the child, we'd leave the village, if he would only let me go. He told her to go away and said that if he saw her at his gate again, she would share a jail cell with me. She told me this herself, because the people at the jail were more merciful, they had a heart and let us talk. Then they shut me up in the railcar. I don't know who told my mother that we were all there, at the train station, many people's relatives came, with bundles, small sacks, thick clothing, food, which they gave to those who had been loaded into the railcars. A little bit of what my good mother packed for me made it to me. I'm guilty because I didn't listen to her. I want to die when I think about how many people whose names I wrote on those lists are suffering now. They're suffering like me or maybe worse. I wrote you down, ma'am, and you all, and you! I ask you all to forgive me, I pray for long life for you, but even if you can't forgive me, I'm going to die anyway. My guilt is too great and it can't be forgiven. You, at least, please forgive me for lying to you and making you suffer," she said to the kind woman. "May God protect your children. May God give you strength. Forgive me, forgive me!"

Then the kind woman said to her, "Don't think about those lists anymore, because you didn't mean to harm anyone and you didn't know what you were doing, you were a weak-willed woman. If you hadn't written them, someone else would have, they would've taken us even without lists. Because already, starting last April, our strong, young men were rounded up and taken to the depths of Siberia. You were wrong, but you will be forgiven, you endured a lot, be at peace and God be with you."

The woman smiled and she took her hand to kiss it. Then other women came up to her, with their children or without, and they squeezed her hand and said: "God be with you." Then we all prayed for her. Then she hugged Aglaie's straw doll. Later, she died. None of us children wanted to take anything of Dora's, though she was alone and didn't have anyone to leave her things to. We were afraid she'd bring bad luck. She didn't have much and what she did have was very dirty, she had no way of washing herself after giving birth. Everything around her stank. Soon after this, the train stopped and we cleaned, we breathed fresh air and took the dead out of the railcar.

I've lived through this too, Lord. Suffering cleanses sin. Receive misfortune with joy, misfortune is a gift from God. It is impossible to reach your soul's peace without enduring many wrongs and difficulties. Oh heavenly Mother, bride of the All Holy Spirit, come close to our hearts when we repent! He who bears the weight of a sin can't die without being forgiven. Let flow the spring of tears in us so that it can wash away the heavy dust which saddens our eyes. All Holy Spirit, beat out and scatter the unclean stench and infirmity from that women's soul which she had stifled, and guide her mind darkened by despair to repentance. We bow before You and fervently pray! O our Eternal God, look with mercy toward the candle that is going out and cleanse the flame. The bones of those who are bitter dry up, it cuts short the soul's delight. Shatter the soul's narrowness, illuminate the mind! Give us patience, Lord, and wipe away all our tears, so that death will be neither mourning, nor outcry, nor pain . . .

After the air had cleared out a bit and the dead bodies were no longer with us, people felt that it wasn't right, just throwing them out and that's it. And we started, one at a time, to follow a burial ritual, to which each of us added a custom. As if we were burying them properly, except only with words:

When someone is sick and about to die, a candle is lit so they can find the way and have light in the next world. If they die without a candle, a candle is lit every day when the Holy Gospel is read in church, maybe it will lighten their path. Where we come from, it's called the candle for the soul of the dead. At the feast of the Presentation of the Blessed Virgin Mary, candles are also lit for the good health of children, grandchildren, and relatives.

When you have a death in your household, as a sign of mourning you place an embroidered shirt, a white towel, and a black headscarf outside over the door. The shirt is given to the cook. You also put a wooden cross next to the shirt.

It's a sin to put a yoke in the fire. Whoever does this can't die. They will be able to die only if a yoke is placed under their head.

Don't steal anyone's comb! When you die, even lice will run from you.

If someone dies between Easter and the feast of Ascension, they will go straight to heaven because heaven is open for all mortals at that time.

The water in which a dead body has been washed shouldn't be thrown out carelessly because whoever steps in that spot will become paralyzed.

A small waxen cross, a little scarf and some coins, in case they have to pay any tolls, are placed inside the dead person's clothes. The expression "to give the priest an ort" means to kick the bucket—an ort was a small silver coin, of little value, during the time of the Germans in Bucovina.

We also put in a vencică—a folded up piece of paper with writing on both sides. A prayer to the Mother of God is written on the front, and on the back is the deed of the dead, a prayer in which all the dead person's sins are forgiven.

The burial staff is a candle made out of pure wax, as tall as a man. It's lit three days after a person dies, three days after they are buried, and then it's divided into three parts, which are made into candles for burning inside the church for the remembrance of the dead's soul.

The apaoz is a small carafe filled with wine and oil, a woman brings it to the cemetery. Before putting the lid on the coffin, the priest sprinkles the dead with the apaoz in the form of a cross. The little carafe is then thrown in the grave.

The funeral dish coliva is prepared from grain, which is the image of Christ.

Back home, three colivas are made, one is given out on the way to the cemetery, another at the cemetery, and the third on the third day.

After you've had a death in your household, the house has to be whitewashed: the dying person struggles and the walls are stained with blood that we can't see.

The dead person is watched over so that they aren't visited by evil spirits, so that children don't play pranks on them, so that the cat doesn't eat their nose.

In the coffin, a cross is placed at their head, on the sides, at their feet, the bottom is made of spaced out slats, over which are placed reeds or cornhusks.

Water for the dead is placed in windows, because they're thirsty.

In our village, five memorial gifts are given for easy passage.

Back home, they're given at each crossroads where there's a troiţa cross.

The dead are taken to the cemetery with twelve ceremonies: at the gate, at the crosses, at crossroads.

A feast is held for the dead at three, nine, twenty, and forty days after their death, at half a year, at a year, then once a year for seven years either at the church or at home.

That's how we buried our dead. The mound of words grew, it covered them, we even added the cross, as was proper. Someone from the village of whoever had died said nice things about them, the person would say who they had been, what a hardworking man, what a good person, what a mayor, principal, priest, excellent mother, wonderful wife. "May you rest in peace in this ear—," someone started saying and then stopped. What earth? But Grannie Anghelina bravely continued: "May you rest in peace in these words! God have mercy on his soul!" We all breathed a sigh of relief, because we had buried the dead properly, with all the rites . . .

⟶

I didn't notice how so many had died. Death was so easy, like getting a mosquito bite. We had gone through so much suffering that what could death mean anymore, if not the long awaited peace, the end of terror and pain? When you were at the side of a sick person who you had no way of helping, someone maimed by scarcity and lack, you almost wanted them to die, finally, and be free. I had Mother and Jenea with me and I didn't at all want them to die, I didn't want them to suffer either. My heart would've been broken if anything were to happen to my loved ones. I know that whoever God loves, He chastises and allows to suffer. Whoever forgets God takes on the role of God and worries about what is to come. We mustn't forget this, we mustn't forget!

The mothers stood there, weak and frowning, like a group of birds watching from a mountain peak. Their only care was for their children not to die. At least three out of five, at least two, if only one out of five would come out of this alive! Then they, too, would have a reason to live, someone to fight for. Mothers without children would break, they'd become soft, mushy, they'd melt and dissolve, they'd become inert, passive, and indifferent bodies, which everyone would wait to be thrown out from the train before they started reeking, before the flies set in. There wasn't enough air in the railcars, but flies found a way inside.

When people die, the survivors are glad. That's how it should be, probably. You were glad that what the dead person had stored up would be divided among everyone and you'd get something too. I remember how happy I was when I'd bring Mother a small plate or a headscarf, taken from a woman who had just died. If she had relatives or children, they would guard all the dead woman's belongings. We left them to it. We, the ten or so children still moving about that increasingly putrid railcar, were staking out those who were alone. We could hardly wait for them to die, to stop moaning at night, to stop stinking, so we could take their goods, because they couldn't use them anymore anyway. We studied what we might take, not just us children, but the older ones did as well, who were nearer to the dying person. The railcar was big, all sorts of larger and smaller groups formed, some kept more of a distance from us, with their backs turned, we didn't really talk much, we didn't know them. We didn't pity them, we didn't want to pity them, we only had a little bit of pity left hidden inside us and we kept it for those who were close to us. We waited to get some kind of windfall and then we wanted the dead person out of there. We'd look at people to guess how much longer they had to live. The way animals do. All kinds of objects were left over from the dead people, the most desirable being their woolen blankets, because the weather was getting colder and the nights were increasingly chilly. Whether a blanket, a rug, or a tapestry with colorful stripes, a bedspread embroidered by some grandmother for someone's dowry, or a throw, everyone had treasures like that and an extra wouldn't hurt. Mother and I had a beautiful, warm woolen carpet, with a stag on it. We also had a blanket, and a woven rug, and I wasn't interested in the woven goods of the dead. I had eyed a small pot belonging to a dead person, they also had a pair of good galoshes on their feet, but the grownups would see to those, not the little ones. A child was standing next to a dying person, and at one point she announced: "She's dead!" We hurried over quietly, so it wouldn't be too obvious, and we took her possessions, she was a woman alone, the child she had had died earlier, so we could divide up her things among us.

There were also cases when people started dividing up the goods when the dying person was still alive, maybe they could hear and understand what was happening, but who cared anymore? Man saves up for a rainy day, when he dies it all goes away. Others, when they felt that their time had come, offered what they thought might be helpful to those around them or made their dying wishes known, who would get what. Their word was law and no one went against it, everyone did exactly as the dead person had said. After the person died, everyone received what was intended for them. But that only happened a few times. Death usually came unannounced. We were all weak, hungry, sick, but death chose only some people, hard to say according to what criteria. Usually, the villain with the scythe kept pretty much all of us neither dead nor alive, it rocked us all the same in that increasingly unbearable train. The women around me, including Mother, were very ashamed to receive things from the dead. But it wasn't right to just let them sit there after the dead were thrown out of the train either. We children solved this problem without a twinge of guilt.

And, while everyone circling around the dead woman was pulling on that long, thick blanket in every direction, I grabbed the small pot. Someone, with their tiny hands, grasped the handle at the same time as me, a little girl, who I, without wanting to, scratched when I was trying to make her let go of the pot. I was bigger and stronger than her and I brought the pot back to Mother. Mother said: "May God forgive her soul!" blessing the dead woman. I turned to see what the little girl was doing, I found a cup and I put it in her hands so she wouldn't cry and she stopped crying. She was happy that she wouldn't go back to her mother empty-handed. Two children were left holding onto that blanket from different ends and neither of them were letting go, they looked like two chicks who can't share a worm and stretch it out from both sides. Jeni came over and cut the blanket into three equal parts, he took the middle part for himself, I thought, and everyone went away happy. People said prayers for the soul of the dead woman, then came the entire burial ritual, which we knew almost by heart, and each person said exactly their part, nothing else. And we children enjoyed our spoils and waited for the dead woman to be taken out as soon as possible, meaning thrown out, before the body started to rot. Mother had seen how I had ripped the small pot out of the little girl's hands and she asked me to please give it to her, because we had pots, and their family was bigger and needed it more. I gave it to her and she gave me the cup. An extra cup never hurts.

Jeni put the piece of blanket over the woman's face. When the soldier came to take the dead out, he asked him to keep her face covered with that piece of blanket so that the birds wouldn't peck out her eyes. Maybe there'd be someone who would take pity on her and give her a Christian burial. It's very cruel to live a dignified and prosperous life, fearing God and loving all that's holy, observing holy days and folk traditions, helping your neighbors and caring for your family, but then to be thrown out like a dog, on the side of the road, when you leave for the next world.

At first, I didn't understand what those noises meant. The doors would open and you'd hear thuds, bangs, besides the muffled crying of others. People in our railcar started dying later and we didn't know that those thuds were the sound of dead people being thrown from neighboring railcars. They died though they weren't full of years yet, no one died willingly, but given that they did die, I think they liked it even less that they were thrown out on the side of the road like stinking trash. The survivors cried when the dead were thrown out, even if they weren't their relatives. I didn't know who the others were, I couldn't see anything, but just as in our railcar there were only people of high standing in our village, the pick of the bunch of Bucovina filled the other railcars as well.

I can't forget those sounds. I hear them even in my dreams. In my dreams, at first I still don't understand what I'm hearing, then I realize what it is as I'm closer to waking up or even after I've woken up. It seems as if the dead are moaning, complaining, angrily: how could we just throw them out like that, as if they weren't still people? We, meaning the soldiers who were alive and powerful. And them, the humble cadavers, decomposing, helpless, stinking. Thud, bang, splash! Then I saw what was happening when we also had our dead. They'd grab the children from behind and throw them out face down. The bigger ones, who were heavier, would be picked up by two soldiers, they'd take them out of the railcar, and they'd swing them two or three times so they'd fly as far as possible when they let them go, falling at random. After the first dead body was thrown out of our railcar in this way, all our old people, but the youngest among us as well, fervently prayed that we'd reach a place where we could be buried, and not thrown out, as soon as possible. Help us, Lord, get off this death train, so we may close our eyes on the good earth. We children didn't know what to ask the Lord. That we arrive safely, but where? So that our mothers wouldn't die, because what would we do without them? That we'd receive water when we were thirsty. The old people dreamed of dying in their own homes, at their hearth, in their yard, beneath their sky, they were like plants that had been cut on that journey. They dreamed of returning to their homeland and dying, on the soil where they had been born, had gotten married, had built their houses with their own hands, had raised and sent off their children. Death in their own land, at home, in their sweet Bucovina, that's what kept them alive. We who were young didn't think about death at all. We didn't think about life either. "Don't worry, we'll get there just fine," Mother said. "They'll be waiting for us with pies," she joked. "When we get there."

And we prayed, and we prayed again, until the railcar was lifted up by our prayers and floated in the air.

God of mercy, lay Your good hand upon us and comfort, Lord, our troubled souls. We don't want to die on the side of the railroad, Lord! We don't want to be thrown from the train, like a bunch of potato sacks, without candles, without crosses at our bedside. We want a Christian burial, Lord, if not in our land, next to our people, at least when the journey ends, somewhere in a Christian land. But even better would be if we didn't die yet.

Lord, keep us alive, so we can help our children grow up. We're not asking for much, all we need to live is a bit of water and our prayers, and a breath of air when the railcar door opens! You, Lord, who sees into our souls as in an open book, regard our tears, our heartfelt prayer!

Help us, Lord, do not allow us to lie uncomforted, thrown out on the side of the road, like heathens.

Cast out, Lord, the shadows, poison, and vapors around us, give us a speck of Your light, Lord, a breath of air!

You, victor over death, You, haven from our whirlwinds, pull us out, Lord, from the flood trying to drown us! Because You, Lord, gather our tears of repentance and humiliation and redeem them.

Give us strength and patience to carry Your cross, give us sacrifice and love to treasure it! To You, Lord, belong all honor and worship, together with the Father and the Holy Spirit, now and until the end of the ages.

Amen.

I don't remember how the book by George Coşbuc got into my pouch. Books were the last thing I was thinking about when they rounded us up. Maybe Mother stuck it in, maybe it was already there, or maybe I picked it up and forgot. Mother had been very careful to bring her Bible which was always by her side, but inside the train, she hid it carefully so she wouldn't lose it, so it wouldn't disappear. With how thin the paper was, perfect for the soldiers'

cigarettes, it would've been gone in the blink of an eye! She took it out later, when we had a room to ourselves, which we shared with our cat, but animals, as everyone knows, don't steal books. Mother guarded it even from the animals, when she'd take it out a night to read, but from people she kept it well hidden. But poor Coşbuc was sacrificed in our railcar. That book was a lifesaver for me! We weren't lucky enough to have a soldier who knew Romanian, ours only spoke Russian. But we were lucky that he was halfway decent. We were also lucky to have Miss Eufrosina, who knew the language and translated for us. I was able to communicate with the soldier even without knowing Russian. When the train stopped, he opened the railcar door and saw me with the book in my lap, on a sunny day. I don't know why I had felt like reading right then. Maybe there had been more light in the railcar or people in the train had asked me to read something? The soldier's eyes lit up and he came over to me, with the intention of taking my book. And when I screamed at the top of my lungs, the soldier took a step back. He told Miss Procopovici that he was asking me to give him just one little page from my book, just one, just enough to roll himself one tiny cigarette. No, I answered and looked at him menacingly, squeezing my book in my arms. I defended my treasure with both hands and my entire body, I hugged it tightly and there it stayed. The soldier went out, swearing, it seemed. I didn't understand Russian, but it wasn't hard to understand how angry he was. He went out, but he didn't shut the door, a sign that he was coming back. There was no sound that the train was leaving either. Mother prayed the soldier wouldn't come back, that he wouldn't shoot me, or move me to another railcar, or torture me with beatings. Everyone told me to give him the book, to save my life.

The soldier returned quickly, with a peaceful expression, without murderous intentions and with half a large cookie which he held out to me. *Listocek tolko*—just a little page. I tore out a page from the back of the book without writing on it and handed it to him, in exchange for the cookie. Everyone breathed a sigh of relief, and the children looked at me slightly enviously, though I gave them some of the cookie. Fedor came over to me and together we counted how many pages were left. He could've taken my whole book then, but it was safer with me than with him, because he was in a railcar with lots of other soldiers who smoked and would've quickly ripped it all, so he'd come when the train stopped and take a page or two, just for himself and sometimes for the soldier in the next railcar, where no one had books. He paid honestly. If he didn't have anything, he'd allow me to get out to fetch water, though I was only a little girl and children weren't allowed to handle the buckets. I could breathe a bit of fresh air! He'd leave us an extra piece of bread, including the dead in his count as well, he'd give us more water or a bigger fish or similar very useful treats. Sometimes he'd bring me a bit of his own bread. His bread was also dark, but it seemed less gummy than ours and tasted better. Even though the book was all mine, I shared what I received with Eugen and the children around me, especially with those who had eaten all their provisions from back home and were very hungry. So that we wouldn't feel bad about the torn out pages, we'd read and memorize the poem on the page that was to be torn out next, both front and back. We'd recite it, by turns, sometimes the mothers would give heartfelt recitations as well, then I'd tear out the page. Only one page didn't have words on it but a drawing that took up the entire sheet, of a horse with its mane waving in the wind. It was very beautiful. We had nothing to memorize on that page, but I saved it for last anyway. Our soldier wasn't in a hurry either, we'd flip through what was left together, sometimes we counted the pages, each in their own language, but we'd leave the horse. Maybe he, too, had a horse at home, and he missed it? When he came for the horse, he didn't bring me anything. A page this beautiful deserved something special. But I gave him the horse without saying a word. That was during the time we had been invaded by lice and our heads were scraped up from scratching. Then Fedor came with a little bottle of brilliant green—*zelyonka* he said and showed me what to do with it. We applied it, it was enough for all the children and our mothers prayed for his health and thanked him. We put in on all the wounds we had from the lice, rashes from sweating, from not washing. Soon after this, the railroad ended and we all got off the train. When parting, the soldier gave me another small piece of bread, though I didn't have a single piece of paper left, not even a little one, to give him for his cigarettes. Smokers didn't eat, they'd give their last breadcrumb for some rustic tobacco and they were the first who died. I'm talking about the deportees. The soldier who guarded us wasn't doomed in this way, but how did our men locked up in their railcars fare? Families separated from the heads of their family didn't know anything about their fate. I'd hear them praying for their husbands and fathers. Most of them never saw each other again.

⚓

"My three have not a bite to eat!
My children's mouths are dry with heat;
And bitterness gone on so long
The stream of milk which once was strong
Did from my wife deplete!
He's mine! For this brave horse of mine
I'd fight with God at every shrine—
Take pity! For you know you can
Find better horses in the land,
But, master, how could I?"

Mom, I thought the poor laptop would completely crash! I looked up the poem on the internet for Cuța and found it easily, she knew several of the lines but had forgotten the title of the long poem about the horse. I found it quickly: *El Zorab* by George Coşbuc, and pressed play. Cuța listened with her eyes closed, she was breathless and as happy as a kid, she opened her eyes only to follow the stanzas she recognized. She recited along with "the machine." (That's what she calls the laptop.) We haven't learned this poem at school yet, but when we'll get to it, I'll get the highest grade, because now I know almost the whole thing by heart. The poem would be over, that clip would end, we'd both be quiet for a moment, then Cuța would ask me very, very nicely, whispering, like a kid on their best behavior: "Let's ask the machine if it doesn't mind repeating the story of *Elzurap*." (That's how Cuța pronounces it.) I'd hit play again. When it was over, we wouldn't say anything, then I'd ask her, without Cuța mentioning it: "Again?"

"Yes, again. But isn't it tired, doesn't its mouth hurt?"

"Nothing hurts it!" I said, "Look, Cuța, you push this and it talks by itself."

I went to the bathroom, I stood around, I went outside, walked around a bit, and when I came back, she was still listening to it and was just as happy. I told her I'd play it for her tomorrow too. The people on the train would get tears in their eyes when she'd read for them from that little book, turned into rolling paper for the soldiers' cigarettes.

They, too, had left behind cows, beautiful horses, just as majestic as that stallion . . . "It would've been better if I had stuck a knife in my own horse than leave it for those wretched stribocs," some of the old men in the railcar said. There were two stanzas on each page and I'd read them until Fedor came, when I'd tear out the page. And I'd read, and we'd all tear up. Not because it was awful and hard and agonizing in that railcar, no! Our hearts ached for that horse and for its master!

—⊶—

After many days, our train reached a large body of water. It stopped and I heard some of the railcars open but ours remained bolted. We listened to what was happening and watched through our small makeshift window. The water proved to be a river, in the opinion of our mothers, but it was so big that you couldn't see to the other bank, maybe that was also because our window was too small. We heard a lot of people outside, we could see them only after they had gotten close to the edge of the water. There were three boats on the water, two big and one small. A big one was already full of people and had started heading out. It went upstream. People were crowding around the second ship. On the gangway, there were lines of soldiers, it wasn't easy to get onboard. One line of soldiers drew up lists and chose people who were stronger, they'd push some of them and the people would fall: if they jumped up quickly, they got back up, the soldiers would take them, if not, they wouldn't. They wouldn't give a second glance to those who could barely stand or had a hard time getting up, or were unsteady. They looked for others. We watched and said what we saw. They ignored the women with children, they pushed them aside. These women were outraged, they pushed to the front. Some of them, who were sturdier and more insistent, with older children who didn't need to be carried were chosen after all and they quickly ran inside the boat with their children after them to get a better spot. Those with younger children weren't able to get past the soldiers. The second boat also filled up fast, in just a few minutes, it let out a long whistle, blew smoke from its smokestack, the way our train did, and it began to sail in the opposite direction, downstream on that huge river.

Among those who were shoving to get into the last boat, I noticed a woman with three children, she was carrying a little one in her arms and two were holding onto her skirt. The woman tried to get past the line of soldiers, she had seen that they were looking for people who were stronger, and more or less healthy, who could get up quickly off the ground and were steady on their feet. Maybe she realized that those who would be left behind there were doomed to perish, abandoned, without food, without help of any kind. So she didn't give up and kept moving up to the front. A soldier pushed her, she didn't fall, but others got ahead of her, it was hard for her with three children, who she was holding onto tightly so she wouldn't lose them there. Meanwhile, the small boat was getting full too. The woman was agitated, desperate, maybe, she kept walking around next to the soldiers and didn't know what to do. She took out some head-scarves, some ribbons, from our window it wasn't clear what, she tied the baby she was holding to her back, and the two bigger children helped her, she tied him up well, with tight knots, and with one hand held onto another child, the hand with which she had held the baby was now free, and the third child was holding on tightly to the second child. The hardest thing was to get past the first soldiers who were selecting people, then the others formed a line on the opposite side all the way to the boat, they'd notice something else, they'd check something out, maybe they'd ask you something, but only the first ones would turn you away, they'd push you and throw you to the ground by hitting you, the ones after didn't. We were watching to see what the woman would do. Would she get past? Would they let her? No, she hadn't gotten past yet, we could see who had climbed in, the small boat was closer to the train and we could see more clearly. We could almost hear the woman and the soldiers yelling, but also the moans of the deportees in pain. Maybe there were also people from our train there, maybe the people taken out to the boats were fellow Bucovinians.

At one point, the woman got a running start and rammed into one of the soldiers selecting people. He lost his balance and fell, and the woman started getting past. The soldier next to him caught up with her and kicked her in the rear, she fell on her knees but got up quickly, her children helped her as well and she ran ahead toward the other line of soldiers by the ship. I told our railcar. "Oh, the poor thing, oh, the crazy woman! Will they shoot her?" the people in our railcar asked. "No, she's past! She's getting on the boat now!" The soldier who had been knocked down shook himself off, he yelled something, he pushed the people in front of him out of spite, but the woman was far away and he left her alone. I saw how she got on the boat, how she quieted and stroked her children, how she untied the little one from her back and held him again. She beat a soldier, the villain collapsed when she let him have it, the wicked man, and she climbed in with three little children. People made way for her and the other soldiers treated her with respect. We talked about it passionately. Meanwhile, our train began moving slowly, ever so slowly, because we were crossing over water, probably that same river which the three boats traveled away on, slowly, so we could throw out the dead into the water. The brave woman and the boat slowly disappeared. The small boat was now full and it went neither up nor down but across that great expanse of water. "Maybe it will come back for the others," we speculated. We were crossing over a branch of the great river, it was only when we were on the bridge that we saw the course of the river. It was the second time on our journey that the train was stopping on a bridge and we threw the dead into the water. At a turn, I saw that there weren't many railcars left, that the train was shorter now. There could be fewer railcars on a certain portion of the road, except that sometimes when we lost some, others would be added. But now it was shorter than ever. At this bridge, we didn't have any more dead, two more had died on the way, but more than half of our people were still alive. The grownups discussed how it was better for the dead that had been thrown in the water than those thrown out on the fields, abandoned there to the crows, hyenas, and other wild animals. Lucky them, people said. The train kept moving slowly to allow the soldiers to enter all the railcars. A soldier waved something, he motioned and the train moved a bit more, then the doors shut and it took off.

Telling long stories at night is very good, the story circles the house three times so that nothing unclean can get close to it. The story guarding the house turns into a wheel of fire and it keeps the Devil from getting close. And it was even better to tell stories inside the railcar. At first we had only four storytellers on our endless journey: Mother, Grannie Anghelina, Eufrosina Procopovici, and Nicanor Gherman. Then Baba Tudoriţa once told us a long story. Then we all started telling stories. Mother and grandmother Anghelina told beautiful stories from the Bible, Mr. Gherman knew Romanian stories he had heard and learned from his grandfather, and not only stories but riddles as well, and Miss Eufrosina knew all kinds of stories, even from other countries, because she had read many interesting and rare books.

Mother told us the story of the miracle of the loaves, the story of Jesus, when there were thousands of hungry people on the edge of a lake and only one boy had a basket with only five small loves and two fish. And Jesus performed a miracle and filled all the baskets with bread and fish and everyone ate and was satisfied.

As for us, we also received bread and fish. But Jesus's fish wasn't salted. And we never had enough.

We loved the story of the child Onufrie, we could never hear it too many times. Grannie Anghelina would tell it to us when we received bread. "The Life of the Holy and Venerable Father Onufrie the Great . . ." She would begin slowly and we would chew the bread softly, so we could hear her better. She wouldn't tell us the entire story of the saint's life, only the part that fit the moment:

"When he reached the age of four, the child Onufrie often went to the refectory, and taking a small piece of bread with him, he'd go out to the church porch, where an icon of the Immaculate Virgin Mary holding the Christ child was painted. There, innocently and without ill intent, he spoke to the child, saying to Him: 'You are small like me. But I go to the refectory, I ask for bread and eat it. But You never eat, You never say anything and You suffer in silence. Look, I brought You my bread. Eat some too!'

"And the child in the icon reached out his little land, took Onufrie's bread, and ate it.

"Since Onufrie took bread rather often, the refectorian monk noticed and decided to snoop to see what the child did with it. So he secretly followed him and watched, listening to everything. When he saw the Christ child reaching out his little hand and taking the bread, he was terrified and went running to the abbot. He told him the entire story of the miraculous incident.

"The abbot didn't fully believe it and he said: 'When Onufrie comes to you for bread, don't give it to him, but tell him to go ask the Lord Jesus from the icon.'

"That's what the refectorian did. When Onufrie, who was terribly hungry, came to ask him for bread, he said what the abbot had told him to say.

"Then Onufrie went to the icon and lamented: 'I didn't receive bread today and I'm hungry. Give me some too, just as I gave you some.'

"Immediately, hearing his complaint, the Lord Jesus gave him a loaf of white bread that was so big that Onufrie could barely carry it.

"'Look what a big, fluffy loaf of bread the Christ child gave me!' he said to the abbot . . ."

Since returning from exile, I no longer want for bread. They've allowed us to bake bread, with our own grain, these last years. The smell is intoxicating for me even now and I silently pray: "Lord, give us all our daily bread and see that no one ever goes without."

One day, Baba Tudoriţa, who only cast and broke spells, started on about how stories are powerful, stories cast out the Evil One, and they cast out even death. And then she told us a wondrous story, which at times she screamed, other times sang, sometimes mumbled, which scared us, amazed us, sometimes we'd laugh, other times tremble with fright. And when she finished telling the story, right when her story ended, the train stopped, the railcar doors opened and we received water, several bucketfuls! We received bread, a slice each, but also a pail of hot stew, with bits of beets and cabbage floating in it, but it was a hot meal and enough for all of us! The first time since being on the train! Look what a good story can do! After this miracle, we couldn't tell enough stories. And we told stories, and more stories, until the spirit of the stories took pity and stopped the train, that's what we thought. But the mothers said that God heard our prayers. The most powerful stories were those from the Bible, many of them made us cry, many seemed written especially for us, and we left them as a final argument for stopping the train. We told them at the end, when there weren't any more of the other stories or, having been constantly repeated, they weren't powerful enough. However much we repeated the Bible stories, they never lost their power.

When we were getting ready for bed and wanted to fall asleep, we'd leave the story unsaid, like a fire flickering on the hearth. "And then the ginger fox said: . . ." And we'd go to sleep. And in the morning, whoever woke up first continued with what the ginger fox said next. A story lasted several days, with scenes that repeated, so they could be heard at the other end of the railcar as well, the stories got longer, and longer, in fact, a long story was made up of several stories, which we connected in such a way that everything seemed to be a single story. All you have to do is travel in a cattle car for a month, without food, without water, without anything else to do besides telling stories, to understand this. We took turns telling stories, the younger ones, and the older ones. At first, only two or three people who were better storytellers told them. Then, after having listened to the stories so many times, we learned them as well, we, the others who were shyer or had never told a story in our lives up until that point. Then we learned how to embellish the stories. That's how the older ones would scold us: "You're embellishing here, that's not how it was."

"Yes it was and we're not embellishing." Back home, liars were said to embellish things. But as we couldn't embellish anything in our humble railcar life, we at least embellished our stories, with the help of those who were good with words. My mother-in-law would also say to her son: "Oh, you embellish everything." He did, the poor man, but not because his life was so great. My husband wasn't a liar but a peaceful, happy person, and he told it so that it was more like his own nature. That's what we'd do as well in the train with our stories, we'd embellish them, we'd make them better and more beautiful.

I've forgotten many of the stories, but not all of them, because we kept on telling them, we'd repeat them, we didn't have television, or as many books as we do today, sometimes we didn't even have work all year round, we'd gather to warm ourselves in winter at the mouth of a little stove and oh how we'd tell stories, what fun we'd have! Or out in the fields, with the women, while working, or in the tailoring shop, during a break or when the lights would go out for hours on end . . .

✦

Mom, Cuța made baked potatoes, she taught me how to make them too, how to put them on the fire and when to take them off. They're better than french fries, or chips in any flavor, or mashed potatoes with milk and butter. They're the best! I also ate fire-roasted corn for the first time, we've only ever boiled it. But roasted corn tastes different and it's more delicious. It's not at all hard to keep a fast. Cuța said I can eat whatever I want, because "Look, your pa filled the fridge with all kinds of good things." But I want to keep the fast and we make all kinds of dishes without meat or dairy!

Cuța had a friend on the train whose name was also Jenica, like mine. But this friend was actually a boy, Eugen, dressed as a girl. Great Gran had a son and she named him Eugen, that son was Grandpa in whose honor you named me Eugenia as well. And Great Gran's name is Ana, Ana Blajinschi, Anica Blajinica, but also the name of Grandma on your side. You named our Annie in honor of them and that's how you made both sides of the family happy. But the funniest thing is that Annie's boyfriend from Iași is also named Eugen! All these Eugens and Eugenias!

Mom, I told our Blajinică about Eugen Țarev and she seemed to come alive, she took my hand, she asked me to tell her the story of how this boy came to Iași. Annie had once told me his real last name was Țară, like the Romanian word for country, not Țarev, but the Russians butchered it. That he, basically, wasn't Russian, but Bucovinian, that his grandfather had been born in Bucovina. "His name is Eugen Ţară?" Great Gran asked, filled with emotion, and she cried a bit. "Don't cry, Cuţa," I said to her, "don't cry."

"I'm not crying," she said, "I'm just happy." She also said: "What long roads our memories take us down . . . And how winding are the ways of Lord! Let us pray for this Ţară, who has returned to our country," she said, smiling now. She didn't ask me anything else. And Annie hasn't written me for a week.

⎯⎯❧⎯⎯

On the train, we'd all have our different roles when telling stories, we all learned them so well that all of us participated and played along. Eufrosina was the author who began with "Once upon a time," then she'd get to "and then the sparrow said: . . ." and she'd stop. The sparrow quickly answered. "The woodpecker went to the fly . . ." and again a pause, someone among us always wanted to be the sparrow, and someone else the fly and the bee. But no child wanted to be the mean elephant who stomped on nests, a bad character who would meet a terrible fate. Then a mother would join our game or, usually, Eugen's grandmother, who scared us, that's how well she played the part.

In a forest lived a sparrow couple who had made their nest in a tall tree. One day, while the mama sparrow was laying eggs, an elephant, who was boiling from the heat and wanted some shade, sat down underneath the tree. Then, just for fun, he pulled on the sparrow's branch and broke it. The eggs fell down and cracked. Overwhelmed with grief, the sparrow couldn't stop sobbing.

"Why are you wailing like that?" her friend the woodpecker asked her.

"That arrogant, wretched elephant destroyed my eggs. If you're my friend, help me punish him."

"A friend in need is a friend indeed," answered the woodpecker. *"Now you'll discover the power of my cunning. I have another friend, a fly by the name of Whirring-Cobză. I'll go call her and together we'll kill the awful, wicked elephant."*

The woodpecker went to the fly and told her the story. The fly answered:

"We always help our friends, and they in turn help us. I have another friend, a frog by the name of Rumble-Cloud. Let's go ask her for help too."

Then they all went to Rumble-Cloud and told her the same story. The frog said:

"What's one measly elephant compared to an angry crowd? Do exactly as I say. You, fly, go to the elephant at noon, buzz sweetly and drowsily, like a cobză, in his ear, so that he closes his eyes in pleasure. Then the woodpecker will peck his eyes out. Being blind now and terribly thirsty, he'll hear the croaks of me and my sisters as we stand at the edge of a cliff. The elephant will think there's water there and he'll go straight for it. He'll get to the cliff, fall down it, and die."

And that's what they did. The fly buzzed, the woodpecker blinded him, and he, lost and following the choir of frogs, fell over the cliff and died.

We loved this brutal story, which we entitled: "What's one measly elephant compared to an angry crowd?" That's right!

But one day, we ran out of stories, they were finished, no one had another new one. Then we decided to listen to an old one, but when we'd ask for it to be told, we didn't say: "We want *The Old Woman's Daughter and the Old Man's Daughter* or *The Goat and Her Three Kids*," but "the story in which the fox helped the man beat the wolf, and the man, instead of thanking her, sicced the dogs on her" or "the story in which Proud Aim-Golden Leaf had to build a golden bridge overnight from his house to the king's palace, with blooming trees on each side and, at the end of the bridge, a gilded well with a bucket that draws water by itself, and with a towel hanging next to it that jumps onto people's hands by itself, and golden jingle bells all around that sing, may the flowers bloom divine with the scent of spices fine and may the sun shine" or "the story with 'a hawkbit and a peach pit, stop, boy, don't say it'" . . .

After a while, it was no longer interesting for us just to listen to what we knew almost by heart, we'd jump in as well, play the parts. Then we no longer wanted the grownups' stories, we wanted a new one all our own. We'd start telling a story, we'd all gather round and someone would begin: "Once upon a time, in a land far away" and they'd say something about a king, and they'd go on until someone else would cut them off.

"No, that fox was in fact the daughter of a king and she ran away and fell asleep, and an old couple who wanted a child of their own found her and took her as their child, they cared for her and healed her. And what a good fox she was, she didn't eat chickens, she didn't steal from others, she was neither crafty nor lazy. The old couple was overjoyed to have such a comfort in their old age."

Another child continued the story, "Then the fox said: 'Mother, Father, it's time for me to get married. Go to the king searching for a maiden fitting for his son and tell him that I will be the best of wives' . . . The old couple was very scared, but they went . . . "

We avoided scenes with food. In our version of *The Old Woman's Daughter and the Old Man's Daughter* the little oven was never tended by either, so that the oven was never waiting for either daughter on her way home with a tray filled with toasty pies, neither hot, nor cold, but perfect for eating right then. We were all thinking about that scene, our stomachs were rumbling, but we avoided it, we quickly skipped over the little oven . . . And the apple tree wasn't plucked free of pests, no matter how much it might have asked the girls who passed by. Oh, apples! In June, there weren't any apples from the previous year, or from the current one. In the aul of Belial, one night I dreamed of an apple tree, no, I think it was a quince or a pear. I dreamed of a tree laden with fruit, its branches were bent from so much fruit, ready to break. I picked one, held it under my nose, what a delicious scent! But when I was about to eat it, I opened my mouth and thought: "What's the name of this fruit? Apple—no, it doesn't seem to be an apple. But what's it called?" And thinking about it intently, I woke up. I was sorry that even in my dreams I wasn't able to take even a little bite. I told Mother what I had dreamed. Mother listed off several names of fruit, but I, after years of not having seen or eaten one, had forgotten their taste and names. The Kazaks in the area where we worked had some bread, some animals in their yards, maybe even some money, they wore thick clothing, but I didn't see fruit there like back home in Bucovina. And compared to our rich, blessed life, they were very poor. Compared to what we, deportees, were now, yes, they were kings, but if they had seen us when we were masters in our own homes, had they come to see our village of excellent landowners in our beloved Bucovina, they wouldn't have laughed at us anymore.

A man was once going home after threshing wheat and he met with a wolf on his path.

"Please, put me in your sack and carry me, because a hunter wants to shoot me right now."

The man opened his sack, the wolf got in, and the man kept walking with the animal in the sack. The hunter appeared and asked him:

"You haven't seen a wolf, have you?"

"No," the man said and continued on his way.

"*Now,*" *the wolf said,* "*let me go.*"

The man let him go and the wolf said:

"*In return for the good you did me, I'm going to eat you.*"

"*But how's that,*" *said the man, surprised,* "*good begets good!*"

"*No,*" *the wolf said.*

"*Let's keep walking a bit and if the first person we meet agrees with you, then you can eat me,*" *the man said.*

They walked a while and met with an old dog. They asked the dog if good begets good.

"*I've served people all my life, I guarded a farm, but now that I'm old, they chased me away and I'm dying of hunger. I did good in my youth and received evil in my old age.*"

"*See,*" *the wolf said.* "*That's it, I'm eating you.*"

"*Wait a bit, let's keep going.*"

They met with a horse.

"*Is it possible to repay good with evil?*" *they asked him.*

"*Yes, I worked hard, but when I got old they threw me out to die of hunger on the side of the road.*"

"*Let's ask once more, and that will be the final answer,*" *said the man.*

They met with a fox, and told her everything. The fox was surprised:

"*Come on, that's not true, did you really fit inside this sack?*"

"*I did!*"

"*That's impossible, you're lying, how can a wolf as big as you fit inside a sack like this?*"

The wolf said to the man:

"*Hold the sack.*"

And he got in.

The fox said to the man:

"*Tie it up tightly and throw the shaggy thing around.*"

And he kept throwing the shaggy thing against the ground until it was completely dead. Then the fox asked him:

"*What will you give me for saving you from death?*"

"Four chickens!"

The man got home, but his wife yelled:

"I only have four chickens in all, how can I give them to the fox? Take those two dogs (they had two big dogs) and stick them in the sack, but tell the fox not to look inside until she's in her den."

That's what the man did and he told the fox not to untie it or the chickens would escape and they would be hard to catch. But the fox thought to herself: "As if I'd have trouble catching a chicken" and she untied the sack. The dogs jumped out and ate her . . . And that's the end of the story.

We weren't at all satisfied with the death of the fox that had done a good deed. "Let's make her an enchanted fox, the daughter of a king, and find her a prince and castle, in which she can live happily to a ripe old age . . . We loved the stories, we, us children, sat and listened with our mouths open wide, everyone sat and listened, we made up new stories too, we passed the time with something, so we wouldn't go crazy. We told stories nonstop. Those who didn't tell stories died. Whoever began telling a story would suddenly liven up, brighten, their eyes would shine, blood would flow through their veins, the spirit of a person would also listen to the story and couldn't bear to leave the storyteller.

Then, the grownups on the train sometimes also got tired of our embellished stories and started to reminisce about Bucovinian stories, the legends each one knew about their village. The story of the village of Straja. This village is more toward the border, there used to be a stone pillar there, and Stefan the Great's străjeri, his watchmen, faithfully defended the country from its enemies. On that spot, a settlement was founded and they named it Straja.

Molniţa, what a beautiful village, nestled in the Prut's picturesque valley! The name comes from an incredible mill that made the best flour! First mentioned in sources written during the time of Stefan the Great and Holy, the village prides itself on its inhabitants, whose faces are pleasant and whose souls are good, and who for centuries have lived there loving the land and having faith in God. They kept the customs and traditions passed down from their forefathers, bravely defending the ancestral hearth in times of plague. Poiana: they say that one day all the bees of a beekeeper disappeared, he searched for them and found them in a poină, a truly marvelous meadow. What flowers, what scents! The man stopped there next to his bees and named the place Poiana. There's another village, named Beehive, Prisaca, not far from us. The son of a lord caught the queen of the bees: "Don't kill me," the queen begged him, "let me show you a place where the water is clear and cold, next to it are rich pastures and the forest is also close by." The young man listened to her, he followed her and built a noble estate there, he also built a palace for the queen of the bees, a beehive that was also noble, and that village was named in honor of it. Crasna means beautiful. It was a very beautiful settlement and a nobleman from Galicia came and marveled: "*Crasna, prekrasna, krasiva!* More beautiful than beautiful!" And so it remained, though no one knows anything about the nobleman anymore, not even his name.

Our village, Albina, whose name means "bee," also owes its appearance to the brave deeds of Ştefan the Great, like many other villages in our sweet Bucovina. He had just returned from a battle against the Turks, crushed and with his army in shambles. In our area, in villages such as Prisaca and Poiana, there were many landowners who knew how to harvest the finest honey from bees. An old beekeeper had once told the prince that his bees were so fierce that no Turk would withstand their attack. Their honey was the most expensive, and they didn't produce much, but it was also the most sought after and only a few great noblemen had ever tasted it. The people who know the story maintain that the bees of that beekeeper were rather wild indeed. The old man said that it would be enough to steal the queen of the biggest beehive, the matriarch, for all the warlike bees to set out in search of her to defend her. He had once served his fragrant honey to the prince and had told him this. After having lost the battle, Ştefan, downcast, went to the old beekeeper and they came up with a plan of attack in revenge. "We need a brave, swift-footed soldier to run up as close as possible to the Turkish army, during the day, not at night, because bees sleep at night, then, when he reaches the Turks, to release the queen. He must smear himself with heavy oil and after he releases the bee, he must drop to the ground and remain motionless. And the swarm will attack the enemy." No sooner said than it was done. Ştefan's soldiers then killed many Turks who were terrified, stung by the fierce bees. The site where the battle took place was called Albina, and the land there was given to the soldiers who had won the battle, and is inhabited by brave people to this day. Others say it was a swarm of wasps, not of bees, because bees die if they attack, while wasps don't, as the beekeeper well knew. Whatever it was, bee or wasp, something so small conquered the enemy. Then the village spread and part of it was called Old Albina, and the other was New Albina. A large village.

There's the legend that says that Ştefan the Great's mother was the one who sent him back into battle. What a mother he had! He's our most beloved prince, founder of churches and villages where we come from. Everyone knows stories of his heroic deeds!

"How could he come back home, defeated in battle, and his mother not receive him? I couldn't do that, what kind of heart would I have to not receive him, to not comfort him, when he was going through so much!" a mother said.

"No, she's a good mother, fit for a hero, a true prince, not a striboc!" Grannie Anghelina answered back. "Coddled and patted on the head, and at the first sign of trouble they go over to the enemy's side. Enemies are enemies, but how could you become a traitor! How could you fight against your neighbors, against your own people? The people from the village you share a well with? More heartless than the enemy! What kind of mothers raised them, what kind of milk did they suckle? How could the enemy have drawn up lists of deportees without a striboc like this, a local communist, a bastard and scoundrel? Where are Ştefan's descendants? Where is Ştefan's mother, who put the interests of her people above her maternal pity?"

Nicanor Gherman calmly broke it up with a different kind of "story" from his village:

"One Sunday, soon after the 'liberation,' when the villagers were going to church, a major in the Bolshevik army was talking to a pauper. Looking at the polished boots and expensive clothing of some of the more important landowners who were passing by in front of them, the major kept prying to find out from the man who those people were. 'Mr. Maior, sir, do you think we'll ever be dressed as well as them?' 'You twit, do you think we've come to make you like them? We've come to make them like you,' the officer replied . . ."

Papa Gherman taught us how to come up with lingotwists. People don't know what those are anymore, no one still speaks in such a complicated, flowery way . . . Eufrosina didn't know the lingot-wisty language either, but she liked it and quickly learned how to speak it with Papa Gherman.

"There once was a Bucovinian shoemaker who could wield a hammer in the smith very skillfully. Because he was such an excellent carpenter and could work the planer so finely, he made such pots as had never been seen before, that's how good a shoemaker he was!" This is the simplest example.

"Because I was craving cherries, I went out in search of apricots. I reached the plum trees, and yelled at someone stealing from the neighbor's, 'Hey, you with the nectarines, stop stealing apples, because the pears belong to that man.' And when he threw a lump of pebbles and hit my heel behind my ear, it hurt for a day and a week until a month went by."

Then we'd go into ones that were a bit harder, real puzzles for us: "How I tried to steal sheep: one morning toward evening I climbed onto a proceeding and I forested at an arrival. I pathed onto a slant, from where I eyed that a shepherding was sheeping some grazed. I groved down from the climb and yearlinged about three stolen. But when the shepherding eyed me, he crooked me so hard with his struck that my bibs roke, that my bulges eyed out!"

No one in our railcar knew how to crack a joke like Papa Gherman. He could also tell us riddles from morning until night. "What could it be? What could it be? Let's see! Let's see!" we'd scratch our heads. "Should I tell you?" "Yes," we'd beg him. "No," our dear Eufrosina Procopovici would say and she wouldn't give up until she guessed right, sometimes she'd think about it for two days and then answer correctly.

Whoever makes it doesn't need it, whoever buys it, doesn't buy it for themselves. Whoever needs it doesn't know and can't see it: A casket.

What, though it is small, very, very small, makes a ruler take his hat off: A louse.

A comb on its head, a tool for cleaning flax on its back, spurs on its feet: A rooster.

Marshmallar, issmaller, a curly springflower. A tiny bird as white as a boll climbing up a pole. It doesn't have wings, it doesn't have feet either: Beans.

In darkness I come to play, I borrow a light to guide your way: The moon.

A little chicken, tongue in cheek, gathers ashes in its beak: A pipe.

Old woman and old man, quick! Hop inside the pot of curdled milk: Păcornița or dihornița, a wooden container for heavy oil used to grease wagon wheels.

"Where are you going, Swirled?" "Why are you asking, Unfurled? My tail's all gold": Fire flames.

What is bundled up during the summer and unbundled during the winter? Ears of corn.

What goes over to the well but doesn't drink water? The bell around a cow's neck.

Lump in a stump, sit down and pump: A butter churn.

I have a herd of horses—the weak ones jump the fence, the fat ones stay in place: Chaff and wheat.

Tassels, passels, slowly going up the hills, Old tassel-passel walks along behind them with his song: Sheep and their shepherd.

What, you only knew the answers to three riddles, you and Dad put together? Well those were the easiest ones, for kindergarteners: *It has leaves and many branches, whoever understands it, advances*: A textbook. *A white field, black sheep. Whoever sees it doesn't believe it, whoever chews it over, knows it for sure*: Writing. *A fork with five tines that your parents provide*: A hand.

Mom, I also know a riddle or two and I told them to Cuța and she didn't know the answer: *How many eggs does a chicken lay on the moon?* None! A chicken has never been to the moon! And another one: *A hunter climbed up a tree. Suddenly he saw a lion below, and above him, on a branch—a snake. The snake was coming down toward him, below him was the lion, and he had only one bullet. How did the hunter get out alive?* He climbed down, picked up the lion and put him in his pocket, and shot the snake. Haha! Cuța was amazed!

Give up? Should I tell you the answer to the riddle from last time? I didn't know the answer to this one either. Well, it's a spindle, as if I knew what a spindle was! Mom, is there a museum with spindles in Chişinău? So I can see how people used to live. Even with the answer I still don't understand sometimes!

Bunny under a little tree, whizz up, whizz down, by night he's got a potbelly: A spindle.

Through the warp, through the shed, a clumsy horse to grass is led: A shuttle.

The old man's sittin' on his noggin, the old woman his moustache is tuggin': A gas lamp.

What has a mouth, but doesn't talk: A stove.

With water I'm replete, food I don't eat, but food is my feat: A water mill.

An iron nose into the earth awkwardly goes: A plough.

I have two sleighs: at night they're empty though they're full all day: Peasant shoes.

Who is the stranger who passes by the gate but all dogs tolerate? The wind.

What kind of thing is this? The longer it gets, the shorter it becomes? Life.

———

They took us out to pasture a couple times. The first time, we picked greens and made sarmale. The second time when the train stopped, next to our railcar there wasn't any grass at all, not even a blade, either others had picked it before us, or we were now in the steppe where not enough grass grew. They wouldn't allow us to walk away from the railcar, but we saw that a few railcars away, there happened to be a small meadow with juicy grass. Many women got out, they ate what they found there and then went blind. The entire train heard about about it, and at the next stops we'd ask: "Did their sight come back?" Maybe it wasn't from that grass, but from too much sun? A few people in our railcar went blind from the sun, but after a day they were able to see again in the darkened railcar, and better than before at that. We would've all gone blind, but only those women went blind, the ones that ate that grass. When we were taken out to pasture the third time, Mother was very afraid that I might go blind too. Many of us had picked grass but we were too scared to eat it. "Let's take the grass with us," Mother proposed. "I'll eat some first and we'll see if this weed causes blindness too. I'm old, I'll die with or without my sight, but you're young, you need it." Then Anghelina heard and she wouldn't let Mother touch the grass either. "How can you leave your child with a blind mother?" We put the grass down and were afraid to touch it. I was the first to see Kot pick up a blade of grass and chew it with relish. "Mother," I yelled, "Kot is eating our grass!" Then all the people who had picked grass ate it quickly and no one went blind. Cats know what's good. We kept asking the soldiers if those blind women could see yet. "No, they can't see." They were helped out of the railcar by those who hadn't gone blind. They were so skinny, bent over, and seemingly defeated by fate! When I saw them, I realized that their days were numbered. That death was waiting and watching them. I felt it stalking us all, grinning and sharpening its scythe.

Lord Jesus Christ, Treasurer of all good things here on earth, Master over life and death, be gracious toward us in our weakness and keep destructive and wicked temptations far from us. O Lord, what fount of salvation is near us and where can we find refuge?

Despair weakens you. Those who had fallen into despair were

the first to get sick. We, those whose faith was strong and who prayed often, held up the best. The Devil's great joy, that's despair: satanic power, poisoned thought, demonic influence. Trouble gives rise to humility, but great sadness casts out true prayer and repentance from the soul, and brings weariness, bitterness, and hardening to the heart.

You're overcome with sadness, because you've turned away from God. A person whose heart is pure and who has faith in God doesn't despair, they must never despair. The hope that God is taking care of them never abandons them even in the hardest of hard times. And if you're struggling, it's because God is putting your faith to the test. If you start with that, no matter how crushed you are by fate, you never lose your respect, or pity, for others. But those whose hearts are hard, whose faith is weak, or whose conscience is heavy aren't like that.

When the storms of trials bear down on us, keep us, Lord, from being blown off the path of our faith. Sprinkle, Lord, over our souls, which are full of sinful thoughts, a drop of Your holy blood to cleanse us! Help us, Lord, fight against despair!

Our endless train was sometimes shorter, sometimes longer, we parted with some of the railcars, some headed up, others headed down, but we kept going straight ahead. The train for the work camp, the train for the village, to the south, to the north. They also added on a railcar of Polish people, who we would die of hunger with afterward. Later, they also brought us some Germans who had been deported once already, but were being deported again, so they wouldn't get comfortable where they had been settled. The Germans were very hardworking. The Soviet Siberians, who had barely moved on from hovels, had never seen houses like theirs. They'd wait for the Germans to build them, then they'd banish the Germans and live in them themselves. Where people lived more underground than above ground, they'd bring in a couple of Germans and, in a few years, the first decent houses would appear. Then they'd banish them again, but the Germans still wouldn't resign themselves to living underground as the Siberians did and they kept building house after house. Good, hardworking people.

From time to time they'd give us a small salted fish. I'd give the tail and a bone or two to Kot. Eugen would also bring Kot food. And Aglaie once came with a handful of tiny bones. I was so happy! My kitty wouldn't die! Someone I didn't know, from the back of the railcar, brought some bones, saying: "From us, from Ciucurul Mare, for your cat." That's how we divided ourselves, we gathered according to village, in the middle were lots of people from Mahala, there were less of us from Albina, there were more from Poiana, a few from Prisaca, Plaiu, and Tereblecea, we made up the entire map of Bucovina. We didn't have anyone from the cities, only the villages.

From going about in the dark for so long, my eyes adapted and began seeing better at night. One night, I felt my cat slip out of my arms and he started sneaking through the people sleeping on the ground. Since I hadn't fallen asleep yet, I wanted to know where he was going and what he was planning on doing. It was quiet, quiet enough, I should say, because some were snoring, others moaning softly, and you could hear the sound of the wheels turning. I lifted my head and scanned for the cat. Jumping over the people spread out on the floor or going around them, the cat was headed for the hole we used as a toilet. He started sniffing it, then circling it, then he began chewing on the wood that was dirty with excrement. So that was it! That's why my Kot hadn't died of hunger yet! At first, I felt like throwing up, then I felt very sorry for him. The poor cat! How he was trying to survive! He'd chew on dirty wood, then come to lick my hands, and not only mine. After this, I didn't let him drink from my cup anymore (I had done this, hiding it from Mother, a couple of times) or lick my fingers, as he liked to do. So he wouldn't get upset, I'd pet his fur so he didn't think I was rejecting his expression of love.

When the hunger became more and more unbearable, I could tell by the way people in the railcar looked at him that they wanted to take my cat. He felt it too, he wasn't at all stupid. Before he'd meow and didn't want to stay in his box, but now he went in obediently without me having to coax him. I tied my box to my hand so I could feel the slightest movement. I had carved out a little window with a knife and checked up on him through that. I'd stick a finger in and he'd bite or lick it, so I'd know he was still alive. This was during the day, until evening. At night, when we went to sleep, I'd put him inside the almost empty trunk and lock it. There were fewer and fewer who would have defended my cat and every day there were less of us. They looked at me hostilely, as if they'd have eaten me, too, and not just my poor cat. Then Anghelina picked him up, she raised him up high, and yelled so that the hungry people could hear:

"It's all fur and bones, not a bit of meat on it! It's not fit to eat!"

We, children, would eat the dead's bread until their bodies were thrown out and they were crossed off the lists. We'd pretend the dead were sick, lean them against the walls of the railcar staring at the ground, and we'd receive bread and other food from them. That was until they started decomposing, before they stank so badly that we couldn't get that little piece of bread down our throats. Then, at the next count, we'd declare them completely dead and wait for them to be taken out of the railcar as soon as possible. We'd lean them against the door, so they might fall out when the soldier came in. They couldn't always be thrown out, either because the train wasn't stopping or because it was stopping somewhere people lived and we couldn't throw the bodies out of the train because it would scare the locals. As punishment for our greediness, we'd be stuck with them another couple days. We wouldn't receive bread for them, because the soldiers had crossed them off their lists, and our railcar wouldn't be rid of them either. Both hunger and stench. It's terrible to make those around you suffer even when you're dead!

After one incident, I stopped eating the dead's bread. We had just received some bread and the parents were happy that they could give their children a bigger piece or an extra crumb and they praised God who is merciful and magnanimous that when some go to the Lord, the rest of us can enjoy their portion of bread for another two days! I thought to myself, *That's right, I'm stealing bread from a dead person.* I was little, but thoughts like that would enter my head and I looked with pity at the dead in our railcar. While I contemplated this, one of the dead people next to me suddenly opened an eye and stared at me, intensely, insistently, without blinking. He was looking at the little piece of bread that I was just then moving toward my mouth and I froze with it in midair. As if he were reproaching me for eating his portion of bread. I was so scared I couldn't scream or even move. I don't know how long I stood that way, but someone nearby moved and the eye took off, buzzing in annoyance, in search of another suitable spot. It was a black fly that had landed on the eyelid of the dead man and made the eye look open. I snapped out of it, but for a long time after this it seemed to me that the dead, whether their eyes were open or closed, didn't like that their bread was taken. They didn't want you to eat their bread, but to leave it somewhere near their bodies, they needed it, it belonged to them.

I can feel that little piece of bread stuck in my throat even now when I think about it.

Mother had also taken a sack of beans when they rounded us up, and after we were given water, she'd leave a couple drops at the bottom of the cup and put in a few beans, so that they'd expand a bit and we could eat them the next day when the beans were larger. All the children looked forward to Mother's beans, because we shared them, especially with those who didn't have any food left. We were capable of chewing on that bean for a whole hour! It was our favorite food, because we could nibble on it for such a long time. First of all, the bean was hard, it didn't expand enough and had to be chewed a while, also, we knew that we wouldn't receive anything else to eat any time soon, so we weren't in a hurry. Everyone did the same thing, not just me. We'd compete to see who could take longest to eat the bean and the winner was the person who could stick out their tongue and still have bean on the tip of it while the rest of our beans had disappeared without a trace. First, we'd move it from one molar to another, happy we had something to eat, then we'd lightly suck on it, so we wouldn't somehow swallow it by accident, then we'd separate the skin from the bean and we'd chew it for a long time, as if it weren't the skin of only a single bean, but of at least ten. Then we'd divide the bean into two equal parts, because that's its natural shape, two halves stuck together. Then you had to play with the two pieces for as long as possible, maybe while listening to a story, but being very careful not to crush them between your teeth. And when you decided that, enough, it was time to move on to the next stage, again you had to be very careful not to mash them at the same time, because otherwise you'd immediately swallow them and have nothing left in your mouth. You had to take them one at a time. After you swallowed the first part of the bean, you were overcome by a terrible sense of disappointment, because look how quickly it melted and you barely felt it, you barely tasted anything . . . So as not to be disappointed again, even worse, you delayed finishing off the bean for as long as possible. But that moment would come as well, then you'd roll your tongue around your mouth a couple seconds in search of the tiniest bit of bean, no matter how small, that might have been left in between your teeth randomly or through carelessness.

In Mother's sack there were three kinds of longer beans, and one kind of short bean that was roundish and beady—crab's eye. We ate all the crab's eye beans first. The three longer kinds were big white ones, big black ones, and pink ones with lilac colored polka dots or splashes, which were the same size as the first two. I got to choose which bean I wanted first and each time I picked a different one, so I could try them all and see if they had a specific taste. But I couldn't tell. So much time passed from one bean to the next that I always forgot the taste of the one I had eaten before. I think they tasted the same, but I liked the beans with the polka dots the most because they were the prettiest.

A prayer against hunger. Lord, make this word disappear from our thoughts, and with it the fatigue that it brings to the body. Lord, feed our spirits, our souls, so that it reaches even our swollen bellies. Illuminate and warm us. Pour Yourself into our souls, so that we will no longer think of food. Temper us, Lord, You, who knows our sins, see our hearts which are melting like wax and hear our sighs. Do not reject our prayers and laments, but receive with Your clean hands our tainted souls! Our souls are beaten down, Lord, by storms of doubts and worries. The consuming fire of all our sorrows terrifies our souls. Come, Thou clean and gentle light, and allay our consternation, bringing us Your peace, which we crave with such thirst. Place in our voices, Lord, the strength of faith, the perfume of love, the sweetness of hope, the power of goodness, and the comfort of patience, so that we can arrive safely at our ordained haven.

Bring us safely, Lord, to the end of this journey!

A journey as long as a lifetime. A lifetime is too short even, given how many lives it took away! A journey as long as all the lives of the Bucovinians who died and were thrown from the train, as long as those of everyone who later died of starvation, sickness, or from freezing throughout the entire expanse of the foreign steppes. And if you stop to think about it, a journey longer than the string of people thrown out along the entire length of the railroad. If we lined up the dead, one next to the other, it would reach farther than the end of the road and even the world. Lord, how vast is our Bucovina now, with its living and its dead! From one end of the earth to the other. The entire world belongs to us. To our dead.

Everything stopped. We got out. For good. Putting on its furry cuşmă hat of smoke, the train started the journey back, like a mare tossing its mane in the wind. For the first time, we could see the entire train, getting smaller and smaller, farther and farther away. The train melted away fairly quickly, as if it had never existed, but we still carried it within us, it rattled and jolted us inside and that's how it was long after we got out of it. Actually, when I think about it, it jolts me even now . . . We were just a handful of people, those of us who got out . . . Maybe some people were still inside. Were only so few left from a train this long? Did that many people die on the journey?

After three and a half weeks of travel, we reached the end of the earth. I heard people around me moaning that, for us, this wasn't just the end of the earth, but the end of the world. Forgive

us, Lord, for we know not what we say! I thanked the Lord who
had allowed us to get this far and touch this heavenly sky not just
with our tortured souls, but also with our thin, withered fingers.
Because of so much light, at first we couldn't see a thing. We covered our eyes. After being in the train for so long, the sky appeared
so suddenly, it was as if I had just been born and was seeing it
for the first time. At the end of the earth, we were afraid of step-
ping too hard, we walked gingerly. You could fall from the earth,
which ends here. And so we had taken the train to get to the heavenly skies. We climbed out into the sky, the train left, everything
turned into heavenly air after the suffocating train, even the grass
was made of air, and you could see the sky through it. Here I saw
how round the earth is, like a mămăligă or a little watermelon.

Longer than all the roads and deeper than all the seas, more
beautiful than all flowers, more precious than icons, heavier than
cannons, brighter than candles and darker than cellars? The sky! I
looked around for a stick, a hill, a pond, anything, a sign of something earthly or something human. But only the high heavens
greeted us. Welcome! it said. And we held it up with our shoulders
and our hands, so it wouldn't crush us completely.

I was a little girl when I had gotten on the train and I climbed out a
woman. At the end of the road, we received more bread than usual,
they had us get off and the train went back, with a long whistle.
Fedor, the soldier from our railcar, waved his hat at me, maybe not
just at me, but at everyone. Maybe not at anyone in particular, but
just because—from the joy of being done with his difficult mission. We watched the train until it disappeared past the horizon.
Though it had been horrible in the train and the entire way we
had wanted to reach our destination as quickly as possible, to get
out, to breathe, finally, clean air, to have more space for our sweaty,
unwashed bodies, when the train disappeared, we almost felt bad.

The train kept getting smaller, all around us, just us and the sky, no human dwelling, no village or town, work camp or prison, kolkhoz or place to live, nothing . . . What we had around us, we later found out, was something called the steppe, an endless field, mirroring itself wherever you might look. The train was our connection to our previous, normal life, which we would later forget, but which now we still painfully remembered and missed. The train had come from our dear Bucovina, it connected us to the place where we had been born. I cried a bit, the weight of the sky was overwhelming, as if they had sent us here, at the end of the earth, the end of the road, to shoulder the sky, to hold it up so it wouldn't collapse. We stood bent over, humbled by such majesty and the miracle of the change.

I was crying because we had arrived here and now it was my time to die. I could feel the blood draining from me. At first, I didn't know what was leaking and then I touched it and saw that my hand was all bloody. *It's over, I'm dying. Many have died on the road, and now it's my turn*, I thought to myself. I felt the blood drain from my head, chest, fingers, pool into my belly, and trickle down from there, sticky, hot, unpleasant, onto my pants, which were already dirty. I cried. Mother was calm, or at least she tried to seem so, and attentive, she kept trying to cheer me up, to hug me, coddle me, trying to hide her own feelings and fear. "Cheer up so you don't freeze, so you don't catch cold. See how cold it is now, in the middle of the day, at night it will be even colder. Move around, walk a bit."

"What good will it do if I'm dying?"

"Why are you dying?"

"I'm losing all my blood, whatever's left of it, and I'm about to die." Mother smiled sadly, to my confusion. I was dying and she was making light of it!

"So much sky and now your blood! Now it decides to come," Mother mumbled, rummaging through our suitcase for a pillowcase, which she tore into strips and handed me one to put there. She told me that I wasn't at all dying, but growing, my blood was changing itself out, filtering itself, and that I had to live, give her grandchildren, and return to sweet Bucovina. She also told me about girls and women, she hadn't had time to tell me before, because, look, I had been a child and now I was entering the world of childbearing women. There was a lot I didn't understand then, just that I wasn't dying, not even close. Just so, how could I die when I still had a good crust of bread and some food hidden in our suitcase which could keep us alive for at least two more days, why was I in a hurry to die right now? Mother calmed me down and I looked around some more. That's how I camped out in the middle of those heavens, a woman. Maybe from the joy of too great a sky.

Evening fell, our first evening on the steppe, under the great open sky. And as evening fell, a chill settled in as well, freezing our bones weakened by the journey and prolonged bumpy ride. We wrapped ourselves up in whatever we could find, but a violent shiver from the cold would still shake us from time to time. The Gherman sisters from our railcar, who I had become friends with on the train, came over with a few younger girls from their village.

Mother said we should move around, because otherwise we'd die of cold here before morning, we'd freeze.

I don't know how it started, we gathered tightly together, we hugged, we began stamping our feet, humming a song, singing it with more feeling, louder, we began spinning around, improvising, in the end, a circle dance, a horă. Well, what do good Romanian girls do to keep from freezing? They start up a little horă! We were still young girls, we hadn't come out yet at the village horă, but we had already been dreaming, before the deportation, about some handsome boy, maybe we secretly liked someone, we were preparing our festive blouses, which we were learning to embroider beautifully, we were waiting for the little boots in which, in two or three years, we'd steal the hearts of all the young men of the village. I was my mother and father's youngest daughter, my older brothers who went to horăs would ask me to dance at home, meaning they practiced on me, so they wouldn't embarrass themselves in the village. I liked dancing with them as well, I could hardly wait to grow up too. I knew all different kinds of horăs, some with more steps, some with smaller steps, some with more spins. The mothers looked at us lovingly and with a kind of cheerfulness. Other girls and young girls came up to our horă and would yell louder, above our song, and we'd unlink our arms and let them in. So our horă got bigger and our song grew stronger:

> *Come in closer, gather round! All together stamp the ground!*
> *Left, right, left, and to the right, so our horă lasts the night!*
>
> *I'll keep dancing, I won't stop, even if it makes me drop!*
> *But these boots they aren't my own, they were given to me on loan,*
> *Da-da-da and da-da-dem, hope that I don't ruin them!*
>
> *My poor feet you're getting weak from my dancing up a streak!*
> *But you'll have to stand the test, 'cause I'm not about to rest!*
> *When you dance the horă right, you'll be dancing through the night!*
> *That's how Mother danced the tune when she had me in her womb!*

The dancing and singing warmed us up, cheered us, and kept us from thinking black thoughts about what was to come. Then all the women who had survived (most of us were women), even the oldest ones, surrounded us and gathered their courage to join us in the horă. Including our Baba Tudoriţa, who was weak, bent over, she seemed barely able to move. She came over limping, bundled up in all her clothing. We unlinked arms to receive her in our bountiful horă, but she walked into the center and sang the horă calls to us, some of them happy, others less so.

If we knew before our birth, all the pain we'd feel on earth
We'd no longer take the breast, we'd go straight to heaven blessed!

Leaves of silver, leaves of gold, people say that I've grown old
Let them talk, what care have I? From my boots I make dust fly!

Meanwhile, all the mothers and housewives had joined us and were singing and doing fiery footwork, some became rosy-cheeked, others were smiling as if this were their first horă in Bucovina and they were unmarried women, with slender waists, without a care in the world. Where did all their vigor come from? They had been staggering when we got off the train! After she sang and called out for us, Tudoriţa began to dance amazingly too, the way she whirled around and all her different steps! We couldn't stop marveling . . . She got warmed up and started taking off some of her clothes. She'd go up to some child who was more lightly dressed with a headscarf or blouse and put it over their shoulders or tie it around their waist, while the horă kept going. We were afraid she might fall, or feel sick, she had cast off all her clothes until she was wearing only a white underdress, with nothing under that. She danced a bit more, then she left the circle, she laid down on the cold grass and breathed her last. When we came over to her, we saw that she had died with a smile on her lips. What a beautiful death! We danced some more until we heard the whoops of the Kazakhs that had come to get us. They had heard our whistles in the distance and had answered back.

Then, in the horă, Jenea held me tightly and took me to the center to dance as boy and girl, he led as the boy and I said:

"You lead so well! How nice it would be if you were a boy and protected me!"

"I will protect you," Jenea said and kissed me on the cheek, blushing like a virgin. It wasn't his first time blushing, he'd blush especially when I'd kiss him on the train thinking he was a girl. And me kissing him on the cheek as my best friend! I told him that I had grown up and my blood had come, "Did yours?"

"No," he said, scared, and turned red again.

When they had come to round them up, they had asked if all the members of the family were present. His parents had said yes, hoping that their oldest son wouldn't return right then, thankfully a neighbor had gone to his grandmother and had told her that the Țarăs were getting taken away that moment. Grannie Anghelina hid Jeni, and then, later, when they were picked up together, she dressed him as a girl so they wouldn't be separated. Jeni had been to the train station to search for his parents, he had a handbasket with things to eat. He saw them and gave them the handbasket from his grandmother. It's wrong for children to see their parents humiliated, brought to their knees, it's enough to make you cry, scream, but everyone was standing around as if nothing had happened. His father had been separated from the family, Jeni had seen this as well. His mother was left alone with three small children, only two reached the destination, the youngest had gotten sick on the train, he was just a few months old. The soldiers had counted, father, mother, three children, when his mother had, in fact, four, but the people with the lists hadn't found out. Then the enemies came back and took his grandmother as well, not because she had been political or too rich, but because they needed her house, his grandmother was old, they also picked up the child and added the name to the list only when they were already inside the railcar. Then Grannie Anghelina said this was a granddaughter of hers, Jenica, who was visiting from a village in Romania. Jenica had on a coat of his grandmother's and looked like a little girl, his hair was even long and curly, exactly how little girls wear it. I was really embarrassed when he told me that he was actually a boy. I realized that Mother knew, that maybe the entire railcar knew, I was the only one who rushed to kiss and hug him. It was easier for me to believe that Jenica was a girl, I didn't know how to act around a boy, especially after all that had happened in the train. I was very embarrassed, it was my turn to blush.

And when I thought that this was the end, that we had finally arrived, that there was nothing beyond this, there was no going farther, fate was laughing at us. There is no end to life, dear child. When the people from the nearby kolkhozes came to pick us up in wagons, I saw them from a long way off, most of the wagons were driven by oxen, but a few of them by camels. There were no camels back home in Bucovina and I was seeing that animal for the first time then. An old woman crossed herself and said: "Holy Mother of God! Lord, good God! Look what the antichrists have done to the beautiful horses! What state will they bring us to? What will become of us?"

God of heaven and earth, You who have dominion over all time and bestow all good things, have mercy on us! Blessed are the meek, blessed are the merciful, blessed are those who suffer, blessed are those who travel in cattle cars, just as Christ was also born in a manger for cattle. Blessed are we, those of us who the Lord has given days to and have reached the end of the road. But Lord, do not be angry with us, who speak from bitterness of heart. Lord, Your will be done with us sinners. When the storms of trials blow over us, do not allow us, Lord, to be thrown off the path of our faith. We ask you, most merciful Lord, to give us Your wisdom, so we can shun all that is not pleasing in Your sight, so we can know how to speak and choose only that which is pleasing to You, so that we may be saved. Give us the strength to count all the vanities of this world as nothing. Amen.

- PART TWO -

THE EXILE

Train, may you never touch another rail, or ever keep another wheel,
'Cause you took us far away, in dark foreign parts to stay. Oh, oh!
Railcars went, several hundred, and so many died of hunger,
Then we who survived the ordeal with the Kazakhs had to deal:
Their language we didn't know, so what we meant, we couldn't show.
We had nothing to eat, nothing on our feet, nowhere to sleep.
I was eleven years old, my youth was wasted out in the cold!
If I had a father, mother, never again would I cry and suffer;
If I had a brother, sister, never again would my heart be bitter;
If I had some land to keep, never again would I want to weep!
My God, what did we do so wrong, that You should punish us so long?
Guilty, of what? I cannot understand.
They took us to a godless land and from sweet Bucovina banned,
To our own country never to return, and forever there to yearn,
Lost among aliens, all because we're Romanians.
Sing it out, if you can, we found ourselves in Kazakhstan.
Ravens have their chicks and home, we were left there all alone.

Quday! Yelled the women with narrow eyes when they received
the black pieces of paper, notices announcing the death of their
sons or husbands. And their despair echoed throughout the
entire Anarkhay steppe, desolate and indifferent, whose small

hills or knolls looked as alike as two drops of water. *Qu-day!*
Quday! and the poor Romanians they were housing were kicked
out, even if it was cold enough for stones to crack. *Quanysh!*
they'd yell when they were happy, but usually not in front of
us. *Masqara!* they grumbled when they were upset. When they'd
see that we were upset, they'd say, "You dirty muskrats!" That's
how we interpreted their displeasure but that's not the word for
muskrat. There, *masqara* is a kind of "poor me," "goodness,"
"oh no," or "sigh." *Sen beybaq* were swear words, we were on
the receiving end of those as well. We were exiles on this earth,
and exiles aren't surprised by scorn and curses. There, we were
"the enemy of the people," we were Romanians and Romania
was fighting against the Soviet Union, so it was our fault that
their sons and husbands were dying on the front lines. What can
you expect of strangers when your own neighbor, from the same
village, your supposed friend, had no mercy, understanding, or
compassion and he wished you evil, sending you to the end of
the earth? Why would these people treat you well? How could
we tell them that we meant them no harm, that we had never
wronged anyone in our life, that we weren't the enemy of the
people, or anyone's enemy. How could we talk to them when we
didn't know their language? We had barely learned a few words
in Russian, because some of us knew that language and thought
that we'd run into Russians in the heart of Russia. But Kazakhs,
Tatars, Uyghurs, Kyrgyzs, Uzbeks, and who knows what other
peoples were all thrown together there, and there are as many
notions as there are nations. Each worshipped their own god
and you didn't often meet with someone who spoke Russian.
All kinds of Asiatic peoples lived in those parts, besides those
who had been deported there before us, and then those who
came at about the same time as us, and others after the war. We
thought that they looked the same and spoke the same language,

of which we didn't understand a word in the first years. We communicated with the locals through gestures at first.

They had picked us up from the steppe in their strung-together *arbels*, a kind of wagon, some of them covered, and they brought us to an undeveloped, godforsaken settlement named Ozek-Belely (Belial, we called it), to the kolkhoz named "The Way to Communism." They brought us to a place where bells don't ring, houses aren't swept, dogs don't think to bark, the enchanted bird never flew. Their word for city was *abad*, a bigger village or even a district center was a *kishlak*. We had arrived in a *kishtak*, a small village, and Eugen and his family lived in a *yurt*, not far from our kolkhoz. A kolkhoz was composed of a few smaller *kishtaks* or one big *aul*. So, a *kishtak* was a small village, *ail* also a kind of small village, and *aul* a big village, and a *yurt* was a large wooden house insulated with felt made out of sheep's wool. They would say so-and-so is from the Uyghurs' yurt, meaning that respective people. Yurt could also mean the whole village, the entire gathering of yurts.

On the first day, they left us in a large, abandoned barn belonging to the the kolkhoz, which was full of bedbugs, fleas, lice, rats, and other creepy-crawlies found in the steppe. Then we spread out among the locals, because there were too many of us in the barn and we were afraid that winter was coming and we'd freeze. We received a small hut from a Kazakh family in exchange for a beautiful rug we had brought. It was big enough only for Mother and me and you had to bend down when you entered. It had been built when the Kazakhs were poorer. They were decent and brought us some straw as well, and we had a kind of bed made from three wide planks, and a wooden chest which served as a table. We would've died there if we hadn't also had a *tandâr*—a small oven made of earth for baking bread. We didn't have anything to make bread with, but we warmed ourselves with it when the harsh winter came and Mother used it to prepare a soup traditional for all deportees called *balanda*, made of boiled water with a handful of flour in it, and on rare occasions a few stray potatoes found their way into the pot. We only had a satchel of corn flour left and we were being cornered by our hunger. Millet porridge there is called *tary botqasy*, but we had so little millet left that our botqasy was practically soup.

Only one thing mattered to our poor mothers—saving us children. That's why, after we had gotten somewhat settled there and had a roof over our heads, right from the first few days, we went to the director of the kolkhoz and asked him to give us some work so we wouldn't die of hunger. Meanwhile, the war had started and almost all the men from there had gone to fight, so there was work to do. The weight of all the farm work fell on our shoulders. There were also some who didn't want to work, they'd steal, run away, or die. But our Bucovinians were very hardworking and they never avoided a job, no matter how hard.

At first, for about two weeks we were taken out to weed the wheat fields, we'd pick thorns until our fingers bled. A kind of camelthorn grew there, a plant with purple flowers, about half a meter tall, that blocked all the wheat's sun. Then they sent us to gather hay and harvest produce. But God forbid we touch a grain of wheat! Jail awaited us, you'd get ten years of prison. They'd give us a stew to eat, *mashhurda*—they made it like a watery soup, with some vegetable peels floating in the bowl or, less often, *mash* porridge, meaning mung bean porridge, which was somewhat gooier, more filling, and we liked it a lot. I'd work alongside Mother and receive food as well. Toward evening, hunger would begin to torment us again. When darkness fell, a few of us children would get together and steal into a potato field at night, we'd crawl on our hands and knees and pull up a potato or two. The guard would fire into the air, but we wouldn't get scared, we'd keep going, because nakedness makes you hide but hunger makes you march right out.

Afterward we were directed to plow the steppe. Here our backs almost broke, that's how hard they worked us, that's how much we suffered. A six oxen plow was pulled by only four of us. That *hirman,* meaning the field, was so vast that if we started out in the morning, at sun up, we'd get to the end of it as the sun was getting ready to set. The oxen were weak, scrawny, mangy, and either they wouldn't pull, or wouldn't keep the plow in the furrow, or they would stop and we'd have to push them until they'd drag the plow again. This is where I helped out, because I wasn't pulling the plow but carefully guiding the oxen. At the end of the field where we'd turn, there was a ravine and the oxen would rush to drink water. They'd get in the mud, sink down into it, and we'd use up all our strength pulling them out and getting them to plow another furrow. We'd be so tired that, on the way home, we'd lean against each other so we wouldn't fall.

The beautiful landowners from Bucovina were unrecognizable—we looked like a bunch of walking skeletons in that cursed land overrun with thistles. The younger people took courses for three months to become tractor drivers so they wouldn't have to pull plows anymore. I was too young for the tractor, and Mother rather old, so we got jobs at the farm. Those who worked there each received three hundred grams of cereals (wheat, barley, millet, or oats) daily. Old people and children, being unfit to work, received only one hundred and fifty grams. We didn't receive oil, sugar, potatoes, or vegetables, and we were never full.

We couldn't even say "salt and bread is all we're fed," because we didn't have salt either. In the first year of the deportation, those who had something left from home got by better, if they had provisions or woven rugs, towels, headscarves, blouses, they traded them for a handful of wheat or a glass of milk. Out of hunger, people would eat even the peasant shoes made out of pigskin or cowhide that they had come with from home. But smokers had it the worst, because they would trade their portion of cereals for a rustic cigarette. They were the first to die.

Mother was a skillful embroiderer and she had brought a floral tablecloth with her from Bucovina. She wouldn't sell it to anyone but used it as a sample: "See, I'll make you one just like it." First the Kazakh housewife who had given us the hut came. It took her a while before she understood that we weren't selling our treasure and that it was just for display, and then she brought one of their tablecloths, *dastarkhan*, as she called it, and Mother embroidered little flowers on her dastarkhan. She left us some wheat and brought me a *chapan*, a kind of warm robe, worn and a bit small, but it served me well. *Qolonershi* —craftswoman, they called Mother because she embroidered, only Bucovinians called her Aspazia. For her work, Mother later also received a pair of *ichigi*, footwear our Kazakhs wore, a kind of soft-soled boots over which you'd put on shoes or galoshes. You couldn't find anything better around there.

Mother also embroidered flowers for the Kazakh woman on some pillowcases and she then brought us the best *qurt* I'd eaten in my entire life, it was flatbread made with hard cheese which we didn't make back home in Bucovina. So what if we hadn't heard of qurt, they hadn't heard about our pastries either . . . They were also poor, they couldn't give us more than that, and we were happy with what we got. In the evenings, we'd go through the village calling out "Dastarkhan!" Sometimes I'd bring one of my mother's tablecloths, for display. Then, at school, I found a drawing of a swan in a book, a big one with its wings spread out, next to its young. I copied the drawing and we later embroidered the swans, which were very popular and our work was in demand. A Russian woman brought us colored thread and we made her a large swan with six little cygnets, in different colors, because you can't embroider white on white. We'd embroider more during the winter, when there was no more work out in the fields. The hut was dark and we were afraid we'd go blind. But hunger pushed us forward and we worked away, listening to Mother's stories about our little house in Bucovina, about our ancestral customs and traditions, about the foods that my dear little mother would've prepared if she had had any ingredients. When we had gotten past the toughest times, I didn't want to embroider anything anymore, not one flower, not one swan! When I'd pick up my needle, I'd remember the dark, cold evenings when I'd embroider with Mother so we wouldn't starve to death.

Mother would ask me, during those freezing evenings, something about Father and I wouldn't know how to answer. I couldn't remember Father, I couldn't remember his face, his smile, I couldn't remember my sister or my brothers either. Mother would get sad and begin to tell me anecdotes about what I did when I was a little child in Bucovina, about her and Father and Bucovina, my brothers and Bucovina, my sister's wedding in Bucovina. What the people were like, what life was like, she told me so I wouldn't forget, here, in this dark foreign country. When I returned, my mother's Bucovina had disappeared, all that was left were her stories about my dear birthplace.

Whenever Mother managed to bring me some milk from the farm, she was so happy that her eyes seemed to sparkle and she was younger and more beautiful, she'd sit down in front of me and watch me drink the milk. At first, I tried to give her some as well, I wanted us to share it, but she kept saying no, that she had tasted some at the farm and that this was my portion. I noticed that each time I'd swallow, she'd swallow as well, I'd glug-glug noisily, and she'd glug-glug right along with me though nothing was going down her throat. Then I, to make her happy, after I had finished it all, would say: "I'm full," though I would have wanted three times as much, and I'd wipe my mouth. "I'm full too," Mother would repeat after me and she'd wipe herself as well, as if a trickle of milk were going down her chin. I'd laugh and she'd laugh too or just smile. She'd always do that when she brought me food, not only milk. She'd chew and swallow at the same time as me, as if just by looking at me and imitating me something of that tiny bit of food would get to her as well. I laughed for a while, then I thought about how she was giving me everything she brought and wasn't eating anything. And how skinny she was, and how sickly! Even if she'd bring me only half of a little cup, when I would've wanted at least three to drink my fill, I began leaving a tiny bit for her. I'd swallow slowly, so it felt that I was drinking more, and then I'd say, "I can't finish it, I'm full, drink some too." Or: "My stomach hurts, I'm not used to eating so much." Mother refused, saying she drank some at the farm (you wouldn't have said that by the looks of her). But when I handed her the cup and said I'm not drinking the rest, she began to cry while holding it. "Don't cry, Mother, or your tears will fall into the cup."

"It's fine, there will be more to drink," she said. When Mother took me to the farm with her, I saw how hard it was to take even a drop of milk home from the farm and how hard it was to taste it there. Mother was lying, so I wouldn't feel I needed to share with her.

In the evening, after we'd return from the farm, we'd go through the field and look for ears of wheat through the piles of straw. We'd bring back a handful, we'd rub it, lightly crush it, boil it, and that's how we fooled our stomachs. We were looking not only for ears of wheat, but also bird nests, ground squirrels, mice, anything we could add to our meals. One time, I saw a big wolf in a field, who took off when he saw us. There were wolves around there, they attacked the sheep, the cattle as they were grazing, the flocks of geese, and whatever else people had, they'd even come into the kolkhoz. But this one, what an animal it was, as big as a calf! We watched him go and looked at the spot where he had been before we had approached. Why had it been standing there? It was evening, we couldn't see well and it was a bit far off. We got a big scare when a person stood up in front of us. It was a woman, in fact, who when she saw the wolf running toward her, had gotten down on her knees and from fear began praying to God to save her and, behold, He had brought us by right in the nick of time. The wolf had gotten scared and ran away. I recognized her as Maria Gherman, the mother of the five girls everyone just called Aglaie though they each had their own name. She told us that she had been looking for ears of wheat too. She had reached some stalks of wheat, decided to rest for a moment and sat down, and when she looked more carefully, she saw a trail of wheat ears on the ground and followed it, then she rummaged through the hay and found a satchel of pure wheat, which the Kazakh kolkhoz workers had hidden during the threshing. She picked it up joyfully, she had never returned home with so much wheat before, now she had something to quell the children's hunger. As she started quickly for home, suddenly she saw something rushing toward her. It was a huge wolf. She got down on the ground and began praying: "Lord, have compassion on my plight, let me take this wheat home to my children, so they won't die of hunger, Lord, how can

I accept being eaten by a wolf now of all moments, with so much wheat on me? Allow me, Lord, to take the wheat to my girls and then I'll come back so the wolf can eat me. At first, I felt its wild breath, and then, when you came along, it took off running." The frightened woman asked us to walk back together, Mother knew she had many children, she didn't ask for a single grain of wheat from her full satchel, though we hadn't caught a ground squirrel, or a sparrow with a broken wing. We hadn't managed to gather ears of wheat either and we were going home empty-handed.

When we reached the village, she put two fistfuls of wheat in Mother's apron and she said that her husband and daughters had made a trap for catching ground squirrels, and that we should go catch them together, so I could learn from them, and they could make me a trap as well. I didn't know how to use a trap to catch things, you might wait even for several days until something fell into it. The surest way was to find a tunnel of theirs and pour water over it, and at the other end, the second exit, be waiting with a stick. But you couldn't find any animals near the village, either they had been eaten, because we were all hungry, or the animals had gotten scared off by us. But farther from home, it was hard carrying water and we could never bring enough of it with us to flood their underground houses. If at first the wild animal got scared, and the moment you poured a little water, it hurried out, sometimes six animals, the entire family, came out, the next time, if any had escaped, they were used to the water, which stopped midway in the tunnel, and they would then burrow into the ground and not one would come out. We were looking for the places where they were storing up food, where they would spend the winter, we poked around in the ground with sticks, with our hands, maybe we'd get lucky with baby ones that couldn't defend themselves. It was hard by yourself, children with more siblings did better. I went a few times with Mother, but Mother got tired,

it was hard for her after a day of work to run after ground squirrels. And ground squirrels don't just stand there waiting for you
to catch them, they're nimble, slippery, they slide right through
your fingers and they're gone! The people from there considered
us backward, but it would be several years until we had our own
pig, and four geese that we'd later sell when they were full grown.
"Plant corn and you'll harvest bacon," Mother would say. If only
we had corn then! They'd laugh at us and call us savage Romanians who eat mice and sparrows! But we, the savages who caught
animals out in the fields, survived, while the others who lived off
only what the state gave them died left and right. What joy when
we'd catch a mouse without lifting a finger or find a baby bird!
We'd boil it with a handful of wheat or oats and have a meat dish.

I also lived to see the day when there was enough bread in stores,
when we were paid for our work in potatoes, even up to twenty
kilograms. It seemed like a lot to me, "Finally," I said, "now we
can eat until we're full," and I'd get mad at Mother who still kept
me at a potato a day. Now I know that she, poor woman, was
making sure we didn't finish them off in three days because that
was the allotment of potatoes for the entire year, until the next
harvest. She was saving up for lean days, afraid that we might die
of hunger. How many times would she give me food, but gulp
only air herself. She'd be filled with joy when I'd eat everything
with relish, I'd say how good it was, nothing hurt anymore and I
wouldn't moan from hunger in my sleep.

People get accustomed to the good life really quickly. When it's
good, they want it better, it's not enough anymore, it's never
enough. But I'll never forget that first year of exile, which was also
the harshest year of famine, when all I wanted to do was eat until
I was full. At night I'd dream I was holding a steaming hot potato,

which all I had to do was peel, wait, no, I'd eat it as is, skin and all, sometimes I'd pop the whole thing in my mouth, sometimes I'd bite into it. The same potato, night after night. Sometimes I still dream of that potato even now. Back then, I'd search for potato peels, at the pig farm, at the kolkhoz cafeteria, I'd pick through trash piles looking for scraps that were more or less edible, which Mother would wash and then boil with three ground up blades of wheat, if we were lucky. In the winter, I'd search the fields for frozen potatoes, I'd come home with my fingers frostbitten. What a hard winter! Sometimes I'd return without anything, but one time with bruises as well, when two older boys stole my potato or that frozen piece of something that seemed to be a potato. They pushed me, I fell down, but I kept holding onto the potato, I defended it, then they kicked my hand and my potato or whatever it was flew into the air, like a ball. It was freezing, snowing, it had gotten dark. I couldn't see anymore, I didn't have time to search the field for anything else, everyone was leaving. I saw Mother, who was waiting for me to bring something to put into the pot. I came in, shaking from the cold, hunger, and the blows from the boys. Mother helped me undress, she sat me down next to the hob to warm up. When she saw my injured hand, she asked me:

"Does it hurt?"

"No," I said, "but I feel like it hurts God."

She didn't ask me anything else, she didn't say anything else, she put the plate of boiled water in front of me, after fishing for who knows what out of the pot, it didn't taste like anything but it warmed up your stomach. Well, and when I did bring home a frozen potato! We didn't get much out of the rotten, smelly thing, but at least a tenth of it was still good and we put it in our pot. And the feeling of victory, that I found it, that I brought back something, the light in Mother's eyes, who'd say with lots of praise in her voice: "You brought a darling potato, my, our meal will be so good now, we'll lick our fingers." She'd say a "potatowee" or a "potatowo," giving it a pet name and making the word longer. As if a longer word would mean a bigger potato: "Potatowooo!" She'd be so happy it was as if I had brought a ground squirrel or a frozen mouse!

I once did bring back a ground squirrel. Actually, I don't know even now nor did I know then what kind of animal it was, I'd bring back home whatever I found, to ease our hunger. An animal meant more than a frozen potato or some peels picked out of the trash. The food was much better, we'd chew even the little bones, suck on them, until they melted in our mouth as well. Our boys called them ground squirrels or gophers, while the Russians called them *suslik*. Its snout was something like a rabbit's, its fur like a squirrel's, and it most resembled a mouse, especially if it was small. There were two kinds, the little ones, as small as mice, and the big ones, weighing about a kilo, yellow or gray with stripes on their back, with a tail shorter than a mouse's and which dug underground tunnels a meter deep or even three meters, people said. In the winter they would stay in their den and sleep, if you found their home, you could catch them all in one fell swoop, because winter was also when they had their babies. The boys would go out to catch ground squirrels, they'd set traps, we, girls, had a harder time coming across them. But sometimes it happened that the boys would scare them, chase them out of their nest, and we'd find some frightened animal. We had better luck with the baby ground squirrels. They'd catch the daddy ground squirrel or the mama ground squirrel and the babies would be left defenseless.

I was once out looking for potatoes, and suddenly I saw something move in the ground and a tiny head. Gotcha, I grabbed it, I squeezed tightly until it stopped moving and I tucked it carefully into my pocket. Then I started acting as if I were distracted and moody. "Did you find anything?" a child near me asked. "Nooo,"

I answered, "but I'll keep looking!" Later I said: "I'm not feeling very well, I'm cold. I'm going home."

"Don't go, it isn't dark yet. The boys have found ground squirrels, maybe we'll find one too, there have to be babies as well."

"Tomorrow," I said and I left with my hands visibly empty, so everyone could see that I didn't have anything. *Lord, help me get home safely with this ground squirrel! So no one steals it away from me!* Our hungry children weren't the only ones who might have stolen my treasure, but also the Kazakh children, who'd play with it, then take it with them, maybe they'd give it to their dogs. And not even their dogs would eat it, they'd say, while we, savages that we are, eat anything that breathes. "All the birds and all the animals will go extinct thanks to these deportees! They'll wipe everything that moves off the face of the earth. Some say that we, Kazakhs, are backwards, because we live in yurts and don't know how to make cheese out of milk. But look at these people! They'll even eat the bark off of trees!" They called us all sorts of names. They came to respect us later, but at first, when our people were dropping like flies of starvation, they laughed at us.

When I brought Mother the ground squirrel, she looked at it as if it were a Christmas pig. So much meat, she didn't even know what side to start from. It was a young, skinny thing, longish and with striped fur, it was pretty. But I came in frowning so Mother would think I hadn't brought anything. Mother looked at me out of the corner of her eye: "It's alright if you haven't got anything, we'll get by." Then I came up to Mother, I stopped in front of her and pulled out my kill triumphantly, the treasure in my pocket! At first, Mother didn't understand. Then she whispered, unable to believe it: "Meat!" She didn't say anything about how good our meal would be, the way she did with the potato peels. We now had a whole ground squirrel, as big and as wide as my palm, and as thick as three fingers! We wondered if we should split it in half, because we didn't know if we'd catch another one tomorrow . . . We decided that it would be better to eat it all now though, because who knew if it wouldn't go bad by tomorrow, or if the cat wouldn't come by and eat it up.

We ate it all, mostly I did, but Mother tasted it as well. The fur was the only thing we didn't eat, but Mother scraped the fat off it. And the little bones were softer than the chaff and straw found in the bread we received, which could puncture your guts. We had to be grateful even for bread like that, because there was a war, soldiers were dying on the front lines, and those who didn't die had to eat so they could defend the country. And who was fighting against the country, on the side of the evil Hitler-lovers? "Who's killing our sons on the front lines? You, Romanians! And you think we owe you bread! Oh, it has too much straw in it?! You vile invaders!" We, Orthodox believers, hold that peace on earth is a gift from God, same as good weather, and a good harvest, rain, health, and life itself. We prayed for the giver of all gifts to give peace to the world. If virtue weren't so shaky in this world, people wouldn't talk so much about peace because peace would come naturally, from kindness and understanding. Because who else could be the foundation of peace on earth other than the only one who is called the Prince of Peace?

One day I also caught a kind of darker-colored sparrow, actually I didn't catch it but found it out in the field, frozen. I was looking for cabbage leaves, which made a stew tastier than potato peels. One time, the cook at the kolkhoz cafeteria saw us rummaging around and she came out with good, unspoiled cabbage leaves and passed them out to the children looking around there. Leaves, cores, for everyone. We went back home to our mothers happy.

Eugen told me that in their kolkhoz, children weren't allowed to search for ears of wheat out in the fields. If they were caught, they were punished, yelled at, threatened, and their ears of wheat, of course, were confiscated as well. It didn't matter that those ears of wheat would rot out in the fields. The children were taking Soviet property and food from hungry soldiers. If they caught a ground squirrel, they'd say a prayer of thanksgiving to God and eat it with great relish. Ground squirrels weren't Soviet property and weren't being taken from hungry soldiers on the front lines.

On that day, a child from the village came to tell us that he had found a frozen sheep out in a field and that we should come with knives and axes even, if anyone had one, to slice off meat. We all rushed out, I took our hatchet and told Mother that we were going to go bring back some meat frozen in a field, so we could eat it. Mother wasn't able to reply, that's how in a hurry I was, so that the delicious sheep wouldn't all be gone somehow by the time we got there. There weren't that many of us children, about three, and another three little ones, younger than us, followed in hopes that something good might drop into their laps, meaning that we'd take pity on them. We were hungry. Our eyes shone at the thought that we'd finally eat something decent, meaning meat, and not the meat of some sparrow or ground squirrel, but sheep. In Bucovina, we didn't eat sheep meat, but we heard that people here did. In Bucovina, we ate chicken and rooster, geese, pork, turkey. In any case, all things we didn't eat here, so sheep was a real windfall! The child guiding us didn't have either a knife or an axe, but he knew where the treasure was. He'd have taken it all home, but the frozen sheep was very heavy and stuck in a mountain of ice, so it weighed three times as much and couldn't be moved. He thought that if he left it out there for too long, someone might come and take it, maybe a man with a cart. So it was better to tell some children who would share than for someone to steal it from under his nose and not to get a single piece. We had at our disposal two knives and my hatchet. At first, we hacked through the ice with the hatchet, we had a lot to clear before we could remove the sheep. Then we cut it up, it was hard work. I cut off the first piece, but it wouldn't have been right for one person to eat or leave with their portion while the others kept working. I said that everyone should get a piece first, and only taste it after. We decided to chop up and hack away as much as we could, to split it evenly and then to haul back as much as we could take. Frozen meat could be sucked on raw as well, in little pieces, without having to boil it, you kept it in your mouth a bit, then you chewed it, we were drooling at the thought. I was already dreaming about the choice pieces Mother would cook as well. I was proud that I'd be bringing her food, that I wasn't simply waiting for someone else to put food on my plate. But first we had to cut it up, in any case it was ours, no one would take it. The little ones circled around us, they were keeping watch, supposedly. We weren't strong enough, the hatchet barely went in, the knife slipped along the meat that was frozen solid. We were weak from hunger and the cold. Ever so slowly, I dislodged a nice hip, some pieces from the chest, I was lucky that a part was already flayed, someone, clearly an animal, had tried to eat it before us and gave up who knows why or maybe it had eaten it, but had left some for us as well. We gnawed away at it with our knives, we'd dislodge another piece, our hands had frozen, that dead sheep wasn't giving up, but neither were we. And right when we had cut off all we could cut, when we had reached the long awaited moment in which we were preparing that tiny bit that we could suck on all the way home, when one of us was looking to see if we really had taken all that we could from the sheep, when okay, okay . . . I heard the scream. It was something that made our blood run cold, even frozen as we were, it was a terrifying, unearthly scream, but I recognized Eugen's voice. It was he who had let out that scream. We went off to go save him, some children held onto their portion of mutton and ran more slowly through the snow, but I dropped everything and raced breathlessly.

Eugen came to our village about once a week, he'd find a reason to come, his grandmother would send him, he also worked a lot and we didn't see each other as often as we would have liked. He had come to our house that day to visit us and Mother told him what she knew, that I was out in the fields to bring back, together with other children, a frozen sheep that had died. Eugen headed out toward us, to help us, but on the way he met with Bubusara Abdusaidova, our beloved teacher, and he told her as well where we were. Bubusara grew pale, then she yelled, she explained that he had to run and stop us, that the sheep wasn't out there in the field just because it was nice, but that it had died from some terrible sickness and we'd die as well if we ate its meat. That other people had died because of dead animals. Eugen ran as fast as he could, he saw us, we were far away, he yelled to us but we didn't hear him, he screamed for us not to eat it, but we still didn't hear a thing. Then he imagined me dying if he didn't stop me and he screamed at the top of his lungs: "Ana!!!" Even Mother heard, and the teacher, and that entire aul village. More people gathered and they knew as well that you shouldn't eat the meat of a sheep that had died in the fields, that even adults who had eaten it had died, let alone a bunch of skinny children, everyone knew except for us. I ran as if my soul were on fire, but even though I was terribly anxious, I was also sorry about my portion of meat that I had left behind. Eugen was running toward us as well and he kept screaming: "Don't eat the meat!" Only when we got closer to each other did we understand what he was saying. We, the older children, had been hard at work and hadn't had time to touch the meat, but the little ones who were standing around put some in their mouths. "Did you taste it, did you swallow it?" They started crying, thinking that we were going to beat them for stealing our meat, their parents made them throw it up, only one didn't survive, he had eaten a lot and died the next day. And Eugen was hoarse until spring.

When we arrived in the kolkhoz, Kot quickly became the center of attention. The Kazakhs already had dogs, especially those who took animals out to pasture, but they didn't really have cats. People asked me what his name was. "Kot," I answered. But those who knew Russian wrinkled their noses: "A cat this pretty and his name is Kot." It had seemed rather a strange name for a cat to me too, but that's what the girl who had given him to me had said. With us were some Ukrainians from Dobrogea, Haholi, who understood Russian, but they also understood a bit of Romanian. When some of their boys, who were livelier and quicker and got by better there, also asked me what his name was, they said with deference, "Ahh, Kot. You mean to say Kotovsky?" in the sense that Kot was a nickname for that name. They respected Kotovsky. Later I learned that Kotovsky even had a statue in Chişinău, so he was the king of the cats then, except that he was proudly seated on a horse, not on or next to a cat, that statue doesn't even have a little kitty near it, I know because I passed by it several times, and each time I thought of dear Kot. The Russian women liked the name Kotovsky better too. "Such a brave cat and no name!" For them, Kot wasn't a cat name. But Kotovsky sounded fitting and cat-worthy.

The Russian women especially adored my cat: "What has Kotovsky been up to? Where's Kotovsky?" they'd ask me. I still called him Kot, or sometimes used the pet names Koty, Kotsies, but they liked Kotovsky more. Kot didn't allow himself to become a victim, he got his own justice. Since he saw that we wouldn't share our food with him, he started coming by home less often, sometimes he didn't even sleep with us. He'd go to the houses where there was less hunger, where the children, to lure him in, would hold out bread, he'd allow himself to be caught, petted, scratched, he'd endure it for the bread, then he'd return home. He no longer brought us sparrows or mice, that was just at the beginning, when he was scared that we'd abandon him on the steppe, though we never wanted to abandon him. We once took him out to a field so he could hide and so that no one would eat him. But he came back. The steppe might be full of mice and yummy bird eggs, but cats are domestic animals and they need people. They'd still rather be around a house. The poor cat, scrawny and famished as he was, so skinny you could count his ribs, like us, he still went out and looked for food for us too. It was a real lifesaver for us then. But we wouldn't give him bread, because our people were dying of hunger and Mother said it was a sin to give the bread to an animal when we don't know if we'll make it to tomorrow, and cats catch mice, you give them bread if you have extra, not when times are hard, in hard times it's a great sin. We'd sometimes give him some of our stew, but he didn't like it. He got by however he could, but he was attached to us. He knew that he was my cat, though he played with other children too.

I remember how he got in front of me and pretended to be dead right before a storm. I got such a scare then! It was at the beginning of March, with the first sunny, warm days, the snow had begun melting, which made us happy and revitalized us. Look, we made it through such a hard winter and we didn't die! Now we'll go out in the fields, maybe we'll find something to ease our hunger. The grass had sprouted, we'd grab a handful and bring it home. We hoped to find other things as well, even the time seemed to pass by more quickly.

Evening was a bit of a ways off, it was about three in the afternoon when I got home from Mother's farm and found Kot waiting at the door of the hut. "You came back, you little beggar? You finally remembered us? Or did someone chase you away? You race hound you!" Where we're from, "race hound" is what we'd call men who'd wander through the village and come home late at night. Kot stood there with his tail up and didn't want me to hold him. He was mad. Maybe they had been mean to him where he had been, maybe they had yelled at him there too. I left him alone. I took my little bag and started for the fields, because at night hunger would gnaw at us the worst and I couldn't wait until then, thinking about food for hours on end. I'd search for something, take my mind off it. I'd pick a couple green blades of some grass, the way I had last time, and our meal had turned out so well with those grass shoots. You'd have thought it was wild garlic, it smelled like meat! We, us children, liked searching everywhere. As I was about to go out, Mother came home and began puttering about. She'd find herself something to do as well, to not think only about what we'd put in our mouths.

I thought it was hot outside, but I wore my usual clothes, I had put everything I had on. Kot was meowing from hunger or something else. I went outside, but he kept meowing, as if he wanted me to take him with me. I put him inside and left, though Mother would let him out when he meowed, because maybe he needed to relieve himself too, he couldn't go in the house. I looked back, there was no one there. I hurried to catch up with the children I could see already searching the fields. The sun was high, I had enough time, all was well besides a rather cutting wind that had started up. I was a fair ways from home when what should I see before my eyes? A creature completely splayed out right in the middle of the field! I was frightened but then I went up to it because maybe it was something to eat. When I got closer, laid out dead in front of me was none other than our beloved Kot! What a scare I had! How did he get here, what happened to the poor cat! I picked him up, I shook him a little so that he'd come to, maybe he wasn't completely dead. I hugged him and I saw that he seemed to have moved his tail a bit, to open an eye for a second. He was alive! But something happened to him. What could I do, how could I save him? I'd run home with him, to Mother. So that was it, why he was meowing, there had been something wrong with him when he came home, maybe he swallowed some poison, maybe someone hit him, though he didn't have a scratch on his body, neither a broken paw, nor a torn ear. I walked back holding him.

I hadn't gone very far when I heard a long howl, a roar so fierce that my hair stood on end, even with the scarf around my head. Before the count of three, it grew dark and the entire sky was covered by heavy clouds. I had never seen a storm, I didn't even know something like that existed. I had never been caught in one on the steppe before, and from my hut, I wouldn't have realized what it was. Something scary in any case, and I started running toward home. Being weakened by hunger, it was hard for me to run with Kot in my arms, but I wouldn't have let go, let him die there, for anything in the world. I hurried as fast as I could. At one point, Kot jumped out of my arms and ran ahead of me. It had started to snow and I was having trouble seeing, and after a few seconds, I couldn't see anything anymore. Because of the blizzard, I couldn't make headway and I was afraid the wind might blow me off my feet. I walked as far as I could but the wind stung my face, I knew I was close to the village, not far from our house, I yelled for help, because I didn't know which way to go, but even I couldn't hear my voice, then I stopped because I couldn't take another step. I couldn't move at all. My tears froze on my face.

I wasn't thinking about anything then, not that I might die

there, at the edge of the village, not that I could pray then in that trying moment. We aren't prepared for the difficult experiences of our lives and it's so easy to die. You go out to the field for shoots and grass, a blizzard starts up and there you stay, you're the shoots and grass of the following year, I'm only thinking of this now, because back then I wasn't thinking of anything. Then I was slowly turning into a snowball, a snowwoman . . . When Kot and Mother found me, I was still alive and warm, they brought me home, they unthawed me, I didn't even catch a cold, and Kot was so happy, nothing hurt him, nor was he hungry, he snored quietly and lovingly in my arms. The village was buried under the snow for two weeks. We had brought many things from back home, a knife, a hatchet, spoons, but we hadn't brought a snow shovel and had no way of clearing the snow-drifts. The snowstorm lasted all night, then it just snowed, and in the morning, we couldn't move the door. Me, Mother, and Kot all pushed, but it was no good.

I remember how Mother picked the cat up and kissed him, and then crossed herself. Our dear pet! She couldn't have saved her child in a blizzard like that, but Kot did, he pretended to be dead, and brought me home in time! For two days we thought we'd die of hunger, not even Kot could leave, he tried to tunnel through the snow but he came back. As if all that weren't enough, a huge gust of wind blew off part of the hut's thatched roof. Now it was really snowing, right on our heads. Aglaie's father made it to us, using a long stick with a plank tied to it, a kind of makeshift shovel, and he got us out of there. The three of us moved to their place and we were saved from freezing and starving. Not that we had anything to eat, but we made a fire and received a little some-thing from the kolkhoz, some lifesaving breadcrusts. We were so happy. Many children never made it back from the fields that day . . . Not even after the snow melted and spring finally came, the children never turned up. Sometimes you'd come across some rags and bones out on the steppe.

Many died that winter, they were hard times. How many dead bodies stacked up had I seen and counted? What a long death we were subjected to! During the war, a terrible famine raged and the cases of theft grew accordingly. Because of this, the cows belonging to the Kazakh were chained by their horns, and weights were locked to their feet. The Kazakhs also sometimes had gardens next to their homes, they kept animals and birds. They'd steal something now and then from the kolkhoz, so hunger didn't cut them down the way it did us, who didn't have anything and were considered the sworn enemies of the people on top of that. All we had harvested was taken by the state, and we only received a kilogram of wheat per month. With these reserves we went into the winter of our calamities.

Actually, the most Romanians from Northern Bucovina died the following winter, in 1942. They, the poor things, weren't prepared to live in the harsh conditions of that climate. They had neither winter clothes, nor shoes, nor enough food, and that's why they dropped like flies. How could a helpless old man or a fragile child live off only 150 grams of bread a day? Because of his terrible hunger, a boy who worked in the kolkhoz kitchen reached out for a piece of meat. The act was considered theft and during the trial he was sentenced to seven years in jail. People died one after another. Seven or eight were taken out to the mass grave daily! But the grave wasn't a real grave either. It was dug in the snow, because the ground was frozen, and the dead bodies, all together, were dumped into it without a coffin and without a Christian ceremony. On rare occasions the relatives of the deceased managed to cover the body with a rug or plant a makeshift grave marker. That was more toward spring.

The smaller children went around begging and they'd find old people who were frozen, almost dead. Mayors, teachers, village leaders would also beg for a crust of bread. Whoever didn't work hardly received anything and they were ashamed to be a burden on their children and to take their grandchildren's food. If some child survived, but their parents died, they could disappear at any moment and no one would know what was happening to them. There were orphanages somewhere, which terrified us more than anything in the world, and we'd pray for our parents, we'd ask God to keep them alive, so we could grow up by their side and not be taken there.

Come to our aid, Lord, because we are surrounded by the thorns of all kinds of troubles. Remember, Lord, that though we are sinful, we are not Your enemies, but weaklings. Defend us from all Your foes, Savior!

Help me, Lord, to keep going! Help me return home. Help me meet with Eugen. To You, Lord, I call with great sorrow, oh holy God, come and help me! May the voice of my prayer reach your ears, may I not suffer this punishment beyond measure!

Mom, stop sighing over there and coughing so much when Cuţa is telling her stories! She understands everything, do you know how smart she is? She said that this machine listens and sighs if her story is sad, that technology has really come a long way in our days. "A person passes right by you without caring about your life, but the machine, look, it cries and moans."

"Yes," I agreed, "in our days, the machine can even sing if people around are happy," and I played a folk song on YouTube for Cuţa.

She liked it, then she asked: "Does it want to sing any more?" I answered, "It does, it can sing as long as we want to listen."

"Goodness gracious," Cuța said amazed.

At first, Cuța crossed herself three times, then she got closer to the computer. "Great is Your mercy, Lord, if You allow people to discover such things. I hope they are from You, and not from the Devil. Nothing can live without the breath of life, every living thing is necessarily brought to life by something. Repent, entrust yourself to the Lord. The fight against the passions—"

"Cuța, tell me, is my machine good or is it bad? Is it from God or from the Devil?"

"What is just a bit, a smidge, is from God, what is too much is from the Devil. God gave us everything, He also gave us the evil one, to test our faith. But we sometimes let the evil one get too close. And you can't enter the kingdom of heaven just because you feel like it. God has allowed us to choose between good and evil, otherwise we'd be living in hell, and it's on earth that we choose. When we have to make a choice and find the right path, then heaven is here, on earth. Being close to God is being close to heaven. How light this world becomes, when we put it on the Lord's scale!"

I really liked reading and learning, but I was scared of trying to get into the institute. That was later, when I arrived in Moldova, because at first they wouldn't even consider us. My file wasn't clean and I didn't know the language well. Neither Russian nor "Moldovan." I could read and understand Russian, but I was nervous about speaking and writing it for exams. And the Romanian language didn't exist, though at school in Bucovina I had written it using the Latin alphabet, not the Russian one, as they used here and then called the language Moldovan. If you had tried to say Romanian was being forbidden, what's Romanian?

I went to school there too, on the steppe. One year they gathered all the children, older and younger, and they put together a special class, we were from all different nations from half of the globe, but we didn't know Russian. We had learned a little something, we understood a word or two, but that school didn't last long because they sent us back to go work in brigades. In the end, we finally learned some Russian, but we also knew the Kazakh language, which others didn't know as well as us. We didn't get much of an education because we had to work and there was lots to do, but students each received two hundred grams of bread daily. It wasn't a small thing, if we added it to what we got from elsewhere, from the farm or out in the fields. In our kishtak there was no school, so we went to a neighboring yurt. Lots of Uyghurs lived there, who were neither Kyrgyz, as we thought at first, nor Kazakh, but a people that had been scattered by many troubles. We had lots of Uyghur classmates and we got along really well with them: Kamran, Abdullah, Alimjan, Kurban, those were the names of my classmates. Only boys. Their girls didn't go to school. They were a kind of Uyghurs called Ili Uyghurs.

We didn't know Russian well and those who did thought we were stupid, they laughed at us. Only Bubusara Abdu Saidova, our Russian teacher, didn't laugh, she looked at us with compassion and kindness. Her eyes were black, she was tiny and had a very beautiful *kimeshek*, that was the name of the headscarf that Muslim women used to cover themselves. We addressed her as "Bubusara-*hanym*," which means "Mrs. Bubusara." Everyone there was surprised that Jenea-Eugen could be a man's name because it sounded like the word for sister-in-law! We only called him Eugen, because if we said *Jeni*, they gave us dirty looks. And we'd address the school's principal as "Karimberdi-*myzra*," *myzra* was a term of respect for men older than us. *Agha* was also for

men, and it means older brother or uncle. Grandfather was *ata*.
In general, you'd use *ata* for older men. You added *bala* after a
boy's name for a pet name. "Eugen-*bala*," I'd whisper into Jeni's
ear, but he wasn't crazy about it. We learned more words in those
languages, because children naturally talk. When you got good
news, you had to give a *suyunshi*, a present, so it would go well for
you, a kind of adălmaş of ours.

Once a week, on Saturdays usually, after we had our last lesson
with Bubusara-hanym, she'd take a few of us with her, she'd bring
us to a little house where she had one big room, maybe there were
more but we always sat on that same warm bench. From a small
oven she'd take out a pot filled with *pirozhki*, a kind of savory
pastry that was smaller than our plăcinte, she'd check to see if they
were warm, yes, they were warm, I didn't know if she had made
them in the morning or if maybe the woman she shared the house
with had made them. Just for us she'd also make *kompot* to drink
from dried fruit and she'd treat us. The pirozhki had potatoes in
them, we'd eat slowly, we savored them, meanwhile she'd read us
all kinds of stories in Russian. We'd eat and listen. I've never had
better pirozhki anywhere in my life! It was as if she put honey in
them. And her gentle voice would blend together with the taste
of the delicious food, so we associated our teacher with the good
things she made. I really liked the Russian language back then.

I loved our teacher, I loved her stories as well, and I never
again had pirozhki like hers, I've never eaten anything like them.
May God give health to that being who took food from her own
mouth to give it to some hungry children. She told us that we
couldn't flunk a grade or they would take us to a special school
for the mentally handicapped, but that she knew we were smart
and that we'd learn the language. Not even all the Kazakhs knew
how to speak it. If we could handle math, if we had gotten this far,
we'd keep going. I don't know what ever happened to her. She left

after the fight with the brigadier. But I recall her stories even now, I still remember them, she'd repeat them to us until we had them memorized. After we had eaten, we'd say everything we knew in Russian. She'd laugh, she was glad we were so smart.

She'd read us all kinds of wonderful books, I cried at one and she gave it to me. I brought it with me, I also read it to my children. Maybe I still have it, if some grandchild hasn't taken it. Bubusara told us how she had been engaged since she was little, but really little, since she was two, to a boy from her aul, just as little, that's how things were done there. *Bel kuda* is the name of the tradition when two couples decide that their children will marry each other when they grow up. *Soiko saluu*—the earrings brought by the two-year-old boy's parents for the girl as a sign that they have a marriage agreement. But our Bubusara, when she grew up, refused them and wouldn't do what her parents wanted her to. She left the village, went to the institute, studied, she married someone of her own choice, but her husband was sent to war.

I really liked it at school, especially since I shared a desk with Eugen, I could never sit next to him long enough, time seemed to pass by too quickly. I'd bring him something good from home and he'd bring me something good as well and we'd exchange. It was hard for him, because dear Grannie Anghelina was bedridden. When he didn't come to school one day, I raced over to their house and I found them both lying in bed sick. I ran home, Mother was at the farm. I told her I wanted some milk for Eugen, because he was dying. Mother brought me a bit and I took it to him. Then I kissed his forehead and cheeks and he revived, but I didn't kiss Grannie Anghelina and she stayed sick, and then she passed away. Eugen had become friends with the Uyghurs from that village and I got to know them better too, though they were completely different from us. I once went over to their house, it was a round yurt of theirs, it was beautiful and filled with colorful carpets, like a storybook. From then on, I liked my Uyghur classmates who told stories during history class.

A great number of people had been deported from Eugen's village, more than half the village. His village was in the former county of Dorohoi, Târnăuți, I think it was, and many families there were named Țară. But the Russians, when they heard that name, thought of their deceased Tsar and who knows what others tsars from Russia's past and they were surprised that now they were getting tsars from Bucovina. Meaning they thought to themselves "Didn't we exterminate all the tsars?" They'd write his name as Țarev on the lists, in vain Eugen would correct them: "My name is Țară, not Țarev." They always heard Țarev. They said that no school would admit us with names like ours. Well, the trade school admitted me, because all the "hooligans" needed to be put to work, so we wouldn't be fed for nothing.

At first, they were all surprised at our names: "With names like that, you got off with an easy deportation, they allowed you to stay here among good people, they didn't send you to the bears, to the northern tundra." They couldn't call me by my name, Bojescu, they said Bozhinka, in Russian *Bozhe* means God. *Bozhe moi!* I heard the Russian women say. "How could your name be Bozhe!" There was another boy, Bucovinian like us, very handsome, with curly hair and huge eyes, his name was Bogdescu. *Bog* is another word for God in Russian. "Ah, all of you come from Bogovina, you're named after tsars and gods."

"Bucovina," we'd correct them.

"Bogovina," they'd insist. "Does your Bogovina still exist on the map?" We didn't know. *Bogo-vina*: "vina" in Romanian means fault, "God's fault." Divine guilt, guilt and innocence, we all share the same fate. Vina means the same thing in Russian as it does in Romanian, we were surprised, we didn't have to translate it. And

God is the same for everyone, even if everyone uses a different word.

Our Russian teacher was beautiful, understanding, and kind, but our history teacher was a different story. She would scold us, we could tell by her tone and facial expressions, because we didn't really know what she was saying, she'd smack a ruler over our hands and insult us, calling us worms, lice. She'd call the boys *buzaqy*— hooligan, and the girls *soyqan,* meaning sinful, slutty women. And at both she'd yell *Şhaytandar*! meaning devils. And the Kazakhs would translate her words and say that they weren't but that we were. It was from our Kazakh classmates that Aglaie-Trandafira heard "*Zhalmauyz Kempir*" which she understood to be the name of our history teacher, that's what they called her and we really thought that was her name. And, at the beginning of class one day, Aglaie wanted to ask her something and she said, in a polite voice: "Zhalmauyz Kempir" and the teacher jumped as if burned! Then she slapped Aglaie-Trandafira across the face, who fell on top of Aglaie-Aculina, her sister and classmate. The Kazakh boys who giggled weren't spared either: she grabbed one by the hair and threw him against a bench so hard his head sounded like a gourd, the other rotten Kazakh boy managed to get out of the way and got off easy with just a slap upside the head. That's how we found out that "Zhalmauyz Kempir" in their stories is a baba with claws and a brass nose, a kind of Baba Hârca or Baba Cloanţa of ours, and you can't call schoolteachers that or they'll get mad.

One day, three school inspectors came in and stood at the front of the class. History teacher Baba Cloanţa started to ask us, in a fake and smarmy voice:

"Children, who is the beloved author of the great October Revolution?"

"Lenin," we answered in unison.

"Bravo! Who is the secretary general of the Soviet Union?"

"Stalin," we said, to the delight of the three inspectors.

"Who is the father of all peoples, who takes care of us and loves us?"

This time the children hesitated between Lenin and Stalin.

"God," I was hasty in answering and scared the inspectors. The teacher pounced on me:

"Who taught you a thing like that?"

I couldn't get a word out, but the children defended me, saying all together while looking at the inspectors:

"Zhalmauyz Kempir, the history teacher, our comrade teacher, she told us!"

That's how the children, insulted by her so many times, took their revenge. We didn't see her in school again after this incident. I hadn't meant to cause her harm, I didn't want her to suffer because of me, but I believe that God rewards good and punishes evil and He gave her what she deserved. I also believe that neither Lenin nor Stalin love us, only God does. He has us at heart and cares for us.

After they fired the history teacher or moved her to another school, or maybe she decided on her own to leave, our dear Bubusara would come to our history class and she'd tell us: "Read the lesson from the textbook, then say it out loud in your own words." There were no other teachers and we were on our own, sometimes someone or other would look in just to make sure we weren't too noisy. We'd get down to learning the lesson, a child would begin reading, we'd listen on our best behavior, then the teacher would leave to go to her own classroom, to other students. We'd change the subject and tell fairytales. Everyone had to tell a story when it was their turn, whoever didn't know one would bring in a storybook and read from it. We listened with delight, quietly. Gradually, after a few lessons, we chose a couple children who were better storytellers, who included more details, spoke more dramatically, while we, the others, would listen. We kept our history books in front of us, and when we'd hear footsteps down the hall, we'd change the subject and read out of the textbook, pretending to concentrate. We never got another teacher.

—Cuţa Ana, and what stories did you tell all the deported people? *The Purse with Two Coins? The Goat and Her Three Kids?*

—And the story of the brave Cinderer, about a twelve-headed monster who stole the sun one day and threw the earth into pitch darkness. And a man's youngest son said: "I will go free the sun from the dragon!" Because he liked to play in the ashes, they called him Cinderer. Haha, he really gave those dragons a beating . . .

I didn't know Russian well enough to tell stories nicely, I told stories in Romanian and Dasha and Masha, two Moldovan sisters, translated for me. The sisters had been born there, their grandparents and parents had arrived in those places during the time of the Tsar, they had received a lot of land, they worked hard and gotten rich, except then the Bolsheviks came to power, they took all their land, their sheep, and their cattle, but they wouldn't let them go home, to the place they were from. The Moldovan girls didn't know any stories, but they loved listening to the ones we told. Though they spoke Russian well, they also understood Kazak, they talked to their parents in Romanian so they knew it exactly as well as we did.

Kamran and Alimjan, the two Uyghur cousins, were the best storytellers in our class. Kurban called them *dastanchi* which means storyteller. What a hush would come over us when they started to tell a story! In their stories, instead of wolves and foxes, like in ours, all kinds of tigers would show up, not one of their stories was without a tiger. They said that a long time ago there used to be tons of tigers around there, maybe even now there was still one left. Where they were from, some people believed that if a tiger lived to be a hundred, then it changed color and became a white tiger, and if it lived to be a thousand, it became black. Those animals became vârcolaci who could turn into people. We listened to the story of the beautiful tigress, where a woman was, in fact, an animal, with our mouths open. Then the tiger and the monk, the tiger and the magic flute. Good tigers and bad tigers, stories where even a god turns into a tiger and walks among people . . . Also stories about the brave Chin Tömür . . .

But first, let me tell you the story of "Buddha and the Tigress with Five Cubs": *One day a prince was walking through the jungle and he saw a tigress with five small cubs who was dying. The tigress was so weak that even though she saw the man, she couldn't move a muscle. The prince looked at the hungry cubs and understood that if their mother were to die, they would die too. The thought gave rise to a feeling of immense pity in his heart and he decided to save their lives and feed them with his own body. The prince went over to the tigress, so she could attack him and tear him to pieces, but the animal didn't even have the strength to do that. Then he cut his hand with a dagger and fed the animal with his blood. Once the tigress tasted blood, she got her strength back, she pounced on the man and ate him. The prince then transformed into the Buddha of the steppe peoples, and the five tiger cubs transformed into people and they were his first disciples, the* arhats. They're similar to our saints and apostles.

"The Tiger and the Magic Flute": *A poor family lived at the edge of the world. The husband never slept, he'd work in the fields in the summer, and in the winter he'd go out and hunt tigers. One time he went out and didn't come back. The wife was sewing something in the winter by the light of the moon and waiting for him, but he never came home. By her side, her three sons kept asking: "Mother, where's Father?"*

"He's out hunting tigers."

"Why hasn't he come home yet?"

"The tigers have probably torn him to pieces. You'll grow up and avenge him." The sons swore to avenge their father. They grew up and learned how to handle a bow and arrow. First they took aim at rabbits and deer, then wolves and foxes. Then they began to hunt tigers as well. They had learned to aim and hunt so well that they were without equal in their realm. The time came for them to leave home, they came before their mother and said to her: "We're going to go avenge Father."

Their mother said to them: "Fine, but first you must undergo a test" and she brought out a jug filled with water from the house, she placed it on her head and said: "Each one of you must shoot an arrow in such a way that the jug will remain intact and the water not spill."

The oldest went first. He bent his bow and the arrow pierced straight through the jug. Then the middle son shot an arrow that went in through the first hole and plugged up the second hole. And the youngest stopped up the first hole with his arrow and no water was spilled. The mother, very pleased, said: "Now I am at peace. You may leave right away." The brothers prepared themselves for the long journey and off they went. They traveled far until they reached the big forest filled with tigers, where they parted ways. The forest was thick, the trees reached up to the skies, filled with never before seen birds and animals! As the youngest brother was walking through the forest, a beautiful girl appeared before him, laughing, running, and wanting to play with him. The brother understood that something wasn't right, that he was dealing with the spirit of an enchanter, he picked up his bow and shot her right in the heart. The girl fell to the ground, she spun around a few times and disappeared, and in her place a big, furry tiger lay dead. Suddenly, from every direction, tigers began to gather, roaring and growling threateningly, surrounding him. He was a good marksman, but what could he do when faced with an entire ambush of tigers!

He quickly scrambled up a tree, he climbed up toward the top and what did he see? The leader of the tigers held a shining flute in its teeth. It approached the dead animal and played the flute. The tiger came back to life and jumped to its feet. The young man was amazed: what kind of flute was this? The tigers began to jump up next to the tree to chase him away. He climbed even higher. Then the biggest tiger leaned up against the tree, another climbed on top of it, the next jumped up onto the back of the second one, the fourth on top of the third, and so on, until they nearly reached the boy. Then he carefully took aim and let his arrow fly with such force that it passed through all the tigers and killed them all at once. They fell to the ground, dead. Then the boy climbed down, he took the flute from the teeth of one of them, and when he looked at it closely, he saw it was made of pure gold. He put it in his pocket and set out in search of his brothers. He traveled over mountains and valleys, and there was his middle brother, dead under a tree. The youngest was sad until he remembered about the flute, he took it out and played it, and the middle brother came back to life. He jumped to his feet and recounted how a beautiful girl dressed in white brought him there and killed him. They set off in search of their oldest brother. He, too, was dead under a tree. They played for him as well, he came back to life and recounted how the girl in white had killed him. The brothers were overjoyed that the youngest had killed the tigers, they took the animals' hides and went home. On the road, they thought about what they should do with the magic flute. They decided to take it to the king to hide it, because if everyone came back to life, there wouldn't have been enough room on earth. The king hid it extremely well and no one has said a word about that magic flute since.

In our stories, no hero would take such a magnificent flute to a king just like that, for nothing.

Long ago, old people, when they reached sixty years of age, had to be killed, because they were no longer useful. Those were the king's orders. A son loved his father so much that he couldn't kill him, but hid him in a cellar instead and would steal away to bring him food there. One day, that king's castle was attacked by giant beasts, as big as cows, with long snouts and long, thin tails. Everyone was terrified and they didn't know what to do. Then the old man in the cellar said to his son: "Find a cat that weighs eighty kilos." The boy brought one that weighed seventy. "Feed it until it weighs eighty kilos," the old man said. He fed the cat and then set it loose in the city. When those animals saw the cat, they shrunk in fear until they became mice, who to this day run from cats. And old people were no longer killed.

A king had a sort of counselor, an important governor, who was very wise. The king decided, to show how much he valued him, to hold a celebration in his honor. All the nobles came, great and small, everyone who was anyone in the court. They feasted, they caroused. In a jolly mood, the king said to the wise man:

"Why don't you treat me like an equal? You're my best friend, after all. Let's joke with each other."

"Jokes with kings end badly, and I value my life."

"You're a pig, my dear," the king then joked.

"And Your Lordship and Highness is a Bodhisattva!" (meaning a divine follower, who understands the Buddha's teachings better than anyone).

"What are you saying, my wise friend, how can I be a Bodhisattva, I'm a mere mortal, the same as you. Have no fear, you can joke around with your king!"

"A pig, Your Highness, sees before him only a pig, but the eyes of a Bodhisattva can see the Buddha himself."

———⟐———

Pelagheia took classes with us, but she never said anything to anyone, she never spoke at all in school and the foreign children nicknamed her "thick," meaning stupid. She was cursed by fate, not stupid! Once, when we were returning home from school, she came close to me and asked me to walk with her. I was surprised, I usually walked home with the little Aglaies, the two I was friends with. I said: "Alright," and walked with her. We didn't speak the whole way, but when we came up to the barn in which her family lived, little Pelagheia said to me: "Help me with something and I'll give you half my bread." Again I said: "Alright" and followed her into that big barn. From the outside, it was run down and ugly, but inside it looked like a human dwelling, with beds and rugs. Several families lived there and they had once been numerous. Now, in the dark, some withered, bundled up old people who looked dead were lying on those plank beds.

Little Pelagheia's mother was also lying down, with her eyes closed, and sprawled out on top of her was a child, two or three years old, with a red face, dressed in a thin little shirt, his small hands buried in the breast he was rhythmically sucking on, which had stretched out and dried up from so much sucking. "Help me bury my mother, because everyone here is old and sick, dead or dying, there's no one else. Their younger children or grandchildren have died, and the grownups are away at work, in the mine or on the railway, and they come home only Saturday night, I can't wait that long." While she was talking, the child continued nursing and paid us no attention, he seemed not to understand. The dead are very heavy, and we were weak and fragile. Little

Pelagheia tore the child away and I expected him to cry, but he didn't have any tears. He kept on moving his lips, as if he were still sucking on something. His sister put a small piece of the bread she had received at school in his hand. The child squeezed the bread, as if expecting milk to come out of it, but he didn't put it in his mouth. He looked up at us and he didn't seem all there to me. "I'll bury him by myself, but Mother is heavy." We tried to pick her up but could barely move her. Then we rolled her onto a rug and pulled on the same end of it together, we finally managed to get her outside, but where could we take her? We kept pulling the rug a bit and stopping, to catch our breath. From a corner of the barn, Pelagheia brought over two sharpened sticks we could use to scratch into the ground. "People threw their dead into that abandoned well. I also threw in two younger brothers, with my mother, because the ground was frozen and we couldn't have a Christian burial . . . But now the well is full of bodies, it's overflowing," she said. I felt really bad that there wasn't any more room in the well. In the spring, when the snow melted and the ground thawed, the dogs would tug on our dead because they weren't buried deeply, it would've been better for them in the well . . .

Our sticks were useless against the frozen ground. We kept going and not far we found a place with some straw and branches. We poked around there a bit trying to create a hollow and I, for one, thought I'd faint from exhaustion. We prepared a place as best we could and put the body there, covering her with the rug. On top of the rug we put straw, branches, and big rocks. It was pretty, but maybe no one would steal it, this woman, too, deserved at least a rug to cover her face. We couldn't hold a candle over her mother, or keep a wake for her, as we do in Bucovina, or wail for her, as is the custom. "Let's cover her well," little Pelagheia said, thinking the same thing as me. In the barn, they didn't have a small stove, they'd make a fire in the middle from straw, branches, or whatever they found. They didn't have matches either, and when the fire would go out, because straw burns quickly, they'd go to a nearby hut to bring fire back. She gave me her bread but I didn't want it. Little Pelagheia was the same age as me.

Her mother gave birth to the fourth child when they arrived there, a woman alone with small children she had to feed and take care of. She went to a house-raising and broke her leg when she fell from a ladder. House-raising is a fall activity in our steppe, dedicated to the completion of a house after the harvest is gathered. The men come with their wives to offer *asar*—to help at the house-raising, they drink *boza* and eat. Then the *jigits*, the brave men, climb up a narrow ladder with a sack of wet dirt, they leave it on the roof and are rewarded with gifts, for a sack of dirt put on the roof you could receive a sack of grain in return. That's how they raised their houses, with sticky, wet dirt, and putting it on the roof was the hardest and riskiest part. But during the war, where could you find jigits? So they coveted our Bucovinians, meaning the Bucovinian women, because there weren't really any men in our kishtak. But among them were weak, inexperienced women and some fell. It was dangerous to climb up that ladder even without hauling sacks. That's how little Pelagheia's mother fell. She received some wheat, people helped her out with what they could, but she and her children got sick, everyone in that barn got sick, and without medicine, without a stove, with just watery balanda to eat from time to time, it was hard to survive. After the little child died as well, Pelagheia left our kishtak and went out into the wide world. I don't know what happened to her.

Lord! You raised up all forms and put Your seal, the seal of Your wisdom, upon them, You made all these vessels from clay and filled them all with the song and joy of the Holy Trinity, but Your shadow left a drop of sadness in each vessel, with which those who are saddened press their sadness onto You.

~~~

After school, we'd go to the farm to help our parents, many mothers worked there. We weren't paid anything, but there was a chance we might get to taste a little milk. Of course, we weren't allowed to touch such a delicacy and we appeared to be completely indifferent to the much desired milk. No, we hadn't come here to feast on the riches of the kolkhoz, we weren't attempting to steal the food of soldiers on the front lines, but only to help our mothers and that's all! But our mothers who were milkmaids discovered a method which we brought to perfection. Drinking milk through a straw. It's not what you're imagining. For such a feat, it took us a week to prepare the straw and to practice. The straw wasn't a regular one, but had to be the longest one, half a meter long if possible. Straws that long don't grow anywhere, so we had to connect shorter straws together. You'd stick one as thin as possible into another that was a bit thicker, then you'd stick it into one even thicker than the first two, you needed about three straws. You'd put this long straw down your sleeve and you had to keep your arm straight so that it wouldn't break, but so it wouldn't show either, or you could attach it to your stomach somehow to be on the safe side. When you found yourself next to a source of milk, a jug or a bucket, you'd busy yourself around there without getting too close to the milk, so you wouldn't make people suspicious, the straw wasn't visible from a distance. You had to learn how to approach inconspicuously, to put the straw in quickly and drink. Of course the mothers and the other children walked to and fro and distracted the guards.

We were so hungry and so inventive that we soon became experts at drinking milk through our straws. Almost all of us managed to stick our straws in pails and get a few gulps of fresh milk and we were so happy! So people wouldn't be surprised that we were doing so much work for nothing, we acted tired, and we really were, we complained that we were hungry. Every once in a while a kolkhoznik would feel sorry for us and bring us a few crumbs of bread from somewhere, only once did we receive milk as well, when the mothers far surpassed the quota. They, the poor things, would have always surpassed it but it was more important to them for us to have some. I once emptied half a bucket, you usually couldn't drink that much because it was really uncomfortable to hold your straw out straight, and it would also get soggy after the milk passed through it. The straw wasn't dangerous in the event an enemy approached, with all the straw lying around there, you'd quickly throw it down, and there, you were in the clear. It sometimes happened that they'd make us clean up, somewhere far from any milk, and no straw, no matter how long, could help us then.

Worse, hungry and weak as we were, we could slip and fall in the manure around there. Because what we were made to clean up was manure, in fact. What a tragedy it was to fall! The middle Aglaie fell, she got up and left. She didn't come to school for two days, because her mother had washed her clothes, and when she came, she stunk up the whole classroom. It was very hard for us with the clothes, actually the rags, we wore. We didn't receive new clothes and the ones from home were completely worn through. Nor did we have detergent as we do now, if it existed, it didn't for us, very few people possessed even the tiniest bit of soap, and the stench of manure didn't come out of dirty clothes easily. Aglaie shared a desk with her younger sister and the other children laughed at them: manure sisters, stinkers, cow-lovers. They sat there, embarrassed and unhappy. Our first lesson was with the

Russian teacher, our beloved Bubusara. When she came into the classroom, the pungent smell made her stomach turn. She put her hand up to her nose but quickly took it away so we wouldn't see, but we saw. She didn't say anything, but the children were making a ruckus, they put their hands over their noses and yelled that they couldn't stand it anymore. I thought it stank too but I felt bad for the sisters, we were friends and I didn't know how to defend them. The girls got up out of their seats at one point and left the classroom, crying quietly. Afterward I told the teacher that we had been on the farm to help our parents and they had made us clean manure. I didn't tell her that Aglaie had fallen because she had leaned over too far, since her straw was too short, unsuccessfully trying to reach the bucket of milk. She had piled some manure into a heap, and focused only on her straw, she lost her balance and fell right on top of the heap. And we didn't have a change of clothes, or even soap. We barely had a crust of bread . . . The thing about the clothing I did tell the teacher, who was listening carefully. "Aglaie won't come to school anymore, because she doesn't have a change of clothes," we thought.

But two days later, what should we see? Headed toward our school was a tsarina in a *sarafan* dress with a blouse embroidered with little flowers and a woolen vest, dressed as if she were going to Cinderella's ball and the pumpkin had just turned into a coach, and the fairy had touched her with her magic wand and transformed her into a princess. Our mouths hung open in amazement, and who should the vision entering our school be? Aglaie herself! We were stunned at how beautiful she was! And how ugly the rags covering us now were.

Scattered throughout our aul, a few of the homes were *izbas* belonging to the Russian women deported here before us, and our Russian teacher, with her heart of gold, asked them if they didn't happen to have any clothing leftover in a trunk to help out a little girl who didn't have anything to wear and couldn't come to school. Someone took a blouse out of an old trunk, someone else the sarafan, the vest, but what fabric, what good clothing, fit for royalty! Clothing from the time of the tsars! What finery, what beauty! Only the crown from her head was missing for us to think she was off to the ball! But when she went to the farm she'd put on her smelly clothes.

And Aglaie was so proud, so happy! She told us how she had gone home crying and had said to her mother that she wasn't going to school anymore, because she stunk as badly as an entire farm of cows! And the next day, she found of satchel of clothes at the door, with a note written in Russian: "Enjoy them! We're waiting to see you back in school." The clothes seemed to be made for her, that's how well they fit. A Polish neighbor, who knew Russian well, had translated the note for them.

"What good deed, holy Paisius, is the best of all good deeds?"

"The one that is done in secret . . ."

The tree is known by its fruit, the person by their deeds . . . There were good people in that place and they helped each other, taken there and brought together by the same scourge.

The Gherman sisters were an example for all the Bucovinian survivors. When things were hard for Mother she'd say: "It must be so hard for Maria Gherman with five girls, I have only one. I'll manage!" That's what others said as well. The oldest Aglaie, the only one whose name actually was Aglaie, was taken to a mine, after about a month she ran away from there, and so she wouldn't be put in prison, she signed up for a course to be a tractor driver, like many of our girls who were a bit older. I really wanted to become a tractor driver too, but I was too little, then after the war, the Kazakhs returned and the girls no longer took classes to become tractor drivers. Aglaie, after studying for three months, received a small "Universal" tractor, in which she went around the entire steppe. Those who drove trac- tors were fed better than us. Because she did a good job, she then received a more powerful HTZ, which she used to plow, harrow, and sow the fields of the kolkhoz. In winter, tractor drivers repaired tractors and related equipment at the SMT. The second one also got very lucky, and her whole family along with her, because she worked as a cook at the kolkhoz cafeteria and there she prepared food for the brigade that worked out in the fields. Everyone praised her for her delicious food and for not stealing. Papa Gherman had taken the president of the kolkhoz golden earrings so that she'd get the position. And she quickly became the top chef, the one who sprinkles salt in the food, as they say, because it's not the person who cooks the food who is the expert, but the one who adds salt! While making the food, she'd sometimes stick her spoon in it, to check the taste, she'd sometimes bring a crumb back home for her starving family and she got the Ghermans through that hard winter. The next two girls went with their mother on the farm and would take out the garbage, later I went to school with them. But the littlest one didn't lie around doing nothing either, waiting for something to fall into her lap, to be handed to her, brought to her on a silver platter . . . She guarded the geese of a Russian woman and one day a wolf stole one of the birds, the girl got scared, she didn't know how to explain what happened and she was crying. The Russian woman didn't beat her or send her away. No one paid us any money for our work back then, everyone was very poor and people would the work their fingers to the bone for a handful of grain or a couple potatoes, sometimes we were happy even with potato peels. It was wartime, there was a famine, they were dark days.

On the train, when the girls were asked their names, they said: the first one, "I'm the oldest Aglaie"; the second one, "I'm the second Aglaie"; the third one, "I'm the middle Aglaie"; the fourth, "I'm Aglaie-Trandafira"; and the last one, "I'm the youngest Aglaie."

In fact, their names were: Aglaie, Margareta, Aculina, Trandafira, and Antonina. Whenever we called them by their names, they were tickled pink. When we'd ask them where they were from: "From the village where the Siret meets the Siretel River. I'd tease them: "The Siren meets the Sire," and they'd correct me "Siret and Şiretel, not Siren and Sire." We'd entertain ourselves.

In 1943, a decree was announced which stated that if our men, the Romanians who were deported, declared themselves Moldovan in documents, they'd be sent off to war, and if they didn't, they'd remain in Kazakhstan forever. They tried to convince us, but we wouldn't give in and we stayed to face the ordeal. They called Nicanor Gherman to the police station to register him. "Either you write that you're Ukrainian and we'll let you go and you'll get a passport, or you stay Romanian and remain under arrest and without a form of identification. If you don't want to write down Ukrainian, at least write Moldovan." "I was born Romanian, and Romanian I'll stay, you can do whatever you want with me!" The man escaped the war, but he didn't receive his papers and he was left to continue living and working in the kishtak along with his family.

When our hut fell apart, Papa Gherman took us in. They lived in a small abandoned house made up of two large rooms which they had fixed up. Meanwhile, Nicanor Gherman was building a new house, with the permission of the bosses around there. First, he found, not far from the village, some stony ground. He had never built houses before then, he wasn't a craftsman, but he went ahead, necessity drives people forward, and with the beautiful Bucovinian houses in mind and with the help of the Kazakhs who sometimes gave him materials, though later with the hidden motive that his house might become theirs, Gherman built his first house. When everyone saw that it looked like a dwelling fit for humans, Nicanor was permitted to build a school as well, so that our young children wouldn't have to go to the neighboring village in the snow and rain and with wolves lying in wait behind the bushes.

Gherman asked for materials for the school, which he also used to repair a hut or shack of ours from time to time, because they were really run down. Then they all moved into the new house and let us stay in their old one. They built a dividing wall between the two rooms, they put in a door in place of a window, and now the little house had two entrances, each room had a door and a window. We lived in one room, and in the other, a young Polish couple, whose children had died in their first year of deportation, moved in. We didn't understand the language and we didn't really talk to each other. But on chilly nights, when the weather was ugly, rainy or freezing, when Mother and I would sing, they'd come over, they'd sit on the edge of a bed and listen. When they had something to eat, they'd bring us some. Sometimes they'd bring us herbal tea. Then they'd sing as well and we'd go over to their place, with a bowl of warm balanda or a crust of bread. That's how we'd feel everything was alright, that we were still alive. Then other families started coming as well.

Whenever you'd hear a song coming from inside a cabin, it was a sign for whoever was passing by that they could come inside and join in. At first, it was us Bucovinians gathering with the Poles and Russians, then the Kazakhs started coming around. In the winter, they would gather at a *mereke,* and hold a kind of şezatoare like we had back home, and play music on the *dombra,* while serving their *boza,* sometimes called *buzà,* a slightly alcoholic drink made from fermented corn or millet, a kind of kvass, what we call bragă. We'd also go over to their places. When it was warmer, our Kazakhs would serve us *ayran*—yogurt mixed with water, or *jarma*—a non-alcoholic drink made from crushed grains that seems to have milk in it but doesn't and sometimes resembles a soup. They'd make it when it was hottest outside and it's considered a refreshing drink.

We'd seen Kazakh children plucking away on the dombra before, but we'd never heard how beautiful it actually sounded. But if a *bakhshi* or an *akyn*, meaning a musician, picks it up, then its wonderful music soothes your soul. And the Kyrgyz play the *komuz*, also a kind of *dombra*, which the Russians call the *balalaika*. All of them look like our cobza, that cow that takes a bow, at its tail, nails, at its belly, melodies . . . When we were lucky and the *koyshylar*, the shepherds, came down to their *zhailau*, summer pastures, we'd hear the most beautiful songs: *shyryldan*, the song of the horse herders, and *bekbekey*, song of the shepherdesses . . . I also learned Polish words not only Kazakh ones: their word for brother is *brat*, which is unfortunate. They'd also say, when they were happy about something, *milo mi*, to us it sounded like "me why me," and for thank you, the Poles said "chin gooey." I scratched my head over it for a long time: what could anyone have on their chin here that would make it gooey? When they saw that we didn't understand, they switched to Russian, *spasibo*, which we knew meant thank you. And a "tack" meant "yes."

After Papa Gherman finished building the school, the village leaders kicked him out of his beautiful new house because they needed it for a post office or some other state institution. And they sent them back into an abandoned house. Now it was only them and the last Aglaie, the youngest, since the others were scattered among different work brigades, I wasn't still in the kishtak either then. Mother took in the youngest Aglaie, while her parents built a new house, small, as pretty as a toy. But they never moved into it, instead they sold it for a lot of money to a Kazakh, and with the money they got they bought tickets to Bucovina. For the whole family. They divided what was left of their possessions among the people there, they said goodbye to us, took their five girls, hardworking and as graceful as fairies, and they were off . . . The Ghermans had worked so hard, they had never said no to anything and where they put their shoulder to the wheel, God also put in His favor.

I had been turned into a plant that sways with every gust of wind, no, worse than that, into an object, into arms for work, into a beast of burden, into nothing. Forget what a wonderful house you had in Bucovina, forget your family, your language, your relatives and your friends, your big white bed, sheets with lace and embroidery, your elegant clothing, specific to each season. Summer clothes, fall clothes, winter clothes . . . Forget the village horă where you waited with the other little girls to grow up, so you, too, could beat those tiny steps and twirl your skirt when taken by the hand of a neighbor's boy or a friend of your two older brothers, forget the dowry chest where so many treasures had been stored up for your wedding, expensive and beautiful things . . . I was my mother's pride and joy, the spoiled baby of the family, and all that was most precious from my grandparents and from the markets ended up in my chest for when I'd be older. Mother's daughter, Daddy's girl, little sister, the family's pampered darling. And now? I could've cried for hours on end, from gratitude and great joy, if I had received a piece of soap. Life improved on the steppe, it became better than in those first years, I escaped the danger of starvation. But I couldn't forget what had been worse. What had been better, yes, you had to forget that, so you wouldn't become overwhelmed by all the suffering.

I can't forget bringing home a few loaves of bread when they did away with the ration of a few hundred grams . . . You'd receive more if you worked, less if you were too young and couldn't work, too old, weak, sick, and sluggish, other than that, if you wanted to eat, you went to work, five hundred grams, three hundred, one hundred and fifty . . . then just like that, all at once, as much as you wanted! I bought bread with all the money I had, a few big, freshly baked loaves, steam rising from them, I put them on the table and didn't know what to do. Mother didn't either. We stared for a long time at the bread that only a short time ago we could only dream of. What if it was a prank and tomorrow the bread would disappear and we'd be hungry again? How could we store it better for dark days, where could we hide it? What did that mean, to eat it all, until we were full, without putting some aside, without worrying about tomorrow? Who knew if they would bake more every day? "Yes, we'll put aside some bread for dark days, of course, but first let's eat some of it." I picked one up and pressed it to my chest: my love, my salvation! Mother also kissed a loaf and crossed herself. "Blessed be, Lord, for we have before us a table laden with bread!" I thought about Eugen. Where was he now? Did he have enough to eat? I thought about all those who would never make the return trip to their homeland and who would never experience this great moment of happiness because they died on the train. Their dried out bodies, thrown out into the fields, into the water, on the side of the train tracks. Did they have crosses? Would anyone place them there?

I saw this affectionate gesture again many years later when a granddaughter received the first doll she ever had, I wasn't the one who bought it for her, but I was taking care of that granddaughter who had been promised the doll so she'd be good while she stayed with me because her parents worked in the city. The doll had curly blue hair, dressed in a schoolgirl uniform. The girl took it out of the box and stroked it, with great delight. Exactly the same way I had once stroked our first whole loaf of bread, a big, round one, all to ourselves, our first deportation loaf . . .

Mother had also stroked the loaf as if she couldn't believe it, but more quickly, secretly, as if she were ashamed to do it in front of me and afterward we looked for a place where we could dry it out, and when we'd buy another one, we'd first eat the dried out one. That way our reserves of dried bread never ran out. Evenings, we usually ate dried bread, which we'd dip in tea or milk. For a long time, I'd eat dried bread dipped in sweetened milk in the evening here in Moldova. No one understood why I liked it so much, but I couldn't break the habit and I thought it was delicious! Not even your cakes and cookies taste as good to me as that rusk soaked in milk with sugar.

And then clothing appeared as well. After all kinds of rags and old patched up things, whose colors had faded and whose shape was stretched out from being worn so much, in the winter as well as summer, having a new dress was an event. After I had been happy when Mother dressed me in sacks and I had something to cover my body, how do you imagine I felt when I got a new dress! It was a great joy! Not like today, when children aren't happy even when you buy them a real car! When I put on a dress, I felt like I deserved a different kind of life. I seemed to enter a new world, one I didn't have access to before. We always faced closed doors, our desires were few, simple, for a minimally decent life, but for years on end we couldn't satisfy them.

All the girls could study, but I couldn't, and no one asked me why. But I didn't complain. I tried to see the side of it that was a blessing from God. I wasn't accepted at prestigious schools, but I've been given a long life, I married a good man, who I had children with, we always had bread on our table. If I would've asked myself pointless questions, if I had gotten upset, I never would've made it. There were many times when I'd say: "Great is the Lord's mercy if I made it through today, may the Lord allow me to get through tomorrow as well." If God made the leaves, frogs, bugs, ants, and all kinds of creatures that don't complain and don't get outraged, we should also try to live in peace and joy. God put meaning in everything, everything that happens to us comes from Him.

I remember the day our comrade principal came into our cow-shed and said that whoever signs up to go to school would receive bread and tea every day! More of us signed up, it was nice at school, even though I was older and had to repeat a grade because I didn't know Russian, but many of the children of deportees were like me. It was hard for us because we didn't know the language, classes were only in Russian, I couldn't enroll in fourth grade, where I belonged. They put together a class of children, some older, some younger, who had all studied in their mother tongues, back in the schools where they were from, but none of them in Russian. We learned what we could, but in the spring and fall, and all summer, they'd send us off to work. How schoolchildren slaved away back then! Years later, my son also went off to work, they took him to the sovkhoz, the state farm. During communism, it wasn't only in Siberia that they had to work, but everywhere. But at least here in Moldova they fed the schoolchildren, the boy had food at home too, they'd bring them a soup or salad and a main dish up on the hill, the children could eat grapes or tomatoes if they were out harvesting, no one would beat them up for that, even though they were told they weren't allowed. But we were really hungry then, during the war, and people were mean to us, because soldiers were dying on the front lines, how could they stuff the enemies of the people who dared to complain of hunger?

At around the end of May, they sent us out to pick potatoes in the fields of the extended area, we'd start off in the morning, before sunrise, the entire class with Bubusara-hanym, the field was big, the rows long, dug up by a harrow, and we had to gather potatoes into big piles, about every five meters. We'd put the potatoes into a kind of mesh bag to carry them over to the heap. If the bag was too heavy, two children would lug it together. Some girls had buckets. Complete silence, the work was very hard, but we were used to hard work, even though most of us hadn't really had anything to eat in the morning and we'd arrive on the steppe hungry. We hadn't had a scrap of food and were very weak, we weren't dressed appropriately either. We'd get tired quickly, and the row seemed endless. We weren't allowed to take a single potato, they were for the soldiers. We'd get our portion of bread or maybe a potato at the end, as had been promised. But who could make it to the end of the day with their belly rumbling and their hands frostbitten? We were also always hunched over and would have dizzy spells.

A girl fainted and the teacher saw, she went over to her and picked her up, she tapped her on the cheek, the girl opened her eyes and whispered: "I'm hungry." It was our voice, the voice of all the young workers out in the field. Then our beloved Bubusara told us all to pick a potato, one that wasn't too big so we wouldn't get in trouble with the brigadier, and to go to the edge of the field, by the road. We gathered some straw and some twigs and we lit a fire. Bubusara lit it, she had a matchbox with her, we took turns putting our potatoes on it, each child watched over their potato while the others brought more hay or twigs for the fire. We didn't keep the potato on the fire for very long, I don't know if it was long enough to cook it or merely to heat it up so that it wouldn't be completely raw, but I'd never tasted anything so good in my entire life. Right when the teacher was taking the wonderful potatoes from the fire and handing them to us, oops, the brigadier showed up on his horse, snapping his whip like an ogre and breathing, all the children could've sworn, fire out his nose. He was, brace yourself, furious that we had lit a fire and were eating the kolkhoz's potatoes. How dared we?

Poor Bubusara wanted to explain to him that we were hungry, we were feeling unwell and couldn't work because we hadn't eaten anything that morning, that a student had fainted out in the field from hunger and because she had to stay hunched over and dig up potatoes, that it was hard for us to haul all the potatoes we gathered over to the big piles, that it would be better if we made more smaller piles, the netted bags were too big and heavy for children as skinny as us, how were we supposed to work if we kept dropping here in the field, and what could she do all alone, if God forbid, we didn't come to again, were we supposed to die here among all these potatoes? She had no time to explain all this. That Mahmudion-Kasim-Bai stamped out the fire, swearing, he didn't even pay attention to her, then when he waved his whip and hit her with it, it threw her to the ground. I don't know how it happened but our communal indignation was so great that after the first potatoes, which we happened to be holding already, many others landed on top of the brigadier's head, then dozens of clods of dirt threw him off his horse. We took his little whip and maybe we gave him a healthy lashing, trying it out on his back, or maybe we just used it to tie up his hands, I can't remember anymore, we dumped a bag of potatoes on his head to stop him from yelling, because he was scaring us, but he kept yelling, then we stuffed a potato in his mouth and he stopped. And we walked away, leaving him there.

We all agreed to each take two potatoes, for the work we put in, we would've taken more, but we felt bad for poor Bubusara, they would punish her because we took the potatoes of the soldiers who were off at war. We picked her up, we comforted her as best we could, assured her that the brigadier had it coming to him, that we, not she, beat him up, that we would defend her if need be. She didn't say anything, she granted us the right to take two potatoes and sent us home. I remember how she spoke those beautiful words to us: "You may take two potatoes for your work." Someone with many siblings asked if they could take, instead of two big potatoes, three very small ones, the smallest ones, one for each little brother, because it was hard to divide two potatoes in three. "You can, but that stays between us. *Shh*," she whispered, putting her finger up to her lips, and her eyes filled with tears.

Well, and what do you think happened . . . They kicked us out of school, also because the school year was finished anyway, they shut down our class and we had to find work. The children told their parents what had happened, they explained where the beautiful potatoes had come from, why they weren't just the tossed out peels that we had enjoyed until then. Bubusara Abdusaidova disappeared from the village. The parents went to the principal, they went to the kolkhoz to ask them not to punish her. But she left all the same. Quickly, in secret. We were told that she was fine and teaching at another school, in the city, where they actually study and don't pick potatoes. In any case, in order to survive, you had to work. I went back to the cowshed, I'd take out the manure and be given something, I wasn't feeding off Mother. I'd also help her with embroidering sometimes, when she'd get an order from someone better off. We'd save up some from here, some from there, it was hard, but, by the grace of God, we got through it all.

You couldn't find potatoes for sale and they didn't give them to schoolchildren, and when I came home with two big potatoes, Mother asked me where they were from, where I got them. She didn't touch them, she stared at them and thought. "And did Aglaie also take two potatoes?" "She did," I nodded, "all the children each took two potatoes." "But she has more sisters at home, there are seven mouths to feed there, they have to split two potatoes among seven people, while we'd each get an entire potato." I began to see what Mother was getting at. But I wanted so much to eat an entire potato, all by myself, and not to have to share it with anyone! I didn't say anything, I only thought it. Nor did Mother say: "Take a potato over to the sisters, share it with them."

My dear, kind mother only said: "Dear Lord, may the potato harvest be so great next year that there be enough for everyone, for all the kolkhoz pigs to get their fill and there be some left over for us! So that we won't fight over a potato. Lord, I strengthen my prayer with a good deed. We'll give of the little we have, give to us, too, out of Your mercy, whenever You think is right. We ask You, most merciful Lord, to give us Your wisdom, so that we may keep far from all that is not pleasant in Your sight, so that we may know how to speak and how to choose only what is pleasing to You, so that we may be saved. Give us the strength to consider all the vanities of this world as nothing. Because today we are sorely tested by this dark enmity and we'd immediately fall prey to it, if You, Lord, didn't keep close watch over us. Our enemies want to turn us into animals. May we stay human! Help us, Lord! For to You, Lord, together with the Father and the Holy Spirit, belong all glory and praise, now and forever and ever. Amen."

We were sure, then, that because of our good deed, we, Bucovinians and others oppressed like us, would have food to eat the following year, the earth would be fruitful and yield many potatoes, so many that there wouldn't be people enough to harvest them. A mountain of potatoes it would be. Full and thankful people . . . With these glowing images in mind, I headed out to the home of the Aglaies with the bigger potato in my hand. Actually, both were about as big. Back home, I later made two meals of one. I called out. My classmate came outside, scared, followed by her mother. I just handed her the potato, because I didn't know what to say. "All of it?" she said amazed, as if she couldn't believe it. The younger little Aglaies came outside as well and looked at that potato. I couldn't say a thing, I was ready to burst into tears. They passed the potato around and were overjoyed. Their mother

put her hand on my head and said: "We thank you, God preserve you." I nodded my head that I understood and left. I arrived
home with tears in my eyes. Mother wasn't looking. She was preparing half a potato for me to eat, we kept the second half for
the next day. She didn't have a bite, so that her prayer would be
powerful and efficacious. How was she able to resist it? How is it
that hunger couldn't transform her into a miserable animal, as it
had so many others? How is it that she didn't forget to teach me
to share what little I had with those who were needier than me?

The next year, the potatoes didn't do too well, the spring of 1944
was a harsh one, grass staggers swept through, the mass death of
cattle because of insufficient nutrients. In 1945, there was another
drought. And hunger mercilessly cut short many lives. Finally,
in 1946 God was gracious and watered those thirsty lands and
there was hope that death would pass us by. In the third year after
that incident, yes, so many potatoes came up that there weren't
enough people to gather them, because the young people had left
for better paying jobs. They were calling us to go build the railroads. I had food there and I had the Gherman sisters with me
through thick and thin, they had received us in their house as well
and we were now as sisters. We helped each other out. Wealth
divides people, makes them strangers. Times are different now.
Supposedly you shouldn't eat potatoes, because they're fattening.
I think stupidity is the most fattening thing there is . . . The hard
times ended, stores popped up where you could buy a thing or
two. Well, at first you'd receive three rubles for your work and
that's how much a loaf of bread cost. It was very expensive, but we
were happy that we weren't working for free, that we at least held
rubles, it was something, not nothing as it had been until then.
We felt better. That year Papa Gherman bought a sow, and when
it had piglets, he gave them out to people, we took one home too
and raised it inside. We later sold some of the meat and saved up

something. We'd sew clothes for ourselves out of sacks or pieces of sackcloth, when we embroidered an item, we'd receive something for it, some potatoes, some grain, everything was of use. I once earned a satchel of potatoes, about twenty. But I couldn't eat until I was full because winters were long and hard times could come again at any moment, when they might not pay us anymore, or make us leave, when we'd have nothing coming in. We constantly thought about what tomorrow might hold. Also then, in 1946, we received joyful news: the war had ended and we were being allowed to return to our homeland.

—Cuţa, but don't pigs stink? How could you live with them, in the same room?

—My darling, no animal stinks worse than people! Pigs stink if you keep them out in garbage and filth, but ours, kept in our room, was a clean animal, it would drop its manure in a corner and it would be glad when we'd gather it up and take it out, it would sleep on straw, which we'd change, it never climbed up on our bench, it knew its place. It would sleep next to Kotovsky, who would rub up against its back, as a sign of friendship, both of them snoring quietly.

There was also a clinic there, with a doctor, who was a deportee too, and a nurse, but they never had enough medicine, or gauze bandages, because it was wartime and everything went to the front lines. We had brilliant green, the same antiseptic that the soldier on the train had first given us, but it didn't work on all illnesses. They helped people as best they could, sometimes just with advice. We suffered most from hunger and the cure for that illness didn't lie with them. The doctor was tall and thin, and when he'd see the children of the deportees, hungry and skeletal, he'd take a little round thing out of his pocket, he'd show it to the children, then, like a circus clown, he'd quickly stick it in his mouth, waving around his long arms. We, children, were scared at first, but he'd do the same thing to our mothers, to the women he'd meet on the street who weren't as easily scared as us. The women understood him, even though they didn't speak Russian or whatever other language he spoke, we never found out because he soon disappeared, they say he was sent off to fight . . . We deportees, supposedly, didn't need medical care, all the men should go off to fight . . .

Anyway, the mothers came in closer and took a better look at the little ball the doctor held, they examined it from every angle, they smelled it, then the doctor would take it back, he'd put it up to his mouth again, but first he'd make wide gestures toward the fields of the Soviet fatherland, which at the time were our source of mice and ground squirrels. "Gather and eat," the doctor's wide open arms said. We gathered and ate: they were a kind of sour berry that never softened or became sweeter with time. They could be dried out, that's what my mother and other mothers did, storing up a supply for the winter. Maybe we survived thanks to them, may God grant health to that doctor, who treated us with berries from the field! They gave us so many vitamins in those cold winters. The Kazakhs would use the weed they called *ermen* to heal themselves, we'd gather it from the fields as well.

I think it was the exact same year the war ended, but we hadn't received word yet, around the beginning of summer, I think, I can't remember exactly, that they wrote up lists of young people who had become stronger and hadn't yet been registered for work. Fishermen, and not only, were needed somewhere, they were forming brigades made up of girls and boys. They needed at least one member from each family and even though I was still just a child, they put me on the list. Mother didn't know who to appeal to, who to beg not to separate us. She asked and was told that I'd be back in three months, because the river freezes in September, it actually freezes beginning in August, but we'd return sometime in September, because the road there is long. Mother said she'd go with me, that she wouldn't let me go alone, but they wouldn't take her. I had grown, I'd gotten taller, I seemed ripe and ready for even harder jobs, as if everything I had done until then had been a walk in the park.

Eugen's grandmother, our dear Anghelina Țară, had died and Sevasta, his older cousin, was taking care of him. He wasn't on the list, but he wanted to come with us willingly, he had just found out that his mother and siblings were in Khanty-Mansiysk, a human settlement much farther north, on the river Ob, and the ship was taking us exactly in that direction. He didn't even have to pay for a ticket, because he was going for work, and there he'd meet, finally, with his family. They gathered all of us young deportees from the kolkhozes in the area. Mother said I should at least take the cat, so he could take care of me. "It's not often you meet with a cat like this, he's practically your shadow." Before I left, she picked up the cat and whispered in his ear: "Take care of her and bring her back!" Kotty must have promised her that he'd do just that.

First we traveled by cart, then by bus, they picked us up from many places and brought us to the edge of a fairly big river, whose existence I knew nothing about until then, called the Irtysh. There we waited for a ship to arrive from somewhere. We were divided up into several groups, people from the neighboring town came as well. It was us, the deportees, who were watched, we couldn't move about freely, also citizens going off to work of their own initiative, because you could earn more money up north, the people who were traveling by ship to a far away destination, there were also some local youth organization pioneers who were going to a patriotic work-and-rest camp, numbering, as always, more women than men. They told us we'd come back in the fall, either to school or, most likely, to a work practicum, because during the summer all young people work for the good and development of the glorious Soviet Union, and in the fall, they help with the harvest at the beloved kolkhozes.

Notable among the free citizens was that group of very pretty and young pioneers, who were dressed, I don't know why, in school uniforms, with their ties and little aprons, though it was summer and they must have been on vacation, but they seemed dressed for a parade, not for a long journey. I had never seen clothing like that! We didn't have uniforms, only the students in our textbook drawings were dressed like that! Where were they going, so beautifully done up? In any case, we weren't all heading to the same place. There were more than a hundred of us waiting for the ship. I had never been on a ship, and when it came, rattling and creaking from every seam, I was scared. It didn't look like a water train, as I had been imagining, but like an old animal, who had trouble breathing, was puffing, sneezing, and was disgruntled and capricious. It was a gigantic vessel, named "Vesna," a girl's name, which means "spring," though it sailed only during the summer.

The free citizens and the pioneers in uniform were allowed to stroll wherever they wished, yelling enthusiastically, climbing over everything, while the wind billowed the pioneer dresses which were really quite short and you could see their underwear and rosy butt cheeks. The prisoners, whose fierce faces looked like those of real criminals (they called us criminals as well, but what kind of criminals were we?) could see this too. They were already on the ship when we embarked, coming from farther away and heading to a different destination than us. They were locked inside a barred cage, but they watched us and yelled awful things at us, and at the pioneers who, hearing what was being said to them, no longer felt like waving their pleated uniforms under the prisoners' noses.

They also locked us inside a cage down below and the criminals couldn't admire us, only swear at us, though we hadn't done anything to them.

At night, they bribed a guard to let them visit us, the female deportees. They weren't allowed to touch the women who were free citizens or the young pioneers. But us, the female deportees, yes. The few male deportees who had gotten on with us were in a cage next to ours, but Jeni had mixed in with the girls, and not only Jeni came in with me, but also the husband of a deported woman, among all the pushing and shoving. My heart was thumping out of my chest. Jeni also had grave fears related to the criminals. The cages were right next to each other, the rooms were, in fact, divided only by some sheet metal corridors. They cut the lights, said it was lights out. We curled up in a far corner, Jeni was holding me tightly in his arms, the waves rocking us also nauseated us, and when the mayhem began, Jeni took out his wooden spoon with the heavy metal handle, preparing himself for an attack. The criminals removed a metal sheet and began pulling our girls into their cage. It was a great commotion, pushing, screaming. The cat was sitting and paying close attention to what was happening, and when I felt some hairy paws try to get me out of the corner, he immediately understood who the enemy was and jumped to my rescue. "Jeni," I screamed, "save me!" I also yelled for Kot, who already had his claws in the enemy's hand. After Kot had sunk his fangs and claws in a choice spot, Jeni added some spoon handles across the back of the criminal's neck, he yelled and started retreating, Jeni gave out a few more handles to the right and left, to the other two, because three had come in, but we couldn't move too far away from our corner and the other two managed to pull some girls out, then they returned to save the third man, who we were stamping all over. They got him, because they were strong, we couldn't see anything in the dark and Jeni was afraid that he might accidentally hit a girl. When the enemies managed to leave, Kot came back, I stroked his fur. Then we heard the screams of the kidnapped girls, then other screams, during which time not a single soldier and no one in charge of the ship intervened, it was as if their ears were stuffed with cotton. We yelled for help, we banged on the walls. In the morning, our dead girls were thrown into the water. In the river floating next to them were two beautiful and bloody pioneers.

The next day, those savage prisoners were taken off our ship, on the shore were many soldiers with guns who watched them, the criminals got off, other more peaceful groups got on, poor women and much better behaved prisoners, dressed nicely and who sang mournful songs at night. The ship also stopped near human settlements, we passed through many cities, where some got off and others got on. Then the water became much wider and we reached the river Ob. "Ob, Ob!" the people on the ship yelled. What beauty! Despite the terror we had been through, we, too, marveled at such a flood!

In the end, we arrived at our destination, we got off the accursed ship, which continued on its way along with dear Jeni. That was the last time we ever saw each other. Before we parted, Jeni tied a scarf with three tulips on it around my neck, I did the same to him with a checkered scarf, and we promised each other we'd survive, we'd meet again and return the scarves. When I was about to get off, I went over to him and kissed him. On the lips, like a bride and groom. Everyone was looking at us and we were embarrassed. But I thought to myself that if I didn't kiss him now, I'd regret it for my whole life. And it's a good thing I did, because I would have regretted it my whole life. We didn't think then that we'd never see each other again. I wrote to him for years, I looked for him. But I never found a trace of him. On the shore, I waved the scarf, he was getting farther away, the ship was shrinking, I could barely make out my scarf in his hands anymore.

—Do you still have the scarf?

—I do, of course I do, it's like new! I kept it safe, it's all that I had left of my Jeni.

I never traveled again by ship in my life, we returned by train. I said to myself then: *When the bee from the skep and the parr from the valley meet and have a drink in the tavern with the lords, the villagers, the locals, that's when I'll get back in a ship to go downstream to the valley or upstream to the wide waters in a galley!* Lord, preserve me and keep me! I never got on another ship again! But I again heard how ships shriek: like girls abused by criminals and then thrown in the water! Lord, You protected me then, and Jeni defended me, and Kot! I escaped with my life.

After they got us off the ship, they put us on a small train, a kind of wagon with seats that moved down a train track. I went with the first group in one of the three railcars, then the train went back and got the other girls. We looked around, what settlement was that, we were leaving behind us some long and windowless dwellings that looked more like farms or factories than houses to live in. We didn't really see any people there, meaning inhabitants, besides our boss, the brigadier of our detachment, as he had introduced himself, who stuffed us inside the train until not a single seat was left, and he sat down in front. After he turned a crank like a pedal, the train began moving down the very narrow train track.

We arrived in a wilderness without a living soul, in front of us was water, behind us was taiga and some barracks. We got off and the train went back for the other girls. We, the first ones, chose the better looking barrack, that seemed to be newer, the door shut tightly, we had a small table, some long planks that were beds, and a small stove. Other people had probably lived there until our arrival, but now we were the only ones there, no one from the previous brigade. We had been expecting something else, and until the train came back, we started wailing, that they had brought us here to die. Tethered on the shore were some boats that were so banged up that we didn't for a moment think that we'd be taken out to work in those wrecks. They looked like they would sink if you even touched them with a single finger, no way you'd go out into open water in them! We had completed our dreadful journey on a large vessel and we thought that you went out into deep waters only in large ships. Those of us girls who didn't know how to swim at all were especially terrified. It seemed that if I were to flick or poke a craft like these it would break apart. No, I wouldn't get in, God forbid, a boat like that! I'd rather die on the shore, I'd rather they shoot me!

By the time the other girls arrived it had gotten dark. The train left and didn't come back until the next day. It returned with different railcars, for transporting fish, and one in which there were some mattresses and blankets for us, so we wouldn't have to sleep on the bare planks (that's what we had thought at first) and to cover ourselves, because even summers were cool there, sometimes you could even get frostbite and puddles froze overnight. The mattresses were thin and short, as if they were for children, maybe that's what they actually were, we had never seen ones so short and narrow before. But having them was better than sleeping on bare planks. In the morning they also brought us bread, drinking water, they dropped off a cardboard box for each shack with canned food in it, they would bring us water and bread every morning, but we'd only get cans now, at the beginning, they were for the entire season. We were happy. Among the canned food were two kinds of jams: plum jam and one made from another fruit that no one could identify and I still don't know what it is, it was like a marmalade. The men came in the morning and went back in the evening with the railcars loaded with fish, and left us there alone. At first, when we were very scared and inexperienced, about five men would come, one for each boat and they'd teach us what we had to do, then only the brigadier with an assistant would come, two at most, who sorted through the fish in the nets and packed them onto the railcars. We'd work in teams of four: four girls in the boat, another four waited on the shore and they'd pull the net of fish out of the water, then we'd switch.

We also received some tall rubber boots, but when we'd pull in the fishing net, water would get in our boots and we'd be left with wet feet all day. During breaks, until the boat reached the shore, we'd run constantly so we wouldn't freeze. A fishing net could hold up to a ton of fish. We worked nonstop, until we filled all the vessels with fish. Late in the evening, sometimes even at night, the train loaded with fish would leave. Most of us didn't know how to swim, the danger of drowning was very great and we'd cry, terrified that the boat might capsize. The man overseeing us would yell at us and say that masses of people were dying on the front lines and if we were to die by drowning it wouldn't be a loss.

My first time in a boat on the water! When we reached open water, the first thing that stood out to our eyes and ears was how quiet it was. A quiet that conquered everything, it swallowed any noise. So much silence scared us and we yelled, we slapped the water with our oars to diminish, to drive out that chilling silence, but everything we did, even the shortest word of ours, seemed to draw attention to the silence, as if any movement of ours, any word, spoken or yelled, was mute. The small, gentle waves swallowed the sound, as if it had never existed. The word would hit against the mirror of the water and then bounce back defeated, helpless. If all you hear is silence, that means that sounds don't exist. The water slowly quivered, with ruffles that were the same wherever you looked, we couldn't even tell what direction it flowed in, its only care was to hunt down yells, the noise of the boats, words, to catch them in a delicate spider's web and destroy them. Its silence was also dangerous, it knew how to scream, to lash out, and to swallow up anything and anyone who dared to defy its order and its stillness with foreign sounds. It seemed to be the silence from before the Creation of the world, before the first human, before the first days. The silence from before language, before the speaking of meaning, the silence of the child inside his mother's belly. And we had ended up there through a time hole, by accident. It was a silence that didn't give us a sense of peace, it wasn't comforting, nor was it benign. It was heavy and oppressive, and we felt how our presence there disturbed that empire of silence from the foundation of the world which seemed to recognize neither the natural order of things nor God's laws. Because that was nearly the truth as we later realized.

The sun rarely showed itself there, and the clouds and sky were also waters, a single color, an inseparable whole as well. The fish allowed themselves to be caught to escape all the silence, they, too, were prisoners of this stillness, which could swallow us up at any moment and much sooner than we imagined. With us were two Moldovan women from Bessarabia who also marveled at this strange water. They had fished before on a seashore, where waves rose as high as houses, but the sea spoke to people day and night. Waves, even if they crash over you, still allow you to live and they deliver you to shore. The sea is very agitated, noisy, whirring, and dangerous if you don't know what it's saying to you, but it's alive like an animal, like a person, and its mouth is never silent. While here everything is at a standstill. Nothing moves, the sun doesn't rise or set, day isn't day, night isn't night. It's the same silence mirroring itself. Hearing the silence in your own scream was so horrific that we preferred to keep quiet. Better the silence from everyone keeping silent, than the silence from everyone screaming. It was only on the water that we felt this mysterious silence, on dry land everything went back to normal. We heard words, we'd say them and be glad. We'd revive, become human again, that water would make our blood run cold. But that fear was a treat compared to what would follow. When we experienced the first whirlpools, with the water's terrifying roars, I would've chosen the water's initial silence, which at least allowed us to return safely to the shore, with our nets full of fish, a thousand times over the death that intended to teach us a lesson, spinning us around it, as in a cruel and dizzying dance.

They also told us to keep the doors shut tight and not to go out at night. We wouldn't have gone out, of course, even without these directions, but we had no idea what was awaiting us! The first days we learned how to maneuver the boat, to row, use the nets, find more and bigger fish. We weren't supposed to go far out into open water, we were told that if the water began to rumble, and waves arose, if we heard any suspicious sound, that we should quickly head for the shore. We were surprised: how could this silent water rumble, how could waves arise? We would've wanted at least one man to stay with us, we were really happy when we'd see them again the next morning, we waited for them impatiently.

The bears began sniffing around from the very first evening when we opened the containers of jam. The forest was farther off, not right up against our barracks, not right around the corner. How could the bears smell something sweet from so far away? How could they sense that we had something that they, too, would like and that we'd share our treasure with them? That was the only treat we received in that wilderness, and we had to share it. Had someone taken out, had someone thrown out, before we came here, empty containers like these? The bears circled around the barracks, they leaned up against the walls, pushed the doors, mumbling in all kinds of ways, sometimes they seemed like drunk men who nitpick on their wives, mumbling unintelligible things, we'd hear them snoring, breathing. They made so much noise all around us that we had the impression there were hundreds of bears outside, that the entire taiga had come to feast on our plum jam! At our door, there was a big mother bear with two cubs, we could see her clearly through the spaces between the slats. The animals spoke freely to each other in their bearish language and weren't bothered in the slightest by us. Inside our barracks, by contrast, you could hear a pin drop. Unlike the bears, we were so scared we could barely breathe. It seemed to us that nothing could save us. That's it, we would die. Let us pray!

Then, when he saw what was happening, when he saw that we were just a bunch of scared girls, weak women who couldn't defend themselves against the bears' attack, Kot, as the only man who didn't lose his composure, started to meow quickly and repeatedly.

"What do you want?"

"Meow."

"To go out, you mean, but aren't you scared?"

"Meow," our dear cat answered, pleased that I had understood him without needless explanation.

"I'll let you out, but please be careful. Please come back, Kot. What would we do here without you? How could I return to Mother without you?"

"Meow," Kot said succinctly.

I opened the door for him and he almost ran out, that's how much of a hurry he was in, as if he wanted to go to the bathroom. He went over to the river and caught fish for the mother bear and cubs. He called them over, lured them over to the river, he swished his tail around the cubs, then played with them. The cubs were very cute and we took turns watching them through the openings in the walls. Then we saw them all take off toward the forest. My Kot, as well as the bears. We breathed a sigh of relief and went to sleep. We'd live at least until tomorrow. Tomorrow we'd tell the brigadier who was visiting us, we'd ask him if we were brought here to catch fish or to be food for a battalion of bears. We'd ask for matches, came another suggestion, we'd gather a lot of wood before nightfall. Dry branches, we'd light them and scare away the wild animals, so they wouldn't consider us dinner.

While the girls calmed down and thought of ideas, I thought about my cat. Kot, come back, come back. We curled up next to each other and dozed off, some started snoring peacefully, tired, as if they hadn't been nearly almost, a short time ago, eaten by the forest beardom. I heard a light scratching at the door. "Kot?" "Meow." I opened the door for him, I hugged him, how he stunk of fish and how ruffled his fur was! I fell asleep too while holding him, he was warm and snored slowly. I was so tired! I didn't know what he had told the bears to make them leave us alone. I thought about asking him the next day, but I forgot.

After that invasion, we survived alright until the following day, when the men stayed later than usual and fired guns to scare the bears and drive them away. Only the mother bear who was lame and her cubs weren't scared and they continued coming until we gave them our last container of jam, to convince her that we had nothing left to offer. Only then did they leave for good and leave us alone. The mother bear with the two cubs wasn't afraid of our men, she'd wait until they left, she knew they would leave, eventually, and she'd come back. Either she was used to people, or she was desperate and needed help. We guessed that she had a thorn in her paw, that's why she was limping. She seemed to be begging at our door, she'd stay there until we gave her something to eat. Something, meaning just jam, not fish. We'd return in the evening with a fish each and we still had some containers of that unknown fruit jam. She was interested only in the jam, I don't know how she could tell that we still had some. We made a kind of wooden spoon out of a branch, we'd spread jam on the tip of it and hold it out to her through a small chink. She'd lick it carefully, without biting or chewing on the spoon. So we wouldn't have to make another one the next day. She'd mumble contentedly and wait for us to give her more, she'd leave only when she considered that she had received her portion for that day. The cubs were really adorable and I think that after their mama gave them some of our jam, they felt like playing and frolicking. They'd roll around like balls, jump up, jostle each other. We would've played with them, we would've brought them inside our hut a bit, but you don't mess around with mother bears. When we ran out of jam, they disappeared.

Women cost less than men. Especially after the war. At Smert-Reka we were all women, out on the water, only women, rarely would a man go out, just in the beginning to teach us how to deal with the boats. As we later discovered, the men caught fish in special ships, in which they had ice chests so the fish wouldn't go bad when they were out on the water for a long time, there were many of them, they didn't have to row, they weren't afraid of waves the way we were. But fish like the kind we had here could be found nowhere else. We had a bunch of run down boats and only women, many who were seeing such a flood for the first time in their life and they didn't know how to swim either. As was the case with me. We had a pond in our village, a bit farther off, but I hadn't learned to swim in it. Nor did the name *smert*, death, for this river draw our attention, though we knew how to jabber away in Russian pretty well, we had also been to school. The river as a whole had a different name, the river was Ob the huge, the long and wide, unlike any other. Smert was just our part of it, a kind of bend in the river, but so big that it looked more like a sea than a river. The water touched the sky, and it seemed to us that we were fishing not in the river but in the sky. Men fished in the river, on ships, but women, in the sky, on boats. Sometimes, in the evening, I'd try to look at the horizon to find the line that divided the sky and water and I couldn't find it. Like the steppe when I first saw it getting off the train after a month of travel, when the sky was above and below. Here, too, the river and the sky seemed to have an understanding to take on the same colors, so that they formed a complete whole.

At the thought that we were fishing, after all, in the heavens, so close to God, I'd get up my courage, because at first I was so scared of that water, of those waves, like the many, small teeth of a saw, that I kept the cross from around my neck in my mouth, I clamped it between my teeth and prayed ceaselessly to God to get back to the shore safely. I thought that the newly arrived specialist was also searching for the divide between the sky and the water. There was a small hill there, on the shore, a hill with lots of rocks. I liked climbing up there during our short breaks and looking out, then I fashioned a cross from small stones and tended it, I'd arrange it, put back the stone that had moved out of place and was ruining the cross. I'd go there and think about Mother who had remained alone in the Anarkhay steppe, about Father who I didn't know anything about, and my brothers and sister who had stayed in Romania, I thought about Eugen who had gone by ship farther along the river, I wished them health and for God to protect them. In that solitude I could think about them, I could pray. There was no church there, there weren't even houses. A great wil-

derness, water-sky, waters-skies! I'd look at them and marvel. I'd
pray at the end for the Lord to bring me safely out from the waves
tomorrow as well, so that I could again pray at my cross of stones.
Then I'd see the boat approaching shore and go help pull in the
fishing net from the water and get ready for my turn to go out.

———

One day I saw that my hill was taken, a man with all kinds of
instruments set up there was looking through them at the sky or
the river. When I approached, he gave me a friendly greeting, he
spoke Russian, he asked me if the cross made of stones was mine.
"It's mine," why should I lie? He was respectful, calm, so I wasn't
scared, I didn't run away from him. He kept mostly quiet, I kept
quiet as well, not far from him. "Do you catch fish here? Do you
work in the brigade, on the Smert?"

"Yes, here, on the Smert," I confirmed.

"You're working on death, so to speak, you know what smert
means?" the man asked. "Death, death itself," he said, as if to himself.

"Death?" I was surprised, I had heard the word before, but I
wasn't completely sure and I had hoped that maybe I didn't know
Russian that well and smert meant something else too, the name
of a big fish, for example, or a murkier branch of a river. Death!
Why, Lord, forgive me, death and more death? How much death
must I keep carrying with me? The specialist didn't say anything.
He looked into the distance through a long tube, I minded my
own business but it was as if I were waiting for him to call me to
see, to let me look through that long, beautiful tube too, I didn't
say anything, but I really wanted to see as well. He seemed to
guess it and he handed me that wonderful tube.

"Kiril Sergeyevich."

"Ana Bojescu."

"Annushka, come see what the water is doing here!"

At first, I didn't understand what I was supposed to be seeing, where I should look. "Do you see it," the specialist yelled at me, "do you see death?"

No, at first I didn't, then yes, I saw circular waves, water spinning around in an eddy, I saw a cauldron of water form out of a whirlpool, and around the cauldron, waves crashed and went underwater. There were many whirlpools in that area, the water had strange and murderous currents, I don't know what the Russians called them, we called them whirlpools. Because of them, the men never took their sloops into that area, but there was so much fish there, so very much, that it would be a shame if someone didn't go out to catch them, someone you didn't care if died, you cared more about fish. In the face of this danger, the fish would become still, they stayed stupid and motionless, to the point where even we, who had never tried fishing before, caught a lot, without being very skilled at it. But what the fish felt, fear, the closeness of death, humans didn't.

When a boat would disappear, we wouldn't know what had happened, we'd be told, "They moved on." They might have moved on, not to another part of the river, but to be with the Lord. They had brought us there when the brigade of girls before us had gone completely to be with the Lord and the barracks were empty and there was no one to tell us what river that was and what we were fishing. God have mercy on the poor tortured souls! So as not to scare us, they didn't tell us anything, because we would've refused to go back out into open water. In any case, the boats didn't sink the very first time they went out, as happened at first with the ships, the vortex wasn't as angry with us, it allowed us to catch some fish, but it didn't like men and it destroyed their ships, which were expensive, and they didn't come to fish in that dangerous zone anymore.

The specialist wasn't much help either, that's not why he had come there. The whirlpool would change its location, sometimes heading to one place, sometimes to another, and on certain days, all the water was turbulent. We didn't go out to fish then. We would've all died. Once, when I was praying at my cross on the hill, the specialist pointed to the water and said to me: "There's a magical animal at the bottom of the water. See, a whirlpool appears, you see it, you feel it pulling you toward it and you row with all your strength, as far as you can from the roar, in the opposite direction. That's a mistake, it swallows everything that opposes it. Don't run away from it, don't try to distance yourself, try to float next to it, parallel to it, or merely to wait, don't do anything."

A whirlpool seen from the hilltop, with that instrument made of glass, doesn't look anything like a whirlpool from the water. Kiril Sergeyevich told our brigadier that we shouldn't go out in the river to fish, because many whirlpools had started up those days and they were swallowing everything and making the water swirl. "But the quota has to be met—today, no, tomorrow, no, then when? We have only a few days left until the water freezes, what kind of whirlpools are these that can't even be seen from the shore? Every day the girls go out and they come back just fine. To the boats, everyone!"

They took us out in the morning, we had the fishing net ready, we let it fill with fish and then started back to shore. Suddenly, in that perfect silence, we heard the whistling, the roaring, we had no clue what it was at first, as if a fighter plane were flying above us, right over our heads, then the wheel of water, then the void. Next to us, a few meters away, a wall of water rose up, and right by it, the hole, the roar came straight from hell, I'd never heard or seen anything more horrifying in my life. Lord, we came to the heavens to fish, but hell is sputtering a breath away from us! The fish froze and stopped struggling in the net, hell was sizzling, bubbling, boiling, roaring, it was threatening and calling us. The boat was headed straight for the hole in the river, despite all our efforts of rowing away as hard as we could. Death was baring its fangs at us, with a menacing and terrifying grin. We were powerless and desperate, but we fought, we were rowing as hard as we could, trying to get away. Lord, take your fish back and save us! "Let go of the net, girls!" The fish in a hurry to swim away now that they were free were quickly pulled to the bottom of the cauldron, their joy was short-lived and they disappeared in the blink of an eye into the the mouth of the greedy, hungry sea serpent. Now it would be our turn. Lord, we're dying, Lord! Let us pray!

When the vortex pulls you toward death, when you hear the pits of hell roaring, you have no time, or you do but very little, to think that only a miracle, only the will of God can save you. I remembered that the monster that slept at the bottom of the water and sometimes woke up, opened its mouth and, snap, swallowed everything in its path. I remembered the specialist's advice: don't fight it, and I told the girls to stop rowing. We were at the edge of it. When you're faced with such a terrible enemy, you don't resist, you just float, plain and simple, you let go completely. From the other side of the boat, near us as well, a smaller hell appeared, as if one wasn't enough, a smaller whirlpool, a little pot compared to the first one, the great cauldron. The big hell immediately sensed it and was furious. Our boat was wobbling aimlessly but with many prayers to God. For the big whirlpool, we now seemed an enemy that was too weak and we no longer mattered, we no longer interested it. Then, in a crazy surge, the fierce big hell, that had first appeared next to us, hurled us out into the open water, so that it could get close to the small whirlpool and swallow it, while we were more just getting in the way.

Our boat was thrown right toward the shore. We heard the triumphant roar of the big whirlpool, now even bigger after their terrible union. We no longer saw eddies in the water, we only heard the rattling, the bark, the roar of all the devils in cursed hell. When the beast in the water no longer felt any resistance, it bellowed, whistled, hissed again, and we saw it move away into the open water, farther from us. The whirlpool went away as quickly as it had come and it no longer seemed like a cauldron, but a spinning spiral that sucked water down, toward the bottom, as if a watermill at the bottom of the river were spinning it. Then it went under with such screams that the few fish we had left in the boat stuck their scales up, exactly the way the hair on our heads stands straight up from fear.

The boat brought us to the shore by itself, without us putting in effort, without us rowing, with a few fish, not empty-handed. Everyone was waiting there for us, or to be more precise they were already no longer waiting for us, because they had heard the water's screams, even though the holes of water weren't visible from the shore. Only the specialist could see them. He came toward me joyfully and hugged me, as if I were his dear brother. It was a miracle from God that we escaped. "Smert," was the only thing he said.

"Smert," I replied as well, as if we were greeting each other after a long separation. "Nature is chasing us out, we've occupied all its territory and it, too, needs a bit of solitude." The bosses would give Kiril Sergeyevich dirty looks when he'd repeat this to them.

Another boat quickly went out and returned loaded with fish. Now tons of fish were in the water! Then we, too, learned how to read the water's signs, how to escape from whirlpools, to defend ourselves. Not even hell is so terrible, humans become accustomed to everything. That is, when you could, if a whirlpool opened up right under you, there was no escape.

Kot was agitated that day, he clung with his paws to my clothes, he probably wanted to warn me in Cat that I shouldn't go out fishing. When I returned, he was very glad, he had brought me, the dear thing, a mouse as a gift. He knew that I had once been crazy for mice, during the great famine, except that now they'd leave us a fish or two, they also gave us enough bread, I no longer ate mice. I shared my food with him, he'd also fish something for himself, it wasn't hard in those waters teeming with fish. He knew this, but he wanted to show me how happy he was, he didn't come to meet me empty-pawed, a reunion which could well have never taken place.

When I helped unload the fish, I looked for the most beautiful of all the fish, the king, the little golden fish, I called it, the magic, lucky fish. Thank you, Lord, for saving us from hell, as a sign of gratitude, I'll let the most beautiful fish from today's catch live. After that, each time I pulled up the net, I'd always choose a fish and take it back to the river. All kinds of species, big, little, were floundering in the net, I'd secretly pick one, the most interesting one or the smallest one, one that could've been swallowed by a bigger fish right there in our net. It was always one that stood out from the others, I'd find it right away and give it its freedom, life, just as God gave us ours. I'd ask the river and its inhabitants to allow me to live. I'd pray to God as well.

Every morning, I'd get in the boat, I'd jump into it actually, and I'd think that I was going to my death. I surrendered myself to the will of God. I'd tell myself that I had lived long enough on the face of the earth, others had died young just in the train, I had seen enough, I had even had enough, I could die now. No, I shouldn't, because I was young, I had left Mother rather sick and alone in a hostile and foreign place. But when I'd see that rickety boat and the waves maliciously trembling, with fish as big as me, there were also some ugly ones with mustaches and fangs that would've eaten us without much difficulty, I'd pray earnestly to get back to the shore alive. I'd say to myself that I escaped yesterday, I escaped the day before yesterday, but today, as the Lord decides! We were so happy when we'd gather in the evening in that barrack! Then each morning when I'd go back out into open water, I'd again pray to God that we'd return safely in the evening, and each evening I never forgot to choose one little fish and let it go in the water.

They sent the specialist packing, he wrote reports about us, about how nature didn't want us there and was chasing us away, as best it could, how it was even killing many, about rare species of fish on the verge of extinction, which are in the red book and which we are forbidden to kill and eat, about the risk people who go fishing out there are exposed to, and who knows what else he wrote, but one day we didn't see him anymore. They didn't keep us there much longer either, they sent us back at the end of summer, they even gave us money at the end, so we'd have some for the journey and some left over. About the rare species of fish, I think that Kiril Serge-yevich knew about them from me, because he was up on the hill all day, how would he know what kind of fish we had in the river? But I'd tell him about them: "Today I threw back a little golden fish, small, roundish, yesterday it was a silver one, thin, longish, that shone like a king among the others, another time I found a fish with a flattened snout and colorful designs on its scales, another fish had a cross on its back, really pretty, one with a front tooth, one with a plumed tail, like a horse's." Out of that net with hundreds or thousands of fish I'd choose one that was different and let it go. I'd give the best back to the river. But if I found a special one that was already dead, I'd take it to the specialist.

I savored every sunrise, every return to our barrack as if it were a gift, I even liked the mother bear. Compared to killer vortexes, what's a hungry mother bear who was crazy about jam, and was trying to find food for her cubs? We, too, had once searched for food in our first years of exile . . . How many girls never returned from out in that water and how close we can be to heaven and hell without knowing! How small we are in God's hands . . .

Hell wouldn't have been hell in the truest sense of the word if we hadn't been tortured there by mosquitos as well. We made shields for ourselves out of blankets and clothing, which we used to cover our faces so we could get a little rest. From all the swarms, our cheeks were completely raw. A devious tribe, these mosquitos, but they helped some of our girls get married. When they attacked, you had to give them something precious and dear and only then would they leave. Not even the entire army of bears tortured us as much as the far more numerous and buzzier army of the mosquitos. There were so many that if you were to throw a neckerchief in the air, it would float down very gently, because the mosquitos would be holding it up. Or worse, it would start floating away and you'd have to chase it to get it back. Leida, a young Estonian girl from the city, polite and shy, who washed herself each evening, was attacked most often. The mosquitos adored moisture, but salt, a salty body, they didn't particularly care for. We'd wash ourselves once a week and our skin was saltier and smellier and the mosquitos would bite us less often, usually our faces, which we washed every morning with fresh water, not river water. The river water wasn't very salty, but I think it was still a bit salty. Leida always washed herself and the mosquitos always bit her, they'd eat her alive. Only after she threw them her neckerchief did they leave her alone, the swarm left, with the airy treasure and all. One day, the girl saw her neckerchief around the neck of a sailor who often came to pick up our fish, a handsome man, tall, good-looking, a real Prince Charming . . . *You dragon of nine tails, with golden scales, go find my charmer* . . . Leida stared at him, he stared at her, they explained, my neckerchief, your neckerchief, do you want it, I want it, they liked each other and the match was made. Others threw up their neckerchiefs as well, but the mosquitos weren't able to find other true loves as easily. To be fair, there were only women here and a couple men who came to pick up the fish. Then it was as the One Above wished. But there were many instances, we'd hear about them, even if we couldn't all get married with the help of the mosquitos. I never threw my beloved scarf with the three tulips in the air, the one I received from Eugen. I knew that mosquitos can't fly that far . . . Leida had a happy marriage, they left together, they must still be together, living in peace and harmony, if they haven't died . . .

After I got married, I'd go fishing with my husband. Here, in our Troiţa village pond, only men fished, it was unnatural to see a wife. Women didn't go fishing. But I'd go, I'd sit down at the edge of the water and listen, and watch. I'd think about those who fished in the sky and never made it back, I remembered that killer whirlpool. I didn't catch anything while sitting by my husband, not one fish, he didn't have much luck either at fishing. There are whirlpools in our pond too, a couple of people have drowned. God reminds us of his mercy sometimes, and of His wrath. In any body of water, the sky is close and there's much of it, if only from being reflected as well. We throw a twig or a pebble in the water, to watch the sky tremble. That river, too, and the limitless steppe had so much sky, and so much death! As if they were afraid of the heavens, people block them from view and hide themselves. As if that were possible, as if you could hide from the wrath of God. You can't, no roof could hide you well enough or protect you.

I don't know how to swim, I never learned after that and I'm afraid of water. I see images from then before my eyes, when the waters split open, I see the chasms that emerge in place of the calm, gentle waves, with whirlpools that pull you toward them, to drag you to the bottom, to kill you. I never told anyone this, but I was on the hill with the specialist, he was looking through his spyglass, I was praying, the water was calm, nothing separating it from the sky, united with it in a kind of embrace, up, and down, the same water. And suddenly, the water began to play, to spin. I saw how the rings of water played with each other. A bigger whirlpool and two smaller ones next to it danced together, from the hill they looked like a big wheel and little wheels. It seemed like a game, it was pretty, then I understood that it might have been a game at first, or it just looked like that to us, but they were fighting. The small ones to survive, the big one—to swallow up the smaller ones. The closest small one disappeared, the big whirlpool grew, it became more powerful and it was only a matter of time before it swallowed the other one as well. The remaining small one was also spinning energetically, it was trying to pull away. Quickly it flailed and shook its tail, but the powerful one kept cornering it, squeezing it, it lured it, embraced it, until they merged and only the big one was left. Then it sank down to the bottom, like a beast glutted and full, off to get a little shut-eye after a plentiful meal. We looked at each other without saying anything, we left without a word.

Before leaving Smert-Reka, I chose four of the stones from my cross on the hill and I took them with me, to our Troiţa de Sus in Moldova. The big whirlpool had swallowed the little ones, just as powerful, ravenous animals do to the ones that are weak, just as people do.

⁓

The Lord was good and merciful and I made it out of there alive, I returned safe and sound to my dear little mother. From all that fishing, I came back with a big, fat cat, with shiny fur, I couldn't even lug him around anymore, that's how heavy he was. I brought Mother two big and very salty fish that didn't go bad on the long journey, and a couple rubles. The war ended in 1945 and our lives changed a bit for the better. People no longer looked sidelong at us. In stores, baked bread started appearing. They'd still take us out for heavy labor, but they'd pay us a few rubles for that.

After we returned, the honorable Kotovsky disappeared after a few days, he didn't come home for about a month and we thought he was with the Russian women. Well, and lo and behold one day he turns up proudly with a raggedy, ugly, skinny, hungry cat. He had brought his sweetheart over to meet us: "Here's my family."

We wrinkled our noses: "Where did you find her? Did you have to look hard? You brought her here to give us all lice, because we barely just got rid of them, you'd guess she had other sins as well" . . . Kot, when he wanted to, could pretend to be like other cats that don't understand our human language. He asked for bread. We normally wouldn't give him any and he knew this full well, but so we wouldn't seem like skinflints in front of his beloved, we gave him some. We felt sorry for him. Where could he find, the poor thing, a more decent cat, better suited to him, in this wilderness? Who knows how hard it was for him to convince this one to offer him a bit of tenderness . . . Kot delicately picked up the bread and, as if he had already eaten an entire family of mice and was completely full, like a true gentleman, allowed the strange cat to eat everything herself, which the stranger did with the urgency specific to dogs. Cats usually eat slowly, delicately. Then, they both took off before Mother and I could become truly outraged at such lack of manners and rudeness!

When the wind blew off the roof to our hut, Kot knew, cats sense things, but he didn't abandon us. He could've chosen a sturdier house for himself, where he'd been before, where the women spoiled him, where there was more food, but no, he stayed with us until the Ghermans discovered us and took us into their home, cat and all, though they themselves barely had enough room since there were more of them.

Then the cat again disappeared for a long time. I thought he had gone after girl cats and I wasn't worried that something had happened to him. Then one day, a day like any other, I was walking through our village and what should I see before my eyes? I saw Kot's tail, then Kot's fur, then I took a closer look. It was a Kyrgyz from there, who had made a fur cap for himself out of my cat and was strutting around with it on his head. "Kooot!" I screamed and burst into tears. "Kooot! How could you, you wretched scourge, make yourself a fur cap out of our beloved Kotovsky?" Kot had become like a member of our family and Kot had known it. "How could you kill him and turn my little Kot into a fur cap? Our dear little Kotty! Kot, why, Kot?" I wailed until the Kyrgyz understood why I was crying and he said something to me in his language, but I had a feeling he was swearing at me. His wife, by contrast, didn't say anything, she didn't speak a single word.

They walked off, I followed them at a bit of a distance, calling my cat, whose tail swished in time to the Kyrgyz's steps. I was waiting for him to come down from the Kyrgyz's head and jump into my arms so we could go home together and I could give him as much bread as he wanted! "Do you remember, dear Kot, how

you survived the great hunger on the train, when Grannie Anghelina said you weren't fit to eat, and you also survived the famine in
Kazakhstan, hiding in the steppe from hungry people? And now,
my beloved cat, now, when there's less hunger, and life's not as
hard, when you found your catmate, who's maybe even given you
kittens in some hay pile, how could you let yourself be made into
a fur cap by an evil Kyrgyz?" The Kyrgyz family wearing my cat
reached their house. The Kyrgyz with my beloved Kotovsky covering his pate yelled something at me again, I thought he wanted
to beat me up as well, but his wife pulled him inside the house.
"Give me my cat back!" I screamed through my tears. Some of
our people who understood why I was crying came and took me
home. I told them, too, how Kot saved my life, how he'd bring us
mice, I told them how much I loved him. The people were quiet,
than someone said: "All that matters is we're healthy." Maybe they
were surprised at how many tears I shed over a cat, because they
didn't wail that way even over their parents, even their children.
I understood and calmed down a bit. I cried some more when
Mother came home, together we remembered the things our poor
little Kot would do.

A few days later, I found Kot's fur at the door to our hut. I was
glad and buried him not far from us. Later, many people told me
that they found cats and ate them during the first years of deportation, now no one eats cats anymore, but back then everyone ate
whatever they could find. But no one could eat my Kot, because he
looked at you as if he were human and could tell when your intentions were bad, he'd run and no one could catch him. And that's
what people who were my friends and from my village said to me,
as if it were a given! They, my dear Bucovinians, would've wanted
to eat my cat but they couldn't catch him! What's the point then of
getting mad at a Kyrgyz archfiend? But the Bucovinians would've
killed him because of their great hunger, not out of vanity, to wear

him on their head afterward, now that we had returned from Siberia with his silky and shiny fur, from getting his fill of fish . . .

❦

When Mother first asked me what I wanted to be and where I wanted to study, I said "a milk maid, like you," certain that she'd be pleased with my answer. I sincerely believed, after having learned to drink milk with our straws, that you were safest from hunger only by the side of a cow, and that there was nothing better in the world than fresh, warm milk! I was still a child and having milk in the house seemed like supreme happiness to me. I also liked the calves, I'd play with them, it's true that I didn't care for being up to my knees in manure, but that could be cleaned off, it dries, the smell didn't bother me. You don't die of hunger if you're a milk-maid, I reckoned to myself. Mother, however, didn't jump for joy, as I thought she would, she sighed and her chin trembled a bit, as if what I had said were a cause for tears. I didn't understand what I had said wrong to make her face fall that way. "A milkmaid, you say," she repeated, thoughtfully. "But times are not so hard any-more, we can go to the store and buy what we want, even sugar, the rubles will add up in our pockets as well . . ."

She was quiet for a moment, then said: "What would your father have said if he were here to hear you, him, a school prin-cipal, with his beloved daughter who dreams of becoming a milkmaid? With older brothers who are doctors, lawyers, engi-neers. And you're the only milkmaid."

"Is that bad, Mother?" I asked, ashamed, trying to imagine my brothers dressed in beautiful, elegant clothes, and me, as I was then, patched up, in rags, and a milkmaid to boot. I found it hard to imagine and I didn't really understand how I was wrong.

"It's not bad, my dear. Whoever works lives to see another day.

If that's what the Lord ordains and you're satisfied . . . But I say you shouldn't be so quick to choose your profession, and should attend more school first. We travel far in these cold and distant steppes and we don't know what fate awaits us tomorrow, so consider what you'd do if there were no cows around. Because to milk a cow you don't need much expertise or schooling, all the farmers' wives do it, but maybe if you learn something else too, so you can make a decent living wherever you go, a bit easier and without having to steep in the stench of manure. There are many good things to do in this world, and from every good trade, no matter how small, if the gold coins don't flow, at least some will fall."

I agreed with my mother, such a tenderhearted and wise woman. She didn't speak of it any more, but I began to think about it on my own. I quickly settled on the idea of being a seamstress, it was enough to walk into the classroom and see beautifully dressed children, in expensive clothes, because they had more money, and poor children, barely dressed to cover their bodies, with few resources but sometimes with taste. In fact, I wasn't the only one who thought of this idea. After I returned from fishing, they called us back to school for about a month, I went without Eugen this time. When I asked my desk mate what she wanted to be when she got older, she answered as if everything had already been decided: "I'm going to be a seamstress, there's a school not far from us *deportees*," she stressed that word. "They accept us there, because they won't take us at the institute, we're not allowed, my sister wanted to be a doctor, but she didn't get in, they wouldn't accept her and she went to that school there, she said it was good, they have dorms, they feed you, you also get experience working at a factory, and they hand you papers, which you can use to go wherever you want. People always need all kinds of dresses and clothes, a good seamstress never dies of hunger. You should come too," she urged me. "You embroider so beautifully, you're a born seamstress!" I immediately accepted and we agreed on going together to that school which was somewhere called Kant. I told Mother and she seemed to cheer up a bit. In her opinion, it was better to be a seamstress than a milkmaid. She said: "It's a good thing to have a trade, it will come in handy, maybe times will change and you'll be able to continue your studies, but having a good trade never hurts. You can milk cows at any point, if there's ever a need." Almost all us girls who were deported together studied at that school for seamstresses. After I came back, I worked a bit more at our "The Way to Communism" kolkhoz, I'd help Mother out, I'd tend the calves, they'd sometimes take us out in brigades for construction work, but we still managed to exchange new patterns for suits and dresses among ourselves. So many of us there were seamstresses that we couldn't really find anyone to hire us, we did whatever work we could, but we came up with new designs on paper and dreamed about the time when we could use them to sew real dresses. A little while later, people began returning to their homelands and a kind-hearted classmate called me over to Moldova, to her village, where she was about to open a tailoring shop, a "services cooperative," and I went there, because they needed workers and I needed a roof over my head and a place of employment.

Sevasta, Eugen's cousin, and her family had been on the same train as us but in another railcar. Her family had been seized one day earlier and the relatives didn't know what had happened to each other. Eugen moved in with them after his grandmother, Grannie Anghelina, died. Sevasta was on the ugly side, a bit hunched over, and she walked with a limp. She was also as skinny as a thread, and kept her long hair in a braid. She was well past twenty years old, gone was the time for marrying, and who would have her now, as she was? *The grass is past mowing, her beauty is past growing, well, her eyes are nice and her clothes are fine*, as our saying goes. But she was a modest, hardworking girl, she always had her head bent over something she was sewing on her sewing machine, to help her family who supported her, to not be a burden to those around her. On June thirteenth, when all the mothers were loading up things to eat and expensive objects that might help them survive, dear Sevasta took her sewing machine. That machine was a lifesaver, she really helped out her family and the needy people around her! Her machine got her through the entire famine and all those hardships. She was hardworking, honest, with a good heart and a spotless soul! All the deportees came to her, from their yurt, from the neighboring villages, and she'd help and please everyone. We weren't given clothes, not a chance, they'd barely give us a slice of bread! Our clothes got old, they turned into rags, ripped, she'd sew them, put in a patch, repair whatever she could however she could. She also helped the Kyrgyz, and the Kazakhs, and the Russians, whoever would come for help. After the war, the brother of the president of the kolkhoz, a handsome Russian, returned to the village, he saw our Sevasta, fell in love with her, and married her. The village was full of young and beautiful women, each more beautiful than the other, the country was full of them, but he chose our Sevasta out of them all. And so what if she limped a bit, and he had lost a hand in the war? They were a beautiful couple and we were overjoyed that at least one of our girls, a deportee considered an "enemy" by everyone, found here, far from her country, happiness. And now Sevasta helped those around her even more zealously, and she put in a good word at the kolkhoz, and didn't forget them when the gifts were distributed. And her kind-hearted husband nearly surrounded himself with hardworking Bucovinians who made the kolkhoz better. He didn't treat them as foreigners. Then Sevasta had a baby girl, then a boy, sturdy, healthy, with two hands, two feet, it was a great joy for the parents. Great is the Lord and great His reward for the worthy and obedient. Then Eugen left, to search for his family. I think that it was because of her example that we, all the young girls, dreamed of becoming seamstresses. Beautiful memories, beautiful places . . .

—Cuţa Ana, what places, where are you now? I can't always tell when and where you're talking about.

—In Kant, my dear, I'm in Kant. There where I went to school for a year and a bit. I got a skirt there, I mean I bought myself one, then I rode on the swing carousel, a big wheel, it's a common sight for you now, but then was the first time I'd even seen one and I was amazed and happy, and after all that, I still had a few rubles left, maybe five. I had received money for our work practicum, because they put us to work for two months and they gave us money.

—What is this Kant, Great Gran? An aul as well?

—A town, my treasure, not an aul, a beautiful town. It was far from us.

—Kant? Was it built by our Moldovans from Cantemir?

—Well I don't know, maybe. It was a lovely town with a really good school for seamstresses and with a factory where they accepted us for a practicum and they gave us diplomas which allowed us to work anywhere in the Soviet Union. It wasn't far from Kazakhstan, the Kyrgyz called it "the sweet town," on account of the sugar factories there, but we weren't interested in sugar, though that's where I ate my first piece of candy in exile! We didn't pay money for it, they had taken us on a school trip, so we could see how the nation of happy workers labored, as if we had descended there from fluffy pillows, not from cleaning barns and chopping down trees and repairing train tracks. Well, there weren't that many of us and after they had shown us through that factory, it seemed really interesting to us, it was the first time we were seeing something like that, we each received a piece of candy.

Kant was a small town, not far from the city of Frunze, the capital of Kyrgyzstan, which was named after a brave Moldovan, Mihai Frunză, who had once been deported there. Then this Frunză fought heroically in the war and he rose very high up, but I didn't make it to his city. Studying with us were lots of Moldovans and a couple Bucovinians, a few Russians, Ukrainians, and then all the Asiatic peoples. There, I no longer mixed up Tajiks, Uzbeks, and Uyghurs, or Dargins, who even have a Republic of Dagestan, I knew who was Korean, who was Bashkir. I knew them all. The language of instruction was Russian for everyone, and when I arrived in Moldova, I had no problems, we understood each other in sewing very well, because the girls in Troiţa also studied in Russian, only at Tiraspol. Almost all the professional schools were taught in Russian and you could find work more easily. *Podkladka, vyshivka, nakidka*, words which all of us in Moldova understand, but which my Bucovinian grandparents didn't know, words like that weren't used there. Hard times teach you everything! Everyone did as best they could, it's a good thing I studied at that school and then had an easier life, because it was very hard for a girl to find easier work.

We went by train to the town of Kant. I don't like traveling by train either. Not a single train doesn't remind me of our long journey, of the terrible thirst and the wait for the doors to open for a drop of water or for the dead to be thrown out wherever they might land, of that musty, stale smell, that rumble of wheels which remained in our ears long after the railroad had ended and we waited there, abandoned to our fate. I like going by horse and wagon. For a while now more horses and wagons have reappeared in our Troiţa. People today now go to markets in their wagons again, like in olden days. My husband also wanted a horse. I no

longer want anything, where would I, an old woman, ride off
alone? It's better for me to wait for death in my own home than to
go looking for it on unknown roads.

Everyone said that the best school for seamstresses was in Kant,
I went, I learned, then I started working, so we could pay off our
schooling and get experience. That's how it was done back then,
theory as well as practice. I worked in that small town, a big city
for us, who were accustomed to the scattered auls and desolate
kishtaks of Kazakhstan and Siberia. I worked, praise God, because
I could, everywhere, on the railroad, and on the farm, and out
in the fields, and out on the water fishing, and hauling garbage
(voluntary and safe work but which paid very poorly). I'd work so
that we'd have a bit of bread to eat. We didn't realize how poor we
were, we had forgotten how rich our lives had once been in our
Bucovinian home, we remembered only the deprivation from the
beginning of our trials. Mother would laugh at our poverty and
say: "We have a horseshoe, all we need is three more and a horse."
We didn't have many clothes, at first none at all, then a single
dress, but I felt like I had everything I needed. Mother wore a pair
of ugly felt boots both summer and winter, she was dressed so
simply, but she was happy for me when I got my first dress.

Now we have everything again, everyone has lots of clothes
crammed into their closets, even their attics, all kinds of different
objects, but I still dream about that simple dress, the first one Mother
bought me so that I'd have something to wear to school. The smell of
ermen tea and the taste of the balanda that would warm your hands
and body. That Siberian winter when I'd go to the neighboring yurt
to school, barely able to trudge through the snow. And in March,
we'd celebrate *Navruz Bayram*, the coming of spring, alongside the
Kazakhs. They were joyful, we were joyful too. Another winter was
over and, behold, we weren't dead yet. It was hard living there, but
we knew how to enjoy every moment, little things. But now, when

we have it all and things are going well for us, it's as if something were missing. Little pleasures, a simple life, don't give us the satisfaction they once did. I feel this weight on my heart sometimes.

At the trade school, I made a friend, Varvara Țărnă, a Moldovan woman from Bessarabia. I went to stay with her afterward, when I didn't know where to return to. Varvara had been deported together with her family and tens of thousands of other Bessarabian families on the same day as us. Her entire family had died, but she wasn't sad and closed off, instead talkative and cheerful. Our young seamstresses took notice of the boys from a construction school, not far from our school. One day, Varvara showed up on the arm of a handsome boy with blue eyes, a Russian, I thought. "Constantin Cojoharov," he introduced himself. And Varvara smiled, triumphant and happy that she found, here in the middle of the steppe, a true Moldovan! The boy didn't know a single word in Romanian, he spoke only Russian.

"What does Cojoharov mean?" we poked.

"It comes from Koja-horde, meaning Koja's army, and Koja means master!" the boy said proudly, though Russian was written in his papers and he looked anything but Kazakh.

"What are you talking about?" Varvara said, getting upset. "You never heard of a cojoc, mister cojoc maker? Just listen to him, Horde-koja-bai! Go back and ask your grandmother want kind of *horde* you are."

He had never heard of a cojoc, but he did ask his grandmother. Varvara later told me that of course he was one of us, from Sturzeni, a village in northern Bessarabia. His parents no longer remembered this, but his grandparents, who had come here during the time of the tsar, did. It's a good thing his grandmother was still alive, otherwise he would've considered himself part of Koja's army, both him and all his descendants, if Varvara hadn't run into him. In the end, she took Cojoc-bai-the-Moldovan to be her husband, I danced at their wedding, they were the witnesses at ours. Varvara didn't stay in Troiţa long, because she had a husband with a Russian passport, which allowed him to go to Chişinău, and she got a job at Zorile, the best shoe factory in Moldova.

When we finished school in Kant, Varvara brought a piece of paper from her sovkhoz, named "Serghei Lazo" after the revolutionary from that area, in the village of Troiţa de Sus, Orhei County, the Soviet Socialist Republic of Moldova, saying that they needed seamstresses there and would guarantee them a job and place to live. I was lucky that Varvara had them write me a similar piece of paper, with my name on it, because it came in very handy when I left, when I didn't have any other form of identification. And when I arrived in that village, I really did receive a job and a place to live, just as it said in the document.

I was once on a train, with many other girls, they had sent us to build a road, because they didn't need seamstresses, in the meantime I was looking out the window, amazed: Good Lord, all these crosses! There were many of them, all along the train tracks, all the same, narrow, tall, made from light-colored wood. Varvara looked as well and she didn't see anything. I looked out the window again: "Now do you see them? Look how many there are, I can hardly count them, there's one and another one, a whole row, even two rows, do you see them now?" She looked again and again, she didn't see anything. She thought she couldn't see them for who knows what reason, who knows what kind of blindness she might have, and she went over to our girls and said: "Look out the window." And the girls looked.

"Do you see crosses along the railroad?" No, not one of them did, not a single cross. But I saw them even in the cities, where they were taking us to go work. They had been raised for those who had died there. Varvara said not to tell anyone so they wouldn't think I was crazy. From time to time she'd ask: "And here, are there crosses in this spot?"

"Here no, but a little farther off" and I'd show her where. I didn't end up living in a city because of those crosses. I didn't see crosses in villages. Or rather I saw them but the ones others saw too, where was fitting, in the cemeteries.

I prayed to God to help the souls of those dead people who were thrown out wherever they happened to land, without crosses. I prayed to the Lord to open the eyes of others as well, of those who were more powerful and were from there. The second time I passed through, after years, I again saw crosses on the side of the road. I asked my children: "Do you see these crosses?"

"We see them," the children answered and I asked them to describe them for me, so I could be sure we were seeing the same thing. Then more crosses appeared and again I asked: "Do you see them now too?"

"Mama, there aren't any crosses here, you're imagining things!"

The crosses they didn't see were made from light-colored wood, narrow and taller, exactly like the first ones I had seen so many years ago, during the time of exile. Great is Your mercy, Lord, and how much work there is still left to do on this earth! Many eyes to open and many hearts. I prayed the whole way, I prayed long after that as well, I pray even now, I light candles for the souls of the dead. If God shows me the crosses that should have been placed there, it's a sign. My heart mourned that I couldn't change that sign, that I couldn't do anything. That I have to bear on my shoulders this burden of knowing of the dead who had disappeared, un-Christian-like, from among the living, without the comfort of at least a candle at their head, but especially without crosses on their graves. That those crosses, that only I have been given to see, follow me around, they pursue me and ask for justice.

Forgive me, Lord, that I didn't right then stop the trains, the journeys, the trips, when I was young and had my strength, that I didn't get off in those places and I didn't yell to those around who wanted and were able to see and hear: "Place crosses here, good people! At the heads of the Christians who suffered the cruel scourge though they were completely innocent! Because if you dig here, just below the surface, you'll find many bones! And dig here as well, just below the surface, and you'll find hundreds of other bones! The dead don't ask for much, they only want a cross on their grave! A tall one, narrow, from light-colored wood!"

Forgive me, Lord, that when I could have yelled this to the people whose eyes were closed and whose souls were captive to those sins, I was scared by Your signs and I didn't listen, I'm listening now, but I'm overcome by old age. So many crosses have gathered around me that I could build an entire country with only them!

I was in the city of Kant and then later in Khabarovsk, the city we called "Hubbub." In Kant I studied, in Khabarovsk I worked, I went there in search of Eugen and Zânel, Sancira's lost son. Mother had moved on from this fleeting life to the eternal one, I had been left all alone, I missed Eugen, he was all that remained for me. I searched for him throughout Siberia, for years I waited for him, then I, too, came back. Word from him never reached me, except much later. After his grandmother had died, may God forgive Grannie Anghelina, he stayed with his cousin Sevasta in the neighboring aul, but he never stopped searching for his family. Siberia is vast, there was a lot of construction, roads, railways, entire cities, with tall apartment buildings, factories, and plants, a lot of work for deportees. When some of them died, others were brought in.

But I was afraid of those places. Siberia: the word alone inspired fear in me, all I could see were skeletons on the side of the new roads, next to the tall houses that shone in the sun. All traces of the deportees who had worked there had been erased, the barracks, the barbed wire to keep them from running away, but I truly saw the thrown out bodies, as I had on the day I found out about my mother's death, as I was working on the railway. You can stroll through one of these brand new cities, and your jaw drop in amazement, what buildings, what great socialist achievements! Who cares anymore what sacrifices it took to build them all, how many people died so that these state successes could be raised. That's why I don't like cities. I don't like Siberia. It's full of the restless, unburied dead, dead before their time, whose souls float next to these great achievements, because they died without a Christian burial and can't find peace, their troubled souls will wander, waiting for the justice and Christian reckoning that they deserve. This waiting of the dead unsettles me. We're not doing anything to ask for their forgiveness, nothing to help them arrive on their shore, a cross somewhere, a candle. Siberia is full of the dead. From hunger, from thirst, from heat, from exhaustion, from longing, from cruelty, from injustice, from the indifference of those in power.

In time, the Bucovinians started heading toward our dear Bucovina. I wasn't given a passport then, because I wasn't old enough yet, we didn't have enough money for the tickets either, and when Mother and I were just about to leave, even without passports, a couple of our people came back, and what they told us put us off wanting to leave. There was a great famine there, as well as in Moldova, the people were bloated from hunger, they ate weeds. The friends of the people had gathered all their wheat, they had even swept their floor, so that not even an ear would somehow remain, everyone was left without provisions, there had been a drought that year, what had been put in the earth hadn't really come up, it was a very small harvest, and the big bosses took almost everything. With spears they poked around in the ground, in piles of hay, in search of hidden grain, everything was taken from hungry families. Whoever still had carpets, farming tools, would sell them for a handful of wheat . . . If you were to go through the starving villages and somehow still find living human beings, you'd be afraid to look at what they were boiling in their pots. The Lord preserve and protect us, but you could find even the fingers of children . . . Thefts and crimes were flourishing, a Moldovan told us how in a deserted yard in his village, he saw with his own eyes a large pot with human bones inside, fingers with nails. He was horrified, he still had nightmares. He left everything and came back here. We were completely terrified and heartbroken when we heard!

Our fellow Bucovinians told us that our village didn't even exist, New Albina was now in Romania, and our Old Albina had been split into two and added to other villages, the people who lived there had left, some of their own free will, others, like us, forced into carts. Some of the landowners from neighboring villages, when they returned, even if there was nothing left of their former farm, came to an understanding with the village president, they brought a little something, their relatives were quick to help them, they were allowed to settle there. But they lived in fear, because if you complained, you were immediately pointed east and urged to go back where you came from, because Siberia was missing you and you hadn't been allowed by the state to return, but came like a fugitive and criminal. And in the border zone no one could enter without a special permit, and you could only get a permit if you had a passport, you'd be thrown in jail without papers. Someone said that even with a passport they didn't really grant those permits, you had to bring a carpet, a sheep, and that was hard to do even if you had half your family there. But what could you do if you didn't have anyone there, if you didn't have either a carpet or a sheep to give? No one was waiting for us in Albina, or anywhere else . . . When leaving, when they finally released us, because many had already fled however they could, they asked: "Did you do your duty to the Soviet regime?" What duty? From that Kazakh aul we had to indicate a location where we had received approval to go. It was possible in Moldova, in Bucovina, no . . . Lucky for me I had that piece of paper from Troiţa de Sus . . .

But we were even more terrified by the fate of the two Ukrainian or Polish sisters who wanted to go near Lviv, which wasn't that far from our Cernăuţi. After the war, people began returning, some with legal documents, but that was only a handful of people, most simply took off, fewer with actual train tickets and more with faith in God and in people's compassion. The journey was expensive and they paid us little, what you got for working in Siberia or the Kazakh steppes wasn't enough, you couldn't even dream of having enough money for a ticket home! Not everyone was lucky, we didn't know how everyone who had left reached their destination or if they reached it. Those who returned told us all kinds of stories.

And the sisters from near Lemberg-Lviv were unlucky, they had papers, people said, but enough money to reach home, not so much. They got on a train that seemed to be a freight train, where they were told that, yes, they could get on, without money, without a ticket, because they were all people and they understood. They locked them inside a corner of a railcar and men took turns going in, the train was in motion, no one heard the girls screaming, asking for help or mercy. Then, when they were half dead, they were thrown from the train. If it had been near a human settlement, the youngest would have survived as well, but there wasn't a soul in sight, only cold, desolate fields . . . The youngest died from massive loss of blood, there on the steppe, the oldest was never in her right mind again. Kind people from another train caught her, because she was afraid of everyone and ran through the fields, and brought her back to our kishtak, since she had papers from our kolkhoz. She screamed, would say something, moan, she had to be taken to some hospital, people understood more or less what had happened and were horrified, especially us, the less experienced young girls, it completely put us off venturing on a train without a ticket and without humane people around us. I had also traveled by ship and was very afraid, because I had seen things, now I heard that in trains as well those who are defenseless can be abused, and I wasn't in a hurry to head home, no matter how much I missed it.

I once saw that girl too, I had gone to school with her sister, in the same class, the younger sister who had died. Then the older one died as well. Some said she had been very sick, some said she had ended her days, a great sin, but her mind was no longer with her. Forgive her, Lord, for she knew not what she did. We were terrified at the thought of getting into freight trains, without people at the windows and without tickets. How costly was the journey home, how costly our precious Bucovina had become!

Mom, did I tell you? I talked to Annie on Skype twice. That Delia, supposedly her best friend! She started making moves on our Eugen, to steal him from under Annie's nose! That she wanted to show him around Bucovina, in her car, to take him everywhere! That she was a real Bucovinian, right from Rădăuți, not like that Moldovan from Chișinău! No, we're the real Bucovinians—not her with her car! Annie was yelling and crying so much as she was talking that it echoed through the house. And right then Cuţa came in and heard everything. She told her that our soul and our roots are from Rădăuţi and the soul is greater than the body, and roots are most important of all! Then Cuţa asked Annie if it was just as hot there as it was here. We chat in here all day long, because it's boiling outside now and inside the house it's cool. "It's sweltering, you melt from the heat," Annie answered.

"And there are churches in Iaşi, isn't that so?"

"We have many and beautiful ones," Annie said as if Iaşi had been her city since always.

"Then go inside a church so you can cool off a bit."

"I will," Annie said. And after we logged off Skype, Cuţa said to me: "Let us pray!" And how we prayed, Mom! Cuţa's icons were shaking from the sound of our voices! And after that, I talked with Annie again and what do you know? Prayer actually works! Our Ana went inside the church of St. Parascheva, to cool off or maybe to pray, everyone was kneeling, she got on her knees too, because she wasn't going to be the only one standing, sticking out like a sore thumb, and next to her Eugen shows up, the sweetie, and they whispered together there, because you can't talk out loud in church, both of them on their knees, and right there he asked her to be his wife. I'm telling you quickly, so you know! Cuţa is off in her corner crying for some reason. But I thought I'd tell you quick and then see what there would be to cry about here.

Now I'm going to throw out that stinky chunk of moth repellent! You know how funky Cuţa's house smelled! I thought that's how the houses of old people smelled, until I found out what was giving off that strong odor, it was a big, white chunk, like a bar of soap, a stinky moth bar hidden deep inside the couch in the main house. "Cuţa, look at what was stinking to high heaven! Let's get these chemicals out of the house and keep only the basil here! I like the smell of basil." Cuţa has two big bushes in her garden, they're green now, but they turn brownish when they dry out. And Cuţa said: "Well your mother put that soap there to keep moths away. You're the ones bringing it here and you're also the ones who think it stinks!" I took it out and I thought about moving it to the attic, or should I just toss it, what do you say? Isn't it expired?

⟿

I graduated from the school for seamstresses, I worked ·for a bit, and I returned to Mother. Life was easier. But I still came down with the yellows, I also had dysentery, like almost everyone else, I was staring death in the face, but I survived. A winter before that, I was almost mowed down by typhus. But God didn't abandon me. I got through the yellows as well and was thinking of finding a more suitable workplace. Our life had barely begun to get sorted, we had finally started being able to save up money, when a car stopped outside our door and they took me to the police station. Mother was at work, but people told her and she dropped everything to come see why I had been arrested. They told her that I was being deployed to the frontline of work, that I'd receive money as well, that I had to. Because we hadn't been brought there to live like kings, to become rich, but as a punishment.

They sent us to work building railroads. So what if I had just finished studying to be a seamstress? The fatherland needed railroads more! We formed various brigades, of girls, of boys, younger, older, about thirty people in each brigade. We worked Monday through Saturday, and Saturday evening they allowed us to return home, we lived there in barracks not far from the work site, half tent, half hut, we had gotten through even tougher times. Here we hauled cement, we dug, whatever we were given to do. We were extending the ends of the rail lines and building parallel tracks, we had plenty of work to do. They'd bring us water and food by car from a neighboring aul, they didn't stuff us but it was no longer just the thin slice of bread from during the war. And they even paid us, that's why no one ran away from there and we worked diligently. I had worked for free for so long, and now that I was being paid, why should I avoid it?

My dear little mother had lost a lot of weight, she could barely do the odd job, but we were short on many things, winter was around the corner, an extra ruble wouldn't hurt at all. Mother would wait for me on Saturdays with food ready, she'd cuddle me, advise me not to slave away, so I wouldn't drop dead from the work, to eat well. I told her they fed us there every day, the work wasn't hard at all, and look, I even brought some money home. At night, after we went to bed, I could hear her sighing in her sleep. On Sunday she'd ask me to read from the Bible, I'd read for hours on end. First, her favorite passages, which she knew and wanted to hear once more, then something that I hadn't read for a long time and she'd listen quietly, paying close attention. She could no longer see the letters, she could no longer read on her own, she stopped embroidering, she kept getting thinner. "Mother, do you only eat when I'm home?"

"I eat, I eat," she assured me. She never complained about anything hurting her, she never wanted anything. No, wait, she did. A month after I left, she said she'd like me to bring her a sugar cube, because she was craving something sweet, not a lot, not something expensive, a single cube. She had never asked me for anything before and I said to myself that I'd buy her one as soon as I returned on Saturday.

I thought about that sugar cube every day, I was afraid I might somehow forget, I tied black thread around two fingers so I'd remember. At night, when I was in bed, I'd dream I went into the store in the neighboring aul, which was bigger and better stocked, they had sugar there too. I asked for a sugar cube. One? the saleswoman asked. No, two, I said. One melts in your mouth too quickly, two is better, no, make it three, because Mother won't take two, she'll make me take one, how could she eat two and me not have any? So three. I don't think three sugar cubes will cost more than a ruble. Mother will say: what a waste of money! For only three small sugar cubes! But she'll be glad. She'll keep the sugar in her mouth for a long time, until it melts. I'd fall asleep happy dreaming about this and I'd have a sweet taste in my mouth, as if I had a sugar cube under my tongue. I was counting the days and could hardly wait for it to be Saturday. Time passed slowly.

Slaving away next to us were also prisoners of war from the Romanian army, some of them from northern Bucovina. That's where I met Nestor Arboroasa from Cupca, and Ananie Bujeniță and Florea Crăiuță from Suceveni. They were beaten by the wind, hungry, exhausted, and they asked me for bread. I didn't have any that day, but the next day I brought them what I could.

One morning, a train arrived on the old train track. We were working close by and they told us not to come up to it because it was full of dangerous criminals. The train didn't have windows, but the doors opened and I could see it was shadows and skeletons that were so weak they could barely move and barely had enough voice left to moan. I thought about how we were also called criminals and enemies. I walked onto the platform, thinking that I might see people I knew from Bucovina among those who were brought there. The railcars weren't even bolted the way they once were. When the train stopped, two armed soldiers jumped down from the steps of each railcar. They went into every railcar and took out the dead bodies, they'd swing them far away so they wouldn't land under the train and block the train track. I felt such pity that I stood there with tears in my eyes. I remembered our train, our dead, thrown out the same way . . .

A girl from our brigade came up to me and said that someone from our aul was looking for me. "If you see her, tell her where I am," I said to her. I watched as the dead were flung from the train and cried. *We'll bury them,* I thought to myself, *and we'll set up crosses, though we don't even know their names.* The others turned their backs so they wouldn't see, but I watched and cried. Someone grabbed me by the shoulders and hugged me, it was a Bucovinian from our region, also brought here to work for the benefit of the fatherland.

"Do you pity them?"

"Look how they're flung, the poor people, look how they're thrown out!"

"Don't cry for others, you should feel pity for yourself and cry for your mother."

She didn't say another word, she didn't need to, I didn't want to hear any more, I didn't want to believe it, I didn't want to think of it. I dropped everything, I ran as fast as I could to the head of the brigade to drive me to the aul in his car, he took me, I bought sugar there, I borrowed money since I hadn't gotten paid yet, a ruble was enough, I bought a small box, with ten sugar cubes, because they didn't sell them individually, I was glad, I hoped that if I bought more, my mother would have more to live. I raced home. "Mother, Mother!" I yelled. Silence, nothing was different in our room. Mother was sitting with her hands in her lap, I don't know if someone had set her that way or she was leaning there on her own. Only her head seemed to bend too far to one side. She didn't normally hold her head that way. I went up to her, I shook her and hugged her. "Mother, look how much sugar I brought you! Wake up, open your eyes!" Mother's full weight fell on me and I had to hold her so she wouldn't fall to the ground. I laid her down on the bed, I put a sugar cube in each of her hands, I tried to put one in her mouth. "How can you die when you have such delicacies?" I left her the sugar, so she could enjoy it at least in the next world.

No one in this world is more alone than the person left without a mother. I didn't have anyone by my side, I didn't have my own family yet, a husband, children, to lean on in that difficult moment. I didn't know what to do and how to go on living. I cried, I wailed, because I was left all alone in this strange land, as if God in heaven didn't want to hear me. I couldn't stand the thought of letting Mother sleep in the Kazakh earth. When so many had returned to Bucovina and we were just about to go back as well!

Lord Jesus Christ, have mercy on us! Holy Mary, Mother of God, pray for us sinners. Pain brings blessings to those who endure it, we suffer because God loves us. Overwhelming sorrow is harmful and damaging. Don't indulge yourself and don't spare yourself. God, heal my soul! Lord, strengthen my faith! Lord, with Your holy grace, revive my soul which is crushed by despair! At least lift me up as high as a young cherry tree, so I can laugh at the serpents that seek to strike my heels. At least lift me up a head above the rotten stench of this filthy lice-ridden bedding so I may fill my lungs with the fragrance of heaven and come back to life. Oh Lord, my hope in hopelessness! Oh Lord, my strength in weakness! Lord, my light in the darkness! How feeble are the heavens and the earth! My soul is mere smoke and ash, if You, my morning dew, vanish and abandon it. Because to You, Lord, together with the Father and the Holy Spirit, belong all honor and worship, now and until the end of the ages. Amen.

Get up, Mother, and send us word about the way to the other world.
The road is long and broken, the way back home unspoken.
The road is long and winding, the way back home past finding!
Turn into a bird of the air and fly through the ground, up out of there,
Turn into a bird so lovely and fly home with me!

Tell me, Mother, do, and I'll come out to welcome you,
I'll clear a pathway through and plant some basil too!
Mother, tell me why you ever had to say goodbye!

Longing, whoever grows you, years of aging will undo.
Longing, whoever loses you, with this living world is through.
Longing for my sisters, brothers, I'd ride my horse through forest covers.
Longing for my mother sweet, I'd ride my horse through cold and heat.
Longing for my father dear, I'd ride my horse through darkest fear.

Get up and look me in the eyes, speak to me your words so wise,
Because ever since you died, this world I can't abide.
I'm left here all alone, without a joy, without a home.

Juniper and lavender, it's hard without a father,
But even worse without a mother.
The day of Mother's decease was the day that mercy ceased.
Mercy at the hands of strangers is full of unknown dangers.

Home I tried to run away, but the Kazakhs made me stay.
So I stayed for three more years, without Mother and in tears.
When permission to go they gave, I first stopped by her grave.
I knelt down on the ground, my words in tears were drowned:
Mother, mother, please come out
And take me home, you know the route,
Do not abandon me, a lonely deportee!
Oh, oh!

PART THREE

ROADSIDE CROSSES

Oh train, you black machine, cursed by all as something unclean.
I've cursed you as well when to my village I said farewell. Oh!
For my village I long, where brothers and sisters get along.
There's no one here to visit me, I'm as alone as I can be . . .
Beautiful oak, friend, just a little lower bend,
So I can climb up your height and of my village catch sight, oh,
My beloved neighborhood, in which I spent my childhood.
I've been left alone in the world, and its name for ages not heard . . .
To the Lord we prayed that our journey home could be made,
To our Bucovina dear, green as a garden, full of cheer.
When home we finally came, boards were nailed to the doorframe
And Stalinists we had to obey, in our own houses we couldn't stay.
God on us will take pity and save us from the committee.
Listen to what I say: the red star will fade away
And in its place will rise the splendid cross of Christ.
And at that time, my friend, joyous days will come again!
Oh! Oh!

That tiny baby crying in the next railcar when they took us to the ends of the earth was probably my very own cousin, little Profira, Sancira's youngest daughter. Who would have thought we'd be on the same train! Sancira had three children, all younger than me, Dochiţa who was six, Zenovie (Zânelu), three, and Profiruca, just a couple months old. I don't even want to think about how this cousin of mine was thrown out from the train. Of course, auntie Sancira didn't throw her out through the latrine. No, surely not, no. Then, when they left us out alone on the steppe, no one really wanted the women with small children, so first the women without children were taken, then those with children who were bigger and could be put to work, then the others, with whiny little children or sick, old grandparents who could barely stand, they took later, maybe on the trucks that were waiting, maybe on those terribly ugly camels. We barely managed to say two words to each other, and they already split us up. About once a year news of how she was would reach me, I'd find out that she, and the two children who were left, were still alive. At first she worked at a kolkhoz near us, then she left for places farther away.

I don't know why the Kazakhs' kolkhozes were so far away from the villages, from where the people lived. If you walked, it could take you more than two hours. It was only an hour from us, but Sancira's village was farther. A car would pick the people up in the morning and bring them back in the evening or people would walk. In the evening, the women would also bring their children something to eat because they hadn't seen them all day. In that village, even the drinking water was far away, and Sancira's daughter, Dochiţa, would go to the well with a little bucket every day, and Zânelu, her younger brother, waited at home.

One day, when Sancira was far away at the farm, and Dochiţa had also gone far away for water, a commission from who knows where came to the village in a truck and picked up all the children left alone, to take them to the orphanage as *besprizornaya*, meaning they were homeless and parentless. Some they took off the street, others from huts, some weren't home alone but with grandparents, who ran after that wretched truck crying and screaming, but it was no use, the truck filled with children and disappeared. The entire village found out. Dochiţa came back but her brother was nowhere to be found. Sancira returned, her beloved son wasn't there. She didn't have money for the journey, she wasn't allowed to just leave her work, she didn't know where to look for her child. Dochiţa was also little and her mother was afraid that someone might steal her too one day.

After my mother died, I went to my aunt so we could search for our Zenovie together. There were other mothers searching as we were, they'd all help each other, they'd exchange information, Sancira, finally, found the orphanage, she had been able to trace where the truck had gone, but finding a child then was harder than finding a needle in a haystack. On the lists and in the children's documents, there wasn't a single Bucovinian, everyone being divided into two nationalities: those with narrow eyes, Kazakhs; the others, Russians. All the boys were Ivanov or Petrov, with first names like Ivan, Kosta, Gena, Grisha, given at random, because no one cared what they were called back home, and the little children themselves couldn't say what their names were, because they didn't speak a word of Russian and, in any case, no one cared. Their ages weren't written down correctly either, just made up. Many were skinny and seemed younger. When Sancira saw this, she was determined to look at all of them, so she could recognize her child's face on her own. She went child by child, but she didn't find hers.

"Oh well," those in charge there said, "we didn't have room for so many children and some of them were taken to the orphanage in Kyzylorda." Sancira worked for another year, she saved up more money, now I was helping her and she was glad I was watching over Dochiţa while she was gone. They had taken the boy almost at the end of the war, about three years had passed since then and she still hadn't found him, but Sancira didn't lose hope. Maybe her beloved child was still alive, and with deep reverence, she prayed to the Lord to help her and to keep her son safe. It is the Lord who wills all that happens in this world.

Sancira worked in the village of Birlik, a large and well-off aul, with hardworking people. From there, we left together for Kyzylorda, which was the capital of Kazakhstan in the '30s and, translated, means Red Horde, we went to that orphanage and they sent us even farther away, and farther south, to Uzbekistan, to Karakalpakstan to be precise, a country whose existence I had known nothing about. Even now the word is like a tongue-twister. *Kara* means "black" in the Karakalpak language, and a *kalpak* is a kind of hat. A very strange country, where we couldn't tell the Karakalpaks apart from the Kazakhs. They were Muslims as well, like our Kazakhs, complete with *Salam alaykum. Alaykum salam*! and morning *namaz*. We communicated with them in Russian. After so many years, both Sancira and I could jabber away in Russian pretty easily. We stopped in Tahtakupir, a village, a large yurt, but the orphanage was in Nukus, the capital of Karakalpakstan. Only Sancira made it there, I remained with Dochiţa in the village, where I worked to save up more money. We didn't know anyone there, but we became friends with Marat and his three sons Kirsan, Sandji, and Zurgan. They came over to us to ask us if we were Romanians, from Romania.

"We love Romania," they assured us. My goodness, how surprised I was! Well, weren't we the enemies of the people? Who could know about us in this endless steppe, who here could love us? We had never heard of the Kalmyks. It must have been the only nationality we hadn't met with in our village in Kazakhstan, but surely there had been some in the neighboring yurt. At first they scared us, we were two young girls all alone, and what did these strangers want with us?

When they heard we were Romanian, the Kalmyk brothers

were delighted and they told us how their Kalmykia was once apparently "occupied" by Germans and Romanians, but actually more liberated, because everyone had welcomed them with open arms, the people went over to the side of the Germans, and if they had won, all the Kalmyks who had been deported ten years prior would've returned to their homeland. In 1942, the Kalmyks no longer wanted to fight alongside the Soviets and switched over to the Germans and Romanians. The Germans even set up a Kalmyk komitet in their country. They're Buddhists, not Muslims, and they don't pray five times a day as the Kazakhs do, and they were deported the same as us, first from 1930-1933, then from 1943-1944. They were still deporting them then, after the war, and bringing other peoples into their territory, lots of Russians and Ukrainians, just as they did with our Bucovina. The Kalmyks fought against the Soviets even after the Romanian and German armies retreated, and after the war ended, maybe they're still fighting even now, hiding out in the forests.

Because of this, when the war was over, it was decreed that this country disappear off the face of the map and the Kalmykia's territories were annexed to the regions of Astrakhan, Stavropol, and Stalingrad. Elista, the country's capital, became Stepnoy. The Kalmyks were sent to Siberia: to Novosibirsk, not far from our Kazakh Belial, Altai, Krasnoyarsk, Tyumen. In Kazakhstan, Kyrghyzstan, and Uzbekistan there were fewer Kalmyks than in Siberia, many died, from the same causes as our Bucovinians. I would've forgotten the names of our Kalmyk friends, I would've forgotten the name of the village too, because I stayed there less than half a year, but when we were leaving they gave me a beautiful old postcard of one of their temples with Buddha, the god of the Kalmyks, on a throne, with their name and address in Russian on the back. I was to write them, to tell them if we found Zânelu.

After 1946, Bucovinians began returning to their homeland, they could travel anywhere in the Soviet Union, the way Sancira, who was searching for her son, did. But the Kalmyks weren't allowed, some tried to run, but the life of a runaway in those steppes wasn't a good one. I wrote them several times at the address on the back, from Khabarovsk and from Moldova, but I never received a reply. Then I didn't write them anymore either, but I prayed to God for their health. I hope they had good, long lives, they were the friendliest to us out of that whole long exile, they were like brothers to me.

There, in that Tahtakupir, a Karakalpak kept crossing my path, because I seemed like a marriageable girl to the man. Whenever a man would take a longer look at me, I'd immediately remember Eugen. I'd wonder to myself what I was doing there instead of searching for him. Sancira and Dochița would laugh at me and say that if they had left me there, I'd now be Kakalpak's wife. "Karakalpak," I'd correct them. But they'd laugh and call me Ana Tahtakupirovna. It's a good thing I left Karakalpakstan in time, it's not easy to get rid of those fierce men who are hot-blooded and quick to anger. To me he seemed ready to draw his sword from under his chapan if I were to contradict him.

Sancira didn't return alone from Nukus. At the orphanage there, an older woman, a teacher, when she heard our story, told Sancira: "We have a boy here—they call him Bucovina, take him, because you'll never find yours, they were scattered throughout the entire Union, so that their trails would be lost, if you do find him, he won't know who you are anyway, he won't recognize you anymore, and he won't understand your language either. Take this boy, who only knows one word and says it from time to time, when he's angry or when he's happy. Take him or he'll die here among the others. Take him because he must be one of yours, if he knows what Bucovina is." What was Sancira to do? Times were no longer as hard as they had been during the war, she'd have a crust of bread to give a stranger's child. She thought that somewhere a mother like her was searching for her son, or maybe his parents died, but he has some relatives somewhere in Bucovina and she'd help him find them. Because in Karakalpakstan they'd surely have lost all trace of him and surely no one would look for him here. And if she couldn't find either his parents or his relatives, then she'd raise him herself, as if he were her own son. Supposedly the boy said the word "Bucovina" when they brought him to the orphanage and he never said anything different. He was small, skinny, and didn't look like he could be more than four but he might have been even six. He did indeed understand Romanian. When Sancira said to him, "Come on, get your things and let's go find your mother," he immediately took off and quickly came back, his eyes shining. He didn't start talking even after he came to live with us, but if we said to him "Put the cup on the table" or "Come here," he understood and did it. He was well-behaved, he didn't bounce around, he didn't cry, but he remained fearful after all he'd been through.

Sancira didn't give up, however, and she went to other orphanages as well in search of her son, that's how we arrived far away in Khabarovsk, where she was searching for her dear Zânelu, and me for my Eugen. All our hope is in You, Lord, our good and merciful Shepherd, we know You are kind and ready to forgive. Help us, Lord, to find our children and loved ones lost in the vast wastelands!

One night, Sancira had a dream. The Mother of our Lord seemed to come to her, in white robes, in radiant light and say: "Sancira, for the faith you all have shown, the suffering you have endured, the tears you have shed, the anguish in your souls,

242 — *Too Great a Sky*

the hope in your hearts, we have had mercy on you and we are allowing you to go home, with all your dear ones whom you will soon find." She woke up and told us, crying. "Dochiţa, Anicuţa, listen to what I dreamed: The Mother of our Lord said we should prepare to leave, because we'll soon be able to go home. We'll find those who were lost and we'll return to Bucovina!"

We were glad and prayed again and with unspeakable joy thanked God. In Your limitless goodness, Lord, keep our souls safe in Your sweet hands. To You, Lord, do we aspire!

The adopted boy, who didn't talk, didn't say a single word, we, too, called Bucovina, though Bucovina is more a girl's name than a boy's. Out of everyone we asked and showed him to, no one recognized him. But many Bucovinians had already returned to their homeland, maybe there we could find out who he belonged to? And Khabarovsk was a big city and full of orphanages. As if all the orphans in the Soviet Union had been brought there. Sancira went everywhere and asked around and then, after searching for so long, one sunny and blessed day, she didn't return home alone again, but holding her dearest Zânelu by the hand, who recognized her, and spoke to her in Romanian, so he hadn't forgotten the language, he recognized his sister as well. She found him in Khabarovsk. We stayed almost a year there as well. He didn't recognize me anymore but we quickly became friends. And he said to the adopted child, right from the beginning, that his parents were definitely waiting for him in Bucovina and Bucovina's face lit up when he heard. So they became inseparable, though that boy didn't speak. Then we got ready to leave. Nothing was keeping us in that Siberia, and no one.

The journey back was shorter, we arrived in the village, at our relatives' home, everyone was overjoyed! Sancira's house was desolate and half-ruined. It no longer even had doors or windows.

We walked up to it, touched its walls, we fell to our knees and said the Creed and the Lord's Prayer, we cried bitterly until our neighbors came to calm us down. "Look, we're in Bucovina now," we kept repeating, "we're finally back!" Everyone teared up, they got on their knees and prayed to God, thanking Him that the hour had finally come when they were seeing people return from deportation. I think that in our village we were the first to return. I wanted to see our house as well, the one built by my parents, Andron and Aspazia Bojescu, since it was nearby and hadn't been destroyed in the war, but it was surrounded by a wire fence and had been transformed into a government building, I even found a locked door . . . I couldn't go in, I looked at it from a distance. A dog barked at us, hostilely.

Everyone asked, looking at the boy who was a stranger: "Who's this?"

"We don't know, he's a little boy who can't speak, and we want to help him find his parents, we brought him here from Uzbekistan." When the child heard us, he gave us a long look and said distinctly in perfect Romanian: "I'm Grigoraş Puiu from the village of Poieni-Bucovina!"

We all rushed to his village to find his relatives and we even found his mother and grandmother. Our house had become a clinic and Sancira's had been destroyed in the war and she couldn't live in it anymore, and in that village, the boy's relatives found Sancira a small house. They proposed she stay there and they held her in great esteem. Grigoraş's mother had returned alone, without a husband, without children, she had thought her boy was dead, because she found only his cap floating in a river, and what a miracle, what joy, for her boy to be brought home safe and sound!

When we returned to Bucovina, Eugen had just left to go back to Siberia, to make money so he could buy back his parents' house and to look for me. But I had just arrived in Bucovina and I didn't have a clue, I hadn't received a single word from him and believed he was dead. Then, because I couldn't live off those people's kindness, because it was hard for everyone, I went to work in Moldova, in my friend's village, Troiţa de Sus, that's where I got married and started a home. There weren't many Romanians left in Bucovina, our numbers had been dwindled by the deportations, and the war, and famine, and poverty. Hmm, I don't really know what happened to the little boy Bucovina, just that he no longer kept silent when he found himself in his mother's arms and no one believed us that he hadn't said a single word throughout all of icy Russia and we had believed he was mute. Sancira said that he was really good in school, and then college, that he was a good boy, and smart. And aunt Sancira lived a long time, more than ninety years, she danced at her grandchildren's weddings and maybe even at her great-grandchildren's. Then she, too, died of old age, all the relatives mourned for her and gave her a Christian burial, in our dear Bucovina. God had been merciful to her, I was also at her funeral, because I was still strong then.

Jeni returned to Bucovina a year before us, then he went to work in Siberia, and he returned and left again, after he found out I got married. His sister had told him. It was hard to find out news back then but it still got around. My husband hadn't yet died when I, too, found out that he was still alive. Then, when I returned to my village, to Old Albina, for the treasure and it was gone, I was even more certain that he was alive. Now his great-grandson comes from the depths of Russia to discover his roots, to learn the language of his ancestors and he falls in love. God brought the two together and made things right. I sensed from the very beginning that he must be his grandson!

For my Bucovinian village, you had to have a special border permit and I didn't have one, I didn't have close relatives in the area either, my closest ones were in Romania and I hadn't had any news of them. I had no word of Eugen either, a major famine was raging there but they said that things were better now, that the worst of it was over, that more had died of hunger than from deportation. Whoever had anything left gave something to those in charge, who turned a blind eye and let them be, to settle in Bucovina. After a while, luckier Bucovinians even got back their houses, they gave money to the state and moved back onto their farms, even luckier were those with good relatives who had taken care of their houses, and when they returned, they had a roof over their heads. I was so poor that I barely had enough money for my ticket. I had worked a lot but I hadn't been able to save up much. We arrived in the village secretly, just to see it, because we didn't have papers, without that special permit, and we were afraid they might catch us and send us back, because what were we doing here uninvited? The people seemed strangers to me, I didn't know anyone, everything was different than when I had left at the age of ten, almost eleven.

I ran straight to our house, now it was a clinic, with a new fence, there was also a big, shaggy dog that never tired of barking. I would've wanted to unearth my treasure hidden in the well, I saw the well, it stood in the shade of the little tree I had planted with Father that was now a big tree, it didn't look like anyone had discovered my treasure. But how could I get in? We were told to go around evening, not to stay in the village too long, and then what would I do with the things once I had removed them from the buried pot, where could I take them, if I didn't have a nest of my own? No one from the village knew who I was, how could they allow me to rummage through the well, where could I even get a spade? Many questions went through my mind and no answers. Ten years don't seem like a long time, but I no longer recognized my village, there was no one waiting for me here, no one knew who I was anymore, I left a little girl and came back a woman. They still knew Sancira and they shared some things with us. Those whose villages were farther from the border were happy, those people could return, they weren't as strict about their documents. But we, those whose villages were cut in two, were viewed with suspicion, they looked at us the way the Kazakhs did in our first year of deportation.

I thought about what I should do, where I should go, and decided to go to my friend in Moldova. She had left me her address, I found her, they took me in. They were getting ready for a wedding. Varvara's relatives asked me what papers I had, what classes I had taken, I had studied tailoring, like Varvara, we had gone to school together. Wonderful. They got me a passport at the village council, except that they wrote I was Moldovan. In any case, we were all the same, we spoke the same language, just that Romania was now another country, and only Moldovans lived in that village. I could've chosen to be Ukrainian, that was allowed too, just not Romanian.

The services cooperative wasn't ready yet, but they needed specialists, so they said they would hire me. They'd give me a spot in the dorm as well, until I was allotted a house, if I decided to put down roots and get married there. I wasn't thinking that far ahead. I didn't have any money left and I could hardly wait to start work. In the dorm lived all sorts of young employees, agronomists, and nurses, and a few young teachers. The dorm was, in fact, a three story apartment building, like in a city, with small apartments that each had two bigger-sized rooms, a small kitchen, an even smaller bathroom, and a hallway. But it was all mine! When I had heard dorm, I thought the bathroom and kitchen would be shared, but no! I immediately accepted, because I didn't feel completely comfortable staying with the girl's relatives either. They hadn't said anything, they were understanding and quick to help, happy that their people had returned. I was really glad to be able to move into my own apartment, they also helped me with some furniture. I didn't even need much.

Until the tailoring shop opened, I worked as a milkmaid. I liked my new job when I started even more. It wasn't hard, sometimes we had orders from the county factories, simple orders, clothing details, patterns to copy, stitching bedsheets, curtains, I'd also sew for the people in the village. When people escaped the danger of hunger and things started getting back to normal, they'd come to us to get clothes made. At the factory, when they saw that we were hardworking and skillful, they gave us harder and better paid orders. We didn't have time to sit around with our feet up. I really liked my apartment, it was bright, clean. I was delighted and the only thing I regretted was that my dear sweet mother hadn't survived her hardships and wasn't with me, so that she, too, could enjoy all this goodness and the times of plenty.

In our dorm there were also many young married couples, I'd hear children crying or laughing, I'd hear them in the evening when I'd come home from work. Little by little, I started eating better, I had money to go to the store and buy myself paté and canned fish, now I can't find those kinds anymore, but they had just come out then and I relished them. I'd eat a baton—that was the name of a longish loaf of bread—with kefir, slightly sour, a kind of buttermilk, what we call chişleag. I dressed a bit better, I bought myself a few things, like any girl. Varvara told me not to wait for Eugen anymore, because what was meant to be mine would be mine, and that I should look around there, in the village, that I should go out dancing at night, to find a husband, because there were many good guys in that village. She'd help me, I had only to tell her who I liked. But I didn't like any of them. Until I found a boy who was kind and gentle on my own, from a family that was god-fearing and devout.

※

In 1941, when they took us away on the train, the journey seemed very long to us, it's true that the war had started and we were kept on sidetracks for days on end or we had to wait for it to get dark to pass through bigger cities, so the residents there wouldn't see us and be troubled, we were allowed to go through bigger train stations only at night. In the '70s, they allowed Romanians to come into Moldova, my sister came then for the first time. Even though we hadn't seen each other for forty years, a lifetime, we immediately recognized each other. She looked so much like Mother that I felt like crying, the spitting image of Mother, while I looked more like Father, she told me, because I couldn't remember. She came with one of her sons, the youngest, and the cousins got to meet each other. Then we decided to go see Mother's grave. She brought me pictures, because I didn't have any photographs, of Mother, Father, her wedding, our brothers, who I hadn't heard from. She even had an old photograph of me, taken at a fair in Cernăuți. We agreed—there was a group of us, relatives of ours and Bucovinians from the village—to go visit the graves of those who had died there, but by the time we had raised the money, by the time we had obtained all the documents, visas for our foreign relatives and those from Romania, it was already 1992. Only then could we go.

I couldn't see my older two brothers until 1990, because it wasn't allowed, and then they died. I never saw them again. Only my sister came to Moldova a few times, when my husband and mother-in-law were still alive. My brothers had left Romania, because they were afraid they'd be expatriated, they went abroad, studied at prestigious schools, one in Austria, in Vienna, the other in Germany. They studied, worked, raised families, they got their children off to a good start. The children I met because they came and together we formed a fairly big group that went to the grave of our mother Aspazia. We arrived more quickly than the first time, but the villages no longer existed. We passed through the cities of Kazakhstan, we reached our steppe, but didn't go all the way into the depths of Siberia. There wasn't a single house or grave left, only fields and fields. I was crying because I couldn't recognize anything, the villages weren't how we had left them, the cities were different, everything had changed. There were more of us Bucovinians and no one could find the graves of their close relatives. We searched, we asked around, and the people there told us that others had come before us, they had asked and had put up crosses in the cemetery of the deportees in the city of Karaganda. We did the same, we took some dirt from the side of the train tracks, we wrote the name of our dead on a large marble cross, we called an Orthodox priest who delivered a sermon in remembrance of the Bucovinians who had remained in foreign soil. People knew there had been villages of deportees around there, they'd find bones, because they plowed and sowed over graves. Everything had changed, other villages, other cities, big ones with many people. Those moments passed quickly and from that journey I remember most clearly the yellow fields and the tea on the train. Oblivion had settled over those years, over our dead, and over our lost youth there.

It's such a shame! I had buried Mother in a real casket, I spent all the money I had been saving up for the journey, for the return, on it, and I still didn't have enough, some countryfolk lent me some too, I placed a cross on the grave as well, I read from the Bible. I buried her properly, so she could be happy at least in the next world. We had been just about to return, but she didn't wait and there, in foreign soil, she remained. I stayed a couple more years, to save up more money, but I didn't regret it, I returned the money I borrowed. Many had remained like me, there were also those who had returned to see their dear Bucovinian land, they kissed a corner of their house, if it still existed, but even if it existed it was no longer theirs, they hugged the trees of their childhood, and returned to Siberia or Kazakhstan.

And now our kishtak, the Belial of many nations, had disappeared, it was plowed and sown with wheat, the symbol of peace between peoples. How can you eat bread grown from the bones of the dead? What does it taste like, the wheat of all the misfortunes that have happened there and all the unfortunate people dead before their time, though innocent, like Mother, like all our dead? We later received, I and other survivors, rehabilitation certificates, on which was written, in black-and-white, that they deported us for nothing, they tortured us for no fault of our own, everything was a mistake. They're living and thriving, but we, because of their mistake, to this day have never recovered. What do you do with so many wrongful deaths? Of course it's a mistake to be separated from your parents, to never see your father or brothers again, to bury your mother far from home, in foreign soil, not to be received in your house, in your village, to have fingers pointed at you for years for being an "enemy," to be told at every turn that you already know the way to Siberia, and if something's not to your liking, that's where you belong, to hear this refrain and tremble from fear for years on end, being at the mercy of a bunch of laughable communists. All the unburied dead demand their right to a burial, they demand justice and the word "mistake" isn't enough for them!

—⟨⟩—

Back then in 1992, Eugen's sister, Parascovia Țară, who had survived also came with us. She told me how Eugen had found them,
just her and their mother, how they had returned without her
other two brothers, who had died in '41 and '42, and without
their father, who had also died around then, whose names she had
written on our shared cross. They hadn't found anything when
they returned, poverty, hunger, strangers living in their house, and
Eugen went back, he started work at a plant and made decent
money. But he had also been to my village in Bucovina, he had
gone to my Albina and hadn't found me. Many from our village
had died, no one had returned, either because it was close to the
border and they wouldn't allow people to return, or because they
had mostly died and no one was left to return. But Sancira and
I returned only in 1951, after ten years of wandering. Nor had
anyone heard anything from us, there weren't little phones like
there are now, people didn't even have big ones.

Eugen sent his family money, so he could buy back their house,
but he was also saving up money for a ticket to go looking for me.
He was one step behind me, he'd find out from someone or other
where I had passed through, where I had stayed. He went to the
Ob River, to Smert-Reka, he also went to Kant, and Kazakhstan,
but didn't find me. We had returned to Bucovina when he was
searching for me on the Kazakhs steppes, then he returned as well,
he spoke with aunt Sancira, when I had just left for Moldova. He
came, but I was married. Parascovia told me how Eugen came
to my village in Moldova, to Troița, he found out I worked in
a tailoring shop, he saw me leaving work and going home, he
followed me, but I had a belly so big, I was pregnant with my
son, that I could hardly walk, he wanted to come up to me, to
tell me that he had been to Old Albina and had dug up the trea-

sure that I had told him about on the train, but he didn't dare, he didn't approach me and then he left for Siberia. And I had no clue, I didn't sense a thing. Is it possible that I had looked into his eyes and hadn't recognized him? Could he have changed that much in ten years? Then my husband, God rest his soul, went to be with the Lord . . . Eugen later got married, in Siberia, with a Lithuanian woman who had been deported, he also had two children, I know that his Lithuanian wife died as well, I know he had grandchildren, that he wanted to move to Bucovina or that he had moved there long ago, so he could be in his beloved land in his old age. He worked long after retirement. Many of his relatives left for Romania after 1990 and the houses were left empty again . . . Maybe he moved into one of them . . .

Domnica, my sister, told me how her husband had been imprisoned, then he returned, but not for long, they were then sent to the Bărăgan, in a kind of Romanian deportation, taken to a backward village as well, that doesn't exist anymore either, they sowed wheat there too or maybe beets. Her family also suffered since she had two brothers who had gone abroad, in addition to themselves being hardworking people with a big house and everything they needed. You'd wake up to find out you'd been declared an enemy overnight. I've never been anyone's enemy, I got along well with everyone, I lived in peace and harmony, but when the Devil pays this earth a visit and his soldiers make the laws, people who have God in their hearts will suffer. It was hard in Romania as well, our Domnica was amazed that my basement was stocked with everything, but for them it was hard to find food, hard to get heating, they kept people in the cities freezing all winter, the store shelves were bare, in the villages, to be allowed to slaughter an animal, your own, you had to prove that it was sick and that if you didn't slaughter it, it would die anyway. People would break the legs of their poor colts, calves, baby goats . . . oh what hard times! My sister visited a few times and I gave her all kinds of things, I'd also send her things through others. Now you have everything as long as you have health and money . . .

She told me about how the war started and how they all returned to our house in July. Deserted, they hadn't heard anything from Father either, people told them we had been deported. How Bucovinians from Horecea, Mahala, and Ostriţa, about four hundred in all, wanted to cross the Prut River and were slaughtered by the border guards, and others drowned. That was around the beginning of February in 1941, and two months later, on April 1st, 1941, people from Cupca, Pătrăuţi, Crasna, Suceveni, Carapciu, and other nearby villages started off for Romania, yelling "Long live King Mihai! Long live Romania!" When they reached Fântâna Albă, the soldiers at the border mowed them all down. A few managed to escape into the forest. But Father wasn't among those who had died. I had heard something about that from the people in the train, but I was little, I hadn't understood everything then.

In Siberia, many looked at Moldovans with a friendly eye, but not at Romanians. "The Moldovans fought against the fascists alongside us, but the Romanians were on the side of the fascists," they said, as the first thing to be held against us. When you'd say: "Bucovina," they'd ask: "Moldova or Romania?" Those who knew a little something and wanted a bit more bread or to keep out of trouble would say "Moldova," others said: "Romania." Who knows anymore that Bucovina was part of northern Moldova, which later became the country of Romania? That it was the union of Moldova and Muntenia that formed Romania? That the great empires each pinched off whatever they could, a piece from the north, that they called Bucovina, another from the east, which others named Bessarabia, leaving the land of Moldova maimed. From 1774 to 1918, Bucovina was under the control of the Aus-

254 —— *Too Great a Sky*

trians, and Bessarabia, from 1812 until 1918 as well, was under the Russians. Father was a school principal, he had rare books and told us many things, especially about history, princes, how Bessarabia and Bucovina appeared, that before it was all only Moldova, how the great emperors divided the smaller countries among themselves. Then I also read about it in my children's books, and those of my grandchildren . . .

Now, even though we speak the same language, people from Bessarabia consider that they speak Moldovan, and those from Bucovina, Romanian. I did three grades, the first ones, in Romanian, then during the deportation I was taught in Russian, and when I arrived in Moldova, my Romanian language was written with Russian letters. One time when I said that I didn't know how to write in Moldovan, only in Romanian, they asked me if I really loved Siberia so much that I was so desperate to go back? What, hadn't I stayed long enough? They repeated that question whenever I had even a slightly sour look on my face or didn't agree with something. Whenever they heard the word "Romanian" it was as if I were blowing sand in their eyes. Now I see that everything is in Romanian again, as it was in our sweet Bucovina as well. I hope those times never return, because you never know what the great rulers have in mind and are capable of.

—Cuţa, why do you say "sweet Bucovina"? Isn't our Moldova sweet too?

—It is sweet, of course, very sweet! But Bucovina is even sweeter. And what you all call our Moldova is just a piece of that Moldova from the past, which I was born with in my soul, and Bessarabia and Bucovina were parts cut out from the bigger country. So Bucovina is also Moldova. The word Bucovina comes from our beech forests, that's what the Germans said. And our house, as you can see, is also next to a forest, there are as many beech trees as you like in the forests of our Troiţa, I have Bucovina right next door if I want it. But it's those times that I miss, those people, that land tended by worthy and kind Romanians of ours. I miss a sweet Bucovina that no longer exists. I went there a few times, I tried to remember the things Mother told me, so I wouldn't forget where I came from. I couldn't find them! Maybe it's not just Bucovina that has changed, maybe everything has changed, and we've changed too, but we can't tell.

"Where is heaven on earth?" our parents would ask us when we were far from home. "In Bucovina, the most beautiful country in the world, the most blessed land of all," we'd answer, "full of fruit trees, so heavy with fruit that the branches bend down to the ground, where the apples smell so dainty, so delicious, from kilometers away from the orchard, and not only the apples, but all the fruit, where the air carries with it the scent of all the flowers, forests, and vineyards, where the sun doesn't burn, but caresses, the wind doesn't whip, but wafts, the blizzard doesn't freeze, but purifies . . ." After the war, we decorated trees in Kazakhstan as well, with flowers made out of colored paper, presents were put under the tree there too, and we believed that Father Christmas, there called Father Frost, came from Bucovina. It was his homeland. That's what the little children believed.

Some of the Bucovinians declared themselves Moldovans and they left sooner. Those who had lived under the former Tsarist rule didn't really understand us. "What does it matter what you are, Romanian or Moldovan, when it allows you to return to your homeland? We speak the same language, we're the same people, what's the problem?" But my entire family line, in all our documents, was Romanian, my Bucovina was Romanian, it had once belonged to others as well but even then in our documents we were Romanian. Those years when Bucovina was ruled by the Austrians was before my time. I was born in Romania, in Greater Romania! We hadn't been ruled by the Russians for hundreds of years, we hadn't spoken Russian! "Then go ahead and rot here, Romanians!"

In any case, then, immediately after the war, things weren't better for those who returned either, the Moldovans, Romanians, or Ukrainians, whatever they declared themselves to be. Given what a famine there was back home! Then the Romanians disappeared, little by little. In Moldova not a Romanian in sight, only Moldovans. In our Troița, after living there for a year, even the Russians also became Moldovans. Dear Varvara's husband, Constantin, learned the language but he actually was Moldovan! But there were also cases when a Moldovan woman married a Russian man and, if she brought him to the village, he'd forget his own language and speak only ours. That's how powerful our language is!

Nobody asked me what I wanted written in my passport. Are you going to Soviet Moldova or Soviet Ukraine? Both sound just as foreign to me! Both were countries I had never lived in, I hadn't even visited them as a child. Wasn't there any way to return to Romanian Bucovina? The ones who left first didn't end up in their own houses, in their homeland, but also in foreign places, with fingers being pointed at them as being "former" or descendants of enemies and kulaks. I hadn't even heard words like that before, but over there any schoolchild knew what they were. You couldn't even dare come close to your own village. In Moldova as well as in Ukraine there was famine in '47-'48 and such poverty, dear Lord, that people died in droves, just as the deportees passed away in their first year in exile! Some got scared and returned, because Siberia didn't seem so terrible anymore . . .

———◦———

I kept dying, I died with each loved one who had left me behind and now death no longer scares me, it doesn't cause me any pain anymore. I died along with my children and I embraced their souls. God allowed me to bury my daughter, and then my son as well. There's no opposing God's will! My mother-in-law, Agripina Blajina, a woman with a heart of gold, also died in my arms. God appointed me to survive my own children. To go through this as well. The scythe of my death must be so worn, it doesn't scare me, it doesn't hurt me. Today I'm alive, today I'm glad. How many times have I seen death with my own eyes, how many times said to myself that this is it, I've reached the end of my life. *This is it*, I said also when I arrived at the end of the steel road . . . But your life doesn't end the way train tracks end, instead, when a person no longer believes in God or anything. What else can I ask of you, Lord? You alone know what I need. Do not allow me to forget that everything comes from You. Lord, give me strength to endure today's toil and endure all that is given to me. Because today, Lord, we are sorely tried by this dark enmity and we would immediately fall prey to it, if You, Lord, did not closely watch over us. And all the evil that people do under heaven is an acknowledgment of our helplessness and infirmity. Our Lord and Savior. The porch to heaven. Our stoop. Our country. Our hearth. Everything that warms our soul and body. Enjoy, Ana, this long life which God has ordained for you.

My mother-in-law never said anything to anyone, because you weren't allowed to speak about those times. Sometimes a snippet would slip out, a word and that's all. But when she was bedridden, sick, her dying wish was for me to tell a granddaughter at least what I had gone through, because it was better than taking everything with you to the grave. The times would change, they'd be more open, I should say what happened. The times have changed, people can talk now, other things aren't possible anymore, but people can talk. Who is still alive? Who can still listen? My mother-in-law had been deported, along with her entire family, with her husband, children, and her husband's parents. They were separated from the men and never saw them again. Her parents took all they had of value, they went to those with the lists and asked for a grandchild, they asked for Anton, their oldest grandchild, to raise him themselves. On their knees they begged them not to take away their entire family where they would perish. So Anton didn't experience deportation. His grandparents gave all their wealth to the kolkhoz, and their cow, and their sheep, and they carefully raised their grandson. Grăchina Blajinschi's other four children died, her mother-in-law died, all the men died, she alone returned from deportation. In that time, there was a great demand for teachers and her son had graduated from a pedagogical school, then he got into the institute, without saying who his parents were, all it said in his file was that he came from a family of farmers. That's what someone advised him to write and he got in, then either someone found out, or someone informed on him, or he was on some list and they knew what kind of farmers his family was. He was a very good student and they recommended him for post-graduate studies, but he was rejected because of his file, he was sent to be a teacher in a village school, then they kicked him out of there was well. My husband would sometimes say something about those times, but my mother-in-law, never. She'd never say anything, and she'd never ask me either. As if it were shameful to talk about it, to remember the hardships and humiliations you'd been through. No one said a word. You don't say anything and it didn't happen. She would tell us, instead, about her happy memories from when she was young, the customs and traditions that had been passed down, especially when something would surprise me: "For Christmas you don't have a Malanca procession here in Troiţa? You don't know about Paparude . . . Now, back in Bucovina . . . !"

Then my mother-in-law would stop and think: "Well, before, we, too, in Moldova . . ." Bright and happy memories, of little Anton when he was a small boy, the children, the grandchildren would listen . . . Of how beautiful it used to be . . . She really loved me, as if I were her own daughter. Not once did she treat me badly, or ever slap me, though, being young, there were many things I didn't know, I'd make mistakes, but she forgave everything . . . She never corrected me even when I didn't do something right, a heart of pure gold. I hadn't known she'd had other children, besides my Anton, then, after many years of living in the same house, on the Feast of the Peaceful one year, I saw her giving gifts in remembrance of the dead and she said each of their names, and how old they were when they passed away. Anton, when I asked him, said that a great many children died in the first year of deportation. He didn't say more than that either, maybe he didn't even know more. That in Siberia it was too cold and they froze, they took them away without warm clothes. Hungry, weak, they dropped like flies . . . I thought they had died on the way, in the train, as many of our children had . . . No, they survived the journey because Agripina Blajina had packed a bit of cheese and about twenty eggs, some flour, some oil. Except that their food ran out, and it had gotten cold. Whoever made it through the first year lived, and many returned, whoever didn't, were left there, the poor things. My mother-in-law would always repeat: "God is great through the good and the bad!" After my husband, her son, died, she became withdrawn, she seemed sad. But she never once complained and she helped me with everything around the house, until she became bedridden. She lay there for a few days and then she died. She said she had had a hard life, but a beautiful one. She thanked God for her share of sunny days and rich harvests. She had buried her son, and all her children, but she had seen her grandchildren growing up. And maybe someone would have compassion and put up a cross at her husband's grave. But when the ground was frozen, the exhausted people only placed one end of a rug over the faces of the dead, and snow was all that barely covered the bodies.

Later, when the times were getting better, I asked a relative of theirs from the village why they had been deported, had they been wealthy or not gotten along with the newcomers? Yes, they had been important landowners in the village, with many houses, a mill, cattle, land, the mill had been destroyed in the war, because the village had been on the front lines, the houses were taken by the communist bosses. "One is a club today, can't you see it looks like a conac, the manor house of a noble family, which the communists added on to, two rooms and a porch. Those bosses left, others came, but these ones aren't in a hurry to return anything to their former owners either. Only her parents' house, next to the forest, didn't interest them, because it was small, old-fashioned, and too far from the main square."

When my mother-in-law Agripina returned from Siberia, they allowed her to move into that house next to the forest, her relatives helped her repair it a bit, she painted it, and the house is still standing to this day. "They also had an orchard, and a vineyard, and forests, you've probably passed by there many times, didn't mother Agripina sigh when she'd go by there?" I never thought about why she sighed. I'd sigh as well if I'd see my Albina in Bucovina again, I miss it so much . . . So many times I thought I should return there, to make a life for myself on our land. But now I feel at home here, my hearth is here. Next to her house, we built ourselves another little house, with our own hands, this is where my son and my daughter came into the world. Mother Agripina stayed in the old house, we lived in the new one. We were close to one another and we got along very well. "Agripina Blajâna!" they'd call her. Now they call me Blajâna, because Blajinschi is too long.

When my mother-in-law was still alive, she was Blajâna, I was Anica Blajânica.

My husband was kicked out of his school, because they found out we had a religious wedding ceremony, a young couple wanted to be our sponsors and they called us to the church.

> *Anton, Anton dear, my heart is beating with fear! And what's more, I feel you've gotten us into trouble here. This couple four times told us to appear at the church, saying it was all clear. I mean it, something's queer. But Anton wouldn't hear, and we went through the church door, and marriage vows swore. The commission arrived to interfere. The sponsors were insincere and signed the affidavit that they adhere, and began Anton's reputation to besmear. The judgment was severe. He was kicked out that school year, they ended his career. What's more, they gave him a scare, saying they could make him disappear, if he decided to persevere in the error of his ways. Anton, Anton dear, there was no staying clear, now you'll be a balladeer . . .*

For a few more years he played the garmoshka, which is a type of accordion, but he became depressed and died soon after.

My Anton was a good teacher, he loved being surrounded by children and teaching them. He pined for it after they kicked him out. One time I came home and heard him talking. I thought to myself: *who is my husband talking to at this hour?* I waited a bit at the door before going in and I heard: "What's your answer, Gheorghiţă? You didn't study? You don't like history . . . But without knowing history you won't get very far . . . Children, stop fighting. What happened? Alright, let's continue, in what year was the French revolution . . ." My husband was playing teacher. He was pretending to be in class with the children. I quietly backed away, I returned to the gate, jingled the handle and started to yell at the dog, that it got tangled in its chain again, that it tipped over its water bowl, so my husband could hear me and finish his lesson before I came inside the house. So he wouldn't be embarrassed.

Then my husband bought some sheep, not many had them then, cheese was expensive and not so easy to find. My husband was hard-working and, a few times, until we found a shepherd closer to us, he took the sheep to water himself, he took them out to pasture, and my son came home from school upset, because his classmates were making fun of what kind of family he had: "Your ma's a seamstress, your pa, a shepherd, and you claim you're a teacher's kid!" My husband also worked at the village museum; there they didn't kick him out, he'd sometimes play the garmoshka for kindergarteners at school celebrations. He wasn't paid much at the museum, but he gathered pieces for it, he made it beautiful.

One day, I found some young boys playing in the street and told them I'd give them some chocolate candies and even 50 kopeks each, if they'd go to the museum and ask Anton Dmitrievich to tell them about the French Revolution. Only not to tell him that I sent them! They should say that they didn't understand the lesson at school well. My husband came home late, he was happy and his eyes were shining. I didn't ask him anything, I pretended I didn't even notice how his face was lit up. Then he started talking without me prompting: "The teachers are a disgrace, they don't teach the children anything . . ." Then I, pretending to be confused: "How do you know?" Well, the children were coming to him so he could explain history lessons to them and they listened with their mouths open, they refused to leave, their parents came to get them, scared because their children had disappeared, and they couldn't find them anywhere. "It's rare to have a teacher like you. Who is teaching them history now?"

"The French teacher, because they don't have a specialist in history." I would've wanted him to be more assertive, I would've preferred he fight for his rights, to return to the school, if not to this one, then to another one, father away from here. Times had gotten a bit better and he had graduated with a red diploma, but they hadn't allowed him to do post-graduate studies, nor was he picked to teach college, though he was first in his class, but to throw him out even from the village school . . . It was too great a punishment for him. He surrendered to his suffering, he took care of his sheep, he'd sometimes teach his imaginary students. People would call him Anton Shepherdovich, but he didn't care, or didn't show it if he did.

I'd ask him what was bothering him, nothing was bothering him. Then he'd ponder something intensely for a few days, and when I'd ask him what he was thinking about, he'd startle, he'd look scared, I'd repeat the question, and he seemed to enter a world all his own. Then out of nowhere, he told me that he was going to go to the hospital because his head hurt. He looked paler than usual, "Fine," I said to him, "go." He hadn't been examined by a doctor in a while, it wasn't a bad idea to get checked out. I laid out nice clothes for him, I packed him food. And he never came back, he had gotten there on his own two feet, practically healthy, and I don't know what germs they found in his head, he stayed there a few days for tests, they kept him there and that's where he died a few days later. He left Monday, Thursday he was dead. He had called me Monday even to tell me he wasn't coming home, that he was staying at the hospital to get tests done. And I buried him the same week. All the teachers came and I gave them all gifts in remembrance of him. He died before his time, he had barely turned sixty. I don't know if they lit a candle for him there, if he had a priest with him before dying. I felt really bad that I hadn't been by his side. To be fired from work because you got married in a church and to die without a priest!

At that time, it was very shameful to be fired from a job, he really suffered, my poor man, who was good and gentle. I wasn't strong enough to help him. At least he had been able to dance at his son's wedding, he had held his first grandchild in his arms. He didn't live to see his daughter's wedding. He was a wonderful storyteller, he knew many things, he'd buy books and have the boy read. My mother-in-law also suffered when she heard the news, but she stayed strong. What a good woman she was too, with a great love of God, such a life enriched by prayer and faith! After I lost my dear sweet mother Aspazia, it was a gift from God that I ended up in my precious mother-in-law Agripina's family! In those times that were against praying out in the open, it was a truly great gift from the Lord. I can't deny, unworthy as I am, the spirit of sadness, of bitterness, which eats at the soul, wears away at everything, unleashes all evil. I had moments of great sadness when I had to take charge of the burials of so many loved ones. The soul is damaged by sadness, the sickness that lies within. Sinful before the Lord is grumbling, impatience, pettiness of the soul, despair, the hideous offspring of faithlessness. The deeds of unconquerable faith are shown not in temporal wealth, not in vain glory, but in poverty and in work. And if these should come upon you, do not forget that this is how God tests those who are pleasing to Him. Joy is attained through troubles and suffering! By going through troubles, people learn to have faith and to hope, the greater the suffering, the greater will be their comfort in Christ, and the best of them will be capable of comforting others in trouble and despair, because a heart without hope is like a quiver of arrows without a bow.

Anton's mother, Agripina Blajinschi, who he loved very much and whose word he respected, told him to marry only a girl who believed in God. Where would the poor boy find someone like that, when everyone was wild about Lenin and Stalin, and instead of a cross around their neck, they wore pins of the communist leaders on their chest?

We saw each other in church. That village had been on the front lines, there had also been partisans in those forests, and when the church was no longer used as storage for construction materials, nor a studio for work and design, the young history teacher was given the mission of putting together a village museum in the Protection of the Holy Virgin church. I passed by in front of the church daily, I thought that I was alone, that there was no one around, I'd stop, say my prayers, a church remains the house of God even if evil people shut its doors or use it for other purposes, and I'd cross myself and bow my head. He'd see me from inside and kept watching me, and one day he came out quickly, I got very frightened, very frightened! He approached me noiselessly, like a shadow, and asked me: "Do you believe in God?" I almost fainted from fright, I had just heard that whoever came from Siberia could go straight back there if they went to church, because we already knew the way and had gotten used to it, they were deporting our believers and all kinds of Protestants. I took off running without answering him. And he took off after me. I was running as fast as I could, he was right behind me. He followed me, he didn't know who I was. I was working as a milkmaid then, the tailoring shop hadn't opened yet . . . I really would've wanted to study at an institute, my dear girl, I really would've loved to learn! But they didn't accept me, so I was left with my trade schooling and was glad that they assigned me to a farm, because I was all alone and it was hard to find work. The cows listened to me and loved me: Gabriela, Daniela, Mihaela, cows with saints' names, then Dumana, Joiana, Vinerica, Mărţica. They were like little lambs, that's how much they liked it when I milked them. If I said a prayer for them, they liked it even more, they didn't even move around, they only twitched their tails to ward off the flies.

Anton didn't catch me then, but he asked around to find out who I was, he waited for me at the farm. With his mother I immediately found a common language. I respected my husband, he was a schoolteacher, had graduated from an institute, had higher education, and I was a simple milkmaid and seamstress. In the village, no one cared that I was a stranger, there were many like me. Three apartment buildings had been built for new personnel, they had opened a winery, a factory for dairy products, a farm for cattle and pigs, a sausage shop, they had everything, how well things were going for the people there. At the same time as the services cooperative, they also built a big, new school, that they were still working on when I arrived in the village.

I would get dressed up on Sundays and make my way past the church. I couldn't go inside, because it was closed, but I desperately wanted at least, at the entrance porch, in front of the church, to cross myself. I had to thank the Lord for giving me a roof over my head, a two-bedroom apartment, with a kitchen, a bathroom and a hallway, like the kind in cities, that I had a job, that my life had turned out so well, that I was healthy and had friends here, in the village, who I could count on if I were in trouble. I didn't know, I didn't suspect, the thought never entered my head that someone was in the church and was seeing me, watching what I was doing. It wasn't an enemy, but it could have been, God forbid!

That *dombyta*, the services cooperative, would soon open and my good friend Varvara assured me that they had many spots open and needed specialists, we had gone to the school for seamstresses together, that's how much schooling I had been able to complete in that vast steppe, I had once promised my mother that I would make something of myself and I kept my word. And there in the village, young workers were offered a salary, housing, then you could start your own family, because there were many young men in the village, Varvara would say, one would quickly lay eyes on you and marry you. I had heard about some of our Bucovinian young women getting into, finally, the medical school in Kazakhstan, but I had no way of doing that, I was working, I had no one left to help me or encourage me. I thought about applying to the institute in Moldova, but I was worried about the entrance exam being in Moldovan. I knew Romanian, written with the Latin alphabet, I had spoken Romanian in our dear Bucovina, I had never studied Moldovan anywhere, in Kazakhstan and Siberia I had spoken Russian with foreigners and Romanian with our people. The classes at the school for seamstresses were also in Russian, I was always anxious about Moldovan.

⟡

—Why do you wear so many crosses, Cuța?

—One was put around my neck by Mother, another was brought to me by my sister Domnica, at our first meeting.

When they rounded us up, Mother freed the dog, she tied a cross around its neck and told it to go to Rădăuți, so our family would know we hadn't died and that now we were completely dependent on God's will and mercy. Our dog had been to Rădăuți with Father before, it had been with him in the wagon, it knew the way and quickly found my sister's house. They were overjoyed and gave him a warm welcome, they took care of him, made him the house's guard dog and that's where it ended its days. When they were putting a chain on it, they found the cross tied around its neck. They removed it and kept it. When I had settled in Moldova, from Bucovina auntie Sancira sent me letters from my family, they had been written to Mother and me, and had arrived at our address in Old Albina, from my sister and brothers. I answered back and my sister was thrilled. She wrote me how back then, in 1941, the cross had reached them safely. I couldn't remember the dog very well, Mother hadn't mentioned anything to me about the cross, in that great hustle and bustle. Or maybe she did say something, but I was scared and I didn't remember? Domnica brought me the dog's cross when she came to visit me.

—Don't you like dogs, Cuța? I see you have only cats. How can you live here, all alone, without a dog to protect you?

—God forbid! I had a dog, what a brave and vigilant dog! But I'm afraid that any day now I'll die and leave it behind, to suffer and bark at an empty house.

A cat is more resourceful and less soft-hearted. It's free, it visits the neighbors too, catches a mouse from time to time for them as well, it can receive an extra chunk of mămăligă from them, it also goes into the forest, it takes its due, it doesn't wait for anyone's pity, it doesn't die along with its master. But a dog, tied up all its life next to its cage, can't take care of itself. Many people left after 1990, so many that I thought our entire Troița would empty out. When someone leaves for a long time, a sheep, a cow, a horse will quickly find a new master, because everyone can make use of them, but who would take someone else's dog? Well, fine, a neighbor might take a dog, if he didn't already have one in his yard, kind souls and those with big farms might have room for two dogs, but no one would keep five. No one in our Troița keeps more than two dogs in their yard.

Those who abandoned their houses freed their dogs to do whatever they liked, to get by however they could. Some of the dogs went into the forests or out in the fields, they formed packs, they became wild. I would sometimes see a pack like that on the side of the road. They never turned on people, they'd only growl, but they had to feed themselves somehow and then they'd attack the animals tied up by people in the fields. They'd attack sheepfolds and steal the lambs, the way wolves do. Or maybe there actually was a wolf leading the group, who knows . . . The men who had remained in the village received approval to shoot them, then there was no more talk of wild dogs, they basically disappeared.

Later, when wild animals again began raiding the sheepfolds, people said: "The wild dogs are back!" But now they were real wolves, that had multiplied unchecked in the Romanian forests and had crossed over into ours, because they didn't need a passport, and now the entire forest was theirs. Being very sly, they stole foals from the mares, the dogs hadn't known how to do something like that. At first they'd come closer in a friendly way, they'd play, roll around on their stomachs, they'd brush the foals with their tails, luring them as far as they could from the mare that was tied up, then they'd eat them as their mother watched, and the mare would neigh, cry out, scream, but it couldn't reach the spot where its offspring was being ripped open. By the time people heard, by the time they got there, the foal was already torn apart. If it wasn't careful to get far enough away, the wolf would get such a hoof to the head from the mare that it would see stars, then it would whimper and whine like a puppy and run away.

But not all the dogs became wild. On our street corner, one sat with its head down on its paws until it died. It withered away from longing and waiting. At first, it would go by people's gates and ask for food. I'd give it the end of a loaf of bread and it would hurry back over to guard its gate. Then it no longer asked for anything, but the people who passed by there felt bad and would leave it whatever they had and could afford. In the beginning it would eat, then it wouldn't touch the food anymore. It would look pitifully down the road and wait for its master to return. Bread, bones were piling up, but the dog died there, at the gate. Then it disappeared; someone must have disposed of the body.

Another neighbor left his dog with a relative, a brother-in-law who had remained in the village. It was a beautiful pup, small, vigilant, a dark brown color, Cip was its name and it barked even when someone came over to the neighbor's neighbors and would announce the arrival of welcome or unwelcome guests to everyone. I don't eat much meat anymore, so I don't have bones to give these poor dogs. The chickens are for the grandchildren, so they can taste real meat, because food in the city has no flavor. But whenever I'd have a little something, I'd take it to Cip. Everyone loved that dog. Maybe others would take it things too, because it wasn't at all thin. It, too, missed its masters, it missed its house, it pined, looked sad, but it barked when needed and it ate well. In the summer, when people come home from foreign lands, the dog felt that his loved ones, too, were nearing the house. It barked, thrashed around, pulled on its chain, dug with its claws under the gate, how could its masters return and not find it waiting at home, at the gate?

It broke or yanked out the chain, it escaped through the small hole under the gate, which was really tiny, it's a wonder how it fit, and it ran, as fast as it could, to its gate. The car, with its masters on their way home, was getting closer, the pooch was jumping for joy and getting worked up. They got out, and little Cip started jumping on them, licking them, whimpering and wanting to be petted. The people, dressed nicely and tired, shooed it away to not dirty them. They went inside the yard, but didn't let it come in, though it really wanted to. And when the driver went to park the car in the yard, he didn't see it and ran it over, smashing its skull.

He got the car in the yard, but the dog remained flattened on the ground, crushed, in a pool of blood. People passed by and saw. In the yard, people having a good time, celebrating, making a racket, and in the road, a dead dog. Someone removed its chain, because you can no longer find thin chains for dogs, they no longer sell them and you never know when you might need one, it's a good thing to have around the house. Some guest must have come in and told them: "There's a dead dog at your gate," and the family must've been outraged, they were upset, who has a bone to pick with them and brought a dead animal to their gate, as a sign of welcome? Then they saw it was their own dog. Who killed him? Well, their very own car, look, a wheel was bloody. The dog had whimpered, it was in pain, but how could you hear when you blasted the music in the car loud enough for the whole village to hear? They didn't want a dog's death to ruin the festive mood of their return, his brother-in-law took it back and buried it. He muttered that the poor critter even broke the tether, that they should come and see: "That's how much it was waiting for you, for two days straight it kept baying, it could tell you were coming back, and you kill it, all while hollering and singing."

In Troița all our dogs are kept on chains, when mine sometimes got loose, chain and all, it would trample the whole garden. One year, it ruined all my peppers. I had spent a tidy sum on seedlings, then watered them every day, I'd wake up at the first blush of morning and haul water . . . I'd water everything, in my garden how could I not grow my own dill, lovage, parsley, carrots, two rows of onions and a row of garlic, a couple plots of potatoes, at least a row of eggplants and one of peppers? It's a shame to go around asking neighbors or buying them from the market! If you haven't grown them yourself, you don't know what you're eating! The well went dry in the summer from so much watering, we ended up drawing out slurry, because the neighbors would draw out water too, not only me. And the dog would ruin everything in a matter of seconds. Sometimes dogs even get a taste for birds. One once slipped in among the geese, it got on top of them and chased them as if they were horses, and when it got a hold of one, in its little game, by the neck, the poor bird went quiet forever. Do you think I'm struggling to raise geese for my own doggy to kill them? The dogs of some of the villagers ate even their grown chickens. They thought it was polecats, but it was their little dog, the dear thing! So, people have kept them tied up since as far back as I know. In Bucovina only puppies were allowed to roam free, but as soon as they grew a bit, they, too, were chained. Small dogs, which are better behaved and afraid of geese, were taken out into the fields, as companions. That's what my husband would do, he'd take the dog with him to keep him company. The dog grew accustomed to their walk and it could sense when my husband was going out into the forest or the fields. How it would bark, how it would beg for him to take it along! Then it would jump up for joy, like a ball. But when it came out onto the road one day, a car passed by and ran it over. Another one, also small, was crushed between the wheels of a cart. Barking, they lunge at spinning wheels and end up caught in them. Then dear Anton stopped taking dogs with him, he was afraid that the speeding wheels would kill our dogs.

When my husband left for the hospital, the dog was crying, jumping up, struggling against its chain. It wanted to say goodbye to him, it knew it wouldn't see him again. Only we weren't thinking of goodbyes at all. How could it have crossed my mind that I would never see my husband again? But the dog knew. My husband went up to it and petted it, and the dog had tears in its eyes. "It loves you," we said. If I would've felt at least something of what our dog felt, I would've struggled as well, I would've broken every chain just to reach my man and hold him in my arms one more time. The next day, the dog began howling and how it howled, we all wondered what reason it might have. A bad sign . . . I didn't understand it, it cried and grieved as if it were a person, hysterically, wailing. Even then the thought of death didn't occur to me. When I brought my husband home, the dog was quiet, it didn't cry anymore, it was so quiet that I was afraid it might die.

━━━━

Mom, let's bring Cuța a puppy. She'll be afraid to leave it by itself and she won't die.

Mom, did I tell you how I went to look for a little dog for Cuța? How could she not have a dog to guard her yard and house? All the people in the village keep a dog in their yard to guard their home, but only one person had a little puppy to give away. His house was next to the school. I looked everywhere in the village. Cuța doesn't know, I want it to be a surprise, I'm waiting for the doggie to get a bit bigger. That man was glad that I wanted a puppy and he let me pick one of the three he had. I told him it was for my Cuța and he said it would be in good hands with Anica Blajinica. He asked me who I was and said, "Aha, you're Jenica Blajinica." I told him no one had called me Blajinica before! And he said that here in the village that's what the Blajinschi family was called. Since he let me pick out the puppy, I picked out the pudgiest, cutest one! White, with brown spots on its back and on an ear, it's so round and chubby, like a little ball. At first, I kept away from the mother dog, I was afraid it wouldn't let me play with the babies, that it would bite me, but after I gave it a bone a couple times, now it's glad when it sees me, it yelps and wags its tail, and it lets me get close to its three puppies. We're friends. I play with mine the most, so it can get used to its new masters. I think the mother dog also knows it will be mine and that we won't treat it badly, we'll love it and take good care of it. When Great Gran made chicken soup and I took the bones after, she saw, but didn't say anything. I didn't want to tell her about the puppy so I said that I had made friends with a dog, and that's where I was taking the bones. "Yes," Cuţa nodded and didn't say anything else. Now I'm scratching my head thinking what we should name it.

My sweet mother Aspazia hid the Bible well, she devotedly kept it and I came back with it. But I wasn't able to hide it as well as her. My son found it and burned it. Both me and my dear mother-in-law hid our tears from him. Then the times grew milder and it wasn't as shameful to believe in God, my son baptized his children as well, though I hadn't told him until he was fully grown that he, too, had been baptized. I finally told him on his wedding day, when I saw that he was marrying a kind woman. As for a religious ceremony, they did that when their children were about to get married, because the children couldn't have a religious ceremony if the parents hadn't had one. The priest asked them if they had been baptized. He looked at me unsure, he thought so, that's what he had been told. Yes, I nodded. A baptized Christian, of course. I think he had forgotten he had burned the Bible, he was little, he doesn't remember anymore.

Mother didn't hide it from me, we'd read it together, then when she could no longer see well, I'd read it to her. You couldn't find glasses back then, maybe some had them, but we didn't, we who were sent to the Kazakh steppes or to hard labor in the depths of Siberia. Mother never hid anything from me. How could I hide from my own child? When he got a bit older, maybe he understood a bit more, but back then, he'd come home from school and try to teach me that it wasn't a God in the sky who helped us, but Papa Lenin, Papa Stalin, Papa Brezhnev. And God didn't exist. My heart would break listening to him. "Religion is the opium of the masses," and it's very bad to believe in God. Neither I nor he knew what opium was. Poison, it seemed, something very harmful, by what he was saying. I couldn't talk to him. I only prayed for him. I'd wait for him to fall asleep to make the sign of the cross over him. I'd pray to the Lord every day not to abandon him, to forgive him, because he was young and didn't know what he was doing, living in a hostile world, where you could even call a dog a bull and ask it to gore something with its horns and bellow. Laws that make humans inhuman change everything, and no one can stand in their way . . . God withdrew into whispered prayers, into making the sign of the cross with the tip of your tongue on the roof and sides of your mouth, so no one would see, so no one would hear. "Lord," I would secretly cry, "save my son! Show him the true path."

One day, my son set fire to the Bible that my mother had left me. In those times, it was easier to find a dinosaur egg out in the fields than the holy scriptures in a house. And Mother's Bible was a treasure! On that day I felt something was happening, a sense of uneasiness was eating away at me, I tried to understand where the disquiet was coming from, then I saw the fire slowly smoldering. It was a spring day, before Easter. The boy had gone to tell his pioneer youth instructor that now he was worthy, that now he deserved to become a pioneer like everyone else. I took the Holy Book out of the fire, without burning my fingers, my burnt Bible, what was left of it, and I hid it inside a shoebox. It was a handful of ashes, but when things were hard, I'd touch it lightly with my fingers and pray . . . They told him that he could become a pioneer and he came home proud, happy, that he, too, was now a pioneer, in line with everyone else. And you couldn't be a pioneer if you had a Bible at home. Because it would upset Lenin, Stalin, or your homeroom teacher, as well as your pioneer instructor. He had suffered because his father had been kicked out of the school, kicked out because he had gone inside a church! And people were whispering about his mother that she had been sent far away as "an enemy of the people." Like his pa, for that matter, he came from enemies on both sides, many in the village didn't know about that anymore, but those who knew sometimes let something slip, "Get this, all the Blajinschis had been dekulakized, miserable money bags that sucked the people's blood!" I was a stranger in the village, not many knew where I had been, but who would choose to go to a trade school in the city of Kant in Kyrgyzstan? Sometimes a few more zealous communists would give me a hard time. They told the child not to take after his parents.

It wasn't only our child who was like that, they all were. They recited poems about the freest country in the world, Lenin's alphabet, they sang songs about the great joy of living in the Soviet Union. The bourgeois, the kulaks, the imperialist enemies, these had to be wiped out. The child probably couldn't understand how his own mother could be an "enemy," but he wanted to be like everyone else, not to be left out and pointed at. So all that remained was for me to pray in secret for him. When they didn't make him a pioneer with the first group of children, those who had the best grades, at first I was glad. He was among those with the highest grades, but they didn't pick him. Then I saw how he suffered because of it and I said, fine, let them make him a pioneer too . . . I just couldn't stand seeing him so sad. These pioneers are children like all children, they'll grow up and then they'll know better. But when they elected him as president of the pioneer brigade, it didn't sit well with me at all. My heart was very troubled. How could my boy become leader of the pioneers? What, doesn't the instructor know who his parents are? I kept thinking about how to convince him to refuse. The boy was terribly proud. I asked him: "What does the president of the brigade do?" He listed off several things, including punishing the children who forget their red tie at home.

"And if Petrică Hanța, who's a mountain of a boy, forgets it at home, you'll punish him too? It might be right to punish him, but he's stronger and he'll beat you to a pulp for it."

My son thought about it for a few seconds, then he said loftily, "I'm the head of all the pioneers and I'm not afraid!"

The librarian came to my rescue, a woman with a heart of gold, God rest her soul. She was our neighbor and we sometimes shared news and our troubles. "Give him something to read," she advised me, "and he'll forget all about the ties, along with all the pioneers wearing them around their necks." She picked out some books for me, about ten, but I didn't give them to him all at once, but started reading them myself first. When he'd return from school or come home from playing outside in the evening, I'd be sitting with a book open to the middle and reading enthusiastically, I'd say a phrase from the book out loud, sighing or exclaiming: "Oh no, the pirates sunk the ship! Oh no, they won the battle! The horse that was skin and bones was magic and could fly as fast as thought!" My son would come over to me, who was the pirate, what was I reading? I'd breathlessly tell him about a scene, but I never asked him to read. I quickly drew him in, until he started going to the library to take out books on his own. He didn't even play outside anymore, and the following year, his classmates chose someone else as head pioneer.

Then the mother of a schoolboy told me about how if her son forgot his tie at home, mine would say: "We'll forgive you this time, but don't let it happen again." That's what he did all year long, today we'll forgive you, tomorrow we'll forgive you, but don't you dare forget your tie next year. Because of all this forgiveness, the pioneer instructor proposed a girl be pioneer president that next year, she said that boys have weak characters and are soft on their friends and that's not good. I felt like laughing when I heard! I think I actually did laugh, heartily and with Mama Grăchina when we imagined our Jene telling a pioneer: "I forgive you for forgetting your tie at home!"

When he went on and got into the Komsomol, I hid his Komsomol identification card and he had to apply again, in the army, so he said. Because if you don't have the document, you're not in Komsomol. When he brought the second card home as well, I set them both on fire and extinguished the flames with holy water. I didn't tell him. If he had to apply to get into the Komsomol a third time, I don't remember if he told me. When my son had taken the entrance exams for the institute and was waiting for the results to be mailed home, I received a piece of paper that he was accepted not at Chişinău, but *v drugikh vuzakh*, "to other universities" meaning universities that were hard to get into, in far away cities, such as Moscow and Leningrad. I hid the piece of paper, Lord, forgive me, and I didn't show it to him. I felt sorry for my boy, but how could I send him so far away, how could I allow him to deport himself? He waited a long time, then he went to college here, in Chişinău.

God also gave me the joy of being a mother. When my son came into this world, I understood that I had a reason to live and that life went on despite all the grief. Then my daughter came into the world as well and she was a great source of comfort and joy to me, it's a shame that the Lord took her to Himself so soon. Now I'm enjoying my three grandchildren, who have gotten married and from their union seven great-grandchildren have blossomed into this world, three little gentlemen and four little ladies, and I pray to the Holy Virgin that they never experience the hardships I had to go through. God allowed for me to bury my children, but my grandchildren and great-grandchildren carry on our line.

⟶

The little old babas in our Troița de Sus made sure that all the children were baptized. Many people risked losing their jobs or getting kicked out of the party if they were caught entering a church, but these old women, who were retired, were in no such danger and no punishment hung over them. They gathered 510 children (in that time many children were born!), they'd leave the mothers at home, they advised the ones who were more fearful to take their children to some relative, and if anyone were to ask the mothers anything, they could say they didn't know, they had left their child for a few hours with their parents, relatives, neighbors . . . Well, and if in that time a relative took the child to church, she had no clue and isn't to blame. It happened, supposedly, against the parents' wishes.

The hardest was with little Joey, the son of the president of the sovkhoz, the staunchest communist in the village, who would rant and rave against our Orthodox religion at every meeting. He was against the reopening of the church in our village, even when times were more peaceful and churches had reopened in other villages and priests had come there as well. Ours served at times as storage for all kinds of parts or construction materials, or, more recently, as the village museum which also commemorated the detachment of partisans who fought against the fascists in the Great War for the Defense of the Fatherland. He named his son, alone in all the village, after Generalissimus Joseph Vissarionovich Stalin, having decided between Vladimir (Lenin), Joseph (Stalin), and Leonid (Brezhnev).

Though he admired all three, he thought that there were too many Vladimirs and Leonids, the world was full of them, maybe everyone was even thinking of a different Vladimir or Leonid. But Joseph was a rarer name, no one had that name in our village. He didn't care that his wife and relatives were opposed to it, thinking it would be strange to name the child Joseph. But no matter, Stalin wasn't the only Joseph in the world, there was also one in the Bible, that Joseph! Joseph, the son of Jacob, the most beloved of the twelve children. Joseph, who his envious brothers threw in a well, Joseph, who became prime minister in Egypt . . . How could they not baptize their Joey! But to go up to his father and suggest that it would be a good idea for him to baptize his child was useless. The boy would turn a year old any day now, he was starting to walk but still hadn't been inside a church! His wife, Melania Alexandrovna, a Russian teacher in the village school, a good, kind woman, agreed to leave her son in the care of his pious grandparents and not to say anything to her husband. He was always busy, always out and about and wouldn't have observed the child's absence anyway. And the baptism would take place at the closest monastery, the priest was waiting for them and it wouldn't take long.

If a child isn't baptized, the enemy clings to him and the holy angel flees, withdraws. In order for this not to happen, until the moment of baptism, you must keep a stick, a broom, or a pair of pliers next to the baby—the unclean one will be afraid and won't come closer, and in the evening the mother must make the sign of the cross over the child. Unbaptized children have to be guarded against the eyes of visitors, especially of sinful women, they can get small blisters. The ones boys get are more raised, the ones girls get, tinier.

After the birth, the midwife takes some bird feathers (chicken or goose) and throws them in three directions, saying, "May the baby grow as quickly and easily as these feathers float in all directions."

If you put the child to sleep as the sun is setting, he will cry all night.

The water in which a child was bathed isn't thrown outside after sunset, because the child won't be able to sleep at night, he will cry and have bad dreams. The water must be poured out at the base of a young and healthy tree, in a clean place, where neither man nor animal steps.

Diapers must be put away before the sun sets, otherwise an evil spirit will enter them.

I hadn't reached retirement yet, but my mother-in-law had grown rather weak and I didn't want her out alone, there were many children, twelve to be exact, so I also went with the grannies from the village to the baptism. It wasn't long before the fall of communism, we were still going in great secrecy.

I remember that on the way to the monastery, we ended up taking a stranger with us in our bus. We had almost fallen asleep, when the driver announced, very worried:

"Dot up ahead!"

"A dot?" we murmured, scared, and Mama Agripina, who was holding little Joseph, startled and looked at the child with concern.

"Stop jolting the bus, because they'll wake up and we've almost gotten them to sleep. What can it be?" a woman asked.

"How can I help that? My bus doesn't have tracks, only wheels. And this road is made for tanks and heavy military artillery."

We, too, knew that this road had been made for the military. I had never heard of another road having a proper name like a person, but this one does, Poltava. What Poltava means, I don't know, but it sounds brave, serious. The drivers complain that the concrete slabs ruin their wheels. But the road is good and that's how it will be even a hundred years from now, while our country roads, after a few drops of rain, are unusable even for the three tractors with tracks from our sovkhoz. Regular wheels are more sensitive when they pass from one concrete slab to another and the passengers are jostled rhythmically. But other than that, you had no cause for complaint.

"I just hope it's not a police officer," the driver continued, as the dot grew until it became a small man vigorously waving his hands.

The women who were dozing woke up and waited for the man to grow bigger, so they could make him out better.

"He's wearing a uniform, but he doesn't look like a police officer, and he doesn't have a baton."

"It's a soldier," the driver breathed in relief. "He must be from the army base next to the monastery. What should we do, should we pick him up? It's not far from here."

We hid the children, I was holding a baby girl as sweet as candy, just a few months old, whose name was Parascovia, and I hid her against my chest, under my big coat, letting just her little head stick out, only my mother-in-law held Joey in her arms, he was too big for her to be able to hide him like the rest of us. When the bus stopped, the soldier got in, and sat down in front of her. He said hello and his Russian was a bit strange. Kazakh, Kyrgyz, Tajik, I tried to guess while looking at him.

"The base at Țigănești?" the driver asked.

"Uh huh," the young soldier nodded happily.

"*Otkuda?* Where are you from?"

"Shabdanbai Sadybekov, from Issyk-Kul, Kyrgyzstan," the soldier introduced himself proudly in military style.

"From Issyk-Kul," the driver repeated.

Kyrgyzstan, so, I wasn't wrong, I'm good at knowing Asiatic peoples. They send us Kyrgyzs, because obviously they're not going to take soldiers from Moldova at the base in Țigănești. They come here from halfway across the world, and our men leave for thousands of kilometers away. It was hot in the bus, so the tired Kyrgyz dozed off. Our little old babas relaxed and fell asleep as well. At one point, the bus had to leave Poltava Road and take a country road that turned toward the monastery, so it began bouncing and shaking. At a more sudden jolt, a child woke up and started crying. Out of solidarity, but maybe for other reasons as well, the other small passengers started screaming too. We lifted the babies up and began to sing to them and soothe them. The army base was close by. The bus was slowing down. The soldier woke up and saw 11 screaming monsters, and some of them were waving around their four hands, each monster's two pairs of eyes glared at him aggressively and threateningly, it seemed to him. Only Agripina and Joey were sitting quietly. The bus stopped and the soldier ran out, yelling something in his language.

"What's he screaming like that for? What, do children cry differently in Kyrgyzstan?" we said, upset.

The Kyrgyz soon disappeared into the forest and our bus was approaching the monastery.

The son of one of the women in our group worked at that very base, he was responsible for supplies for the regiment. It happened that the scared Kyrgyz ran into him of all people and told him about how he had gotten on a bus, at first it was quiet, he saw some heads covered with scarves, he had his back toward them, but when he was about to get off, twenty monsters (we were only twelve women in that bus, Agripina and Joseph and us, the others, with tiny babies) each with two heads and four hands, began screaming at him and trying, probably, to eat him. He was lucky he managed to get out in time. The terrified Kyrgyz seemed pretty certain of what he was saying.

"What monsters? You got on a small yellow bus? That then turned onto the road toward the monastery?" The soldier didn't know, but it was the only road, so it was toward the monastery.

Then our Troiţian started roaring with laughter, and between peals, he asked him: "A big head, of an old woman, wearing a head scarf, and a small one right under the big one, two hands were on its belly, and two much smaller ones were waving in the air?" But telling the Kyrgyz the truth was dangerous, what if he were a staunch atheist and reported us? But not telling him anything was also dangerous, because who knew who else he might talk to, you could imagine the story reaching even bosses who might start making inquiries . . . "So you see, they were old women, grannies taking their little grandchildren to the hospital, for the doctor to see them, to vaccinate them, take their temperature."

"Why were they going to the church?"

"Well today is Sunday, they'll light a candle at the church, the one in our village is closed, and then they'll be on their way."

In order to be more convincing, he took him over to the only mirror in the hallway of the army base, he unbuttoned his coat, he stood the Kyrgyz in front of him, he couldn't button his coat back up but it was easier to explain it this way, two heads were looking back at them in the mirror, one on top of the other . . . No big secret.

"Is that how they hold children here in Moldova?" marveled the Kyrgyz.

"It protects them better from bacteria and diseases. Are you vaccinated against measles?"

"Me?" the Kyrgyz said, scared.

"See, you're not, and who knows what other diseases you brought over from your Kyrgyz steppe! And unvaccinated babies are very susceptible."

"I don't have any diseases," the Kyrgyz said, offended. But he had been completely convinced by these explanations and didn't tell anyone else about his trip to the base.

We found out about this discussion later, but the misadventures of our bus didn't end there. The procession had just started. After the first child was baptized and we were getting the next one ready, we suddenly heard a car horn.

"Inspection, commission here!"

This time, the commission consisted of two members, one from the county and another from the neighboring village, who served more as a guide, since the monastery was in the forest, out of sight and thus harder to find. The man from the county was searching for young couples who were getting married in the church. I well knew what could follow, I had gone through it with my husband . . . We all climbed up into the balcony for the choir, hiding the children who were cooing. The comrades burst in:

"What's with this basin in the middle of the church!" the big chief yelled, disgruntled that not one bride and groom were caught in the act. They had come for nothing, just a bunch of scared babas were rustling above them.

The priest didn't say anything.

"You're cleaning on Sunday?!" the party secretary added in a more conciliatory tone.

The priest answered timidly, "Some women came, you know, the church is big, we don't have a cleaning lady, people help us whenever they can come in."

Then the priest said to us, "Make sure to get all the dust!"

Mama Grăchina looked at the commission, then at the priest, she was the oldest, dressed modestly, in an old patched-up sweater and a housewife's apron.

"We're wiping it all, Father, all of it," and she gave a friendly smile to the party comrade, as a sign of peace and goodwill, a sign which the comrade didn't appreciate, instead he even wrinkled his nose.

The party representative came over to the baptismal font, he felt it and said: "Pretty."

"It's the one we have," the priest answered cautiously.

"It's a nice thing," the chief replied, with hidden intent. But not so hidden from his guide, who commented: "A liturgical object, retrograde, used only for religious purposes, which go against our communist interests."

The priest shot him a look of thanks. Chiefs like that are capable even of undressing you if they like something, they steal and think that's how it should be, because they deserve everything.

At home, Melania, the wife of the president of the sovkhoz, was so happy that, finally, her child, too, would be like everyone else, Christian and not pagan, that her comrade for life sensed something was up and looked at her suspiciously:

"What happened?"

"Nothing."

"What do you mean nothing? I can see that something's different with you!"

"They depaganized Joey today."

She was afraid of saying the word "baptized."

"Did Daddy's little Joey have parasites?"

"A couple very small ones," his gentle wife answered.

I brought her holy water and flower petals from the baptism for her too, to put some in the baby's bath water—so he'd be lucky and have a wonderful life. When the godparents or whoever takes the child to be baptized returns home and hands the baby to the mother, they have to say:

"Our godparent duties exercised, by God Christianized. With his mother, his father, may he live in joy, may God protect from evil your baby boy."

"We bathe him in water and with a toast, may he be given wisdom and luck by the Holy Ghost!"

"The basin spilled its water, long live our granddaughter, it spilled out in a swirl, may you have another girl, it spilled on everyone, may you have another son."

"As dough rises in the trough, may my child's heart be soft, as the fruit grows in the pear, so may truth grow ever there."

I think that my mother-in-law did as the tradition requires when she brought the baptized child home.

Joey became a full-grown man and he followed in his father's footsteps. He became a powerful man in the party. First, with the communists, through family tradition, then with the Christian-Democrats, because he had been baptized after all. After communism fell, the sovkhozes here and everything that had belonged to the party were dissolved, and the land was divided up among the people. But what could people do with so much land? They decided they might as well form associations. Our poor farmers worked more strenuously and harder than they had at the sovkhoz, since they were working their own land now, not the state's, and now it was their only source of income, money from the government—not a kopek. When it was harvest time, Joey would show up with a few of those long vehicles as big as houses, big rigs I think they're called, he'd load everything and off he'd go. He'd buy his children apartments in the city, set them up with good jobs, cushy spots with lots of money and little to do. He'd sometimes invite big bosses out hunting, offering them something or other, so he could get in good, because you never know when you might need them, because they're all just people, they all have desires and weaknesses and they like to be paid attention to. And the people in the village, after much asking and getting upset, waiting to be repaid for their work and produce, would get doled out a little something. Poverty like in the '90s I had never seen! People wouldn't take their children to school, because they didn't have any clothes or shoes for them. Not even the poorest villages in Bucovina in the '30s were like that! The people got mad and left the association, now everyone had to fend for themselves as best they could. And if they couldn't, they'd let the land go fallow and they'd leave the village and the country! Our people have become like migratory birds, except that they live at home only a few days out of the year, and they live on the run almost continually. And they're fine with that . . . Because they didn't leave without rhyme or reason, but because they had to, because no illness is worse than an empty purse. And the women cursed Joey who had stolen from their hungry children. Many stole in that period and woke up rich overnight. Dirty and sinful are their riches. Some became too rich overnight, others too poor.

On March 16, 1990, I was handed a rehabilitation certificate, on the basis of the Decree of the Presidium of the Supreme Soviet of the USSR from January 16, 1989, as it's written on the piece of paper. Well sure, they rehabilitated us, we also have the Day in Memory of the Deportation now. Among those who survived, not many are still alive, here in the village there were also a couple men who had returned from Donbas, from the coal mines, someone had been in Siberia, another returned all the way from Magadan, a few had known the vast steppes of Kazakhstan, as we had, rarely are we able to meet and exchange a few words or tell stories. Until those in power changed, they hadn't even let us talk among ourselves, now old age won't let us anymore. When we run into each other, like everyone in the village, we ask each other how's our health, about the harvest this year, it'll keep raining, it'll stop raining, a grandson or a granddaughter got into college. We're overjoyed that our descendants are studying! We wanted to, but weren't able. We're happy for them. Our whole families are studying, they're among the first in their classes, they earn diplomas, they're even praised on the radio! As for rehabilitation, what can I say, the ones high up did this more for themselves, it was in their interests, so they could be promoted even higher or voted for at the next elections because of their good deeds, not for us.

I don't know exactly what the deportation was like here, because I come from Bucovina, from another village, but word got out, people talk, it was hard for those from Bessarabia too, they also had pounding on their doors, lists of traitors, were crammed into cattle cars, the heads of families separated from the mothers with children, much pain and much death, like everywhere . . .

Because Troiţa de Sus was considered a village with many deportees, here they invited the most brilliant historian of the phenomenon of the deportations, that's how the school principal introduced him with great pomp, to deliver a talk for us. A young and handsome man. The mayor invited all us old people, but the entire village came along, us former deportees had the seats of honor in the first rows. The historian spoke so beautifully that we began tearing up, it was heartbreaking and heartfelt, he spoke rightly and it cut to the core. Before the gathering started, the mayor decided that one of the deportees from the village should go onstage and say a few words after the historian finished. First they proposed that I speak, but I wasn't from the village and then they chose Serafim Opaiţ, the one who had been all the way to Magadan and back.

After the historian spoke about its significance and about our sacrifices, about our merit and so on, in honor of the memory of, and the tragedy of the people, and grief over those who never made it back, we gave a long round of applause . . . When he saw Serafim step up, the man of history walked away, taking the microphone with him, he turned his back and whispered with the mayor and two girls who couldn't take their eyes off him, one the granddaughter of a deportee, the other, not, but no matter, he must've whispered to them that he was running for Parliament, where he would have a lot of money, that they should give him their contact info, because maybe they'd be hiring worthy descendants, the mayor told him that it wouldn't be long now and that they'd go take care of their stomachs, that the people here are hospitable, since there were even special funds set aside for the event at which such important guests were honoring us. We, those of us in the first row, who were actually former deportees, heard everything they were whispering among themselves, but couldn't really hear what Serafim Opaiț was saying, because he didn't have a microphone. Half the village had heard what the historian had said, but Serafim was nervous, he stuttered and not even the people in the first row could completely make out what he was saying. He kept thanking the historian who was sitting with his back toward him and whispering with the young ladies. We could see that he didn't care at all about poor Serafim, our representative. When our man saw this as well, he grew sad. He had gotten onstage in front of everyone, the entire village that was listening, and the historian—the guest of honor—and the mayor had their backs turned toward the person speaking, one could say, with their rear ends toward him, while he, a former deportee, was expressing his gratitude that such important people were paying attention to us . . . He finished what he had to say quickly and got off the stage. The two of them, with the young things next to them, didn't even notice. It was only when we clapped that they turned around to face the people as well.

Then the historian went to go eat. We were expecting him to ask us what our names were, where we had been deported, or at least to say "goodbye" to us. He turned around and left, while Serafim watched him go. I don't know who else had been invited to the party in honor of the historian, but what would the geezers and babas who had been deported be doing there? Our deportation had become for some a way of putting a bit more on their table, deportation interests people, it's studied, with good funding, but deportees aren't of interest, may they all hurry up and die, so we can come in with our truth, with our history. People say the historian also made a movie about deportees, the team asked them how it was, it was a nice initiative, as the principal of the school would say. That might be, but only when the person making it got something out of it as well, otherwise he'd turn his rear end toward us and wouldn't even say "good day." After this, they also held a parade, then another meeting on the subject of the deportations, our mayor called us again, but this time no one went. Then he didn't organize anything else, because he didn't know who would win the next elections and it would be better for him not to have too many patriotic initiatives.

I didn't inquire, I didn't struggle to find documents and proof that I had been wrongfully deported, I didn't write to high courts, I didn't ask for anything . . . Times were tough then too, when the regime fell, you couldn't find anything in stores. When anything arrived, people would buy up all of it, I'd fill entire pantries just with cakes of soap and matchboxes. I, too, received a document that I wasn't at fault for being deported, well of course, at eleven years old, how could it have been my fault, I was just a child! Then I did hard labor and built up socialism in the desolate steppes and on tempestuous rivers more for free than for money. Then socialism disappeared, like a puff of smoke. We had suffered for nothing, so to speak. The rehabilitation was accompanied by payment for the damages we were caused. But what could you do with that money? My husband was still alive then and we thought: "What should we do with the money? A refrigerator, us? We could use one, but the money's not enough even for a little rug." For our goods which were destroyed, for all our property that had been taken, for the tortures and privations suffered in desolate foreign places, for years, I received forty-one rubles as compensation. If you added twenty rubles to this sum, you could buy yourself a headscarf.

My husband said: "We should buy a doorbell, so they can ring in a civilized manner next time they come, and not take us by surprise in the middle of the night." In the end, we added some of our own money and bought a little goat at a very cheap price. People weren't scrambling for them, it had been a droughty year and people didn't have enough feed, because the grass had dried up, so they practically gifted it to us. How pretty it was, how happy we were! We spent all the money from our rehabilitation on it and decided we'd name it "Rehabilitation," it wasn't exactly a goat's name, rather harsh and long, too long for a single goat, it could've been divided among at least three. But we had barely had enough money for one. How we'd call after it when it would climb up and get into all kinds of things! Unruly and headstrong Rehabilitation! Then we shortened it: "Rabilita," like in the foreign shows on television; a goat named Izaura had just appeared in our neighbor's yard. Our entire neighborhood at the edge of the village knew about our famous goat and then I heard others calling after their goats with the same name as ours, though I don't think they realized where the word came from. But maybe they, too, had rehabilitated people in their families who had also bought goats?

Then, the goat's kids also received rehabilitated names: Rabilly, Billily (from Rabillily), Telly (from Rabillitelly), all names derived from rehabilitation. And in honor of the Liberals, the following she-goat was named Lala—in any case calling out "Liberal" in the street didn't roll off the tongue, and the goat's name suited it better than one related to rehabilitation—this, after the members of the county's Liberal party placed a commemorative plaque in honor of the deportees next to the monument for the partisans, as a response to the current communist party's gesture of repairing that old monument. When I arrived in the village, it had already been built, brand new, with the names of the journalists from Leningrad who had been parachuted behind the front lines, into the forest, and those of the partisans who had died in the war and those of some locals from our village who had helped them, not many. I saw that the list of deportees was longer than that of partisans.

Later we also had an ugly and lazy he-goat, which we kept as a breeder, but we quickly sold it. It bore with dignity and spikiness the name of the historian specializing in deportees who didn't care about us at all. Who used deportees to climb up higher on the social ladder himself. Worse than those who didn't know anything about us and didn't care. Ruslan was his name. The man we sold the animal to liked the name as well, he said he wouldn't forget it, because it suited the animal. Now no one gives their children Russian names, the way they had in the past, but you can give them to beasts. So Ruslan is now a male goat name. Fine, you don't come across children with the Romanian names Dumitru, Grigore, Vasile, and Constantin often either. Other names are now in fashion, no one asks priests anymore to look in their book which saint's day it is or which saint's day is close to it. A new era, new names. I remember how the parents of a baby they had named Violet changed her name to Gabriela. A baba who was rather deaf had yelled through the village: "Listen to what they named the girl: Toilet!" The parents were afraid that their baby would be given that nickname when she got older and they thought of a different name for her . . .

Rehabilitation really deserved to be the name of a majestic stallion or at least a colt, high-spirited and with its mane waving in the wind. Not the name of a regular old goat. But we had enough money only for a goat. Other women bought themselves head-scarves, thicker shawls with embroidery that had appeared in the city. Few housewives could boast of having something like that at that time. They kept you warm, they were also beautiful. And what large colorful flowers they had, they were completely dazzling! Those headscarves were expensive! But somehow I didn't feel like dressing myself up with the money that was compensation for those terrible years. But to hold onto money for dark days was dangerous in those times, either overnight everything changed from rubles to coupons, and from coupons to lei, or the money depreciated from one day to the next, and if today you could buy a cow, good, because if not, the next day you wouldn't have enough for a cup of flour. Overnight, a hundred ruble note became a ruble. And prices grew so much, that with that ruble you'd buy a few matchboxes, five at most, if you were lucky enough to find them in those empty stores. People had been saving up and saving up, the sovkhoz had been kind to some. A tractor driver had in his little bank book enough money for three apartments or a few good cars, and when the times changed, you couldn't even get a washing machine with that heap of money. My husband, a teacher, had a salary of 120 rubles, I received 90 rubles, having no higher education, I'd sew something in the village and save up a little extra, but not much. And the tractor driver received 560 rubles each month. The work was hard, he sprayed the orchards with chemicals each year, for example, and, when he was able-bodied, his wife and children enjoyed lots of money, but when the sovkhozes were through and the money was no longer worth anything, the man got sick, he was left out on the street with nothing. The kolkhozes and sovkhozes were dissolved, the land divided among the villagers, tractor drivers were no longer needed, people returned to using horses like in olden times. And he ended up with nothing, neither money nor his health.

Mom, Cuța works all day in the garden. I ask her, "Cuța, doesn't your back hurt? You've been bent over all morning. You should rest a little!"

Cuța answers, "At home, nothing hurts me, as soon as I leave my yard, everything hurts. My house is the best medicine!"

Mom, how could we send our Cuța to a nursing home? Even if the nursing home were made of gold, inside and out, she wouldn't like it there! How mean would you have to be to take her away from the house she loves so much? I'm never going to mention it to her and I think you shouldn't either!

Dad came by, yes, he brought us a bunch of stuff again, he stocked our fridge. He also brought a salted fish, the kind I like, I ate it but Cuța Ana wouldn't touch it. She had already been thinking when she got off that god-awful train that she'd never touch fish again. But when they made them fish out in Siberia, in the morning they'd receive a chunk of bread, and in the evening they'd give them each a fish, not a very big one. The girls would boil it or roast it over the fire, next day boiled, next day roasted. That was in the evening. But they went out to work on the river in the morning, they'd scarf down the bread, but from how hard the work was, from how scared they were, after a couple hours, their stomachs would be grumbling from hunger. Then they'd pull up the fishing net, they'd lift it, each take a fish, and eat it raw, they'd open it up with their hands and gobble it up, while its tail was maybe still flopping. Otherwise they would've fainted of hunger until the evening. Cuța said: "You eat it, because I can't stand the sight of it . . ."

Then I went to the golden apple tree.

Now in June, when the cherries are ripe, the golden apples

ripen too, the first summer apples, small and greenish yellow. There are summer apples that ripen in July, but the golden ones get ripe right after the cherries, before the heat waves. Cuța knows a tree and said that maybe it's still waiting for us.

Cuța taught me that back in the day when a tree didn't bear fruit, our ancestors would go over to it with a hatchet and, pretending that they wanted to cut it down, they'd say: "Without any fruit, there's no point to your roots! With just a chop, to the ground you'll drop." The tree would get so scared that after this that it would bear fruit right away. She also said, "When you go over to a tree, you shouldn't go empty-handed, well, isn't it a living thing too, it's glad when you respect it and give it attention, and it responds in kind. You should at least take it some water from a nearby spring."

"What do you mean?" I said, surprised.

"I would go every year and pour out some water for the tree, I'd give it some horse manure, as fertilizer, I thought it might like something extra, not just dirt. But now I haven't been in a while. You can't find manure anymore, people gather it all for plastering, water isn't close by, that spring has dried up and many others have dried up too. And I'm ashamed to go empty-handed, to just take its fruit and leave. The tree will be upset, everything that belongs to God on this earth is glad when we return a gift for a gift. Trees are the humblest of all, they're happy even if we relieve them of some of their generous fruit and they don't expect anything in return. Well, my delicious tree is a bit different. It's not really accustomed to people, it's a hill tree, solitary, at the edge of a wild grove. People haven't cut it down, but they haven't scrambled after its fruit either, they haven't really eaten its apples. Either it didn't really struggle to give them all that much fruit, or people didn't understand that this was an early apple tree, which ripens at the same time as cherries, not with the grapes in the vineyard, and they never saw it laden with fruit. God directed me to the tree right when its fruit was ripe and fragrant, at the exact moment it was at its peak. Ever since then, I'd go to it a few times a year and tend to it, I'd prune its dry branches, burn off the caterpillars, we had a few very wormy years, I was afraid I'd lose it, I'd water it, because that never hurts, then my legs grew weak, they could no longer withstand a very long road under the hot sun, I didn't go anymore. But I think about it every year, right about now, around this time, and I feel like it's thinking of me too and sighing. People sometimes get together, they stay and chat, but a tree is very lonely."

"Well then let's go, Cuța, let's find it. We'll take a small bucket and give it some water, we'll also take shears and cut off its sick branches."

"Now is not the time for pruning trees, that's after March 30, it's done after Alexius Day, when snakes, lizards, all kinds of creepy crawly things and all the poisonous bugs come out of the ground. That's also when you prune trees. On the same day, frogs stretch their legs, fish splash in ponds, the hedgehogs and the badgers wake up. Alexius, who holds the keys to the ground, releases the creatures who were locked up by the Archangel Michael on November 21. But we can cut off a dried out branch now as well, and in the little bucket, after we water the roots, we can carry the tree's fruit, if it has any. But you carry the bucket, because you're sprier and hardier."

Mom, I swear that Cuța's apple tree understands everything you tell it and it even talks back!

When we got to the grove, Cuța said we should close our eyes, I closed both my eyes and we walked straight to the tree, I didn't even trip, even with the bucket of water I was carrying. The tree saw us from a ways off and it guided us toward it, it called us with its scent, invited us, stretched out its shady branches to us, so I found it first, without Blajinica's help, I wrinkled my nose the way she showed me and that's how I led us to goldie. Cuṭa got there quickly too, we came closer, she laughed at seeing the tree as if she were a child, and talked to it, stroked its leaves, and fruit, and trunk. "You waited for me, dear! I wouldn't lie down in my coffin without saying goodbye to you first! Look how big and beautiful you've become! And you have apples. How sweet and fragrant! You made it through last year's drought, I was afraid you wouldn't make it. Look, I've brought my great-granddaughter. Of course, you, too, can boast of grandchildren, you have your own offspring, I see. They've also reached high up toward the sky! Do you want me to take them closer to people? Closer to water, so it's better for them? If you'll allow me, I'll take two, I'll plant one in my garden, my neighbors will want the other one, because everyone wants golden apples, and one I'll leave here with you, so you can watch it grow, to give you joy in your old age. We'll come and get them when it's the right time, when fruit trees are planted."

Whenever she said, "That's right, dear," the tree would sing and rustle. "Do you hear it?" Cuṭa would ask. "Of course I hear it," I'd answer. Even people sometimes talk to themselves when no one is listening, but who stops to listen to trees, because no one believes that they, too, have something to tell us. Until now, I didn't know either that trees also sing for joy. Then the tree gave us its fruit, small, round apples, golden-greenish, juicy, white in the middle, and they smelled delicious.

There are entire lands where apples don't grow at all, where what we grow, in bountiful Bucovina, is unknown. I lived for many years in a place where we had no access to them. Where people picked berries from the fields, grew wheat and corn, raised sheep, goats, camels, cows, but they didn't have our fruit. I missed our apple tree so much, our pear tree, cherry, quince, the fruit of my childhood, that the first year after I returned I couldn't eat them, I only looked at them, I tasted them with my eyes, then I lightly touched them, then smelled them, I'd arrange them on a beautiful plate and set them on the table. They filled the house with their aroma! The sight of them would comfort me, my soul, until they would almost start to go bad. Only then would I hurry to taste them and each time I felt like crying. Because I would remember the steppe, the deportation, the famine there, the longing for an apple. Every fruit I ate was a kind of banishment of the hunger and longing from the past.

Life changes its scents, as time goes by. The grass smells different, apples have a different scent, now there are even apples that don't smell like anything, but before, they all did and each had its own special fragrance. Clothes, joy, birth, death, all smelled different then than they do now.

Mom, Cuţa showed me a dress. She asked me if I liked it and I said yes. She had made it when she was younger and could see well. I put it on. It was the dress of a good heart, the dress of gentleness. "You're not ready for the dress of love yet," Cuţa determined, after she had me turn around, "not your butt, not your boobs . . ." She said that there's also a dress of remembering. A dress of goodbye, but of all goodbyes. The dress of wisdom. The dress of forgiveness. Wow, a woman needs so many dresses! The dress of fulfillment, the dress of mothers. Mom, did Cuţa give you the dress of mothers? I asked our artsy Blajinica if she had also made the dress of grandmothers. She had. "And the dress of great-grandmothers?"

"Of great-grandmothers, no." She couldn't see anymore. I asked her about why she sewed dresses like that and she told me. I searched in her closet but couldn't find them, I think either she's hidden them carefully or she doesn't have them anymore . . . She said you don't need to have every single one of these dresses, but sometimes you need to know when to take one off and put another one on.

Sometimes I'd get a knock on my door from a poorer wife who wanted a dress, but had enough material only for a skirt. Well, if I liked the woman, if I considered that she deserved a dress fit for a princess, I'd sew her a princess dress. The most important thing was to find something among the remnants of material I had saved that matched the material I received, so the young house-wife wouldn't be ashamed of her new dress, nor I, of what I had made. I'd find something. When the dress was ready and I laid it out in front of her, what joy and what sparkles in the woman's eyes! "God be with you, and enjoy it."

I'd accept whatever she gave, I wouldn't ask her for money, she'd ask if it was enough, because if not, she could borrow some more, she'd bring the rest of it in a month. I never said it wasn't enough. In the '80s, when women started going to seamstresses, we became better off and had plenty, we didn't die of hunger, but most people still didn't have all that much money. But always after this, a wealthier wife would come by, with lots of money in her purse and more material than was needed. God took care of everything.

The first dress I made was for Dochiţa, in Khabarovsk, where I found work at a factory as a seamstress. While Sancira was going around to all the orphanages, I got a job, because I had a diploma from a good school. I'd bring a strip of fabric home every day, until I had gathered enough for a dress. Then I sewed Sancira a dress as well, then I made one for myself. And we returned to Bucovina wearing new dresses.

There are three types of sewing machines now: manual, pedal-powered, and electric. They made their appearance one by one. Electric sewing machines came out in the '60s, until then I had used a manual one at home, and a pedal-powered one in the workshop. We had a Chaika 2, it was blue and not too big, it could sew straight stitches as well as zigzag ones. Later Chaika 3 came out. After that, I don't know anymore, because I retired . . . On our machines, the stitching was made at a stitch point, as we called it, by interlocking the upper thread in the needle with the bottom one from the bobbin. The thread guide holds the upper thread coming from the spool, the tension control knob maintains the tension spring taut, and so on. To stitch straight, which is very important, you have to be careful with the tension of the upper and lower threads. Before starting up the sewing machine, you set the length of the stitch. The stitch length can be adjusted from one to four millimeters with the help of the stitch length dial. On any garment, we can use appliqué, quilting, and turning stitches. So it seems I haven't forgotten, how could I forget, I'd sewn for forty years . . .

And what fabrics we used to have, not like now . . . Fabrics of satin and atlas weaves are fuller and heavier than fabrics of plain and twill weaves. Satin weaves are used to make satin and drapery, and atlas weaves—for ribbed knit fabric, atlas, crepe satin, and satin lining. Fabrics made of satin weave come undone easily.

The choice of material depends on the purpose of the dress: everyday, special occasion, housedress; on the season: summer, winter; the desired pattern, and the particularities of the wearer's figure. Items worn below the waist, skirts, for example, are part of the category of bottom wear, everything worn on the lower part of the body, while those worn on the shoulders, tops, are for the upper part of the body.

Who knows how to take a proper HHW anymore! Meaning half hip width, but also the measurements for the sleeves, the bust, the waist! The length of the garment—GL, length from base of neck to the center of the front—CF. When you calculate the amount of material, you add ten centimeters to the length of the skirt (SK) for fit and alterations, that's only if the skirt is straight. Besides taking measurements, you have to know the size of the seam allowances, so the dress will drape nicely. These allowances are different in each case.

The skirt of a dress can be A-line, pencil, or circle, according to the cut, and according to its style: straight, flared, tapered. Circle skirts are like a sun, we say, or part of a sun. They are divided into seven main groups: full circle, gathered circle, half circle, three-quarters circle, bell, balloon, sunburst. Careful with the height of the waistline and the length of the hemline!

Straight skirts can be modified with a single seam, with two, or with three, with pleats or without, full, simple pleats, double pleats, or fan-shaped, with panels. And the darts, oh, the darts! Back, waist, hip, bust, the sum of all the darts. You don't start making a dress without knowing all this!

Trimmings complete and embellish an item. We use different types of trims, embroidery, different notions, stitching, seams, piping, cords, garment accessories such as sashes, pockets, yokes, bibs, straps. Embroidery can be geometric, thematic, traditional, in the form of decorative foliage. Clothes can be embellished with fringe, sewn along the hemline or the pockets, for some clothes lace is more fitting.

For clothing made of thin silk or batiste you don't use a size 120 needle, a 75 would be more suitable, and for thread number—80 for cotton, 65—for silk. A wool suit requires a 120 needle, thread size 30-40. The details of the pattern are arranged in the direction of the straight grain and the design. Cutting along the cross grain is also allowed.

I thought I had forgotten, but see, the baba remembers everything!

Dear, maybe how to make a dress isn't of interest to you . . . But I've lived through times in our Bucovina when all the fabrics and all the clothes were made at home by women! Those times!

Father was the school principal, he had many books and he'd read, he'd study, we didn't even have that many animals around the house, but I'd go to my grandparents on my mother's side and help them out with all the chores, starting with the preparation of hemp: picking it, putting the stalks into the pond for retting, first using the big hemp break, then the little hemp break, sorting the fibers, scutching, hackling, spinning, weaving on the loom, before the clothing is sewn. The higher quality fibers are used for finer cloth, for shirts for special occasions, and the lower quality ones—for everyday clothes and coverings. Similar work was necessary for sheep's wool before you could weave it into a prigitoare or catrinţă, our long pleated skirt, a brâu to go around your waist, a big or little pouch, a covering, or to full it for a suman to wear in the winter. A young woman had to know how to do all of these household tasks, and many more, to be appreciated by people, in general, as someone who could manage a household, and especially by young men, so she could marry well, a man of means. Even from a tender age, I already had my hope chest, with thirteen shirts for special occasions and seven for regular wearing inside. I also had several good sized cătrinţas, a couple embroidered vests which we call a pieptar or a bundiţă, some of them were from my sister, who had grown a lot and no longer fit in them.

Our grandfather, Constantin Zeiță, also grew hemp. After it grew tall, we'd pick it and then take it to the river to soak it. We'd bring it home, dry it out, and process it with a scutching board and knife. I liked that and asked Grandfather to make me a smaller board and knife so I could help break up the hemp too. Grandfather was a good man and he loved children, he granted all my requests, especially when it had to do with work. He made me a scutching board and knife and I couldn't have been happier. My hair was full of hurd—the multitude of small fibers from the broken up hemp, but I didn't care, I was so happy to be helping. Mother and her younger sister Sancira would come to help with whitening the cloth and carding the wool. In the winter, Mother would embroider, weave, knit, she knew how to do everything . . . People used to work really hard . . . Now who even still knows what a hemp fiber looks like or a spindle . . .

Mom, when I came to stay at Cuța's, one of the first things she asked me to do was stop up the hole under the fence, through which our chickens would go over to our neighbors and never return. I covered it completely, I put a rock there, and a metal sheet. Cuța had twenty chickens when I got here, all beautiful, we ate two and just now when we numbered them, there were only twelve instead of eighteen! Cuța knew exactly which ones had disappeared without me numbering them. She was very upset, because her chickens were disappearing, she was really fond of them, and she doesn't have any other poultry around the house. When our favorite, who was also the rooster's favorite, the barred-feathered Veronica, also disappeared, I went to see if the neighbors had, by any chance, made another hole. They had made two! As long as the chickens were chicks and weren't any good for soup, they wouldn't disappear, but the neighbors would go after fat, beautiful chickens. Worse than polecats!

Since I saw how sad it made our Cuța, I went out in the street and started calling for the chicken. "Veronica, Saint Veronica! Where are you, little chicken, tufted and barred? Are you out there in somebody's yard? Whoever eats you will get the flu, and whoever kills you, will need days to come to!" I waited for our neighbor and asked her, "Have you seen Saint Veronica?"

"What Saint Veronica?"

"Well, a little tufted chicken, whose magic, with colorful feathers, who brings good luck on long journeys, brings its owners health and money, that is, if they don't cut it up for soup. It would be terrible for the person who eats it, terrible for anyone who spills even a drop of its blood! Cuța Anicuța is sitting in front of her icons and praying for our Saint Veronica! She's also praying for the health of the person at whose house the chicken accidentally stopped, because if an animal, the kind that digs holes under fences, catches it, what can you do? Oh but if a person catches it and kills it . . . !"

Ugh, no animal in this world acts more like an animal than people . . . I had thought that if we were fasting, the neighbors must be as well, because they're old, long retired, and since today's Friday, they'd kill it only tomorrow . . . The neighbor got scared, she returned Veronica through the hole under the fence. Cuța thought that something was suspicious about how it came back. I didn't tell her how I had scared the neighbors, it's a good thing they're easy to scare! But they only returned one chicken, how about the others? I didn't tell her how I sainted her chicken either. She never would've seen it again if I hadn't.

Cuța said that regardless of whether you had neighbors who love the chickens of others, or neighbors who don't steal anything (which rarely happens when you're a baba all alone in an abandoned village), it's good to get along with everyone around you.

She had me pick a little bucket of apricots and take it to them. I took it to them and also told them that our Saint Veronica is for breeding and can't be slaughtered except while saying certain prayers, in gratitude to the Lord. Because it lays big eggs and we want it to brood. You don't dig holes under people's fences and steal a person's only bird. I didn't say that, but I'm thinking it now.

We'll talk more tomorrow.

Well, I, too, got angry a few times. Oh! A few times I raised my voice. I yelled holding a fist up to the sky. Strike me, Lord, kill me, break me into little shards of pottery, right now, if I'm to blame in any way! Send Your lightning bolt, strike me with death, so that I know I'm paying for a sin, for some guilt, or strike my enemy who wrongs me and tortures me. Then I was sorry, very sorry, afterward I prayed with humility, all in the spirit of meekness, prayers to the Lord I lifted up, I asked for forgiveness. And God gave me a long life, but my enemies He drove into the ground. So I go on suffering, I thought, sinful as I am, while they have escaped all suffering, but no, my thinking wasn't right, I'm glad that God kept me alive, to live and enjoy all His wonders that are given to us on earth, but by the time a person understands this . . . You die before understanding. You have to be standing next to your coffin, with one foot in the grave, as they say, about to step over to the other side, to be as happy as you should be now, here in this world. Everything comes from God and everything is love. With unspeakable joy I thank God for finding me worthy of this long life, with its suffering as well as its joy. Each day I pray that I may grow in virtue. That I may banish from my soul all that makes me turn from the way of the Lord. Long-suffering, goodness, humility, gentleness, mercy, patience. Lord, strengthen me.

A lifetime I lived alongside people who were good and valiant, who I shared both good and bad with . . . A lifetime, to find out one day that your friend is not really your friend . . .

One day, Mama Agripina took me to a woman in our village who we got along well with, but I had no idea what a secret grudge she held against my mother-in-law, what rancor she had toward her and we hadn't known. She now wished to die in peace, reconciled, and she asked my mother-in-law, who could barely walk, to go to her. I had to accompany her and hear everything . . . It pained me, it felt like a blow, it disgusted me, my blood ran cold, I felt sick, I wasn't expecting it, I couldn't believe it, but poor mamă Grăchina kept listening, having compassion and forgiving everything . . .

"In our youth, you were rich and beautiful, me, ugly and skinny, I took revenge and wrote you down on the list of those who should be sent to their death, though many others had more land, I went to the communists and told them about your family, I gave them everything they wanted, just so I could remain in the homeland, but you I sent away.

"Later, I put a dead ram, with its head and fleece and all, at the corner of your house, I buried it at night after I had tamed your dogs by secretly feeding them every night. So you would have only poverty, sickness, and misfortune.

"I stole the rope used to tie the legs of a dead man together and tied it to your fence, so all your goods and all your joys would be tied up, so you'd be visited only by misery.

"When you bought a horse, how could you have a horse? How did you have so much money, did you borrow, did you save up, to be able to buy yourself such a wonder? With my own hands I tightened the rope around its neck until its eyes bulged out of its head. I also cut some of its mane, but the baba witch didn't know what kind of evil she could do to you with the hair of a dead horse, so I threw it away.

"When your Anton had grown and was a joy to your heart of a mother, I paid some young vagabonds from the neighboring village, through some known drunks capable of anything, to beat your boy to a pulp, under the pretext that he would've wanted to cozy up to one of their girlfriends, they beat him with clubs and a crowbar, and then you had to put him back together, as I dreamed would happen, and when he was bedridden and needed peace and quiet, I sent all kinds of relatives over to you to buy themselves wine and yell, to sing under your windows in the middle of the night so he couldn't sleep and rest. When his classmates wanted to come visit him, I asked them, one by one, not to because it wouldn't be good for him, it would make him worse. But I wasn't thinking about your son and what would be good for him, but about how to punish him and you, so that you'd feel abandoned, alone, so your son would die of sorrow and pain. And then I asked you: 'How is it possible? Not one classmate came to see him? Does really no one care about him?' When I found out that Ana, your daughter-in-law, was just a poor, stupid milkmaid, skinny and ugly, I was glad, but if I had known how well they would get along, I would've run her out of the village from the very beginning!

"I also unjustly punished your grandson, I humiliated him, I was a pioneer instructor then and wouldn't let him become a pioneer, though he was the best student, instead I made him suffer, I wanted all of you to suffer and I told him to burn your Bible . . .

"Then, in 1986, I knew that because of Chernobyl it wasn't good to go to the seaside and I put the names of your entire family on the list for vacations through the union and encouraged you to go, your son and grandson escaped, they didn't go, but your dear granddaughter went and she and her little baby got sick and died of cancer, because of me, they died before their time and you shed many tears.

"When you returned from gentle Siberia, though I would've wanted you to never return, that's where your bones should've remained, I kept all the men far from you, so they wouldn't somehow approach a widow so young, and I didn't let you leave the village so you could have a better life somewhere else either. I wanted to keep you under my control, so you had to depend on me, so things would be the way I wanted them. I wanted to crush your heart, for you to fall, to cry, but you remained upright, serene, and you always smiled, like a dumb cow. You smiled at everyone, you smiled at me too, and thought I was your best friend. You dared to keep believing in your God, who would help you each time and rescue you from troubles by a hair's breath. And I wasn't the only one, so many base women hated you. It was hard for all of us, we would humiliate ourselves, we would butt kiss slimy communists for a better salary or a vacation somewhere, at the sovkhoz's expense. You were the only one who didn't want anything and were always content.

"Every March 8, all the women would receive flowers, but when it was your turn they'd suddenly be all out or you'd receive a broken one, without a stem, which you'd hold in such a way that it wouldn't be obvious that it was different. I managed to do this too! When they'd give us presents at the sovkhoz in beautiful, big boxes, I'd put just cardboard inside yours and wait for you to complain, to be outraged, but you didn't look the least upset, you happily thanked everyone. I wanted you to be unhappy, discontent, but you were all smiles and light. I did everything I could so that things wouldn't go well for your only living child, and for things to go well for my children. Mine became so rich that they could buy half of Chișinău, but what good is it? My only grandson is dissolute and takes drugs and spends all his time with boys with dyed hair who look like parrots, he won't hear of girls, and he said he's not getting married, because all he wants to do for the rest of his life is listen to music. What use is our wealth? His parents live in fear for each leu they've amassed, they're afraid in their own home, that their beloved son will steal from them to buy drugs, or that he'll run away from them and they'll find him in some ravine, dead from the poisons he's swallowed. I can't help him at all. He doesn't talk to me, he doesn't visit the way your family does. I have no strength left, no hope left . . .

"We thought we'd be riding Lenin's coat-tails, that things would go well for us, as they said they would and kept repeating, but it was a stinking lie, we discovered quickly, everything stunk, we were wasting away and drying up in the fields of the fatherland and the party, only you with your God were young and serene. We couldn't forgive you for this. And as if it were yesterday, in a moment everything collapsed, everything disappeared and we were left out in the cold. Without our piles of rubles at the post office, for which we had slaved away for so many years, which overnight transformed into nothing, without the position of party representative where you yelled at everyone and twiddled your thumbs, without our all-powerful communism, great and eternal, that had no right doing this to us after we had served it with such self-sacrifice! Our communism fell and no longer cared about us, it no longer supported us, but your God is still standing, prouder and looking better than ever and he supports you and is by your side, and he also opened up the churches, while we trembled at the thought that we might be thrown in jail. Ours had barely fallen, and yours was opening the gates for true believers and calling them, urging them, enticing them. I swore loyalty to the party until death, faith in the party! And when it was in trouble, I abandoned it. I joined its side to eat bread that was finer, I swore to be faithful, and then I betrayed it, I abandoned it and I'm neither with God, nor with the party, all our people have gone over to new parties, with nice names. A great betrayal and a great punishment to go with it. Betrayal is a sin. Breaking your oath is a sin. The Devil, too, is powerful if you've given yourself over to him, he demands his rights.

"I went to the church to pray like you do, if you're doing well with so little, why wouldn't it be the same for me? I went secretly, because I'm an important person, I had been a party member. I didn't want the village laughing at me that, look, I'm asking God for help. But if God forgives and helps, why wouldn't he forgive and help me? I wanted to ask God for what I didn't have, peace and quiet for my children and grandchild, for us to be a loving family, for him to fix my problems. Kira the witch, who I always went to, told me that whatever someone wished for in front of the icons would come true, she told me where and how to touch them. But there in the church, all I could think of was you, I kept seeing you everywhere, though I tried banishing the thought of you, then I felt I wanted you to die, that I wish for your death. The thought I had in the church scared me and I didn't ask God for that. Kira calmed me down, she told me you were close to dying, that you were in a bad way, your children weren't rich like mine or set up for life, your whole family was weak and sick, so God was on my side. I didn't go back to the church.

"Now I'm at death's door and you're serene as always. Kira lied to me. You're out in your garden hoeing by yourself, and I'm bedridden and a nurse changes my sheets. I will die soon, and you will live, you will enjoy the sun, the gifts of life and of old age, good children and well-behaved grandchildren, who call you 'Granny Grăchinny, Grăchina Blajina' all day long, only with pet names, while my grandson said on the telephone that he doesn't want to see the half-dead baba who reeks of piss. He said it so I could hear it too and not keep insisting on seeing him at least once more before I die. The cherries are ripening and your life will grow sweeter, while I will rot in the ground.

"Your cruel God is removing me from off the face of the earth so I can't sin anymore. I forget what else I did to harm you. Every day I would think up plans, how else I could hurt you, how I could make you suffer. All the neighbors were on my side, I taught them to steal your chicks and chickens, to poison your rabbits, to whistle under your window at night so you'd be afraid that you were home alone. I also killed your cat, because you really loved it, and none of your neighbors wanted to kill it, 'cause it caught mice and didn't steal anything, so they said, a good cat. And it's bad luck to kill a cat. I don't believe in your bad luck. I can't stand cats, only dogs, and only when they're chained up, where they're supposed to be, so enemies and strangers can see them plainly.

"My girl liked your boy, who had grown up to be polite and hardworking, but it's a good thing she didn't marry him, she found herself a rich man from the city, well-suited for her, not a dirt poor enemy of the people the likes of yours, who Siberia awaits at every turn. She would've married your Anton, the little fool, if I hadn't taught her better in time. He found himself a seamstress well-suited to him, a fellow enemy from Siberia. Who besides him would've looked at that skinny thing twice! I didn't stop until your son was kicked out of school, I had those stupid sponsors tell your boy to go to the church, I'm the one who called the commission, I thought of everything the way I wanted it, and that's how it turned out. You buried him quickly, I don't know what it's like to bury your only child, after you've also lost your husband and have no one left, and I still wouldn't leave you alone . . .

"I don't remember how else I harmed you, but how much more it would've been if I still had the strength, I wouldn't have allowed you to get so hoity-toity. Now, it's over, my time has come. I don't believe either in heaven or hell, I don't know how some can believe in God, I'd like to believe as well, but there's no more time. But I think my death would be easier if you'd forgive me. I wanted you to know everything. You have to be able to forgive me, but for real, with all your heart. You, believers, forgive everything. You can hit me in the head with something, you can spit on me, you can do anything because I'm bedridden, helpless, I'd understand after everything I've done to you. Maybe your faith doesn't want to overlook so much evil, maybe your God is saying something else to you now, but I have to tell you everything and ask you to forgive me. Only your forgiveness can free me from agony, I'd like to leave this world reconciled. I harmed others as well, but they returned evil with evil, they weren't to be outdone, they took revenge, a tooth for a tooth. You're the only one who never took revenge, you never did me any evil, I searched long through my old mind. You never did me any evil, and I never did you any good. Do me evil now, great evil. Or a final good deed and forgive me."

Remembering old sins weighs heavy on the heart, it keeps old filth inside you. Guard the peace of your heart and don't hold hatred against your neighbor in it. To be free of despair, don't gather up anger or remain angry at yourself or at your neighbor. Be hard on yourself and lenient with others. If you submit to the will of God, you will never feel the heavy darkness of sorrow, the terrible waves of passions will die down, and in their place will arise clarity of thought, calmness of mind, gentleness of the soul, and the peace that never disappoints, which will bless you from above and make its home in your soul.

"With the measure you use it will be measured to you." If you do evil to another, you will experience evil as well. Do not allow your body to be master over your soul. Endure all things. The body is the instrument of the soul, the entire world is a mystery. The soul that lives in sin is shaken, it has no constancy. May the holy fire burn in your heart. The human heart is full of serpents which are the passions. The passions don't live separately, but together, gathering there one after the other. The disordered life. Lies and folly affect our conscience and we are overpowered and fall. Whoever doesn't fight against sin has no way of overcoming it.

Great sadness is sinful. You do evil—God will punish you, you do good—people will punish you. Throw all your cares onto the Lord and light will be your cross. Sorrow tortures everyone, it destroys the beneficial fruits of self-control for even the greatest people. Whoever has denied themselves through hope in God, what could cause them sorrow? For such a person, "the enemies have vanished in everlasting ruins," as the holy scriptures say. Depression is an invention of the Devil. If you selfishly pity yourself, you'll end up in hell. Jonah didn't lose hope in the bottom of the abyss when he was swallowed by a sea creature, but instead prayed, and you, weak soul, let out blasphemies of despair, doubt, suspicion, though you're enjoying the light of the sun.

When the light of grace can no longer be seen within because a cloud of passions overshadows the soul, and when the power which gives joy has weakened in you, so that your mind is enveloped by an unusual darkness, do not let your thoughts be troubled, but have patience, read the Bible and wait for help. Just as the face of the earth is saved from darkness by the rays of the sun, prayer can destroy and scatter the clouds of passions from the soul and comfort the mind with joy. Whoever spends much time in prayer will be shown the truth. Endure everything with joy and goodwill, because great is the reward of patience.

Keep me held high, Lord, since coming down I do on my own!

When you thank God for your troubles, the unseen spiritual power of faith springs up in your heart, then an unspeakable spiritual comfort. Endure and fight. God, our Heavenly Father, is all-knowing and all-powerful—He sees our misfortunes and if He deems that we deserve them, we will go through them. Those in trouble find themselves right before God. Let us stand with great reverence in front of God, our most merciful Father.

Flee, wretched thoughts and unclean attitudes, go into the wilderness, into the mountains and far away valleys, go to other lands, scatter in the winds! I will love You, Lord, because You are my power and my great virtue in fallen times. You are my refuge and my salvation, You give me great hope in faith!

What can I ask of You, Lord? You alone know what I need. Don't allow me to forget that all things come from You. Those who mock us, making earth troublesome to us, make heaven dear to us. They drive us closer to God. Forgive them and bless them and pray to God for them. Give me strength, Lord, to bear today's burden and to endure everything given to me. Guide my life and lead me to what I should pray, to endure, believe, love, hope. Amen.

Agripina prayed for a long time then, and this is what she answered that woman:

"One time Anton came home with a little crate full of strawberries. You had just been picking some, and he was passing by, he must've looked a bit longer, like children do, more hungrily maybe, you called him over and gave him a crate full of ripe, sweet-smelling strawberries. Don't you remember? How happy he came home and how he popped them in his mouth! I also made a small jar of jam then. No one in the village had strawberries like yours! We planted some as well, but they didn't take, they were too in the shade, then the heat waves came and they dried up. And then, the boy came home with a crate. What generosity, what a good heart! I prayed for your soul. ("I don't remember the strawberries," the dying woman said, sluggishly.) And one time you helped me find a doctor, the best in his field, may God give him health as well, he got my boy back on his feet. And you gave me a Christmas tree one time. I kept it up until March and it was still green. And when everything disappeared from the stores, in the '90s, you took some of us women to Orhei, to a store only you knew about, you had some relatives there who told you when it would be stocked, and we bought things. I still have two of those rugs even now, soft wool, not synthetic material like now which slips and squeaks under your feet. If you ever wronged me, may God forgive you, because I don't harbor any anger against you.

"Forgive our enemies as well, Lord, those who oppress and afflict us, forgive those who do wrong without knowing, and do not allow them to perish. Help them to return to Your path. I've always respected this woman and held her in high regard my whole life, she's had a harder life than mine, only now do I realize that she's had a harder life than I could've imagined. If she wants to pass over into the next life more purified, I can only help her. I said I forgive her, but only the good Lord forgives. Forgive me, Lord, for taking this sin upon myself, I'm not worthy, forgive me, Lord, and also forgive this poor woman who is on death's doorstep. Give us the spirit of true repentance so that, all our sins being forgiven, we may be devoted and righteous until our journey's end. Allow this tortured soul to leave in peace, reconciled. Because nothing stings a person worse than the sting of regret and the weight of sin at the end of one's life."

And I was listening and my heart was bleeding. I had buried my husband, my daughter, and my darling granddaughter, and I couldn't stand hearing such horrors. And that baba was more than ninety years old, and Mama Grăchina was almost ninety, and I was already a baba, going on seventy. To hear how the death of my daughter, my beloved child, was so thought out, with such treachery and in cold blood, and say: "I forgive you, die in peace," as my mother-in-law said, I couldn't do it. Agripina listened with a serene countenance and no poisoned arrow entered her heart. But I couldn't, the poison entered me, the evil in the words of that ghoul struck and whipped everything within me, it threw me to the ground, it laid me low. I would've wanted never to have known it, not to have been there. Every trial comes from You, Lord, and I have made it through them all, but how can I make it through this one as well? Lord, Lord, help me!

A long time passed until my heart learned to forgive. God, forgive me for my wickedness, I had dark thoughts about that tormented, sick woman, I forgave her only halfway, half-heartedly, instead of smiling at her and helping her find peace and calm. I let myself be overcome by some words about the past, a blessed past which, thanks to You, Lord, I lived well. Forgive me for calling up images of what happened to us, I condemned her and didn't smile at her with an open heart.

Lord, I lack the words to give You the glory You deserve! What hard times and with each change everyone hoped things would be better and they seemed to everyone to grow worse. But Lord, I thank You, despite how much wickedness we've accumulated inside us, You are exceedingly good and merciful, and You allow us, vile scoundrels and blasphemers, and murderers, and sinners of all kinds, to enjoy all Your gifts. Even the Evil One who sets people against each other and awakens doubt in our souls would be frightened to know all that people are capable of doing to their innocent neighbor, but You forgive us and love us. I lift up my gratitude to You, Lord, for forgiving us sinners, and also for showing some the true path.

Despair is death's dowry. Guard yourself from somehow hating those who don't believe. For you it would be harmful, for them unhelpful. Regard them with compassion, as poor wanderers. The Lord is in control of everything. Forgive! If the Lord forgives everything He created, if He gives a life of plenty and wealth to

those who don't believe in Him, and a long life, you should forgive
them as well. Maybe they'll enjoy it and grow wiser and, at least in
the end, thank Him for everything. I don't understand how you
can live in the lap of luxury without gratitude. I don't understand
those in high places, the great and rich, who put everything into
their bellies, they fatten their bodies, but don't feed their souls
anything. Even a pig, a cow, has a belly, but a soul . . . To have a
soul which likens you to all that is holy, to what is above, and to
forget that you have it, to neglect it, wrong it! Our soul is a miracle on earth, our godliness comes from our soul.

Many of our society's amusements are pagan abominations.
When I look at today's children, the poor things, who can bring
them closer to the Lord? And where? You turn on the television—
from morning until night all you see are antichrists, jumping and
yelling. What television shows, what schooling . . . Yes, all the
manifestations of the Devil everywhere, laugh and cavort, with
barbed tails. Today's children read many harmful books, but the
Holy Book, the source of God's truth, so necessary for guiding
our lives, they don't even have, they don't even read.

But God is nearby. Why would the Damned One, God forgive me, be everywhere, always at hand, but God not? It's enough
only to think of the Lord to see Him in all right and honorable
things, starting with the sun's rays, the fruit of the field, timely
rains. "God, how we could use a good rain shower!" And the Lord
hears us and sends the blessed rain, which helps the corn shoot
up. The corn has grown, we have food for all the animals and all
the poultry around the house. The devils that travel on the backs
of sinners aren't more present among us than the Lord's angels.
You only need to be less hurried, to have more patience.

How can you be sad, how can you be angry with life because
you don't have something or other? The sun rises even if there's no
rooster to sing. Sometimes I even think that a bit of Siberia wouldn't

be quite so bad for today's youth. Well, of course, not a Siberia like ours, but maybe a two-week journey to get there. Ours had been in cattle cars, without water, without food, without the sun's touch. We once stopped next to a river. And we hadn't washed ourselves for over a week, maybe two, how we all stunk, our clothing was stuck to our bodies, and then we saw that water! We shouted for joy, for the pleasure of it, that water gave us life. We splashed each other, laughed, for three days afterward we felt that cool cleanliness of a washed body. I feel it even today. I lie in bed and remember. Our mothers yelled to us: "It's cold! Be careful or you'll get sick! Don't go in!" But today, weak souls, weak bodies, lacking faith, sick.

I'm the only one left in the house, but I'm never alone, God is always with me, sometimes the wind blows and I hear strange sounds, animals sometimes cry, shriek, bellow, at first you might be frightened, you think of all that could happen, but focusing on God, on His mercy and His will calms all our fears. "Fear gives rise to despair, there is no fear in love, the one who fears is not made perfect in love." Excessive melancholy keeps you from experiencing joy. Steadfast courage faithfully maintained is proof of this love.

Lord, we pray to You so little, we thank You so little!

I enjoy the sun, a slice of bread, the warmth of the stove in winter, peaceful neighbors, children and grandchildren who spoil me, animals with their gentle eyes, all the creatures with the power of speech and those without, all Your creatures, that the church is now a church and that we have the kind of priest who is a rare find, that we have our health, all that we need to be able to go and work the land and feed ourselves, I can even tend the parsley in my garden. All Your gifts, Lord, make me glad. They are countless.

People are divided into several types, not only there, in Siberia, but also in Bucovina, and I saw the same thing happen in Moldova. Some change along with the times, others remain the same, regardless of the times, others, fewer, are the ones who change the times. Some deportees became the guards or overseers of the newer deportees, forgetting how, a short while ago, they themselves were like us. Others wouldn't align themselves with the new regime, they didn't join it in order to live better, and they helped us however they could, sometimes even a word of advice helped us greatly, because they had been living in the wilderness for decades, while we had just arrived and didn't know anything. Some want to forget, others don't, they can't, they don't even know why themselves. Remain human and help your neighbor in trouble. Give, and God will give to you, He'll reward you, help and God will help you. People who are stuffed to the gills, rich, who have everything and can get whatever they want whenever, are farther from God than the afflicted person who lacks many things and is undergoing hard trials. It is good when the person who is tested, who has gone through many things, has wisdom and goodness, the person who has been reduced by hardships to the condition of an animal, and has to return to being human again. It is good when they walk the road back with dignity, with excellence, carrying God in their heart.

Here, a good deed, a nice gesture, is praiseworthy, but it doesn't seem to have the same weight as there. There, a mother who sat on the frozen ground and held her child in her lap knew that the child's life would cost her own life and hoped that this would be the result of her deed. The child understood as well and honored the parent. Whenever anyone shared a piece of bread or a potato skin they knew that they risked dying of hunger themselves the next day and for no one to hand them anything in return. Here, not even when branches are breaking under the weight of their fruit can neighbors bear to share with those around them. If you get a taste of their fruit in the end, don't forget that you probably also have a fruit free with which you can repay them for their good deed. Thank you and God preserve you! There heaven and hell went hand in hand. Everything was short and simple, life and death, one next to the other. Life meant a thick coat or a spot more sheltered from the wind and a crust of bread, and death—the lack of these.

People are the same everywhere, both good and bad. During the war, the Russians, the Russian women actually, helped us, but they, too, were deportees like us, suffering as well. They would ask the Kazakh bosses to bring our children medicine, to give us food, especially in the winter, when it was harder and any bit of help could save a life. They also brought us firewood, when we became a bit better off, we repaid their help, we, the few who survived that winter. They would say that those who brought this scourge upon them and upon us weren't Russians, but communist demons. They said that the Russian people are peace-loving and gentle, and look what a plague has descended on them and is destroying them from within! It's so great a plague that other nations were caught up in the wheel of death as well. From Bucovina to Siberia, we said, the road was sown with corpses and watered with tears. Later I found out that it was not only from Bucovina, that the innocent victims were from different places, from many, many places. We all met there, at the edge of the world.

❧

Mom!

Cuţa sings these songs, she cries while singing them! I've learned how to sing them too, listen:

*Mother grief, when I remember, makes my heart burn like an
     ember. Oh, oh!*
Mother grief is heavy sickness,
To my heart it's fixed, just like sap it sticks

You know for parent grief, nothing gives the heart relief.
Grief of sisters and of brothers, unlike those of any others.
And grief of home cannot be outgrown.
And grief of land is more than you can stand.
Oh, oh!
The linden tree asks me
Where my parents might be
I say that I left them there
In that land far away and bare
Among wormwood wilting
Of this Stalin is guilty!
Oh, oh!

I know others too, every night we sing and talk!

—There are also people who don't sing.
　—Is it bad not to sing?
　—What is the human soul without song? Songs uplift you, they calm you, and cheer you up. Today everyone listens to songs, but they don't know how to sing. I can't understand how you would just sit there listening without allowing your spirit to soar, so it refreshes itself a little. When we used to gather together, we'd talk, nibble on something if we had anything, then we'd sing. Someone would start and everyone would join in, at least at the chorus. Except that when you hear an incredibly beautiful song, that tears at your heart, you can't bear to interrupt it by joining in, to ruin its magic. Before, even an uneducated kolkhoz girl had a notebook with songs in it. Now everyone just listens, young people don't know songs, if you asked them to, they couldn't sing one for you, not even a simple chorus that rhymes. They watch soccer instead of playing it themselves and stretching out their legs. When eating—a dog, working—a fox, sleeping—a log.

—Well then come on, Cuţa, teach me another song of yours, about the deportation.

I had no candle, had no shroud,
Had no cross, no priest's head bowed . . .
Perhaps your tears will hasten
And be the means of my salvation.
Mother, of my bitterness
Ask God to be my witness.
Pray for mercy, grace, amen,
For the country to be whole again,
For you all to be free as well
From these troubles and this hell.
Cry for me and for me grieve
Until this world you finally leave.
Tell everyone, so they believe,
How your child dear
By pagans was killed here
For being a Christian
For being a good Romanian!
Oh, oh!

Mom, as we were singing, we heard a loud noise in the barnyard. I pulled aside the little curtain at the window to see what was happening with the chickens, then I knocked on the window. All the birds were squawking, the rooster was thrashing its wings, and in the middle of them, I saw some kind of animal like a gray ball, that was jumping and spinning around. I went outside to find out more, because I couldn't tell from the window.

"Cuţa! Come quickly! An animal got in with our chickens, and they're running around scared!" I yelled.

The animal transformed into a bird when I got a bit closer.

"A raptor!" exclaimed Cuța, when the animal that was about the size of a fat chicken opened its wings about a meter in length, they were very beautiful, they had patterns and what looked like ribbons, and it made my jaw drop.

That raptor, a buzzard, had chosen a chicken for its prey and was struggling to grasp it better in its claws and fly away with it, but the prey was too heavy, too big, and when we showed up, it took off scared without the chicken. I had never seen a buzzard before then.

"Cuța! It's the enchanted bird, from the fairytales, did you see what beautiful wings it had!"

I was so thrilled to see a live buzzard in our very yard that I forgot about the poor chicken that was maybe injured, maybe dead. The rooster reminded us about it, cackling and crying.

"Well, enchanted bird, you've gone without prey, since you've chosen to feed from my yard. You think I have something good for you here? Because of these people, there's no more room in the sky for you. They've taken everything from you. You poor thing. Well, why didn't you choose the limping chick, why were you greedy for the fattest hen, the most beautiful one? From the high heavens you were drawn to what was beautiful and fat. Woe is you, if you have a hard time capturing a chicken, when you used to steal even lambs from the sheepfold and fly away with them, woe! You must be at the end of your strength! Even eagles grow old. Now, what do I do with this hen?"

After Great Gran talked to the wild bird that had disappeared from the barnyard, she went over to the chicken. Was it hurt or not really, should we cut it up or leave it? We kept thinking.

"Oh, oh, my tufted beauty, the only one to roost two years in a row and is full of eggs. *Cheep-cheep!*" Cuța called out to the chicken.

The rooster kept answering, crowing wisely and butting in. The chicken was out of it and Great Gran asked it how it was feeling. The rooster crowed something instead.

"I'm not talking to you," Cuţa stopped it.

I picked up the chicken, the rooster didn't like that but I didn't pay him any attention. "It's not hurt, just a little bit on its comb, it's not limping, it's heavy and full of eggs, our little chicken." Cuţa let me pet it, then I put it down carefully, to not upset its eggs, and the rooster was strutting around it happily, looking to see what I had done to it.

"Hush," Great Gran said. "See, it flapped its wings, it's just dizzy, it'll be fine."

Then again to the invisible buzzard:

"Come and get the limping chick, if you're dying of hunger, enchanted bird! I'll save it for you."

"Cuţa, I didn't know birds like that existed, I thought they only existed in the past."

"They do only exist in the past, but sometimes a magical bird from our past will come and steal something from us in the present, to remind us of the time that is disappearing, passing, and that it's wrong for us to forget about it."

We have foxes in the forest as well, that poachers from the village hunt, greedy people who sell the animal's fur. Two years ago, they killed a fox that had just given birth, they knew they weren't allowed to but killed it anyway. I found it in a trap, it was whimpering miserably and I heard it. I searched for its cubs, which weren't far from their mother and were crying, and I hid them in the catacombs of the forest, in the underground trenches. Three out of five lived and grew up, very beautiful, then two quickly disappeared, the third one waited for me there to bring it food until it became a big fox.

I wasn't able to save their wounded mother, it died in front of me and I wrapped it in the head scarf of the poacher's wife, to scare him. I had seen the wife's head scarf fall as she was walking,

I called after her to pick it up, she didn't hear and I wasn't as swift-footed as I used to be, I said to myself that I was sure I'd see her later and give it to her, then, when the fox died, I thought that God had planned it that way. Yes, after that her husband no longer went out killing, others got scared as well. The poacher had happily taken the wrapped up dead fox home and his wife recognized her own head scarf, she asked him to stop killing, because it was a bad omen. My cubs escaped as well. When we have little faith in the Lord, we no longer consider the innocent ones, who are weaker than we are . . .

⤙

Mom, I was playing on the computer and Cuța was amazed at how kids today play by themselves, just with the machine. Before they used to play in groups or packs. Mom, do you know about these games from olden times, because this is the first time I'm hearing about them: "Mr. Ioan, where are you?" where the kids stand in a circle, one kid is blindfolded, another kid isn't but he can't leave the circle. The one that's blindfolded asks: "Mr. Ioan, where are you?" Someone from the circle says "Here, here" and claps their hands.

Or "The stone bridge": the stone bridge has fallen down, the rain washed it out of town. We'll build another, farther down the river, prettier and stronger!

Or "Duck, duck, goose," or rolling wheel, milk jugs, strainer, "Don't look back, the old man's in the shack!", little head scarf, țurca, hidden ring, cat and mouse, mother hen and buzzard, pumpkins . . . The games people used to play! If there were kids in the village, Cuța would teach us games, but the kids have left . . .

⤙

My cat Sofron is ruining my refrigerator. Before, when I still had more of my teeth and sometimes bought groceries from the store, I'd let it taste some, and if it gobbled it up, I'd eat it as well and buy more, if it didn't, I wasn't in a hurry to eat it either, because who knows what kind of poison they put in it, if not even a cat wants to touch it? Stores are now full of all kinds of things, colors and scents added, but who knows how fit to be eaten they are . . . And what do you know? I didn't always have the cat taste things, if I already knew they were edible, I'd buy two hundred grams of little sausages for example, without telling the cat, and then it would open the refrigerator by itself with its paw and take its portion. I'd simply marvel: how did it know when I had gotten the good kind of sausages and how did it know when to open the refrigerator? It was a bit cheeky: when the sausages were sliced, it would only take a bit and some would be left over, if not, it would pull the entire stick out, eat some of it, and leave some for me, I only had to search for it under the beds, in every corner, at the bottom of closets. If it didn't smell throughout the house, sometimes I wouldn't even notice it was missing, sometimes I'd forget about it, the cat would eat everything later, just so it wouldn't go bad, or maybe it thought I wouldn't want to eat the sausage after it had bitten into it. The refrigerator was breaking down, when the door wasn't shut tightly, it would heat up, the cat never opened the door wide, it looked closed, at first I thought it was my fault, that I hadn't been paying attention and hadn't closed it all the way, then I discovered the disappearance of the sausage as well. Now I don't buy anything anymore and the cat doesn't open it . . . Cats are good animals, respectful, but if a cat considers you're not being fair, it will right things itself. Why would I eat something and not give it any, when I know how much it likes it? I've never punished the cat in any way, people who kick cats have no idea that this is why their dough won't rise. And if a cat steals a lot, it happens because it isn't being fed sufficiently, because if it were full, it would purr all day by the stove.

Before Sofron, I had a cat, we named it Goon, who didn't open the refrigerator, didn't steal off the table, and I couldn't praise it enough for all the mice it would catch. But when I was surrounded by lots of neighbors, on every side, not like now, one of them, old man Grigore, used to hang-dry a ham that he'd tie to a lightbulb that was at a great height for a cat, in a farther-off room of his house. Maybe even the old man had to climb on a chair to reach it, because it was hung up so high. Well, I couldn't believe it when old man Grigore complained that my Goon would get in through a small window that was cracked open, which the cat opened with its paw when it was shut, then it would jump, slam against the walls, until it reached the ham, which it grabbed onto with its claws, and it dangled there, and the ham swayed along with the cat, while the animal feasted on it and even took some away, he had found a piece of meat on the floor as well. Then it would leave through the small window again. I was scared then for the fate of the gluttonous cat. I said to it: "Don't go anymore, little Goon, because the neighborhood men are waiting with pitchforks to kill you!" But the cat didn't listen, it went and the people stuck the cat through, it came home still alive and looked for a place to die. I buried it. I cried. It had become a big animal, it liked ham. Of course I wasn't making it go hungry, but I didn't feed it ham, because I didn't have any either.

People were faithless and they sinned and then God became angry and punished them. He punished them for three days straight—the first day, cars disappeared, all of them, from people's courtyards, all the garages, parking lots, streets, the earth was left without a single car. The second day, God made all the supermarkets disappear, every single last one of them, not one was left, just a few farmer's markets and a couple small grocery stores. On the third day, all the cellphones and everything like them disappeared.

But as if that's truly a punishment, my dear? The punishment was when they were given all these, when they were allowed to have all of them, the cars that poison the air, the stores—stomachs, and the phones—minds. And now if you have all these, you want to save them. It would be the most just thing. How good it would be if it happened!

In times of trouble, some get closer to God, others get further away. But who I am I to judge them? We lack so much. The world looks only downward, it continues on its way and doesn't see where it's going anymore. Before, people would look at each other, greet each other, everyone knew everyone in the village, they'd exchange a few words if they got along. Now they walk around with their eyes glued to their telephones, what they see there, I can't imagine. In any case it's something very small, considering how small that toy is. When I heard my neighbor Raisa yelling in the street, I quickly came outside, I thought something had happened, that she was asking for help, I got scared, God forbid, what could've happened to her. She saw me and, beyond proudly, told me that she was talking on the telephone with her close friend, she was going to get some cheese from her, then she glued herself to the little box again and yelled: "I was talking to Ana Blajinschi, I told her I'm going to get cheese from you!" Pfft, you crazy woman, yelling at the top of your lungs and frightening everyone! And her friend lives two houses away, Raisa's house is two doors down. Does she have to yell like that just to let her know she's coming over? Maybe she's yelling out of pride, so everyone can see she has a telephone, it's fashionable now to have something like that, even little children have them. Her friend, as long as she's not deaf, could've heard her even without a telephone.

But the young teacher . . . I was surprised that young teachers even still come to our village. Usually it's just retirees teaching, but then, a young teacher! Tall, slim, may God grant that he settle here. He's living in the house of a couple former teachers who have left to work in Greece. Supposedly farm workers are better paid, and they clean around there, because the Greeks don't like that kind of work. What have people come to, without faith, directionless, pulled up from their roots! What the people from this bit of land could've done! What wasn't good enough here, what didn't they have? Just short of milk and honey flowing, a piece of heaven, like in poetry, but in reality, if you don't have money, off you go!

The young scholar walks to school down our street. Sometimes we run into each other. But he's always glued to his telephone. I'm surprised he doesn't get lost, because he's not from the village. One time I was returning from the fountain with two buckets of water. It's hard for me to draw water now in my old age. I take two and fill them just a little, it's easier with two and I don't fill them more than halfway. I don't expect anyone to help me, because we're all burdened and have our own troubles. But men aren't like how they used to be either. My son would help all the women when they were carrying something heavy. That's what they'd teach them at school too, I agreed with them. He'd also draw water if needed, when it came to helping others he never tried to get out of it. Now men have become very squeamish, women carry their bags and totes for them, their backpacks, because they've got a pain somewhere or other, and the poor women would do any-thing just to have them by their side. It's hard with today's men, they're very coddled and spoiled.

Well, and the teacher was coming straight toward me, I'm not saying he should've at least said, "Good day!" or asked, "Isn't that heavy for you, ma'am?" and hurried to help me, in any case I was almost at my gate, you know, it's not far, just a few steps. I was looking at him, maybe he'd take his eyes off his phone and look at me, but no reaction from him and I stepped aside, I got out of his way just in time, because he would've knocked me over, buckets and all. I wasn't upset, I was just very surprised. I kept looking back at him and what do you know? He was walking with his head bent over that telephone of his and he ran straight into a lamp post. If he didn't see me or he saw that I had gotten out of his way, maybe he expected the lamp post to do the same. Well, why not? But the lamp didn't see fit to do that and the honorable teacher hit his head right against it. I quickly went inside my yard so he wouldn't be embarrassed, he probably looked around to see if anyone had seen. He could've split his head open but he wasn't walking very fast, he didn't seem to be in a hurry, he probably ended up with just a lump on his head. I wonder if at school he tells the children something from time to time, or if his eyes are glued to his telephone there as well.

Mom, today I started washing the dishes and I don't know how but two dishes slipped through my fingers, one after the other, and broke, and right after that, though I tried to be really careful, I also smashed a little cup from that set with the red squares and gold line. I made so much noise that I think even the neighbors heard. What a racket dishes make when they break! And I hurried, so Cuţa wouldn't catch me, to pick up everything that had flown everywhere and hide the broken pieces. I was scared. But Cuţa heard, because even if you were completely deaf, you still would've known I'd made a mess. Cuţa came to see what had happened, but I was busy cleaning up and didn't hear her, I wasn't expecting her to show up so quickly and so quietly. She was watching me and when I noticed her at the door, she was laughing. She hadn't come to yell at me, or show how upset she was, but to laugh a little, because no one manages to break two plates and a cup in just a few minutes. It's the first time I've ever seen her laugh.

Mom, when Cuţa is serious or has something on her mind, she looks like a Madonna from an icon, even in her eighties she's still beautiful. But Mom, when she laughs! Her nose seems to touch her chin, her eyes become small and narrow, you'd think they had completely disappeared, her toothless mouth takes up her whole face, gosh, she all but had tiny horns, she looked exactly like a devilish little demon! As I looked at her, I burst out laughing too. We were both dying of laughter, how I was racing to hide the broken pieces! She said that I was like a bull in a china shop but we don't take plates with us to the grave, because we're Christians, not pharaohs!

Something else, Mom, I'm not at peace about today let alone about tomorrow, I'm not filled with gratitude, I don't have the joy Cuţa talks about. I can't say, like our Blajinica, that God has given me another day of rest, of peace. I haven't gone through every-thing she's gone through, but I'm always complaining. I don't have Cuţa's serenity. Do you?

The steppe had entered my soul, it was part of me. Those strange, cold expanses had gotten a hold on us and followed us our entire lives. They formed a trail of memories behind us that we couldn't escape. I see all kinds of moments before my eyes again. Not fear, not sadness. Man is weaker than flowers and stronger than stones. If you're naturally fearful, you'll be afraid even of your own shadow, you'll be afraid someone will jump out at you from a corner, you'll fear the darkness, the sounds of loneliness, anything can make you so scared you have a heart attack, you don't need a mother bear at your door or to wobble in leaky boats, but we get accustomed to everything. And when some time passes, the memories become beautiful, precious, you don't see things like that even in movies.

The steppe hooks you in, you get addicted. That's why I haven't died, it keeps me alive. I have to see it once more and then I can die. It pulls on me, draws me in, it calls me. Its round sky calls me. Here, there's less and less sky, less and less air. It's quiet only when it's dark. Less and less. The songs of the deportees from there, of the Russians, the Russian women, had something of the wolf's long howl in them. I think that's how they felt like singing when they found themselves taken against their will to that huge steppe with no escape. They say some words, and then they start: *Ooooooooeeooeeoooh, aaaaaaaaaaaee-ahah, eeeeeeeeee eeueeuu, uuuuueeuuuuueeeuhuh!* As if the sounds are searching for an edge they can grasp, to hold on, to stop themselves. But they roll back and forth. Everywhere you look, the same land-scape, no variation, no movement, the same lazy objects endlessly. I've never been more aware than in the steppe that man is a creature created by God. We are so small, so helpless, like babies, that only God sustains us and can help us in this world. Today, it becomes harder and harder to understand this. Man believes he is greater than everything, he pretends to ignore God. I don't even know if the steppe still exists, they may have covered all of it with buildings, garages, stores, roofs.

—Cuța Ana, it's not hard to find a steppe somewhere, but I'm afraid that if you see it, after that you'll die, like you said. I don't want that weighing on my conscience.

—I don't want a steppe somewhere. I want my steppe, there

where they left us at the end of the train tracks, where I caught my first ground squirrel and ate it, where I played with Eugen who, from my bashful Jenica, from my best friend, transformed into the boy Eugen, as pretty as a girl, as a *kartinka*, a painting. I would say: "You're my best friend, I love you so much," and she would blush, get flustered, and not say a word. There in the steppe we held hands and prayed together to God to help us get out alive, to survive, and to make it through everything together. Together through the good and the bad, to remain true friends all our lives. There, his grandmother, Anghelina, blessed us and told us to take care of each other. There, in the steppe, we danced a Bucovinian horă, we held each other, his cheek against my cheek.

—Then did you kiss?

—Kissing didn't even enter my mind, we were green, a couple of children, not even old enough to get engaged! Children left to our own devices during hard times. I thought about a kiss when I found out he was a boy. I remembered how we'd pick lice off each other on the train, how I'd lift my shirt and ask him, "Do you see anything on my back?" I'd tell him that my breasts hurt. "Don't yours?" "No, they don't." It was only on the ship that we finally kissed! We kissed then for the first and last time and everyone was looking at us. How I searched for him after that, the other girls were getting married, and I was waiting for my Jeni! Even after seventy years, I'm still waiting for him, I'll wait for him until I die, because love is a fire that never goes out as long as the mystery lasts. Our God, turn Your face toward us and grant us breadth of wisdom and a heart full of gentleness! Because You show Yourself in the earliest hours and You never sleep, teach us to keep awake and to wait patiently.

Not only the steppe, not only Eugen, not only my first kiss, but also my dear sweet mother Aspazia, who gave me life, and gave her life so that I might survive. May I live long enough to return home, to again set foot on Bucovinian land. I know how much she wanted to see our land, home, orchard, again before she died, to say goodbye to her loved ones, to the graves of my grandparents, her parents, to see her husband, who she didn't have any news of but hoped was still alive, her talented and accomplished sons, her oldest daughter, who was married and probably raising children while Mother was fighting against the bitter cold of the steppe. She had probably already had a second child, we supposed. My dear mother's return was not to be. But she arranged things such that what wasn't possible for her was for me. She'd remind me of my siblings' birthdays, we'd celebrate them somehow, we'd make something tasty and offer it to our Polish neighbors so they'd enjoy it, thinking of my brothers' health and of my sister's, we prayed that our wishes would reach them even if our bodies imprisoned so far away couldn't speak to them. And now, before I die, I'd like to have my mother's grave close by me, to tend it, to straighten its cross, lay a flower on it, say nice words over it, of thanks.

Long life is a gift, among the troubles are so many joys! What chills, what bitter cold, what winters, and now God is so gentle with us. Over there, what a howling, like someone wailing, the crunching of frozen snow, the moaning of the wind, as if even the snowflakes were suffering, as if they, too, were cold, and hungry, and had something weighing on their hearts. And the rain seemed to cry there, hiccupping, with tears sprinkled over the cheek of the earth. So many times in my life I thought I was going to die, that I wasn't going to live to see tomorrow, and yet God has given me days even until now, and maybe I'll have a few more sunny Sundays. When we think we've come to the end, that here it is, we've reached it, that there's nothing beyond this, nowhere else to go, destiny laughs at us. Life is endless, my darling girl.

Think of yourself as already dead, I'd repeat to myself, and *you won't feel the coming of death and its terror.* Each morning, consider yourself a miracle and you won't feel old age. Don't wait for the coming of death, because truly it has already come and never left you. Its teeth are always in your body. Everything that lived before your birth and all that will go on living after your death—that, too, is alive in you right now. We worry about tomorrow, but few think about the day after their death.

Oh Spirit of vigor, of the fullness of morning and the peace of evening, You, who art lighter than sleep, faster than wind, more refreshing than dew, sweeter than a mother's voice, brighter than fire, holier than all sacrifices, more alive than life—to You I pray and bow down, be my fellow traveler on the arduous road to eternal happiness!

Any day now I'll be ninety years old, but something makes me hold back from death. I must still have something to do, to feel, to suffer. Just one more thing, and then I can die.

—What does one more thing mean?

—I have to see Jenea, then I can die. My heart tells me he's still alive, that he's thinking of me, just as I'm thinking of him. I know that he dug up the pot, no one else could have, he dug it up to bring it to me, not to take it to his grave, because it wasn't his, and we're Christians, not like those Eurasian kurgans who buried their entire houses with them and their graves look like mountains.

I had walled up the pot in the fountain, I had covered it with rocks and cement. My brothers had dug a kind of hole next to the fountain so that animals could drink from it. That's where I put my little clay pot filled with all kinds of things of mine, I called it "my dowry," I was able to fit inside a teacup, two small silver spoons, a beaded necklace that Domnica forgot to take to her new house, a reddish horse, a toy belonging to my brothers which I liked as well, a small embroidered head scarf, it must have rotted in the meantime from the humidity, some old coins from my grandfather which were in use during time of the Austrians, a little bottle in the shape of a swan that once held perfume . . . I put them all in until it was full, then put a lid over it and covered it well with rocks. They soon deported us after that and my treasure remained hidden there. I told Eugen about it on the train. I described how I had walled up "my dowry" in such detail that he, when he returned there before me, found the pot and took it. And the old doctor told me that someone else had once come by asking about the fountain, who else if not Eugen?

Eugen will come to bring me my dowry.

—Cuța, the power has gone out! Right when I wanted to turn on the computer!

—Hmm, the neighbors' boy must have come home and he's a glutton for work. When he starts welding, the lights go out, but they come back on quickly.

—Well, let's talk a bit then. Tell me a story, Cuța, but a happy one, please!

Long ago and far away, it happened back in my day, 'cause I'm not from back when stories were new, but from the time when pigs were shoed with ninety-nine quintals of iron on each foot, that's right, and they'd jump through the house as if they were light. Back when a flea was yoked instead of a cow and a mosquito held onto the plow. When the fox was the mayor and the rabbit was the flute player, supposedly the bread ran into the cornmeal:

"Good day, corny friend," the bread said.

"I thank you, child's play."
Embarrassed, the bread tried again, respectfully:
"Good day, heartiness of the house!"
"I thank you, beauty of the table."

You give honor, you get honor. Neither is to be sneezed at. Even if bread is good and beautiful, mămăliga helps you through hard times and fills up a family, and bread is given more to small children when people are poor and have nothing else.

—Come on, Cuța, I want a longer one!

—I've told you one in the time it takes for the lights to come back on. But they haven't come back on!

Listen to "The Story of the Wine":

Once upon a time there lived a great emperor who had many officials, but there was one he loved more than the others. He once threw a ball and all the nobles came, but the favorite was also rather greedy and he wet his whistle a bit much. As he was heading home, he fell down. They say that brandy makes you fall face down, and wine makes you fall face up. He was very drunk and lay motionless there on the ground. Some ravens flying by thought he was a corpse and they quickly pecked out his eyes. When he woke up after a while, he did so eyeless. The emperor was so upset that he ordered grapevines be pulled up from the earth and whoever had wine to pour it into a ravine. The people obeyed, that's what they did, but one hid a barrel of wine, because he felt it would be a shame to waste it. Soon after this incident, a lion escaped from its cage and no one could catch it. The emperor sent word throughout the land that a bag of gold coins would be given to whoever could master the lion and stick it back in its cage. But no one dared try. And then the man who hadn't poured out his wine went over to his barrel, he took a couple guzzles, he filled up a little flask as well and hid it under his suman. When he got to the place, he saw that the lion was close by. He reached for his flask and took a gulp, he took a couple more and then went straight over to the lion. He lunged at it, grabbed it by the ears, and stuck it right in its cage.

"Who is the brave man who caught the lion, let's see him!" the emperor said.

They brought out an old man. The emperor was amazed, "What's this? How did you manage it?" *The old man took out the flask from his suman and showed it to him. The emperor grew angry and said:*

"But I had given a dread command and you did not obey."

"Your majesty, I heard the command you gave, but it would've been more fitting if that command had been that each person should drink only as much as needed to catch a lion by the ears, not as much as would cause ravens to peck out their eyes."

—You must have heard that one from some drunk guys, Cuța!

There was once an old man and an old lady who were rather poor. The old man managed to get a hold of some coins and buy a bit of wine. He came home, "Look wife, something to cheer us up." *His wife was glad:*

"But when and with what are we going to drink it?"

"We're going to drink the wine tonight, with measure and prudence."

Right as he was speaking, two young men passed by and heard, and they winked at each other.

The man went to work, and as it was getting dark, the young men knocked on the old woman's gate.

"Auntie, we've come for that wine."

"Who are you?" *the woman asked.*

"What do you mean who? I'm Measure, and this is Prudence.

"My husband'll come and give you some."

"Auntie, didn't he tell you who he was drinking the wine with? Give it to us, 'cause we can't wait around."

The old woman, believing them, gave them the wine. The old man came home from work, they had something to eat, and then the man said to the woman:

"Come on, Wife, let's toast."

The woman, surprised:
"Well Measure and Prudence came and took the wine."
"Measure who, Prudence who?"

—Tell me one with Păcală too!
"Neighbor Păcală, where did you learn all your tricks and how
do you remember them?"
"Everything I hear, I tuck inside my head," Păcală said.
"But the hundred note I lent you a month ago, what about that,
when are you paying me back?"
"Well that one I tucked inside my pocket, not my head, I don't
know anything about it!"
—Do you know the story about the lion and the midge?
—No, but what's a midge?
—It's a small mosquito.
A midge landed on the lion's nose. When the lion tried to catch it,
the midge landed on one of its ears, and then on the other. The lion
was furious and asked the midge who it was:
"I'm a midge," the little mosquito said, "I suck blood from whoever
I want and no one can catch me."
"I'm stronger, I'm more powerful," the lion said. "You won't suck
my blood!"
"Let's make a wager on who's stronger."
"Let's."
Then the midge stuck its snout in the lion's nose and immediately
filled up with the lion's blood.
"Well, see, I sucked your blood. What is it you can do?"
"I can eat even a man, in a second!"
As soon as the lion said that, a child showed up on the road. The
lion was about to pounce on him, but the midge stopped it:
"Wait, that's not a man, he'll only become one later, he's too small."
A bit later, an old man appeared:

"Wait, this one was a man, now he's an elderly person, you'd be breaking your teeth on his stringy flesh for nothing."

The lion left him alone too, when right then they saw a hussar on horseback coming down the road.

"Maybe this one isn't a man either?"

"Yes he is, this one's a man!" the midge yelled.

The lion got a running start, but when the hussar saw it, he quickly drew his sword and gave it a couple lashes! Wanting to escape, the lion took off running, and the midge clung to its ear and asked:

"So, how was it with the man?"

And the dazed lion said, "That man with a mind possessed, when he took a rib out of his chest, and gave me such a blow, he almost laid me low!"

Let me tell you "When You Can Get Married":

A man had only one son, who grew up rather spoiled and didn't really like to work. He became a young man and fell head over heels for a girl.

"Father, I want to get married."

"My boy, before you get married, you have to throw a gold coin in the water. If the coin floats, you're ready to get married, if it sinks to the bottom, not yet."

The boy ran to his mother and asked for a gold coin.

"I have the gold coin, Father."

"Throw it in." He threw it in and the coin sunk to the bottom. "See, you're not ready to get married."

More time passed, but he liked the girl and wanted to make her his wife. He went to his father again and again his father told him to throw a gold coin in the water. He went back to his mother:

"My boy, why are you wasting gold coins? You don't know the value of a gold coin and how hard it is to earn one."

"But maybe this one won't sink to the bottom."

He threw in this one as well and it, too, sank. He cried and went back to his mother.

"You want more gold coins than I have. Go and earn some money and throw in your own gold coin, not mine."

He went to his sweetheart and said to her: "Let's go work and make some gold coins."

They went to work and labored hard and earned a fistful of gold coins. Then they returned home.

"I want to get married, Father."

"Do you have a gold coin?"

"I do."

"Let's go over to the water. Throw it in."

"Father, how can I throw it in when I worked so hard for it with my sweetheart! I can't bear the thought of throwing it in!"

"Aha, now you know how money is made! But when you took the gold coin from your mother, how do you think I bore it? Now you're ready to get married, my boy."

—Got any more? Tell me another one! The lights haven't come back on yet!

There were two brothers, one was very rich, the other was very poor. The poor one went to the rich one and said, "Please give me your cart, so I can gather some wood from the forest." That one was rather stingy, he gave his brother his cart and horse, but not his harness. The poor one went without a harness and drove the horse by its tail, but on the way back, with the cart heavy with wood, the horse bucked and broke its tail. The man returned home and went to his brother and told him what happened. His brother was furious and sued him. The poor one thought to himself that he had better make himself scarce. He reached the train station. But a lot of people were there, a huge crowd, he found a spot on the train by climbing up to the luggage rack, he fell asleep and dreamed about how the horse's tail broke, he startled and fell down right on top of a woman holding her child and the child died. Oh no! The child's mother would sue him as well. What could he do, he jumped off the train, and considered his situation: My brother's suing me, this woman will sue me as well. He saw a high bridge and thought to himself: They'll sentence me for the mare, they'll sentence me for the child. I'll throw myself off this bridge and die! Under the bridge, carts and cars were passing by. He got a running start and right as he jumped off, a wagon with an old man being taken to the hospital drove by underneath. He landed on top of the old man and killed him. The people caught him and took him to the public prosecutor.

The mother said, "I had only one child and he killed him."

"Go stay with him until he gives you another child."

The son who was taking his father to the hospital also wanted justice.

"Alright then, he'll go lie under the bridge, and you jump down from there on top of him to kill him."

And the brother with the tail-less mare asked what he should do:

"You, take the mare to your brother's yard and leave it there for him to feed and take care of until its tail grows back."

And the prosecutor sent them all home.

—The lights haven't come back on yet . . .

—On the Feast of the Peaceful eggshells are released into the water. They say that beneath us an entire people lives as well. If the Peaceful, back home they're also called Rohmans, like you, they take you on as a servant for a year, and if you serve them well, they'll teach you the language of birds. That's what happened to a good-natured boy from a poor family. *A boy worked for a year for the Rohmans and then it was time for him to return home. He reached a sheepfold and he asked the shepherds:*

"Are the dogs doing their job?"

"They are, especially the younger two, the old one is a good-for-nothing, it doesn't even bark anymore."

At night a wolf came and the young man heard: "Rip apart more, so there will be some left for us too!" the two young dogs said. But the old one: "Stay away from the sheep!"

The young man understood their language and told the shepherds: "The old dog is a valuable dog, keep it here for as long as it lives . . ."

The young man kept going, night fell as he reached a forest, and he sat down under a tree to rest a bit.

"What's new?" he heard the birds ask each other.

"Under the willow is a spring of clear, sweet water, but people carry water from the very far end of the village, they don't know they have water right next to them!"

Another said, "Yes, people seem smart, but they're actually very stupid! The old widower, for example, he never eats his fill, he doesn't even have decent shoes, he keeps mending his old ones, and he doesn't know that he has a pot of gold coins hidden within the wall in a corner of his house."

"True, and what about the rich man whose daughter has fallen ill? He has spent so much money on doctors and medicines, but the girl is still sick and he doesn't know that a poisonous bug has hidden in the firewood and at night it sucks the girl's blood. No one knows that the bug must be killed and the girl will be cured."

In the morning, the boy woke up and headed toward the village, he looked and saw women carrying heavy buckets from far away. He went over to the landowner who had the willow and said to him, "Let me dig here." He dug a bit, the water sprang up, the people built a well there and thanked the boy for his good deed. Then he went to the poor widower. He said to him, "Let me help you," he lifted a plank from the corner of the house, and there was a pot of money; the old man was overjoyed, he wanted to give some to the boy but the boy wouldn't accept it. Then he went to the rich man and his daughter, "I'll heal her," he said, "but I'll need wood and oil." He lit a big fire and heated the oil in a cauldron. At night, when the giant black bug

wanted to come out, he poured hot oil over it. The girl became healthy
and the rich man gave the young man her hand in marriage . . .

—Cuța, they've come on! This was the story that lit up the house!"

[Thurs] *** Missed Call from Mom ***
[5:58 PM] *** Missed Call from Mom ***
[7:16 PM] *** Missed Call from Mom ***

Mom, why did you call so many times? Everything's fine. We
just had a little apocalypse and I forgot my phone at home. Cuța
said I didn't need my phone during the apocalypse. We hid in
the forest, in Cuța's shelter for hard times. We had everything
we needed there, bread, canned food, jars of jam, and a bottle of
Coca-Cola, though it was expired. The mosquitos were eating me
alive and I told Cuța that I wanted to go home! "Let's go back! I'm
bored of your apocalypse. It's taking too long and nothing interesting is happening. There's no TV, no internet, and no phone. I
can't call Mom to let her know how we're doing here in the forest."

"You think it's over when we want it to be?" Cuța said and we
stayed some more. There were so many matches in the shelter,
that's where all the matchboxes she had me buy went to!

"In the forest, fire means life. It warms you up when you're
cold, feeds you when you're hungry, protects you when you're
afraid, keeps away bloodthirsty beasts."

Then we left the forest for home.

"Is that what the apocalypse is like, Cuța?"

"No, that was just a test, a kind of dress rehearsal. God is good
and He's allowing the world to go on living. We have time to die.
And to enjoy life in the meantime. My heart is telling me that

we'll have good news waiting for us at home. Let's hurry. Look, even the cat is getting excited!"

When we thought the apocalypse was coming, the sirens were blaring because someone had set the winery on fire, from the alcohol and the chemicals that had gotten into the air, the sky was rainbow colored, like an aurora borealis. And the crash that sounded like a bomb had been the big barrel of alcohol exploding. Today Cuṭa found out from a neighbor that someone had gotten mad at the winery's director because he won't accept people's grapes and makes artificial wine. You can't imagine what it was like, Mom! I thought that's it, it's the end of the world. The end times! The end times! But we had gotten scared for nothing! It was a false alarm.

Now Cuṭa has gone out into the village to get a kilo of cow cheese. I didn't tell her anything, but she senses something. I did tell her that Annie is coming with her fiancé, but no exact date, because I didn't know it either, but she has no way of knowing that the Eugen from their train is also coming! Though I did hear her repeating that Jenea has to come, to bring her pot to her, her treasure from Bucovina.

And Mom, that man with the dog told me that it's gotten big enough and I can come get it. It's a boy dog, not a girl dog. I know what we're going to call it: Kant! Isn't that pretty? Doggy Kanty! It's the name of the Kyrgyz city where our Blajinica learned how to be a seamstress. And Eugen, her love from Siberia, will stay with us and they'll live happily for the rest of their lives and we won't need to take our great gran to a nursing home anymore. Kant will guard them both. Let them spend their last days in the little house next to the forest, in the fresh air, so they can reach the end of their journey together.

I bet our guests will arrive right when Cuṭa is taking the pastries out of the oven. Neither too hot nor too cold, Moldovan pastries, from long ago and far away! And Eugen will put that little pot from Bucovina on the table, we'll look to see what's inside, and he'll hug our wonderful Cuţa, because they haven't seen each other in so long!